ACKNOWLEDGEMENTS

I would like to thank my parents and husband for all their help and encouragement throughout this process, and for turning a blind eye when I spent a little too much time on my laptop. I would like to acknowledge Gaston Leroux for writing *The Phantom of the Opera* and inspiring my muse with his wonderful characters. Finally, I would like to extend a big thank you to all those people who I have met online through my writing. You all have been a continuous source of support and inspiration.

CW01499465

SHADOWS OVER EDEN

A *Phantom of the Opera* Inspired Tale

L.M. BIRD

Prologue

2005

The fate of the country changed in a single moment.

It changed when Jennifer Henderson made her decision at 5:13 AM on a cold Wednesday morning in February, two days after Valentine's Day. Still wearing a pair of black yoga pants and an oversized New England Patriot's sweatshirt, she stared down at her sleeping husband, a frown tugging at the corners of her mouth.

I can't stand this anymore. I'm tired of lying. I'm tired of you. Maybe I even hate you.

She packed her clothes, toiletries, and smaller prized possessions into a black leather suitcase, hurling them in as fast as her perfectionist tendencies would allow. The big stuff would be moved later—and soon. She'd be damned if he got the thousands of dollars' worth of equipment in the exercise room. She rubbed a hand over her face, and her fingers brushed against the tips of her nostril. At least there was no way in hell he was getting the nose job back. The thought almost made her laugh out loud.

Mrs. Henderson, the divorce court orders that you have surgery to return your nose to its former state. Of course, your husband will be performing the operation.

Finding a notepad with floral designs in the corners, she jotted a quick message.

Dear Craig,

I'm sorry, but I can't do this anymore. There's someone else and has been for a while. We're happy. You should be with someone more worthy of you than me. You know that I've always been a mess. I'm sorry for any pain I've caused.

Jenny

P.S. Cuddles is with me. I know you never liked her very much.

With the dog carrier in one hand and a suitcase in the other, Jenny took a deep breath. She tiptoed down the stairs and out the front door, a cold breeze blowing her short blonde hair. The Pomeranian yipped from her carrier at a passing car, and Jenny shushed her. Without a glance back at the three-story home, she climbed into her car, started the engine, and drove away.

***

Craig Henderson found the letter at 6:45. After reading it twice under the light of a solitary lamp, he balled it up in his hands. Silent tears rolled down his cheeks. Maybe he'd always known it was coming. *But Jenny, how the hell could you do this to me? After everything I've fucking done for you? Everything we've been through?* He went through the house and kicked every object that reminded him of her, from the two thousand dollar elliptical to the silver dog food bowl for that squeaking freak of an animal. At least she'd taken Cuddles. Stupid excuse for a dog.

He got mindlessly drunk for the next few days. Wine bottles littered the house, and he ignored the *tsks* of his Russian housekeeper as she picked them up and dropped them into a black trash bag. The bartender at his favorite dive would offer a few words of sympathy and then cut him off by midnight. The alcohol numbed the pain just enough to keep him from finding the nearest bridge.

He drowned himself in terrible 80's action movies and blood-and-guts video games. Porn. Anything to get his mind off her.

Eventually, it was time to go back to work. He'd been 'on vacation' for two weeks, but Monday's scheduled surgery was high priority. It couldn't be delayed. His work had been called innovative, and his techniques had been described as world changing. At least he could be *someone's* hero again.

The sounds of the hospital flooded his ears, intercoms and mechanical beeps and depressed murmurs. He could feel the eyes of his surgical team on him as he approached the pair of blue double doors.

"How was your time off, Dr. Henderson?"

"Do anything fun?"

"How's Jenny? You two still training for that marathon?"

He answered the questions with single syllables.

"Are you feeling well?" asked a pretty anesthesiologist whom he'd known for over ten years. She was eyeing him closely, and he looked away from her. "I know there's been a bug going around."

"Feeling just fine," he curtly replied. "Ready to get to work."

I'm not letting that bitch ruin this for me.

Male. Severe congenital defect. And one of the youngest face transplant candidates ever. Local Channel 4 had already done a feel-good story about it. CNN was going to be following up.

"You're sure you can fix this?" the mother had asked behind the privacy of closed doors, so no one could hear what a basket case she really was. "Some doctors thought he was too young, but you can do this, right? I'll pay whatever insurance doesn't cover. If you can't do it, I-I might just snap. You don't know what it's like, being stuck inside all day trying to homeschool him. I don't have any friends left. I can't take it anymore."

I'm going to snap.

Snap!

The room tilted, but Craig Henderson took a deep, wine-laced breath and entered, the rest of his team behind him. He could only hear the letter, repeated in her voice: *I'm sorry, but I can't do this anymore. I'm sorry, but I can't do this. I'm sorry, but I can't.*

I'm sorry.

Chapter 1

2021

Green icky mush.

Raoul stared down at his sandwich and wrinkled his nose. "Eww." He wrapped it back up and stuffed it into the crinkled brown lunch sack with a disappointed sigh.

"What's that?" asked a red-headed boy, standing behind him as they waited in the gymnasium for the first day of school to begin. Raoul knew he was in the fifth grade and a bit of a bully. Not the kind who beat you up and took your lunch money, but the really annoying kind who wouldn't shut up.

"Turkey and avocado," he muttered. "I told my mom not to make it anymore, so Enid must have made it."

"Who's Enid?"

"The housekeeper."

"You have a housekeeper?" the boy asked. "You rich or something?"

"Um. I don't know." He really didn't want to talk about it. The first day of third grade was shaping up to be bad enough without bringing his famous dad into it.

"Hey," the boy continued to Raoul's displeasure. "I know who you are! You're the Senator's kid. Yeah. I saw you on the TV. My dad said he'd cut off his right hand before voting for your dad."

Raoul shifted uncomfortably. "Whatever." He ignored the boy.

Enid hadn't even put in chips or a cookie or an apple. All he had was this sandwich. Stupid sandwich. Stupid fifth-grader. Stupid third grade. Stupid—

"You can have mine. I don't like peanut butter."

He turned to his right. A girl stood right beside him. Her strawberry blonde hair was done up into a messy braid that went down her back. Freckles dotted her pale nose, and she was missing one of her front teeth.

"How can you not like peanut butter?" he asked.

The girl blushed, but her blue eyes twinkled. "I dunno. Just don't. It's sticky and icky!" She giggled at her own rhyme.

Raoul couldn't help but smile. "Do you like avocado?"

"Um, I dunno. I never tried it."

They traded, and she opened his sandwich and bit into it. "Mmm!" One of the monitors frowned at her for eating outside of lunchtime, and she quickly wrapped up the sandwich and put it back into the bag. "What is a Sen-a-tor?" she asked after swallowing.

Before Raoul could reply, the fifth-grader interrupted, "He goes to Washington and makes all the laws. And my dad says they do nothing but raise taxes!" He turned to Raoul. "Why don't they stop raising taxes?"

"What's a taxes?" asked the girl.

The bully scoffed. "Don't you know anything? It's when you pay money for nothing!"

"Just ignore him," muttered Raoul with a glare. "What's your name?"

"Christine," she replied. "I'm in second grade!"

"I'm Raoul. I'm in third. That means we'll have recess together."

"Good because I don't wanna play with the kindergarteners again!"

"Yeah," he agreed. "They throw up a lot."

"Well, I'm glad I'm not stuck with you guys," said the fifth-grader, annoyed that he'd been excluded. "Your dad is a stupid tax raiser."

Raoul didn't tell him that the feeling was mutual.

Third grade wasn't so terrible after all. He and Christine played together many times that year. She was the first girl he'd met that didn't have cooties, although sometimes it was still hard to convince the other boys of this. Raoul loved how the sun shined off her hair and how her pale face acquired a pinkish glow when she was happy. She was a little shy sometimes, but when she laughed it was almost musical. At the winter assembly, he even got to hear her sing, and it was obvious that his new best friend was talented.

Although they usually didn't get together outside of school, he did bring her over to his house a few times. Christine told him that it was 'ginormous' and 'really fun.' She loved rolling around on the floor with his Golden Retriever and letting the dog lick her face with a giant, wet tongue. In the springtime, she and Raoul would jump and wrestle around on his trampoline until his mother stepped outside and said, "Calm down, or you're going to break your necks."

Over the summer, he didn't see much of Christine. Raoul was sent off to camp with other boys whose dads did important things. Most of them went to private schools, but Raoul's dad always said that "it sent an important message to the people" for him to attend public school. Raoul wasn't quite sure what that meant. As long as he had Christine to play with, he didn't care.

Fourth grade arrived, and Raoul had grown a whole inch. He felt more confident as he walked through the familiar halls of his elementary school. Only one more grade to go and then he would be the oldest! His good mood vanished the second he saw Christine.

Even before they spoke, he noticed that something was different. She murmured a soft "hello" and silently ate beside him at lunchtime. It was still summer, but she was wearing a plain white turtle neck and a long jean skirt.

"Is everything okay, Christine?" he asked.

"Oh…yeah," she murmured, staring down at her folded hands.

"Are you sure?"

"Yeah. Just—well, my mom died. She had cancer." A tear formed at the corner of her eye, and she brushed it away with the back of her hand.

"That's awful. I'm really, really sorry."

"Thanks. And then my dad…he…"

"He what?" Raoul pressed as a heavy feeling formed in his stomach.

"He changed *everything*."

"What do you mean?"

"I dunno. Never mind." She looked up, eyes dry now. "Wanna trade your ham for tuna?"

"Uh, sure." He didn't like tuna, but he wanted to make her happy again. And, for a moment, she smiled.

Christine was never the same. She would laugh, but her eyes held a sadness that he was still too young to understand. Then, one cold day in November, she came up to him at lunchtime. Fresh tears glistened in the corners of her blue eyes; it was the first time that he'd ever wanted to hug a girl. "Raoul." She wore a pine green and black plaid skirt that reached her ankles, hair combed into her famous long braid. "My dad says we're going away."

"Oh no! You're moving?" he replied with a groan. He'd had a friend do that to him in first grade.

"Yeah. Daddy says we have to give up the world."

"What?"

She shrugged. "I don't know. But I'm leaving. Today is my last day. I don't know what to do."

"Oh." His head drooped. "Well, maybe we can…Do you have e-mail?"

She shook her head.

"Well, maybe…" His voice tapered off. To his surprise, he felt her arms wrap tightly around his shoulders. She kissed his cheek.

"Find me someday," she whispered into his ear. Before he could hug her back, Christine ran away, leaving a few wet stains on his navy polo shirt.

Raoul went home and told his father everything. Ethan Chandler finally agreed to give Christine's dad a call and at least find out where they were moving. Raoul was unable to tell what had happened based on the brief one-sided conversation. That night, though, he put his ear to the door of his parents' bedroom and heard them speak in low voices.

"But they seemed like a decent family," said his mother. "I can't believe it."

"The country is changing, and people are afraid," replied his father. "Things like this will continue to happen, especially to trusting people who are down on their luck."

"But that stupid group is no better than a cult!"

"They don't see it that way, Judy. They see it as their salvation. Luckily these people stay on the edge of civilized society."

"That poor, poor little girl. So many awful things could happen to her."

"I know, honey. But the authorities will keep an eye out for anything illegal. They know what goes on in places like that."

"Still. It's so sad."

Raoul barely slept that night as he lay on his pillow and tried to figure it all out. Why had someone taken his best friend away? This wasn't fair at all!

"What's no better than a cult? What do you mean by cult? What happened to Christine?"

His father was reading the morning paper and started as Raoul jumped into the kitchen and bombarded him with questions. Ethan dropped the paper on the table, right into his plate of scrambled eggs, and frowned. "What have I told you about eavesdropping?" Raoul lowered his head. His father sighed, and his expression softened. "I guess you're old enough, aren't you? A cult is…it's when a bad person or group of people trick other people into believing and doing whatever they want."

"How do they do that?"

"By telling lies and making false promises, usually about going to heaven. Things like that." Raoul squinted. "Like what if I told you, if you clean the house, I'll give you a hundred dollars and take you to Disney World."

"Would you really?"

His dad smiled a little sadly. "No. But you almost believed it. That's what a cult does. Except a lot worse."

"Oh." Raoul paused. "What's going to happen to Christine?"

"I don't know. I'm sure her father will keep her safe. I would try to make some new friends, though."

"But I don't want a new friend. I want Christine. Can't you bring her back? You make laws!"

"It's not that simple. I don't have that kind of authority, son. I'm sorry."

Raoul sat down and stared at the table, feeling very helpless. "This really…sucks." His much older brother said that all the time, and his mother always told him that it wasn't dignified language. But it was the only phrase that summed up the situation.

His father rested a hand on his shoulder. "Well, hey. Maybe we should take that trip to Disney World soon. We've been talking about it, right? And I won't even make you clean the house."

"Really?"

"Really."

"Yeah. That'd be cool."

It was a brief distraction. Still, Raoul never forgot about the little blonde girl. Sometimes he'd look for her in the crowds, but she had completely vanished.

As the awkwardness and excitement of adolescence came upon him, Christine slowly became a ghost of his childhood. It would be twelve years before he saw her again.

Chapter 2

2034

"Good evening, Christine."

"Good evening, Spirit." As always, she bowed her head in a show of respect. The glow from the dim overhead lamp cast the small room in eerie shadows, all the while setting her in a spotlight. It was the only time when she was singled out. Special.

The walls were covered with thick midnight blue curtains that hung to a carpet of the same color, creating a cave-like atmosphere. It was always like stepping into another world. The Spirit's world. A place of purity and goodness where even the air was crisper and cleaner. She was so very blessed to be there.

"How are you tonight?"

"I'm fine," she replied, chin tilted upward. Naturally, the Spirit spoke from heaven and so she tried to direct her body language toward him.

"You are lying."

Christine inwardly cringed; the Spirit could always tell when something was wrong. She needed to try harder to keep her thoughts pure. *And now she had lied as well!* "Spirit, please forgive me for not being honest. But it's not that important. I don't want to bother you with it."

"Come now. Sit, Christine. Your lovely voice is always strained when you are troubled by the outside. There are days when I wish to isolate you from all those unworthy imbeciles. Let us deal with this."

She slowly sat on the single cushioned chair in the room, her fingers digging into the silver floral embroidery. Christine had never seen anyone else tread into the sacred space, and she didn't think the Spirit spoke to anyone else, except, of course, to the honorable Cameron Lourdes. Cameron had been the one to announce the Spirit's presence nearly five years ago, citing it as a great blessing that God had sent one of His very own angels down to Earth. The Spirit would ensure that her world remained a secure and just place.

No one ever saw the Spirit, but the Spirit saw *everything*. He knew when people were not acting righteously, and then they were swiftly punished. Or, on rarer occasions, they disappeared and were never seen again.

It was the Spirit who had put all her lingering childhood doubts to rest. She had been frequently punished during her youth for insolence and doubt. But the Spirit was proof of Cameron's declarations that they were God's chosen people. She had begged her dying father for forgiveness after all those years of casting secret glares toward him for bringing her to that place.

Still, there was that rare occasion when something would bring back her doubts. Something would not feel right, would tug at her conscience and make her stomach turn. And this was the reason for her somber mood that evening.

She nervously tugged on a string of her long, yellow hair. "It's just…" *Oh, Spirit, please do not be angry with me.* "Joe Breyer didn't mean anything by what he said at the meeting," she rambled, a quiver in her voice. "He's really a very nice old man. And Mr. Breyer called Cameron a grouchy badger after Cameron banned birthday celebrations. It was a silly joke. But I heard rumors that Mr. Breyer might disappear. So I-I'm hoping for mercy for him. Please?"

She shivered in her thin blue cotton dress and hoped she hadn't crossed the line. If the Spirit became angry, she would have to fall to her knees and beg forgiveness.

"Breyer spoke against Cameron," the Spirit finally replied.

"I know. He shouldn't have done that. I'm sure he'll never, ever do it again, though. And you could grant mercy—"

"My job is not to give mercy. It is justice. You know what Cameron says."

"Yes," she quickly replied. "The Spirit grants Earthly judgment. And then God will determine Heaven or Hell. Yes, I understand. But—"

"It is not your place to worry over such things, my dear. Your focus should be on your voice. Your gifts. Yourself."

He always said that to her. In fact, her voice had attracted the attention of the Spirit two years ago. The first time she had stepped into that curtained room, she had been trembling violently, standing there and waiting for…she didn't know what. And then, as she hugged her pale arms to her chest, wearing her nicest lavender dress with the little yellow roses, the Voice had spoken to her. Just hearing its beauty proved to her that the Spirit was from heaven. Nothing else could sound so divine.

Hearing him still sent chills up her spine and tingles through her skin. The only thing she had to offer this great being was her voice. So far, it had been enough.

"Christine?" The Spirit broke into her thoughts. "You will not worry over this?"

She looked down at the carpet. "Mr. Breyer will disappear now, won't he?" Joe had been kind to her since her arrival. When she had been a frightened eight-year-old, he had even given her a chocolate bar.

"Those who speak against Cameron are unwelcome." His tone was less patient.

She rapidly bobbed her head up and down. "I understand, Spirit. You are the great giver of justice. I don't question you. I promise! Forgive me! Please forgive me!"

"You are forgiven. Now, is there anything else that concerns you?"

She swallowed. "Just one thing."

"Yes?"

"I'm going to be twenty-one soon. I'll have to get married. Will I—

will I still visit you for voice lessons after I'm wed?" The thought made her ill. She barely knew most of the young men and her marriage could be arranged at any time, especially with her father deceased and unable to speak for her best interests. She was at the mercy of the local council. Once wed, she would be expected to immediately bear children, and she felt ready for none of it.

A long silence passed, and she continued to feel her stomach turn in apprehension.

"You have more important duties than marriage." He said the last word with disdain. "And Cameron will accept this. You have nothing to fear."

She felt a weight lifted from her shoulders. Losing the Spirit would destroy her; she had nothing else. "Thank you," she whispered.

"Now is that all?"

"Yes."

"Shall we begin?"

"Oh, yes!" Her eyes glistened with tears of delight as she looked to the heavens.

She was so very blessed.

Chapter 3

2034

"So remember to look for Verma's Veggies at your local supermarket. Verma's non-genetically engineered veggies—one hundred percent natural!" The radio announcer paused. *"And now for the news. National unemployment dropped by point two percent, which makes the current rate twenty-seven point six percent. The White House hailed this as a sign that the economy was improving. Meanwhile, riots continued today in St. Louis over the murder of Jonathan Ramos. According to witnesses, he was gunned down by police during the labor protests that occurred in the manufacturing district. Authorities say that he was armed, but protestors claim he was only holding a sign. That's the seventy-second death during the St. Louis protests this year."*

Another pause. There was a touch of exhaustion in the man's voice as he continued.

"Rioting today continued throughout Atlanta over installment of the eight o'clock curfew. It is the twelfth major city to install the early curfew. As crime rates continue to rise, government officials feel they have little choice. And now for a startling report out of Los Angeles…"

Raoul turned down the radio and glanced at the passenger's seat. "I wish they'd actually play some music. So what should we do tonight?"

"Curfew is down to nine here," Anthony Seung muttered. His baseball cap was pulled down almost over his dark eyes, and his black hair hung down to his chin, framing his face. "What the hell can we do?"

"Board games?" joked Raoul.

"Ugh. More like I'm bored games. Maybe video games. *Tank Master Six* is out in 3-D. You can smell the city burning while you fight."

"You can smell the city burning when you leave your house. Meh, we'll figure something out." Raoul yearned for the days when they could stay out past ten and grab a movie and a pizza, maybe chat with some girls or cruise around the city. The bars were losing a lot of business these days. You could get a special permit to stay out later, but it had to be for work, special circumstances—or you had to know people in high places. Raoul did know people in high places, but the thought of asking for a permit to stay out and get a beer sounded stupid.

"Hey. How's Phillip's campaign going?"

Raoul shrugged. "Going okay. It's only March. Too early to say much."

"But he thinks he has a shot?"

"If he didn't, he wouldn't be running."

For the most part, Raoul avoided politics. Unlike his older brother, he hadn't seen the death of his father as a higher calling to save the country. He still remembered being seventeen, celebrating the end of senior year with water balloons and shaving cream, when he'd been called to the office. One look at his mother's tear-stained, pale face and he'd felt his heart plunge. *"Raoul…at the rally…your father…"*

"Uh-oh. Check that out!" Anthony's alarmed voice broke into his thoughts. Raoul glanced at the sidewalk corner where his friend was pointing. The nearby streetlights were out, and he squinted in the dim evening lighting. Several teenagers were harassing a skinny girl with short, black hair. She was older, probably around eighteen or nineteen, but very outnumbered. They were circling around her and laughing, the biggest one making occasional grabs at her yellow plastic handbag. It wasn't an uncommon sight in the cities these days, where half the store windows were boarded up and the dark streets were filled with potholes.

"Crap," Raoul muttered, slowing his car and pulling it to the side.

The girl took a swing at one of the guys and missed. They began to push her back and forth between themselves, laughing. The largest, a muscular guy wearing ripped jeans and no shirt, managed to grab her handbag. He flipped through it as she started to cry.

"Should we do something?" Anthony asked.

Raoul honked his horn and flashed his headlights, startling the jerks away from her. He rolled down his window halfway. "Get out of here!" he yelled. "I just called the cops."

That threat was no longer as powerful as it used to be; the police only showed up half the time for random acts of street violence. Still, Raoul had a car. It was a cheaper model, a silver Honda Civic, that he used to drive around the crime ridden cities. You still had to be upper middle class to afford most vehicles, but for all they knew, he did have connections to the authorities. They would either run away or, if they had guns, try to rob him. Checking to make sure his car doors were locked, Raoul was hoping for the former.

The larger one hesitated. "Why don't you get the hell outta here and mind your own business, rich boy?!"

Raoul's heart raced, but he held firm. "Police are going to be here in five minutes." He placed his hand on the horn for five seconds. Several porch lights snapped on in nearby apartment buildings.

"The bitch doesn't have any cash on her anyway," said one of the other guys. "Screw it! Let's get the hell out of here."

The larger one continued to glare. After a second, he spit on the ground beside Raoul's front tire and turned to leave. The others sauntered away behind him, and the gang disappeared around the corner. Flattened up against the brick wall, the girl stared after them. When they were gone, she slouched in relief. She smoothed out her white blouse and jeans. "Thanks," she murmured, chest heaving.

"No problem," said Raoul. "Do you need a ride anywhere?"

"Nah. I…" She eyed him and then glanced at her surroundings. "I should be okay."

"How far do you have to walk?"

"About three miles. But it's okay. I've done it before."

Raoul gently smiled. "I promise I'll get you there. We're cool. But if you'd rather not, I get it. Stay safe tonight." He started to roll up his window.

"Wait!" She exhaled. "All right. I'll take you up on it. Thanks." With a trembling hand, she opened the back door and climbed inside. "Thanks," she repeated in a quiet voice. "I'm Megan. Or Meg."

"Raoul," he replied.

"Anthony," said his friend.

"You can go straight and then turn left on Oak Drive. Ugh! I shouldn't even be out here now, I know. But my mom was sick, and I had to go to the pharmacy before she gets worse."

"I get it," said Raoul. "Happy to give you a hand."

They drove in silence and passed a dilapidated brick building with a couple of campaign posters taped to it. They were torn and faded from the rain and winds of the previous week. "I wonder if Cameron the Crazy is going to get very far," muttered Anthony.

"I hope not," Raoul replied. "But Phillip is thinking he might."

Raoul could see Meg's brow furrow in the rearview mirror as she frowned. She seemed to feel the same way about the guy as they did, as most people on the outside did. The problem was—a lot more people were becoming part of the inside. It had seemed relatively harmless at one time. But now?

Many major cities were growing pools of violence, poverty, and corruption, and the government was using most of its waning resources to try and bring peace and stability to them. Only wealthy and gated districts, areas where Raoul was lucky enough to grow up, were safe these days.

A lot of people were leaving the country altogether.

And then there was Cameron Lourdes' expanding sect with its strict and frighteningly antiquated rules. A group of about a hundred or so had marked the meager beginnings of the group in a small southern town. Its growth had been limited until about five years ago, and most people agreed that this coincided with the rapid increase in economic turmoil and violence since that time. Suddenly, thousands began to move there and join. Entire counties were being engulfed by the movement. Cameron promised them food, jobs, safety, and a ticket into heaven. He also promised that they wouldn't have to think for themselves anymore.

"Is Cameron really that charismatic?" asked Anthony. "I don't get the appeal."

"I've heard other things go on there," murmured Meg. "And that's what makes people join."

"Not this again," muttered Raoul. He'd heard these same rumors from Phillip.

"Like what?" asked Anthony.

Megan hesitated. "That people have seen real miracles happen. And that you feel like someone is watching you. Not everywhere. But…but there's something weird going on."

"That's creepy," said Anthony. "But these people are all brainwashed, right? They probably imagine this stuff."

"Maybe. Maybe not," said Meg. "People who sneak in out of curiosity say they get a weird vibe in there, like someone is watching them. And then they get kicked out really fast."

Anthony turned around to face her with a curious smirk. "And how do you know so much about this, girlie?"

"Well…" Megan looked at her folded hands, hesitating. "My mom used to be a member. I lived with my aunt then. But after my mom ran away from them, I came to live with her. She needed a lot of help getting used to things."

"Wow," Raoul murmured. "Good for her. Most people never get away. Still, I don't think there's some sort of creepy *thing* there. It's just a bunch of crazies." *And maybe Christine…*

After a few moments, there was an uncomfortable silence, and

Raoul turned up the radio. The announcer continued to talk about the turmoil.

"There's my apartment," said Meg.

Chapter 4

The Outside.

With the Spirit on her mind, Christine often forgot about the place that lay outside of her community, but she knew that was good. Cameron said that the outside was suffering for its sins and would soon collapse into a pile of smoldering rubble. She was lucky to no longer be a part of it.

After worship services that Wednesday, she overhead two men talking to each other. Keeping her head down and her eyes to the ground, Christine listened. She always sat in the back row with the widows and other unmarried women who didn't have families, but she briefly walked beside the unmarried gentlemen as everyone was leaving.

"You were almost robbed?" she heard one man ask the other.

"At gunpoint. It's a nightmare out there. The end times. They are paying for their sloth and greed. Without Cameron and the Spirit, we would be lost."

"We would be. God be with you."

"And you."

Only the men left on rare occasions; most people didn't want to leave at all. A chain link fence surrounded the perimeters, and certain parts of it were electrified. Cameron wanted stronger reinforcements but, because the population kept expanding, it was necessary to have a barrier that could continuously be removed and rebuilt. Guards were stationed near the entrances at all times to "keep out the influences and dangers of the World."

Christine shuddered and held her book closer. *I wonder what the*

World looks like now. She forced the unwanted thought away and glanced up, now noticing that several women were watching her. They knew she was special. While all of the other females remained silent during the ceremonies each year, Christine had been permitted to sing twice. She would sing again this year, and now everyone realized that she was protected from the normal rules, under the wing of higher powers.

It had been nearly two years ago. She had first sung during the annual ceremony after her father had begged and pleaded with Cameron, the former's health failing quickly. She could only imagine their conversation. *Please give my unhappy, ungrateful daughter a chance at finding a husband. Who else would want such a somber girl after I'm gone? She has a beautiful voice, and that's the only reason any man would marry her.*

For whatever reason, Cameron had agreed to the request. Quivering, she had walked to the front of the massive assembly hall, in front of hundreds of people, and sung one of the few songs of worship that were allowed. That evening, Cameron had requested her presence in his office and had said: "My dear girl. Your sweet voice has greatly impressed the Spirit. He requests to speak with you alone."

She had fainted right on Cameron's gaping-mouthed bear rug and awoken sometime later in her father's home.

"I'm frightened," she'd told him. "I can't do this. I can't talk to the Spirit." At that time, a part of her had even questioned if the Spirit were real. She had never witnessed one of his famous miracles.

An old man had witnessed a pot of petunias levitating. Then dozens of people began to see objects rising into the air or hear holy voices singing from their rose gardens or find notes mysteriously appearing on their dressers with instructions on how to please Cameron or the Spirit. The miracles were now only an occasional occurrence, but everyone knew that the Spirit still watched over them.

Her father had taken her clammy hand into his icy fingers and stared up at her with glassy eyes. "I've always wanted what's best for you," he'd murmured. "That's why I brought us here. Don't you see? Now we know that the Lord is on our side. You are blessed, my girl. It's more than I ever could have hoped for. I can die knowing that you are favored by God." He had passed away two days later. His lungs had never been strong. A final battle with pneumonia had ripped him away from her.

After morning services, Christine walked several blocks to her housing section with her guardian at her side. Each townhouse consisted of four units, identical one-story red, brick homes surrounded by white picket fences that were solely for decoration. In every yard lay a vegetable garden on the left and a flower garden on the right, both somewhat barren at this time of year. Oddly, a few butterflies still hovered around the dead stalks and weeds. Grey concrete steps led to black doors with silver door knockers. One window was situated in the front, always covered by blinds to ensure that no one ever caught a glimpse of the female occupants. The private back of the house had a larger picture window, although the view was obscured by a red stone wall.

It was in the widows' district that Christine had been assigned after her father had died. She was one of the few girls without living relatives who stayed with an older woman until marriage. To her relief, she would be staying with Mrs. Valerius longer than anticipated.

It had been a week since her last lesson, and Mrs. Valerius was twittering on about possible matches. "The Smith boy was looking at you. I think he'd be a good provider; his father is close to Cameron. The Larson boy is nice, but he won't look you in the eye. Or—"

"Um," Christine gently interrupted.

"Oh, listen to me going on and on. I sound like my mother. What are your thoughts, Christine?"

"Well, I have something to tell you," she began, settling in at the round kitchen table. Mrs. Valerius fixed Earl Grey tea on the stove. Christine enjoyed waking up to the sound of the black kettle whistling in the mornings. "The Spirit says that I won't get married soon. I have other…things I have to do."

Mrs. Valerius turned to face her, a strand of grey hair falling out of her bun and tumbling over the side of her cheek. "Oh, I knew you were special," she murmured. "Your father knew that, too. The Spirit must be very, very pleased with you." She winked.

"I hope so. You don't mind me staying here?"

"Heavens no. You're a help to me now with my arthritis. I certainly can't garden like I used to. Did you know that I used to be able to change a tire all by myself back when—Oh, I shouldn't speak about that. See? My mind is not right sometimes."

Her grey-green eyes had a distant look as she turned back to the stove to prepare oatmeal. Sometimes she seemed sad, but Christine never inquired into the older woman's past. That time, on the Outside, was to be forgotten. They were to be grateful for the present and nothing but hopeful for the future. But there was no past.

Christine had mourned the past often in her youth, for years upon years. How could her father bring her to this cold, somber place that had no close friends for slumber parties or classrooms with teachers that made her giggle or television shows with silly talking animals or anything at all that was fun? Her days were spent at services, doing chores, listening to the elders talk about things that either frightened or bored her, or, her favorite activity, sitting outside and daydreaming.

When she could no longer remember the past very well, Christine would make up stories in her head. A fairy witch in a beautiful white ball gown, like the one in that movie, would fly down in a bubble and take her away.

In her youth, she'd been unable to hide these feelings. She had pouted in public and given short, snide responses when asked questions by her father or the elders. As punishment, she had been forced to sit in a dark closet for days or, on one horrible occasion, an entire week. The space contained nothing but a cot and a tiny bathroom. Chicken broth, saltine crackers, and water had been slipped inside through a small slot three times a day.

Her father had gripped her by the shoulders when she'd emerged after that horrid week, her face tear-stained and pale. "Now you will be a good girl?" he'd asked, bending toward her with a frantic expression. "Please be a good girl, Christine! I can't stand to see you cry, but you must be good or they will continue to correct you."

But she wasn't really a *good* girl. Oh, she had learned to control herself and keep her thoughts private. She had learned to force a smile and speak politely to the elders. But anger and discontent had still resided in her heart until the Spirit had arrived.

Curling up in an armchair with a crocheted blanket and cup of tea, she thought about her good fortune. What other duties did the Spirit want her to have? What could someone like her have to offer Him? Her stomach had been in knots over the last few days just thinking about it.

Mrs. Valerius walked through the living area with a black feather duster, cleaning the furniture as she softly hummed a tune. It wasn't an approved song, Christine knew, because it was unfamiliar to her. She'd been there for so long that she no longer remembered most of the music from the outside.

Christine frowned and silently began to chant the mantra that she had learned while lying in the dark closet as a terrified ten-year-old. *I must forget the outside; only evil lurks there. I must forget the outside; only evil lurks there. I must forget...Oh, Spirit, help me forget!*

Chapter 5

"All you people do is have meetings! Hours and hours of staring across tables and talking about how horrible everything is. You never solve anything. Yes, well, I'm right here. Call me. Don't just—Now that's the kind of tone that is taking this country down. Yeah. Same to you." He hurled the cell phone onto the counter. "Jerk."

Phillip had been on the phone most of the morning, pacing throughout the hallways. The volume of his voice had increased with each step. Raoul glanced up as his brother stormed into the kitchen. He wore a pressed gray suit and matching tie in perfect contrast to Raoul's jeans and plain white t-shirt. They had their own opinions as to how people of their class should dress in this type of world, Phillip wanting to set a good example and Raoul thinking it better to blend in as much as possible.

"What's up?" asked Raoul, not knowing if he wanted the answer.

"Look at this," said Phillip in disgust, throwing a newspaper on the table. The front headline read: "Cameron Lourdes. The Answer to Our Problems? A Look Inside His Growing Organization." The picture below the headline featured several smiling members dressed in their bland clothing.

"Okay. So he gets an endorsement and might have a few more guys in the government. It's still not a lot, right?"

"A mentally unstable person is amassing a lot of power, Raoul. It says a lot about where things are heading." Phillip paused. "Why don't you try to start some phone banks or hand out some flyers or something? Get out and talk to people about this."

"Yeah. I'll do that." Raoul pretended to be distracted by the newspaper.

They were at their mother's home, which she had kept after their father died. He and Phillip both spent a lot of time there, usually seeing to her needs and making sure she got out of the house once in a while. These days, Judy spent a lot of the time sleeping or watching ridiculous soap operas. Her eyes were always sad, even when she smiled. Their father had left plenty of money after his passing, so at least that was never a problem.

Phillip also had a small law firm. His clients were mostly poorer people who had amassed complex debts from credit cards, huge mortgages, and payday loans. He also had a new girl by his side every month, saying he was far too busy to settle into a serious relationship. This month it was Sara Lee, like the cheesecake.

Raoul had his own neighboring apartment. Depending on whether his mom wanted company, he switched back and forth. There was some safety in staying together. Raoul was fairly fearless, but even he felt his heart jump upon being awakened by distant gunshots or people yelling during the night. His apartment was looking like a refuge as Phillip continued to rant that morning. "If people your age had just stepped up in the last five years, maybe the world would be a different place—" On and on and on.

Sometimes he thought about following Anthony to South Korea within the next year, maybe taking their poor mother with him and giving her a change of scenery. A lot of his other wealthier friends had managed to leave the country. Phillip would be furious. Still, one thing had been tugging at the back of his mind all week—one mission he wanted to accomplish. Since his youth, he'd thought about her.

"Where are you going?" asked Phillip as Raoul slipped on a light jacket.

"Out."

"You know, you could at least pretend to care," snapped Phillip. "I'm over here working my ass off."

"Yeah, well, I'm going to see this girl I met last week. Megan. Her mom used to be part of Cameron's freak show. Maybe she'll know something useful, right?"

"Really?" asked Phillip, his tone softening. "That's interesting. Yeah. Talk to her and get back to me."

"Sure."

Raoul breathed a sigh of relief as he left and inhaled the polluted air; it smelled like a mix of rotting eggs and burning rubber. His gated area was nicer; the streets were paved and the few businesses there were open, including a couple of cafes and an upscale restaurant. A few men were playing at the golf course down the road, and there was the soft thud of a bouncing tennis ball in the distance. He hopped into his car and drove out of the little haven, soon entering the decrepit areas of the city.

When he arrived at his destination, a rundown brick apartment complex, Raoul smoothed his t-shirt and then knocked on a door with chipped black paint. After a couple of seconds, Meg answered. She was wearing a white robe over a pair of grey pajama pants and a black spaghetti strap shirt. She blinked in surprise and glanced down at herself as though embarrassed. "Raoul?"

"Hi. I'm sorry to show up like this, but I couldn't find your number."

"That's okay. Except I'm not exactly dressed yet. Uh, can I help you?"

"You look fine. I was wondering how your mom was doing."

Meg's face brightened. "Much better. The infection is gone. She's a little tired but doing well. Thanks again for your help."

"No problem. That's great. I was, um, also wondering if I could talk to her about some stuff. About her past, I mean. If that's not appropriate, I get it."

Meg's smiled faded, and she shuffled her feet. "What do you want to ask her about?"

"I wanted to know if your mom, when she was with Cameron's

group, had ever seen a girl who I used to know in school. It's a long shot, I know, but I thought I'd check."

"Can you give me a description of her?"

"Um. She would be around my age now, I guess. About eight when she first joined. Blonde hair. Blue eyes. Freckles. Her name was Christine Dachelet." He hadn't said her name out loud for a long time.

"Sure. Why not? Give me a sec." She dashed away. Raoul stood there for only a minute. Meg returned with a curious expression. "She...says to come in."

Raoul slowly entered, glancing around the worn two-room apartment. The walls were yellowed, and the paint was peeling. From the blanket and pillow folded up on the arm, he guessed that someone's bed was the brown sofa in the living room. A gray and white tabby cat was curled up on the other arm. It raised its head and blinked at him before going back to sleep. A woman in her mid-forties was reclining in a green armchair, her shoulder-length brown hair very gray at the roots. A colorful serape, the only bright thing in the room, was pulled up to her waist, and her mouth was drawn into a thin line. Raoul found himself intimidated; she didn't look all that happy to have him there.

"It's nice to meet you, Mrs. Getten. I'm Raoul Chandler." He held out his hand, and she gave it a limp shake.

"You can call me Caroline. Cari if you're tired." At least she had a little humor in her. Caroline turned to her daughter. "Meg, leave us a bit to talk."

"But—"

"Please, Meg. Go make sure that Cookie has food and water. Then make yourself some lunch."

Meg rolled her eyes. "Fine." She walked back toward the kitchen, peeking over her shoulder several times.

"I didn't mind her listening," said Raoul.

"I did," said Caroline. She glanced down at herself. "I must look a mess. I haven't left the house for two weeks. These bugs seem to get worse and worse."

"I'm glad you're feeling better," said Raoul, settling at the edge of the sofa.

"Hm. Can you believe I once looked like that?" Caroline pointed to a picture in a gold frame on the wall. A beautiful woman with hair in a tight bun was dressed in a pair of black leotards, hands on her hips as she gave a sexy, close-lipped smile for the camera.

"Wow. Were you a dancer?"

"For the New York City Ballet. Back before…Well, anyway. I won't bore you. You want to know about that girl?"

"I'd like to know about you as well," Raoul replied. "From what Megan said, your life sounds interesting. But only if you want to tell me." He meant it. There was something forlornly mysterious about this woman.

"I'm sure you do want to know," she murmured with a frown. "How did that pretty young thing turn into this?" She gestured toward herself in disgust. "I'm only getting into any of it because you saved my daughter and maybe me, and I'm grateful for that. It's hard to find good people in the world these days."

"Like I said, tell me only what you want."

"My life didn't start out very interesting," she began. "I had what you'd call the golden childhood. My dad was a computer software engineer. We had a huge home with a pool in the backyard. We had family vacations in Aspen, all of that. My parents could afford to send me to the best schools, and I got to live my dream. I got to dance all day long and not worry a bit about money. I was pretty spoiled, huh?"

"That sounds nice," said Raoul. "I mean, you weren't spoiled. Things were just better back then, right?"

"I guess. I met a man who was also doing well for himself. Alex. He'd been an intern at my father's company and asked me to dinner one night." Cari smiled with a reminiscing glint in her eye. "He was the tall, dark, and handsome type. A little hard to talk to sometimes, but…We got married and eventually had our daughter. Meg has his eyes. We were very wealthy, and then, well, things started to fall apart. For lots of people, as you well know. We tried to get by, but, when Meg was about seven, we lost our jobs and our house. We fought all the time; neither of us was very good at coping after living such privileged lives. Alex couldn't take it. He drove to the seashore with a gun and, well, I spent most nights after that crying and buying cigarettes with what little money I had."

"I'm so sorry," Raoul replied. He'd heard similar stories over the years.

"You're no stranger to tragedy either," she replied with a shrug. "Chandler. You look a lot like your dad. Terrible, terrible thing."

"It was."

"Well, with Alex gone, I started to panic. I had this sweet little girl to take care of and absolutely no money. Dancers weren't being hired—at least not into positions that wouldn't involve me giving up what little dignity I had left. So I guess you could say I emotionally collapsed under it all. I wanted out. But I couldn't go the way my husband did, like others were doing. I was too much of a coward for that." Caroline glanced down. "So I…I gave Meg to my little sister. She was a teacher and still had work…and I joined Cameron's group."

"Why didn't you stay with your sister, too?"

"We didn't get along so well when we were younger. I was the glamorous dancer, and she was more of a bookworm. I trusted her with Meg, but, you know, I think I was looking for a complete mental escape. Especially after my parents died, I just couldn't cope."

"What was it like?" Raoul asked, trying not to judge her.

"It was honestly kind of wonderful at first. These people fed me and clothed me. They told me I would be one of the chosen ones now. I did simple chores to earn my keep with them. I attended services and ceremonies. The outside world was blocked off, so I couldn't hear anymore awful news stories about who was killing whom. It was an escape into simplicity."

"You never brought Meg there, though?"

"No." Caroline paused. "I suppose, deep inside, I sensed a certain wrongness, especially where it came to the children. It was very strict. Only a narrow list of books and music was allowed. Limited education, particularly for the girls. Very low tolerance for anything outside of their rules. Still, I couldn't force myself to leave. But I wouldn't bring my daughter there either."

"What made you finally escape?"

She didn't answer and stared down at her folded hands.

"Caroline?" he softly asked. "It's okay if you don't want to tell me."

"This is very embarrassing for me. It's the reason I didn't want Meg to listen. I like her to think that I heroically scaled the fences and ran off into the sunset, tossing off my long skirts in favor of a pair of jeans."

"I won't tell her," Raoul assured. "I promise."

"The truth is I completely lost my mind."

"What?"

"I was chosen to do chores and housework around Cameron's compound. It's a beautiful building, enormous and like a Victorian mansion. I was doing well enough there. But then, one day, I heard Cameron talking to someone while I was sweeping the floors. It was this-this voice."

"A voice? You mean another person?"

"No. Well, I don't know. But it wasn't just any voice. It was…it's so hard to put into words, but I'd never heard such a beautiful voice. I was hypnotized by it. I *had* to know who was speaking. But when I opened the door, only Cameron was standing there in the middle of his office. He was furious over my intrusion. He kept screaming at me, 'What did you hear, Woman? What did you hear? Tell me what you heard!'"

"That must have been terrifying," said Raoul. "What a psycho."

"I told him that I hadn't heard anything, but I don't think he believed me. I was removed from my position and left to do nothing but scrub public toilets. But then I suddenly had this feeling that I was being watched. The hummingbirds and bees and butterflies around my little garden—I felt like they were watching my every move. I would hear voices sometimes, right by my ear, singing or giggling, almost taunting me. But whenever I told someone, they said I must be possessed or completely crazy."

Raoul shifted. "Maybe just being in that place caused you to become unstable."

"I felt like I was losing my mind." Cari looked up and weakly smiled. "I was finally dragged from my home in the night. I didn't know if I'd ever see my daughter again."

"You thought they would kill you?" asked Raoul, aghast. "It's that kind of thing we need to stop. If you have proof, we can—"

"But they didn't," she interrupted. "They never said they would, and I have no proof. One of the men who dragged me away said that I was an ungodly woman. He said I deserved hell. But he then said the Spirit had spoken on my behalf. I was banished, but I would see my daughter again." She closed her eyes and smiled. "Thank goodness for the Spirit."

"But you don't really believe in that, do you?" he inquired. "The Spirit, I mean."

"I don't know what I believe or think. I only know what I felt and heard. I simply try to get by these days."

"But maybe you just heard a man speaking that night?" he pressed.

She shook her head and rubbed her right temple. "I don't know. I don't really want to talk about that anymore. It gives me a migraine when I think about it too much. You wanted to know about a girl?"

Raoul surrendered on the other part of the conversation. "Yeah. A friend from awhile back. I don't even know if she was part of your group. She would have joined before you did. Christine. Dachelet." He held his breath.

Cari's face lit up a little. "I do know her. She sang in one of the ceremonies. Had a beautiful voice."

"That would be her." He felt a tugging at his heart. "She sang?"

"It was kind of unusual. Usually women are kept in the background. But not her."

"Was she okay?" A lump formed in his throat.

"She seemed fine. I only saw her that once. She sang and disappeared."

"Thank you, Caroline, for letting me know all of this." He could tell she was getting tired, her head now resting back into the chair. She appeared twenty years older than she was. Life had taken its toll on Caroline Getten. Raoul stood. "I'll let you rest now. I'm sure I'll see you around."

Find me someday.

He paused in his steps. "I have one more question."

Caroline opened her eyes and uttered a weary, "Yes?"

"How hard is it to get in there?"

Chapter 6

No personal cars were permitted, but transportation was readily available. Cameron's compound was too far for her to walk alone during the dark evenings when she had her lessons. Young women were usually not allowed to be alone with men who were not their husbands, but an exception had been made for Christine as far as the male driver was concerned. The elderly man held the car door for her, the enormous building creating a shadow over them. It was both a home and a place of business, a stone mansion and an office complex that curved into a large semicircle.

"Do you see Him?"

Outside of a polite "good evening," the driver rarely spoke to her.

"Pardon me, Sir?" she asked in surprise.

"Do you see the Spirit?" He kept his voice low so that no one else could hear. His soft felt hat fell over his kind eyes.

"No. No, I don't. I don't think he can be seen."

"But you hear him?"

"Yes," she admitted.

He smiled and clasped his hands together. "What does *he* sound like? Is it glorious?"

"Oh, yes," she whispered. "Like listening to heaven."

"Do you think he will ever talk to me? I know that I am unworthy, but I would love to hear his voice."

Christine swallowed nervously. "Oh, Sir. I don't know. He's very mysterious in his workings, and I don't question him."

"Of course. I understand. You will put in a prayer for me with him?"

"Of course. Have a good evening."

She escaped the odd conversation and ascended the stone stairs, entering the building through a glass double door. The carpeted halls were silent as always at this time of day. Still, Christine knew that she was being watched. She made her way into the special room at the far end of the left hall and shut the door tightly behind her. Immediately, that feeling of being part of the Spirit's world came upon her, sending goose bumps down her arms.

"Good evening, Christine."

She smiled and let his tenor voice pour over her, closing her eyes in bliss. "Good evening, dear Spirit."

"You are in a better mood today."

"Yes. But before we start, I was asked to put in a prayer for Mr. Thomas. He thinks so much of you." A silence followed. "Is that okay?"

"They all seek favor with me," he replied. "Everyone wants something."

"Yes. They would all like your blessing. Sometimes things are difficult, and they want hope. Maybe if you spoke to them as you do me, they would—"

"Only you are truly worthy, Christine," the Spirit harshly interrupted.

"And Cameron?"

"Yes," was his clipped reply.

"Is it..." She swallowed and wished her unholy curiosity would go away. "Is it possible to ever see you as well?"

"No."

"Not even as a light? Or a shadow?"

"It is time for your lesson, Christine. Your questions are becoming rather silly. What put these inquiries into your precious head?"

"Forgive me, Spirit. Yes. Let me sing for you now." After warming up, she sang the hymn that she would perform at the upcoming ceremony. It would be here in two weeks, and she could feel herself growing more and more nervous just thinking about all the eyes that would be upon her. No other woman would ever put herself under such scrutiny. Only the power of the Spirit would give her strength on that night, just as it had last year.

"You need confidence," he said when she was finished. "Your technique is fine, but I hear the quiver of fear in your voice. Let it go. You have done this twice before."

"There will be more people there. Every year, there are more. I'm still very nervous."

"I know, my beauty. But you will be fine. I will always be with you."

She nodded, swallowed, and looked at the floor. "Can I ask you one more thing before we begin again?"

"Yes?"

"My father, he forgives me?"

"Forgives you for what?"

"Surely you know. I resisted him. I was not obedient. Really, I was a terrible daughter. I wanted out for so long because of the strict rules. I didn't understand!"

"And now?" the Spirit questioned in a strange tone.

"Now I believe with my entire heart and soul. You showed me the truth, and I will never be disobedient again. I will be good." There was a long silence, and Christine shifted her weight. "Spirit, are you there?"

Suddenly, she heard loud piano music, a beautiful legato cascade of chords that jolted her mind and caused her heart to jump into her throat. Clutching her arms to her chest, she listened and was nearly out of breath when it was over.

The music was new.

And unapproved, as far as she knew.

As the notes continued to echo in her head, she stood there in the uncertain silence.

"Did you enjoy it?" asked the Spirit.

What if it was a test of purity? "Will that music be introduced and approved by Cameron soon?"

"No. It is only for you, Christine."

"It makes me feel strange," she murmured. She would have liked to say that the Spirit's music made her feel purer and holier. But that simply wasn't true. It was as if a current of electricity had flown through her body and made her hair stand on end. "Is it, um, is it right to enjoy that music? Are you testing me, Spirit?"

"Did you enjoy it?" he repeated.

"I…" She froze. If she said no, she would be a liar. And so she admitted the truth at the risk of punishment. "Yes," she whispered. "Yes, I loved it."

"Good. You see, your mind must be on a higher level. You will have an important role in my vision, more important than that of anyone around you. And you must keep your mind open for that role."

"You mean pure?"

"I mean *open*."

She raised her hands up toward him, palms out. "I don't understand. What do you mean by open? Please help me understand, Spirit!"

"Do not fret, my beauty. Let us begin again. You will understand when it is time."

***

"You are crazy."

"Are you in or out?"

"Out," said Anthony. "Jesus, Chandler. You want to be a badass, let's stay out past curfew and get drunk out of our minds. I'm not sneaking in there with Cameron's freaks. You're crazy." He leaned back in the chair across the table and took a sip of his steaming coffee.

They were sitting in a café near Raoul's mother's house. He had wanted to give Meg a mini vacation from the crime and deprivation of her neighborhood, and this place was still in good shape. The walls and floor were made of dark polished wood, and there were street signs from Europe posted all over the walls. He was also trying to convince her and Anthony to help with the new plan that had been forming in his mind over the last couple of days. Anthony thought he was out of his mind.

Raoul rolled his eyes. "Fine. I'll do it by myself. Unless…" He turned to Meg.

She cast her gaze toward the floor. "Um, I mean I'll help out. But, you know, after what my mom's been through, I'm not really sure I want to go in that place. What if the Spirit sees us?"

"Ugh. There is no frikin' spirit," muttered Raoul. "It's a bunch of crazies."

Meg frowned. "Are you calling my mom crazy?"

"No," Raoul replied. "I'm sorry. Not crazy. But I just don't believe that some magical god-like *thing* rules over that place. C'mon. Do you believe in it?"

"No," Meg replied. "I mean, I don't believe that there's something supernatural there. But I think there could be something that we're underestimating."

"Like what?" asked Anthony.

"I have no idea. Just a feeling from what I've heard." She shrugged. "So how exactly are you going to do this, Raoul? Are you going to go all action hero and blast through the fences with a machine gun?"

"I wish. No, all I really want to do is take a look around. I want to see her, maybe talk to her a bit. If she's not happy or in danger or something, then I'll take action."

"Are you sure Phillip can't help?" asked Anthony. "Maybe he has connections to the police? Something better than this?"

"I don't want to take it there yet. When Phil gets involved in something, he kind of goes to the extreme. I want to see her. That's all."

"How's it going to work?" asked Meg. "Did my mom tell you

anything useful?" There was a slight edge of bitterness in her voice, probably from being excluded from Raoul's conversation with Caroline.

"She said there were two ways to get in. So, the first way would be to actually try to join the stupid cult, but that's out the window. It would take a while for them to confirm me. Especially with my father and brother, they'd be extra suspicious. And they'd probably find some excuse to keep me away. I don't want to risk the scrutiny or wait for things to work out."

"Yeah," Meg said. "Plus, who'd want to be stuck in there for very long? No movies, television, good music…"

"Video games," chimed in Anthony. "Pizza. Beer."

"Anything naughty," added Meg with a cheeky grin.

"Oh, God," said Anthony in an extra dramatic tone. He smacked his palm to his forehead. "If those people ever take over, someone get me out of the country or shoot me."

"Yeah, thanks you two. You're really helping here," Raoul muttered but smiled. It was good to have friends in this day and age, people you could relax and laugh with even as everything kind of went to hell. Meg had a great sense of humor, and he was grateful on several levels for having run into her that one evening. "Okay. So plan two—and it's going to have to happen fast. Every year, they have this massive ceremony. It's like the main event where they talk about how much better they are than everyone else. And try to get other people to join."

"Oh, yeah. My mom told me about that," murmured Meg. "People come from all over."

"Exactly. There'll be big crowds around, and it'll be easier to sneak in without their security catching on. Plus Christine might be singing. So it'd be easy to spot her."

"So you're going to dress up like one of them and sneak in?" asked Anthony. "I don't know. Still seems kind of risky."

"Not really," Raoul replied. "The worse that would happen is I'd get yelled at and kicked out. They can't do anything to me."

"He's right," Meg agreed. "His brother is pretty high profile. If anything happened to Raoul, they'd be in a lot of trouble. The feds would probably like the excuse."

"I guess," said Anthony with a shrug. "All right, all right. I'll drive the getaway car when you're done doing what you have to do. Is that good enough?"

"Sounds great," Raoul replied. "I appreciate it."

"And I'll get your costume together!" said Meg, clasping her hands together.

"This is going to be more fun than I thought." Still, Raoul could feel the ache of anxiety and anticipation forming in his stomach. What if he were caught before he ever saw her? Phillip would be furious over the fact that he'd attracted attention to them both for no good reason. But Raoul wouldn't be able to leave the country unless he knew she was okay. He would always wonder.

True to her word, Meg got him looking like one of Cameron's nutty followers. It wasn't that hard—a pair of grey slacks, a dull light blue button-down shirt, a tan cap, and brown leather boots.

"How do I look?" asked Raoul, arms out from his sides as he displayed his full costume. They were in his small apartment. He sure as heck wasn't going to risk Phillip or his poor mom walking in on this circus.

"Like you stepped out of 1930," Meg replied with a satisfied smile. "Nice."

"Anything else I should know?"

"Well, according to my mom, you have to be really careful about what you say. No cursing or talking about anything, you know, normal. Stay serious. Watch the people around you to see when they clap or pray."

"I got it," said Raoul. "Blend in."

"Don't worry; you have a wholesome look about you," said Anthony with a smirk as he leaned back into the plush couch. "You'll fit in."

"Thanks?"

Meg giggled.

As the day drew nearer, Raoul continued to question his plan. There were a couple of times that he nearly backed out, once after Caroline claimed that people occasionally went missing. She could never say whether they had suffered her fate of banishment or something worse. Still, it sent a shudder through him. Then he had found a picture of himself and Christine as kids, displaying the colorful treats they had just bought from an ice cream truck. The plan was back on.

It was about a two hundred mile drive to Cameron's main compound, which is where the ceremony would be held. Driving that distance was always hazardous. People along the highway would try to rob you. Dozens of homeless people were always standing on the side, holding up signs and trying to catch a ride. Then there were a few with the "Apocalypse is Upon Us! Repent!" signs in giant painted red letters. Even crazier were the people who tried to end their lives by jumping in front of vehicles; that happened a couple of times a year.

"Good luck!" Meg exclaimed, hugging him as he and Anthony prepared to leave. "Tell the Spirit I said 'hi.'"

"Will do," said Raoul, feeling as though a rock had settled in the pit of his stomach.

Right after merging onto the highway, they drove past the people with signs and through a couple of near-ghost towns, places where unemployment had become so bad that there was basically no way to survive. Occasionally, you might see some farmers working on their land, people who had found ways to sustain themselves, but they were few and far between. His dad had often mourned farming as a lost art. Otherwise, there were houses with the roofs caving in, and "Closed" signs on cracked store windows. They passed an empty playground where most of the swings were hanging on by one chain, the seats nothing but vertical pieces of rubber swaying in the breeze. A somber silence settled over the car.

I need to get the hell out of here. From Anthony's expression, Raoul guessed that he was thinking the same thing.

As they left any sign of civilization and neared their destination,

Raoul noticed a few more vehicles on the highway. An outline of a large structure was visible in the distance among the rolling grassy hills. They turned off the highway and made their way down a side street. The towering mansion was protected by a chain link fence so long that it disappeared into the distance. Many smaller structures were also behind the barrier, perhaps an entire town. Dozens of people were migrating toward the front of the gate, men dressed like Raoul and women in long solid-colored dresses.

"Holy crap," muttered Anthony. He slowed down at the side of the road, keeping his distance from the craziness. "You sure you want to do this?"

"It's perfect," he said. "Caroline was right. No one will notice me in this mess."

"Yeah, no one will notice if you disappear in this mess either. If anything happens to you, I get your car. The BMW."

"Deal," murmured Raoul. He gathered his courage. "All right. Wait if you can. If anyone gets suspicious, go ahead and get out of here. I might be a couple of hours."

"Yeah, I brought some music."

Nothing that bad can happen. Still, Raoul's nerves were getting to him. The air was definitely fresher here, smelling of pine and the new blossoms of spring. A warm breeze brushed against his cheeks and rustled the leaves and the grass. Other than that and the occasional twitter of a bird, the place was strangely silent. It all seemed so removed from everything that he felt like he was stepping into a foreign country.

Raoul squared his shoulders and treaded toward the entrance, trying to mimic the stride of the men around him. The women and children followed behind, heads slightly bowed. To his dismay, he heard them taking names toward the front. "The Johnsons from Austin, Texas. The Smiths from Jacksonville, Florida. The Browns from Tulsa, Oklahoma." At least it was somewhat disorganized as they tried to rush people through.

A man with his wife and eight, nine, no, *ten* children was in front of him. Raoul wished that the kids were screaming and running around to create a distraction, but they were surprisingly well-behaved. *All right. Time for another plan.* As Raoul and the family approached, he gritted his teeth and stepped in front of the smallest boy, subtly blocking him from the view of the guard at the front. "The Hensons from Tennessee," said the father. "There are twelve of us."

The guard nodded and checked them off. Swallowing, Raoul slipped through the gate with the family. He was about to breathe a sigh of relief when the guard said, "Wait. I think that was thirteen."

"Sir, there are twelve in my family," argued the husband in a calm tone. "Me, my wife, and ten children. The ceremony will begin soon, and we don't want to miss the opening."

With a puzzled frown, the guard looked down at his list again, and Raoul used that moment to duck into the crowds that were heading toward the enormous structure. Cari was right; it was beautiful and mysterious. The entire place was strange, and it was easy to see how people would get caught up in the magic.

He took another deep breath to clear his mind. The adrenaline in his veins was energizing now that he had come this far.

As he stared at the masses of people, all of them dressed alike, his heart fell a little. He hoped she'd sing. There'd be no way to find her otherwise. He'd be screwed.

A bell rang from somewhere high above, echoing around him.

Phillip was right to be worried; Cameron had a disturbing number of sheep now.

Chapter 7

Twisting her hands together, Christine waited behind a heavy red curtain for her time to sing. She was nearly sick with anxiety, her heart pounding in her ears as the volume of the murmurs in the giant room increased with the number of people. The Spirit would guide her, she knew, but that didn't completely extinguish her fear. She prayed to him. *Please let me do well. Please help me make you proud, dear Spirit.*

Finally, the room silenced, and Cameron spoke, his deep, steady voice filling the meeting hall. "Welcome, welcome, my friends. God be with you all. And to those who have traveled far to be here today, to see if you want to become part of our beautiful community, I extend my greatest gratitude. My friends, we are the chosen, and we are the future. If you are still in any way part of the sinful World, take a look around the next time that you are in it. Do you have any desire to be among its ruin? I believe that I know the answer. You know that answer."

Cameron paused, giving everyone a moment to take in his words. He continued, "It is no secret that our strength continues to grow." He pointed to a tall middle-aged man on his right. "We have our first elected member in the House, Adam Patterson." Applause. "We have multiple elected officials at the state and local levels. And, as you now know, I am running for Governor of this great state." The room exploded into cheers of victory. "The polls are already looking good, my friends!"

Cameron spoke for almost an hour, only interrupted by occasional moments of silence and hymns sung by the male chorus. He talked about the coming end of the country and how they would be the ones to survive the collapse and rise above the ruin to form a holier nation that would finally obey the rules of God. It was the same speech given every year, more or less. There were many more people this time, perhaps thousands. Walls in the assembly hall had been knocked down to make room.

She grabbed a cold wall to steady herself. Suddenly, the lights flickered several times. Cameron paused. Then, after letting out a short laugh, he said, "I believe I know what that was, my friends. The Spirit is showing his support for our cause. He will help us in any way he can, but *we* must be the ones to rise above the chaos, asking for his help during those moments when it seems all hope is lost."

A pause.

Then came the part Christine feared.

"And, now, a bit of a special treat for you," Cameron continued. "As you know, the Spirit himself has gifted one of our own with an amazing and holy voice. Not only that, but she has been chosen by him as a beacon of light and goodness. May I humbly present to you, Ms. Christine Dachelet."

She emerged. The view of the room from the stage was dizzying, and she envied Cameron's ability to speak so easily to all these people. He had always been a charismatic speaker who could cause the room to buzz with energy and excitement. All eyes were now upon her with everything from jealousy to curiosity to wonder. Some of the men were also gazing at her in a way that brought discomfort. She turned away from the sea of eyes and focused on the Spirit instead, looking upward to the wooden beams on the ceiling. *Please guide me. Please help me do well.*

Once at the microphone, she paused, smoothing her pine green and white checkered dress and adjusting her lace collar. At least her hair was out of her face and not a bother, clipped back with a matching green bow. Her lips parted, and she sang her hymn. She sang only for the Spirit, not for Cameron and not for all the eyes. She could feel Him give her voice power, lifting it off the ground and making it soar throughout the room. As she progressed, it became even stronger. Though there were no windows, light seemed to shine down from the ceiling, forming a halo around her and blinding her from everything except His energy. Face tilted toward the ceiling, she finished on her highest note. She sighed in relief as the applause began and the light faded, leaving her out of breath, smiling, and in a daze. Even the solemn Cameron was clapping. She quickly stepped aside as he approached the microphone, bowing her head in respect.

"Thank you, Christine," he said with an approving nod. "It is obvious that the Spirit is a part of your soul now. All women should strive to be as you are—chaste and pure. Ladies and gentleman, she is your example."

Christine was still dizzy as she headed toward the curtain, people murmuring as she passed. She merely smiled, wanting to escape the crowds and hear what the Spirit thought of her performance. That was all that really mattered in the end. Would it be appropriate to sneak off to her secret room, or should she stay for the rest of the ceremony? One of the elders was playing a slow song on the piano now. Perhaps she could leave for a bit and then return before anything important happened. If Cameron noticed, the Spirit would explain her absence to him. Her mouth was dry, and she swallowed as she approached the doors to the exit.

A hand grabbed her upper right arm, the warmth of it seeping through the cotton of her dress. She jumped into the air and turned to see a young, attractive man standing behind her. A blush filled her cheeks; no one had ever dared touch her before. It was strictly prohibited. "C-can I help you, sir?" she stuttered, keeping her head down.

"Christine?" His voice was soft and kind. "Christine Dachelet? It's Raoul Chandler."

"R-Raoul?" Her mind was swirling.

"Don't you remember? Third grade? Nottingham Elementary?"

She slowly looked back up at him, mouth falling open as the memories rushed over her. Slides, movies, cookouts, trampolines, skating, swimming, a big yellow dog... "Oh. I can't believe it. Raoul! Raoul

Chandler!" She lowered her voice. "But how are you *here*? Have you joined us?"

"No," he admitted with a blush. He took her hand, and she allowed it. "I sneaked in here to see you after I found out you were here through—Gah. It's a long story. I've always wondered what happened. I always missed you. I wanted to know that you were okay."

"Oh," she whispered. "Raoul, I—" She brought her right hand up and touched his left cheek with the tips of her fingers. "I can't believe it." That was all she could say. She felt as if they were the only two people present at that moment, isolated in another world that was not here nor on the Outside.

He grinned. "I can't believe it's really you either. You look different but kind of the same. Ha ha. I probably do, too, right? And your singing. Wow! You sounded amazing, Christine. I'm glad you still have that."

"Thank you. Me, too. I—" As Cameron spoke again, it finally dawned on her that they weren't alone. *And the Spirit.* What would the Spirit think of this? "You could be in so much trouble being here."

He shrugged. "I'm not worried about it." Raoul leaned in; his breath smelled like peppermint. "I have to know, Christine. Are you really happy here?"

"What?" she whispered.

"Tell me whether you're happy. Tell me if you want out of this. You're over eighteen; there's nothing they can do."

"I-I don't…I'm not…" She stuttered because the question was beyond her comprehension. Several years ago, the answer would have been: *Yes! Oh, please, yes!* But the Spirit. She couldn't leave the Spirit after all he had given her. She was chosen. Her destiny was no longer in her control.

"I swear," he continued. "I'll get you out. Just say the—*Ah!*" Raoul cried out as two hands clamped down on his shoulder. Christine gasped.

Two tall men, wearing the black shirts and trousers that were standard for the guardians, stood behind him with stern expressions. Cameron had introduced the guardians several years ago, saying that the Spirit believed more protection was necessary. "It is time for you to leave now, young man," said one. "I don't believe you're supposed to be here. You don't have Cameron's blessings to be here, do you?"

"Please don't hurt him!" Christine exclaimed as they roughly guided Raoul away. People came between them, curious over the commotion, and he was dragged out of her view and through the exit. He tried to twist away, but his efforts were useless.

She clutched the collar of her dress as a clammy sweat formed on her forehead, still feeling as though she'd been punched in the stomach and yanked out of a dream. The other world. The little boy who hated avocado. Another lifetime, really.

"Did he hurt you?" asked one of the remaining guards.

She looked up. "N-no, not at all. Will he be okay? What will happen to him?" The man turned away and didn't answer her. Too many questions were not becoming of a woman, especially *those* types of questions. There was only one entity who would know.

She rushed into the hall and raced down the stairs. After throwing open the door to the room and nearly slamming it behind her, Christine fell to her knees. "Spirit? Spirit, please speak to me?" Eerie silence answered her. "Spirit, please make sure that Raoul isn't hurt. He's my friend from a long time ago. He only came to see me. Please say he'll be okay!"

Silence.

And then…

"Why do you care so dearly for that boy's welfare that you must run in here and pester me with it?"

The rumbling, angry voice made her flinch. She lowered her head, hands splayed out on the ground. "Spirit, he is a friend from long ago. From when my mother and father were both alive. That's all. Please tell me he'll be okay."

"He is a heretic. An outsider. He is destined for hell. You should not care what happens. He is already damned."

Her upper lip trembled as she stared at the carpet. "Even if that is true," she whispered, "please let him stay safe on Earth."

Another long silence followed. "He will be released to the outside," the Spirit finally replied. "It is not my place to judge those who do not follow Cameron. But he had better remain there."

She nodded, her shoulders relaxing. "Yes, Spirit. I'm sure he will. Thank you for your mercy."

"It is not mercy!" he snapped. "It is the order of things."

"Yes, I understand. Thank you still." She swallowed and tried to turn the conversation around. Raoul would be safe; that was all that mattered. "Did I do well?"

"Yes, my beauty." His voice turned softer. And there was a touch of weariness that she'd never heard until now. "You shone like the brightest star. You were perfection. I have never been so proud."

"I couldn't have done it without you."

"As Cameron said, you will become a beacon for all. A woman of true virtue as you guide others toward righteousness with your voice."

"I don't know if I'm ready for that."

"You will be," the Spirit replied. "I will see to it."

"Is that what you meant when you said I was part of your vision? My voice?"

A pause. "That is a part of it."

"What's the other part?"

"That will be known in time."

"What is it like out there?" she asked, looking toward the ceiling. "The World. I know it is not a good question, but I wonder sometimes. Please don't be angry."

"It is horrid."

"I don't remember it being so terrible when I was a child," she murmured. "Maybe that's why I get confused."

"It has changed since your youth. It is violent and dirty, and the scent of death and poverty fills the wicked air. It is no place for someone like you, dear girl."

"What happened to it?"

"If you have such an interest in the World, then perhaps you have no need of me?" His voice was cold once more.

"No. Forgive me. Please don't leave. You're right. I'm blessed to be here with you, Spirit. Please don't leave me."

"I will not leave you, my beauty. Never. I have used so much of my power for the ceremony today that perhaps I am weary and being unnecessarily harsh. I will always be with you."

"Thank you." Completely exhausted, Christine stayed in that position on her knees for a long time, trying to make some sense of it all. When she was finally ready to leave, she wondered if he was gone. Surely the Spirit had more important things to do than linger in the silence with her. Still, she whispered, "Goodnight, Spirit."

"Goodnight, Christine."

***

Raoul's face was burning hot with anger as he threw open the door of the car and climbed in. He stared straight ahead, taking deep breaths and struggling to keep calm. Anthony watched him in the dim late afternoon light, allowing him some time to chill out before he asked, "So did you see her?"

"I did," Raoul replied, licking his lips to bring moisture to his dry mouth.

"Wow. How was she?"

"I don't know. I was dragged out of there by goons before I could talk to her very long. They questioned me for like an hour and then finally let me leave."

"What did they ask you?"

"What you'd think." Raoul deepened his voice to mimic them. "What are you doing here? Who let you in? What do you want? Are you with the government? Do you know you're going to Hell?"

Anthony shook his head. "Well, I hope you left my name out of it. What'd you say?"

Raoul shrugged. "That I was some stupid kid who wanted to look around and see what it was all about. Maybe I'd join or something. Then I told them I'd get the cops and a lawyer if they placed another hand on me. They didn't seem like they were going to kill me, so I didn't have to use my family name as a final card. Who knows how much they'll figure out? Ugh. Let's get the hell out of here."

Anthony started the engine, slowly turning the car around. The roads were empty. They'd be lucky if they could get back before the city curfew. A ticket was just what Raoul needed right now.

"So could you tell how she was doing at all?" asked Anthony once they were on the highway.

"She was physically okay, I guess. But she didn't look right. Her voice was fantastic. But she had this vacant look on her face half the time."

"Like brainwashed?"

"Exactly. Not the girl I remember. Christine was fun and happy. This girl was like a scared doll. It wasn't right."

"Hm."

They passed several people holding signs. "Goin' My Way? Need a Friend?" "Will Pay $5 to Get to Boston." "Broke and Starving. God Bless U."

"What are you going to do?" asked Anthony after a moment. "Leave it alone, or...?"

Raoul was staring out his window, watching the sun descend and wondering the same damn thing. "I'm going to talk to Phillip," he finally said. "Make some kind of deal with him."

"Calling in the big guns?"

"Yeah."

Chapter 8

Christine desperately sought normalcy over the next few days, trying to avoid thoughts about her voice or the Outside. She devoutly went about the chores she had been doing since she first arrived, gardening and food preparation and cleaning. She turned a deaf ear to Mrs. Valerius as the older woman gushed on about her vocal performance. Every time Christine allowed a thought to enter her mind, it seemed sinful. Pride and vanity over her performance. Curiosity regarding the World and Raoul Chandler.

Several times, she thought of visiting the Spirit for reassurance. Then again, she might make him angry with her stupid questions.

About five days after her performance, she'd begun to find inner peace. Everything would be okay, and life would continue on as it had. She would visit the Spirit for her lesson soon, and he would reassure her that all was going as planned and that he was in complete control of her future. *Why should she worry when the Spirit was in control?* With these thoughts, Christine was sitting in the armchair and embroidering a white handkerchief with little grey doves. Mrs. Valerius was in the other chair sipping on tea and reading.

A loud knock at the front door caused them both to jump. "This is a strange hour for visitors," said Mrs. Valerius, checking the clock as her brow furrowed. She rose to answer it. As Christine heard her talking with several men, another panicky feeling engulfed her. She set down the handkerchief and tried to listen.

"You have got to be kidding me," said Mrs. Valerius. "This just can't be. Christine? You must have the wrong person. Didn't you hear Cameron? She is our beacon. She's a good girl."

Shaking, Christine stood and walked to the door. Three tall men whom she recognized to be guards were standing there with somber expressions. A car with its headlights on was parked at the side of the road, and she blinked in the bright glow. "What's happening?" she whispered.

"You're wanted for questioning," said one of the men, his frown evident beneath his beard.

"By C-C-Cameron? Or the Spirit?"

"No, Ms. Dachelet. From the Outside."

Christine's heart dropped. "*What? Why?*"

"I don't know. They're waiting at the front for you. You have to come."

One of the other men spoke, his eyes gentler. "I'm sure it will be settled. A misunderstanding. But Cameron wants us to comply for now."

Mrs. Valerius had a hand to her heart. "This doesn't make any sense. Christine has nothing to do with the Outside."

"Should I bring anything?" Christine asked, biting her lip to hold back tears.

"A few items of clothing," said the first man. "Just in case you're made to stay. There are only vulgar clothes on the outside."

Christine rushed back to her bedroom and grabbed a large leather handbag. She threw in several dresses, undergarments, and toiletries. As an afterthought, she threw in one of the few photographs she had of her mother and father. They were standing in front of an enormous waterfall with big smiles, their faces tan and their eyes hidden by sunglasses. The picture was one of the few objects she had been allowed to keep from the Outside, and it nearly made her cry to see it now. "Please help me, Spirit."

She ran back downstairs and cast a helpless look toward a crying Mrs. Valerius. "I'll be okay," she whispered. "I'll be fine. The Spirit will protect me." Christine was escorted to the vehicle with men on all sides of her, and she felt others watching from their porches and windows. This would certainly be a scandal. What ungodly thing had Christine done now? Despite her efforts to hold them back, tears fell down her cheeks.

What could she have done? Was this a test of some kind? Was she supposed to try to get away? No, she had pledged obedience. But how could this be happening to her?

Several minutes later, they stopped at the front gate. Christine clutched her bag until her knuckles turned white.

"We are going to give you to them now," said the stern guard. "God be with you. Be strong and silent. Do not let their evil ways sway you."

While silent, Christine felt far from strong; in fact, she was utterly terrified as she approached another awaiting vehicle with a flashing blue light on top. Men in black uniforms with badges approached her. *Policemen*, she remembered. They were the law on the Outside. Turning her head slightly to take one last look behind her, Christine could see Cameron standing in the distance, frowning with his arms tightly folded across his chest.

"You people will pay for all of this," she faintly heard him say. "And you had better return her, or you will see legal action. The girl is happy here. You're taking her against her will, and I won't have it."

As she climbed in the back of the police car, she couldn't hear the reply. Hands folded in her lap, she stared out the window.

"Are you comfortable?" asked an officer from the passenger seat. Christine blinked in surprise at the voice. This policeman was a policewoman. "This must all be pretty scary. I promise it's going to be okay."

Maybe she wasn't being led to her doom. *Oh, Spirit. Where are you? Is this a trial? Have you done this somehow? I don't understand. Is this part of your plan?*

There was no reply, and she was helpless as they drove her away from the place that had been her home for nearly twelve years. Eventually, it became too dark for her to see anything for the majority of the drive, just an empty rolling field or a tree here and there. She was too horrified to sleep, and so she merely stared into the night.

Suddenly, around eight according to the digital clock in the car, there was light. Blinding, colorful, artificial light. Blue and yellow and red. Sometimes it flashed and twinkled on signs.

She looked around and saw things she hadn't seen in ages. Certain restaurants. She remembered the special meals where she got a toy with her hamburger. A movie theater. A female in a skirt that went far above her knees and tall shoes that caused her to rise high over the ground. *High heels.* It was all there, even though it somehow looked sadder, older. Yes, the World had definitely gotten worse, just as the Spirit had said. Still, Christine gazed over all of it with the wonder of a newborn.

City.

Christine was so enraptured by the sights around her that she barely noticed when the car came to a halt. Still clutching her bag, she jumped when her door was opened by the female officer. "Follow me, Ms. Dachelet," she said. "This is almost over." Christine stared up at the policewoman; her hair was pulled into a tight bun beneath her hat, and her eyes were calm. Christine couldn't dislike her.

They were in front of a square brick building with bright porch lights. She squinted as she was led out of the car, surrounded on all sides as they walked toward the glass door. A gust of warm air hit her as she entered and was confronted with linoleum tiles and plain white walls.

"I hope you know what you're doing," said a male police officer to someone behind her. "That was messy. If she wants to stay, we're going to have to deal with them pestering us for a while. If it hits the news cycle, we're going to have to spin it our way."

"I figured as much. Don't worry; I'll take care of it. Let Cameron throw a temper tantrum."

She turned around to see whom the policeman was speaking to. A tall, broad man was standing there, looking rather dignified in black pants and a white dress shirt. He seemed a little familiar to her as a wry half-smile formed on his mouth. "Hey there, Christine. It's been awhile.

Remember when you and Raoul sneaked into my room to play computer games and deleted my final paper? Was that your idea or his?"

"Phillip," she fondly whispered.

"Yeah. How you doing, kiddo?"

Someone spoke behind her. "Christine."

She turned toward the familiar voice on her other side. "Raoul?"

"Yeah." He weakly smiled and walked closer to her. "It's me, Christine."

Chapter 9

"I don't understand. What's happening?"

"I got you out," said Raoul. "I had to. You looked so-so trapped. I got you out, and you never have to go back."

"You did *this*?"

"I wanted to free you."

"Oh," she whispered, arms falling limply to her sides. The bag slipped from her fingers and hit the floor with a dull thud. "What have you done?"

"You told me to come find you, remember? That was the last thing you said when we were kids. Well, I did. I found you and got you out."

She closed her eyes. "What have you done?"

"What do you mean?"

"You can't just take me out of there! You can't just do this!" She started to cry.

"But I…You really didn't want to leave?" whispered Raoul. They soon sat on a backless bench in the police building, and his head was bent as he stared intently at her face. "Is it because of your dad? Is he still there?"

"No," she murmured. "He died a couple years ago. Of pneumonia."

"Oh. I'm so sorry." He paused. "My dad is gone, too."

"How?"

"He was at a campaign rally several years ago. And this crazy anarchist came into the room and shot eight people. My dad held on a few days, but…" Raoul shook his head.

"I'm very sorry. He was always nice to me." After a moment,

Christine added, "We don't have that."

"Don't have what?"

"Senseless violence. We don't have shootings there."

Raoul tried not to be annoyed. "So you only want to stay because you think it's a nice place? It seems so restrictive and, I mean, I don't want to insult it. But I don't see how you could be happy there. You seemed frightened when I saw you."

"It's not about being happy, Raoul. It's…I have a duty. The Spirit says so, and I can't disobey him. My future is his now."

"You believe in the Spirit?" he asked, unsuccessfully trying to hide the disdain in his voice.

"Oh, yes," she whispered. "Of course I do."

"But how do you know he's real?"

"I feel it. And he speaks to me! At least once a week. He gave me my voice. He's everything."

"Have you seen him?"

She hesitated, picking at a loose thread on her dress. "No. I don't think he can be seen. Just heard. And he performs miracles."

"Like what? I hope it's cooler than making the lights flicker." Raoul chuckled at his own joke. Christine frowned. "Sorry."

"He always watches us. He always knows if people are acting righteously."

"That's kind of creepy."

She glared at the floor.

"I'm sorry, Christine. God, I sound like a big jerk. But you're telling me a voice without a body speaks to you. You really hear it?"

"Yes!" she snapped. "And I don't care if you don't believe in him. You wouldn't, Raoul! You're on the *outside*, and you can't understand!"

"You're right," he murmured. He filled his cheeks with air and then released a long breath. "I don't understand. I probably never will, and I'm sorry. I thought you were unhappy there. That's why I got Phillip involved. I didn't want to make you sad. I promise."

"So you'll take me back then?"

He inwardly cringed. "Could you just stay out here for a little while? A couple of days? Please?"

"Why?"

To change your mind? Get de-brainwashed? "So we could talk again. It's been forever, and I've really missed you. That's all."

Her face scrunched up in thought. "I do want to see things out here. I'm sinfully curious. I was terrible about that when I was a child. And I would like to talk to you. But—"

"But?"

"I don't want the Spirit to become upset."

"Doesn't he allow you to have vacations?" he asked, trying to keep his voice as serious as possible. She tilted her head. This was getting ridiculous. "How about three days? Three days of staying out here with me. Please? Don't you remember how much fun we had when we were kids?"

"Oh." She groaned. "Fine. Two days. But then you *have* to take me back! I can't stay away from the Spirit for very long, Raoul. You have to promise you'll take me back there soon, or he'll get really angry."

"I promise," he said. "Cross my heart and hope to die." She nodded, her shoulders slumping now that the decision was made. Raoul wondered how Cameron had managed to trick all these people into believing in this spirit thing. Intercoms? Some kind of weird technology, obviously. It was sick and twisted. "Be right back." Raoul hopped up and walked to where Phillip was chatting with the police.

His older brother turned toward him "What's going on?" he asked with annoyance. "I thought you said she really wanted out. That doesn't seem like what's happening here!"

"She's just scared," Raoul interrupted. "I need a little time with her. It'll be okay. We can take her back to our house."

"Shouldn't we try to find a counselor or something? That's what the police suggested. It's hard to find any mental health help these days, but I could probably call in a favor somewhere."

"Maybe later, but there's no time for that right now. I need some space to talk with her."

"Yeah," said Phillip. "I guess. As long as she's willing. The last thing I need in the news is a kidnapping accusation."

"There won't be. She wants to stay for a couple of days."

"Fine. I'll call Mom and let her know. But I hope that confused kid has some good information for us. And, whatever happens, you still owe me."

"I know." Raoul had promised to take an active role in Phillip's campaign and help in the fight against extremist forces, start phone banks and conversation booths and create flyers. Whatever. Raoul would have promised Phillip the White House if it had meant helping Christine escape.

Phillip had figured that the best way to go about getting her out of there was to bring the police into the fray. They would say that they needed to question Christine, claiming that she might have some information about an illegal incident in the city. It had been somewhat risky, but, as expected, Cameron wanted to lay low and not create a ruckus over one girl. Cameron Lourdes was surprisingly rational for a crazy person, Phillip often said. That's what made him dangerous.

"Will you come with us tonight?" Raoul asked, crouching down next to her again.

"With you and Phillip?"

"Yeah. I thought you said you would come for two days. What's wrong?"

"You're both men," she whispered, her face flushing. "I'm not supposed to be with just men."

"My mom is there."

"So she'll be with us the entire time?"

"Yeah. You can have the guest bedroom right next to her. She can help you if you need anything, you know, that you might feel uncomfortable asking me for." God, this was awkward—a far cry from Christine diving into his arms and thanking him for rescuing her. That had been how he had imagined this would happen, anyway.

"Okay. That sounds fine." She grabbed her bag and slowly stood, looking between them. "But I'll be alone with you in the car?"

"Yes," said Raoul. He rubbed his temples and struggled for patience. "I guess I could ask my mom to drive all the way over here. Or maybe that police lady could come."

"No," she said after thinking for a moment. "As long as it's just the car."

Thank God. "Let's go," he said to Phillip with a sideways nod of his head. After a short exchange with the police officers, his brother followed them outside.

Once they were in the car, Christine looked around and asked, "What happened to all the lights?"

"The lights? Oh. Curfew," Raoul replied.

"I don't remember that. I mean, I had a bedtime. But I don't remember adults having to be inside, too."

"No, that only happened a couple of years ago," said Raoul.

"Why is there a curfew here?" she asked, sitting forward. "And what happened to everything?"

"The curfew is because of crime," Raoul replied. "What do you mean by what happened?"

"It looks different. Not as nice. Or maybe it's because I've been away for so long."

"No, you're right," said Phillip. He loved having this discussion. "Things aren't all that good. Not here and not in a lot of other places in this damn—uh, pardon my language—in this country. Long story short, unemployment kept going up, and no one could find work. Most people can barely get by."

"No one knows why things never got much better," added Raoul. "There was a worldwide recession about fifteen years ago, when we were kids. Most other countries recovered. It looked like it would happen here. People were finding work again. Crime was going down."

"Right," said Phillip. "But then things seemed to get worse again overnight. I've talked to economics professors, historians. None of them have quite figured out the reason."

"I know why." Her voice was barely audible.

"Why?" asked Raoul.

"Because there is so much sin here. This is a very bad world. It's doomed to fail. That's what Cameron and my father said. That's what the Spirit says."

Phillip opened his mouth to rebut her, but Raoul nudged him. His older brother rolled his eyes but was silent. Raoul glanced back at her several times during the quiet drive. Christine was staring out the window, almost as though she were searching for something in the darkness.

They reached the gated neighborhood, and he led Christine into his house, cautious in his movements so as not to startle her. She seemed so jumpy and fragile. His mother was on the couch watching television in a nightgown and pink bathrobe. Christine's gaze immediately went toward the talking box and then back to her. "Oh, Christine! It's been such a long time. It's so good to see you again," said Judy, standing.

Christine smiled, probably relieved to see another woman. "You as well, Mrs. Chandler." They tentatively hugged. "Your house is so nice and different."

Judy shot him a puzzled expression, and Raoul mouthed, "I'll talk to you later, Mom."

He led her to the quaint guestroom upstairs. It had a bright blue canopy bed, and the shelves and four-drawer dresser were decorated with white and blue Ming pottery. The wallpaper was also striped white and blue. His mom had once been an interior decorator, and their house still displayed the beautiful evidence.

"The bathroom is connected to the room, right over there," he said. "Let me know if you need anything." She set her bag on a table, gaze falling toward the carpet. "So, unless you'd like to talk some more, I'll let you get some sleep. You're probably exhausted from all this." Raoul was feeling a little guilty about the whole thing. "Well, goodnight, Christine. It's really great to see you." He turned to leave.

"Raoul?"

He glanced up hopefully. "Yeah?"

"You can come back with me. I want you to be safe, too. I'll make sure that the Spirit protects you."

He lowered his head. "Let's talk about everything later. I think we're both pretty tired."

She nodded, a troubled glint in her eyes. "Okay. Good night, Raoul."

"Night."

Chapter 10

Christine barely slept that night, still confused and shaken. Half the time, she expected the Spirit's voice to boom out of the darkness, demanding to know why she'd left, condemning her to Hell. There was never a Voice, but the noises there were very strange. She heard banging, electrical humming, horns, and sirens. How did anyone sleep?

She couldn't deny her curiosity. Ever since she was a little girl, even after the Spirit had spoken to her, she had wanted to experience the Outside again. It had been difficult to resist the opportunity with Raoul begging her, his handsome face so desperate and forlorn.

Raoul Chandler. He was right out of a fairy tale. If he'd reached her at sixteen, she would have jumped on his white horse and let him carry her far away to his castle. She had missed him. But she couldn't go with him now. *Not with the Spirit.*

A knock awoke her from a shallow slumber as the sun rose. "Christine?"

"Yes?" she hoarsely asked. She blinked several times to reprocess where she was.

"Can I come in?"

"Um, I'm still in bed."

A pause. "That's okay."

"No, it's not. Let me dress." She pulled the covers over her in case he walked in.

"All right. It's cool. Let me know when you're done, okay?"

"Okay."

He was a man, her old friend, and an Outsider. And she had no idea whether to show him respect, friendship, or scorn. She had trusted him enough to take her to a safe place. She'd always trusted Raoul when they were children, and there was still nothing but kindness and concern in his eyes. He just didn't understand how things had to be now.

Christine got up and slipped on a yellow dress with blue clovers over her undergarments. She pulled her long hair back with a yellow headband. She felt far too vulnerable and out of place here to shower.

"You look nice," Raoul said as she emerged. He scratched the back of his head, looking her up and down with an expression she couldn't read.

"Thank you." She followed him downstairs. It was difficult to keep her gaze off certain gadgets—televisions and radios and computers. So many sounds and pictures assaulted her senses at once. On the TV, a man in a suit and a woman in a very short red dress were dancing in a way that would have infuriated Cameron.

"Feel free to watch whatever you want," said Raoul. "Mom won't mind."

"I won't," said Judy. "Unless you turn it to football. Ethan always used to do that." She smiled and turned back to her magazine. Christine found her kind of sad.

She averted her gaze from the television. "No, that's okay. I don't want to watch anything."

"How are you feeling this morning?" Raoul asked. He held out a white box of assorted muffins toward her. "They're fresh. This lady down the street sells them."

She chose an apple bran muffin. "I'm fine, thank you. Um, thanks." The sweet bread was moist and delicious. She never had dinner last night.

"Did you sleep well?"

"Yes," she lied.

"Good." He shifted. "So, uh, is there anything you'd like to see or do? I'd love to show you around a little bit. The nicer parts. Take you to a movie? Anything!"

She smiled. Her one last chance to see the World, and her mind was already going blank. "We could drive past our old elementary school. That'd be fun! And maybe the zoo. Or a mall. Or a park."

"Okay," said Raoul. "Well, I think the zoo is closed for renovation. But the rest sounds like a plan. Awesome."

"Will your mom come with us?"

"Probably not. She doesn't like to get out much." He must have noticed her dismayed expression. "But, hey, I know. There's my friend, Megan. A girl, obviously. Her mom used to be part of Cameron's group! In fact, she's the one who told me you were there. Do you know a Caroline Getten?"

"No."

"Okay, then. I'd invite my friend Anthony, too, but he can be a little over the top. So we'll keep it simple."

His eyes were so hopeful, and his smile was kind and warm. If only he would understand how much trouble he was in out here, being part of the World. As he hopped up and made a phone call, she watched him and wondered if he could ever be convinced to join her. Then he would be saved, too.

"Meg is going to take a bus and meet us at the front soon," said Raoul, slipping on a jacket. "Ready?"

"Yes," she replied. After running upstairs to grab the one knitted sweater she'd brought, Christine followed Raoul outside. His neighborhood was rather lovely in the sunlight, the houses freshly painted and the yards tended. Not everything in the World was falling apart.

Raoul introduced her to Meg Getten, and Christine immediately noted that the girl was her physical opposite. Her dark hair was cut short, and she was wearing tight jeans and a small lime green t-shirt. She had three piercings in one ear and a smile that was somewhat mischievous. "Hi," said Meg, curiously tilting her head to the side. "It's really nice to meet you."

"You as well," said Christine.

"Are you having a good time out here?"

"She just got here," said Raoul. "I don't think she knows if she's having a good time yet, right?" Christine was grateful that he spoke for her.

They drove around from place to place, and Raoul pointed out everything from their past. "So there's the park we used to play at. It's not so nice now. Stupid graffiti. And there's our school. I don't think any of our teachers are still there. Schools are pretty bad these days."

"Yeah, my old high school was turned into a two-star hotel," muttered Meg. She looked back at Christine. "What was school like for you?"

"Umm. Reading and writing and some math."

"But what about high school?"

Christine felt her face warm. "There were some different classes." The truth was that, after age fourteen, academic classes for women tapered off in favor of cooking and other homemaking courses. At least she'd been allowed to continue her music, both piano and voice lessons. The boys were permitted to have more history and science classes, and Christine had sometimes read their textbooks when no one was looking.

Raoul must have sensed her discomfort and quickly changed the subject. "So there's the old museum. That closed two years ago."

"Wow," Christine murmured. It was all she could say about this urban jungle. Even small things caught her attention, like people walking their dogs through the park. Few exceptions were allowed for pets; she did miss kittens and puppies. Children were defying their parents by running away and laughing. Teenagers were smoking cigarettes on a street corner, and a boy and girl were kissing fervently against a wall. The couple giggled and ran off hand-in-hand. Some of the walls had colorful murals painted on them. *Art.* There was so little of it where she was from.

Raoul took her to a pizza parlor near his home. She hoped it was okay to eat pizza and soda. Cameron had never made a statement against the food at least. The steaming mozzarella cheese was divine.

"You look like you're enjoying that," he said with a grin.

She blushed with stringy cheese still half-hanging from her mouth.

"Don't embarrass her," said Meg, giving Christine a playful nudge with her elbow. "So what's next? Shopping? Ooh! Wait. I'm going to play old school pinball first." She jumped up and ran over to a machine that looked ancient. After Meg slipped coins into the slot, it began to clang and beep.

Raoul laughed and then grew serious again. "So how are you doing, Christine?"

"I'm a little tired," she admitted. "This is all a lot to take in."

"Okay. Maybe we'll do the shopping center tomorrow. And the zoo should be open next week."

"I won't be here next week, though. Right?" She eyed him.

"Right," he replied, head hanging in defeat.

***

Raoul's goal for that day was to make this world as fun as possible for her. He took her to the few places that were still nice: well-kept parks and stores where people still bothered to paint the walls and take out the trash. He didn't pry into her life and quietly told Meg not to interrogate her. Phillip also wanted a turn questioning Christine about the inner workings of Cameron's world, and Raoul still wasn't sure how that was going to work.

"Looks like you worked up a sweat playing that," he said as Meg returned.

"I got some bonus balls." She looked between them. "So what's up?"

"I think we're going to call it a day and maybe go back out tomorrow. You can show Christine what's left of the fashion world; I have no idea what's up with any of that."

"Sounds good! So you'll drop me off?"

"Uh." Raoul glanced back at Christine. "Well, she doesn't want to be alone with me in a car. So I'll have to drop her off with my mother, and then take you—"

"It's okay," said Christine. Raoul glanced at her in surprise. "I mean, the car is fine. I trust you."

"Great," said Meg, winking at Raoul. "You can meet my mom."

He was a little nervous about taking her to Meg's part of the city. Then again, it was pretty impossible to avoid poverty and decay in this day and age. As they approached Meg's door, Christine folded her arms loosely against her chest and looked around. With her modest dress and lack of makeup, she appeared very out of place. And, Raoul thought, kind of beautiful, with a few strands of long hair blowing out from under her headband in the breeze. Her lips were slightly parted, and her eyes were a little curious and lost. Raoul gently took her hand and gave it a squeeze. He was relieved when she didn't pull away.

"Yes, I remember you," said Caroline when she greeted them at the door. She was dressed in a black turtle neck and blue jeans that made her appear slender, and she seemed healthier than the last time.

"How are you?" asked Christine.

"I'm well. Happy to be with my daughter."

"Yes, that must be very nice. But I'm sorry you couldn't stay with us. Maybe the Spirit would let you back in?"

Caroline shook her head. "No. I don't want that. The Spirit allowed me to have this life, and I have learned to be grateful for it."

Christine smiled widely. "He did?"

"Oh, yes! It was his decision to return me here. Who am I to question him?"

Christine nodded eagerly. "He speaks to me."

"Does he? I didn't know he spoke to anyone except Cameron. What does his voice sound like?"

"It's divine! Directly from heaven!"

Raoul and Meg exchanged a subtle 'what the hell?' glance.

"So you'll be returning?" asked Caroline.

"Yes. I must for the Spirit. He is in control now."

"I am sure he is. God be with you."

"And you," replied Christine, still smiling. Raoul said goodbye to Meg and then led Christine back to his car. A heavy feeling was gathering in his chest. What could he show her now that would make her want to stay? Why did the stupid zoo have to be closed?

After a silent drive, they were back in his neighborhood. He climbed out of the car and spotted the park down the street where the wealthy could still allow their children to play without fear. Without a word, Raoul dashed over to it and jumped onto one of the rubber swings. Christine stared after him. After a second, she slowly walked to the playground and asked, "What are you doing?"

"Not everything's changed!" he exclaimed, pumping higher and higher. Maybe it was catharsis. Maybe it was one last futile grab at the past.

She laughed and sat on the swing beside him. They swung together, her hair glinting in the orange light of the setting sun and her dress floating out around her. He let out a cry as the swing jerked when he got too high, and Christine giggled. Finally, they both slowed and rocked back and forth.

"Are you going to stay here?" she asked. "In this city?"

"I'm going to help my brother for a while. But if things don't get better soon, I'm going to leave."

"Where are you going?"

"Maybe Europe or Asia. I haven't really planned it out yet. Things are better in other countries, though."

"Are you sure you don't want to come with me?" she asked, glancing away.

"Chris, I wouldn't do well there. I don't believe in any of it. I'm sorry."

"You don't believe in God?"

"I think I do. It's not that. But I don't believe in following strict, old-fashioned rules to get into heaven. I don't believe everyone is damned just because they don't follow some old guy in a beard or believe in disembodied voices. That's a little over the top for me." He saw her expression and repeated, "I'm sorry."

"It's…okay."

"I wish you'd stay with me." He weakly smiled. "I'd take you anywhere you wanted to go."

Her blue eyes were distant once more. "The Spirit, Raoul. I believe in him with all my heart."

"I know you do. I just—"

"What?"

"I don't want you to be hurt if you ever find out that your Spirit isn't what you think it is. Like if it's Cameron manipulating you."

"Cameron doesn't have a voice like the Spirit. No mortal man could. He sang to me once, Raoul, and it was really a voice from heaven. The Spirit is real."

"If you say so," Raoul murmured. He was done trying to argue, at least for now. "But you'll stay one more day. Please?"

"Yeah." She smiled. "I want another slice of pizza. Maybe Cameron would let me make my own version of it there, you think?"

Raoul gave a short, sad laugh. "Maybe."

They rocked back and forth in silence for a long time. Feeling like he was continuing to lose her, Raoul urgently tried to come up with fascinating activities for them to do tomorrow. The thought of her going back to that place was devastating. All because of some horrible mind manipulation. *What the hell had they done to her?*

Was there at least a way to stall her any longer?

Raoul wondered this as he headed to bed that night. He fell into a troubled sleep, only to be awoken several hours later by a deep rumbling outside. Then he heard shouts and another explosion, yellow and orange lights flashing through his window. Jumping out of bed, he threw open the door and ran into the hall. Christine and his mother were standing there in their nightgowns, clasping hands. Phillip was at his own place that night, and so Raoul took charge. "C'mon," he said, leading them down the stairs. "Let's see what's going on."

Signaling for them to stay back, he opened the front door and peeked outside. The smell of something burning was heavy in the air, and he coughed in the growing clouds of smoke. Flames were jumping out of the buildings down the block, around a post office and the café Raoul loved. At least both were closed at this hour. The roof was completely engulfed in fire, and the windows had shattered. "Holy crap," he whispered, taking several steps outside. Neighbors had also come outside to look at the glowing ball of orange.

He approached the street. Someone had probably called the underfunded fire department by now. "I wonder what happened," his mother murmured. She and Christine had followed barefoot behind him, eyes fixed on the jumping flames.

"Must have been an accident. Faulty wiring or something," Raoul replied as they stood together on the curb. He was about to tell them it might be best to get back inside; the smoke was doing a number on his lungs. Before he was able, another explosion shook the ground beneath him, knocking him off his feet and onto his hands and knees. He cried out and heard Christine and his mother do the same.

Smoke filled the air so thickly that he could barely see a foot in front of him. Raoul's eyes watered, and he fell into a short coughing fit on the ground, lungs raw and burning. Once he'd recovered, he rose up from his sore knees, reaching out to grasp at the air around him. "Mom! Christine!"

"Raoul!" his mom cried. She stumbled toward him and grabbed his shoulders.

He hugged her protectively. "Are you okay?"

"I'm fine," she replied. "Oh, what's happening? What's going on?"

"I don't know." He frantically looked through the fog as it finally began to clear. With some relief, he saw that there wasn't another fire—just an explosion of thick smoke. "Christine?" he called, turning around so many times that he became dizzy. "Christine!"

"Christine?" Judy joined him in his search.

"Christine!" He screamed her name as loudly as he could, still hoarse. The smoke had almost completely cleared by now, revealing her certain absence. A massive fire truck was now rolling through the gate, sirens blaring and lights flashing. *"Christine!"* he hollered over the growing noise.

He ran around the entire neighborhood and through the rooms of his house, all the while screaming her name. Maybe she'd become frightened and tried to hide? His mom asked neighbors if they had seen a young blonde woman. But no one had.

She was gone.

***

What happened?

An explosion had knocked her to her knees, leaving her nightgown and hands splayed out on the street. Her hair flew out wildly across her face. Breathing heavily, Christine could only see clouds of smoke rising around her when she glanced up with a gasp, although she didn't seem to be directly engulfed. It was as though an invisible glass wall were protecting her from the billowing grey clouds, allowing her to still see. Her friend was no longer in sight, though.

"Raoul?" Her voice was weak. "Raoul? Where are you?"

"Christine...Christine..."

Her head jerked at the sound of the familiar voice. It rolled over her like the smoke, smooth and perfect. She slowly stood on two unsteady legs, wondering if it had been her imagination.

"Christine..."

"Spirit?" she whispered. *He had found her!* Desperately, she turned around and searched for the direction of the voice.

A black outline of someone or something appeared through the smoke, looming over a foot above her. Two glowing yellow dots shone from the top of it. Christine shrunk back and stared at the silhouette. "Spirit?"

"Yes, my beauty. You will come with me now." Indeed, it was the Spirit's voice.

But what was the shadow? It was coming closer and closer, flying like a black ghost toward her. Her head was unclear, and her mouth was dry. "Are we going home?" she managed to ask.

"Not yet, Christine. There are other plans to attend to."

She thought she heard Raoul's voice somewhere behind her and glanced back.

"Christine." The Spirit's voice guided her attention forward again. She looked down and suddenly saw a pair of shiny black shoes. There was the sensation of cool leather beneath her palm and fingertips.

The Spirit wears clothes…

That was her last thought before she felt a strange and peaceful exhaustion finally consume her.

Chapter 11

"A bomb exploded in a northeast gated neighborhood last night. Officials think it was possibly an attack against the wealthy residents of the area. Citizens Against Classism are denying responsibility on their website, but officials believe that the more militant sect of CAC may be involved. This morning, their Baltimore headquarters were raided, leading to protests in twelve cities against increasing government intervention. The streets had quieted by early afternoon, but authorities are still on edge as tensions continue to rise. Please stay tuned for more news and your local weather."

***

"So she just disappeared?"

"Just like that." Raoul looked down into his soda. "There was an explosion of smoke. By the time I recovered, she was gone." The café was also gone, nothing but a pile of smoldering rubble now. A day later, he and Meg were sitting outside of a rundown hamburger joint and staring down at overcooked food.

"Do you think she ran away?"

"No."

Meg's voice lowered to a whisper. "So you think she was kidnapped?"

"Yeah," Raoul muttered as he nibbled on a blackened French fry. "I know someone took her."

"Wow. Do you think CAC is holding her hostage or something?"

Raoul grunted. "That's just more BS from the media because it makes a good story. The poor versus the rich thing. Me and Phillip are pretty sure it wasn't them."

"How come?"

"Phillip says that CAC always leaves a symbol, like a burnt up hundred dollar bill or a coin with a hole in it. Something like that. But we only found a short note at the scene."

"Ooh. What'd it say?" Meg leaned in.

"It just said: 'She is safe and where she belongs. Interference will be met with retaliation.'"

"That's creepy! Did you show it to the police? What's Phillip going to do?"

"Police were useless. Phillip's going to launch a complaint and make some threats. But we don't have much proof." Raoul sighed. "She didn't want to be here, though. She made that clear. So maybe-maybe I have to let her go." Saying that aloud made his heart hurt.

Meg rested a hand on his bare arm. "Is that what you're going to do?"

"I dunno. The only reason she wanted to go back is that stupid Spirit crap. But what can I do?"

"I know."

"Things are getting bad, you know?" he continued. "I have a feeling that things are going to get worse before they get better."

"I feel it, too. Sometimes I wonder if I could get me and my mom out of here, but we don't have the money."

"Me, you, and our moms. We'll go live somewhere awesome. Like Paris."

"Oh, that *would* be awesome," murmured Meg. "Fresh croissants and brie and wine every day. Anything to leave here. Everyone is a mess."

"You seemed to turn out okay."

She shrugged and poked at her hamburger before tossing it aside. "I remember when things were good, when my parents had money. My aunt was kind of strict but really smart and interesting. It was probably good that I got to stay with her for so long. She moved to Melbourne to teach. I was going to go with her, but then I had to take care of my mom."

"I know how that goes. My mom was never the same after my dad died. I think both our moms grew up during such good times that, when the bad times came, they didn't know how to deal. We were the ones that had to pick up the pieces, huh?" Meg nodded. He put an arm around her, and she leaned her head against his shoulder. At some level, he felt like they were the only sane ones in the world. Or at least in the country.

***

She felt a nest of warmth and softness all around her and nestled her cheek against it. A soft hum of contentment escaped the back of her throat. *What day was it?* Time to get up and go to services, she supposed. Oh, but the bed was *sooo* comfortable. Maybe she would wait for Mrs. Valerius to come in, open her curtains, and say, "Come along, Sleeping Beauty. The prince won't get here before worship services."

Christine lay there half-asleep and wrapped in comfort for another hour or so. *I wonder why Mrs. Valerius hasn't come in yet. It must be late morning by now.* The only sounds she heard were a steady hum and then once a rustling noise in the distance. Something didn't feel quite right.

A memory returned. And then another. *Raoul!*

The fire. The smoke.

The Spirit. The Shadow!

Christine opened her eyes, rolled onto her back, and sat straight up. She gasped. *Where am I?!*

The room was beautiful, even lovelier than the guest room at Raoul's house. The walls and ceiling were painted a pure snow white, and a lavender bedspread with white lace on the edges covered her. Flowers had been placed in vases along two dark oak dressers, purple and white irises and red roses, although she couldn't tell whether they were real or fake. The headboard and footboard of the bed were semicircles filled with gold bars. The carpet was cream, and there were two oil paintings on the wall, one of the seashore and one of the forest. There were no windows and no clocks.

One white door with a gold knob was at the front of the room, and it was closed. There were two similar doors to her right that were cracked open. After taking several seconds to recover from her shock, she pushed the covers off of her and stood. The carpet was soft against her bare feet.

She was still wearing her nightgown, although dark dirt and soot now stained the white cotton. Christine tiptoed to the first open door and peeked inside. It was a bathroom with lavender rugs that matched the bedspread and a pine green shower curtain. A small square mirror was hanging on the wall above the marble sink, but the glass was tilted downward and reflecting the counter. She adjusted it back up to take a glance at her reflection. "I look like a mess." The vain stray thought passed through her panicked mind as she stared at her stringy hair and blotchy, dirty face.

Christine gazed into the second open room. It was a walk-in closet, filled with at least twenty dresses, each one a different color. They were similar to the ones she'd always worn except a little more elaborate, decorated with various pockets and buttons and patterns. She backed up, finding the room a little disturbing, the carpet squishing beneath her toes.

She now stared at the closed door, sensing it led to a lot more than a closet and a bathroom. Trembling, she put her ear to the cool wood but heard nothing but the electrical hum. Her clammy fingers brushed against the doorknob.

Christine backed away from the door and paced across the room. *I can't stay in here forever. But why am I here? I don't understand. Spirit, where am I?*

Finally, she stopped in her footsteps and stared at the knob again. *Okay, just a glance out. I have to. Maybe I'm home. Yes! Maybe Cameron had just put her in a safe house so that she could recover from her ordeal.* Here she was being completely silly when she was probably safe and sound. Maybe Mrs. Valerius was even waiting outside to take her home!

"Calm down, Christine," she whispered to herself. "You're acting crazy. Put your trust in the Spirit."

I just need to get out of this stupid room. It reminded her of a dollhouse she'd had when she was four.

With a deep breath, Christine approached the door again.

But then the knob began to turn on its own, slowly twisting clockwise with a soft squeak.

Christine backed up and ran into the bed, falling over the footboard and onto the covers, hands reaching out behind her for support. She stared as the door opened, praying for Mrs. Valerius or Raoul or even Cameron. Any familiar face.

Her prayers went terribly unanswered.

The shadow from the smoke loomed in the doorway, one gloved hand still on the doorknob. *Only now she had a full view of it!* Black from head to toe. Black shoes. Black suit and gloves and hat and mask. It was well over six feet tall, standing there and watching her with its two yellow eyes. Her mouth fell open, a scream threatening to emerge from the back of her dry throat. She attempted to scoot even further backward until she hit the headboard. A soft groan of pain escaped her lips and then lengthened into a sob of terror. As the shadow stepped into the bedroom, Christine attempted another scream.

But then it spoke.

"I had thought I heard you awake. And here you are, still in bed. Rest if you are tired, of course. You had a rather long night. But then you must dress and come out. This room is only for sleep, Christine. You will grow bored if you remain in it too long."

Her mouth closed as the familiar voice came from behind the mask of the figure, the sound of heaven coming from the sight of horror. The memories of the previous night became clearer. And, suddenly, she understood. Her mind would no longer protect her from the truth.

The Shadow *was* the Spirit.

"Sp-spirit?" she stuttered, clutching the covers with her hand.

"Yes, my beauty. I am. Your dear Spirit." He gestured to himself with his right hand. "For reasons that you will understand in time, these new circumstances were necessary. Your destiny begins here. We have spoken of it many times, no?"

Her eyes ran up and down the wraithlike figure. He was so skinny that the suit seemed to hang off of him. It took her several seconds to speak. "But I don't understand. You're...You've taken *that* form?"

He hesitated and then, with a short nod, said, "Yes, Christine. A more tangible form to finish my work on earth, no? A mere voice cannot accomplish much, can it? But now I am able to walk around like any other mortal."

It made sense. It did. "Is that the only form you can take?"

"Yes," he curtly replied. "Were you expecting something else?"

The question had a coolness to it that made her nervous. "Well, I thought maybe you might...look like-like an Angel. With white light around you. I thought that in my mind for so long..."

"Perhaps you read too many fairy tales?"

"Perhaps," she whispered, looking downward.

"I have disappointed you?" he asked. His arms were down at his sides now, and he made no more motions to come toward her.

Christine lied with a shake of her head, her mind still trying to make sense of it all. "Does Cameron know you look like this?"

"Yes."

She glanced back up, and they merely stared at each other for several seconds, neither blinking.

"I will give you some time to adapt," he said. "To wash and dress. And then we have much to discuss. Much to do." He gestured toward the outside of the room. "You may come out when you wish. You may use any room that isn't locked."

"Are we near Cameron and the others?" she dared to ask.

"No."

"Then where are we?"

"My earthly home," he replied. "Away from all distractions."

He didn't want her to know where she was. "Can I see Mrs. Valerius?"

"Not for some time, Christine. You will stay here. And you will learn, and you will make music with your Spirit and you will soon be very happy. You will. My vision for you is the grandest of all. I will leave you now to prepare yourself."

He left her there, closing the door behind him, and she started to cry. This was her Spirit. It was; the voice was exactly the same. Yet it had been so much easier to deal with the voice when it came from heaven than to deal with *this.*

A moment of panic gripped her entire body. Her breaths turned to gasps, and her heart beat so quickly that she had to lie down again before she fainted. She curled up into a ball on the bed. For a second, she squeezed her eyes shut and tried to escape this nightmare. When she opened her lids, she saw that she was still there. Still trapped.

The Spirit won't hurt me. He is the Spirit. The same Spirit he's always been. He just looks very different, not what you imagined. But he's the Spirit. Yes, he's the Spirit.

She hovered on the edge. If she could convince her mind to believe this, she wouldn't go into hysterics. Yes, the Spirit was out there. Her Spirit who had taught her to sing and been her guardian for two years.

After several hours, Christine convinced herself of this enough to finally get up and use the bathroom. She couldn't convince herself enough to undress and take a shower, but she smeared a soft washcloth with soap and water and scrubbed it over her skin to remove the layers of sweat and grime. She wet her hair under the shower with her nightgown still on and rubbed a little shampoo into the tangled tresses. Still, she looked like a mess in the mirror.

Shutting the door of the closet behind her and noticing with dismay that it couldn't be locked, Christine hesitated and then removed her nightgown. It occurred to her that there might be fresh undergarments in the outside dresser drawers, but she didn't want to ponder the thought for more than a moment. She put on a soft cotton slip and then a velvety midnight blue dress that buttoned all the way up to her neck and reached out to her wrists. It loosely fell all the way to her ankles. The blessed Spirit would prefer the most modest dress, she told herself. Yet it was really a form of protection from those two yellow eyes...

No. It's the Spirit. It's the Spirit. From God himself. He's out there, Christine. You mustn't think ill of Him, or He will know, right?

She glanced at herself one last time in the mirror, struggling to appear calm and not the panicked mess that was bubbling on the inside.

When she looked out, prepared to slam the door shut at any time, the living room she gazed into was empty. It looked surprisingly modern, more like the living room in Raoul's house than any of the simple homes in her community. The most notable object was a shiny black grand piano; it was the most beautiful instrument she'd ever seen. Two black leather sofas and a grey coffee table sat in the middle of the room. There was also a very large television with other complex machines attached to it and enormous speakers that nearly reached the ceiling. The walls were bare except for a single painting of a bright sun over a barren dessert. It was too quiet. Lifeless. And there were no windows or any indication of a door that might lead to the outside.

After glancing around for any sign of the Spirit, Christine walked to the entrance of a small windowless room that was attached to the living area. She was faced with shelves and shelves of books and movies. Hundreds or thousands of them. On her right, there was a blue screen with only the white words: "Press for song selection." Beside the screen were two speakers.

She touched the screen.

"Please choose a category: 1960's, 1970's, 1980's, 1990's, 00's, 10's, 20's, Blues, Classical, Contemporary, Country, Jazz, Opera, Pop, R&B, Rap, Reggae, Rock..."

She stared at the choices and looked over the rest of the contents in the room, most of it completely foreign to her.

"Listen to whatever you like."

Christine jumped and turned around. The Spirit was standing behind her in the entryway, arms behind his back and head tilted. She barely came up to his shoulders. Christine resisted the urge to back up into the nearest corner. "What is it?" she softly asked, gesturing toward the blue screen.

"My song collection," he replied. "All digital and of the highest auditory quality. I dislike ninety percent of it, but it is a very complete collection."

"But these are all forbidden," she whispered. "These books and the music and the movies are all from the Outside."

"I am the Spirit," he said with a shrug. "I must have all knowledge, good and evil, right?"

She hesitated. "I guess so." Perhaps the Spirit couldn't be corrupted by the Outside like the rest of them.

"And you must have this knowledge as well."

"What do you mean?"

He nodded toward his collection. "There are no restrictions. There is nothing there that will harm you." He paused. "The Spirit gives you permission."

Christine gaped, knowing it would take her years to get through all of it. Yet, if she hadn't been so terrified, she might have been up to the task. There was so much to see and read and listen to. But the Spirit was also now blocking the doorway, and this made her forget the collection altogether as her heart pounded in terror.

"Before you begin your musical journey, would you enjoy something to eat?" He stepped out of the room, no longer preventing her from leaving. Still, her stomach hurt, and she shook her head in reply. "Is there anything you want? I have spent months considering you might eventually arrive, as you can tell. Still, I may have been shortsighted when it comes to certain necessities. As a Spirit, I sometimes forget what a mortal might need."

"Can I leave?" she asked more eagerly than she meant to. "I mean just to take a walk or something like that. I promise I would come back."

"No. Not yet."

"Why?" she whispered, and then her voice grew in volume. "Why can't I return to my home? Is it because Raoul took me? I promise nothing sinful happened!"

"Oh, I realize that, Christine." The Spirit's tone made her shiver. "I know you are a good girl."

"Then why can't things be as they were? I would have come to you for my lessons every week. I don't need to be here. I want to see Mrs. Valerius."

"You know too much now, dear Christine. About the world. About everything. And you should know more. You are far above everyone else. Now it is time to go forward and leave that pointless little life behind you."

She rapidly shook her head back and forth, hair flying in both directions, no longer able to contain her panic. "No, no, no! I want to leave here. I want you to be the Voice again."

"You will be allowed out in time. Calm yourself."

"*Please.*"

"No. Not yet."

But she couldn't stop the tears from falling as she raced out of the little room. She ran left and tried another door, but it was locked. She sprinted to a door on her right, and that only led to a closet with folded towels, blankets, and sheets. She ran forward and into a kitchen; she raced backwards and encountered another locked door. The Spirit watched as she finally collapsed onto one of the black couches and buried her face in her hands, shaking and weeping. "I want things back as they were," she said between sobs. "Please! Please just be the Spirit again! Please don't make me stay here! This doesn't make any sense!"

After allowing her to cry for several moments, he knelt beside her.

Christine tensed but kept her face buried. His voice was gentle when he spoke. "Do not cry, my beauty. Calm down. Do not cry. It is me. Your Spirit. I am still your Spirit. Who has guided you for two entire years? Has your Spirit ever failed you, Christine? Have I ever been late to a lesson or disappointed you? Have I, my dear?"

"No," she whispered, gazing into those two strange eyes. "No, you haven't, Spirit."

"Then I will not disappoint you now. You will be very happy."

She looked away and wiped a hand over her sticky cheek. "I'm just confused."

"Do you remember when I sang for you?"

"Oh, yes. I do. When I was so sad about my father one night, you sang for me."

"Would you like me to do so now?"

She nodded again. *Anything to numb the horrible confusion.*

He played the piano and sang an unfamiliar foreign song in that tenor voice, and it was just as beautiful as it had been the first time. Hypnotizing and heavenly. *Spirit.* The music calmed her. When she closed her eyes and could just hear the voice, Christine could almost pretend that she was back in the magic room, that the Spirit was speaking to her from high above and that she wasn't where she was. And, when the music stopped, the silence was almost painful.

"Did you enjoy it?" he asked. She nodded. "You should listen to opera while you are here. It would truly suit your voice."

She was about to ask if opera was forbidden but remembered his earlier words. There were new and bewildering rules to this world—no longer allowed outside but now she was permitted to listen to anything she wanted. How could she understand any of it?

Christine finally dared to open her eyes. The Spirit had left the piano and was standing very near to her. A black gloved hand reached out to touch her cheek. With a cry, she hopped up and ran away into the bedroom, closing the door behind her. Because, deep down, she knew.

Despite her lack of education, she was too smart not to know.

Even if her conscious mind wouldn't yet admit it, her subconscious was raging at her. Her subconscious was rattling the bars of its prison and screaming in alarm.

A man! Not a Spirit! He's a man! A masked man, and you're trapped here and all alone with him!

Still, thirty minutes later, when he knocked on the door and asked, "Do you require anything? Anything at all?"

She replied, "No, Spirit. I just want to be alone for a bit. I'm very tired."

A pause. "Then I will let you rest."

As she pressed her cheek to the pillow, not knowing whether it was morning, afternoon, or night, Christine knew nothing would ever be normal again.

Chapter 12

2006

"Laura. Laura, look at me."

Her black curls tumbled into her eyes as she glanced up. "Mm?"

"Are you feeling okay?"

"Mhm."

"Did you hear what I said?"

She felt her heart sink into her stomach as the sentence left her lips. "You said *maybe* in eight years, give or take."

Her friend and family doctor of over twenty years nodded, his eyes sympathetic behind his glasses. She was so damned tired of sympathy. *Why wouldn't anyone help her?* "That's right. I don't want you getting yourself and that boy in any more messes."

"But I *won* the lawsuit," she said, leaning forward. "We won easily. He lost his license."

"Laura, no surgeon should have been performing that procedure on a child. And you knew that. I told you that. Even if that moron hadn't been half-drunk, things might have gone haywire. No one is going to touch your son until he's at least done developing."

"You're doctors!" She placed her face back into her hands, a migraine threatening to grip her brain. "You people are supposed to be able to fix this kind of thing. Transplants are supposed to fix things like this."

"And they can. They do. But not without risks. Maybe by the time he's ready, the procedure will be even better and—Oh, Laura. For God's sake, don't cry, sweetheart. It's going to be fine."

She looked down. "I always wanted to be a mommy. I couldn't conceive, and *he* blamed me for that. Then fertility drugs seemed to work. Oh, I was so happy! Remember when I called to tell you the news and how happy I was? I pictured birthday parties and play dates and being one of those silly classroom moms who brought in crafts and cupcakes for all the kids. But now…" She looked into the distance. "He blames me for this, too, I think. But…" Laura leaned and whispered, "His second cousin was born with a weird lip, so I think he could have been just as responsible."

"That's ridiculous. Neither of you are to blame. I doubt it was even a genetic problem."

"Tell him that." Laura moaned. "Oh, what am I going to do?"

There was a moment of silence before he placed a hand on her arm and said, "At least your son is alive."

He could say that. Behind him, she saw a picture of his beautiful family in a gold frame. A blonde-haired, blue-eyed woman and twin girls in their teens. He didn't have to go home to a spouse who hated him and a son who stared up at him with those horrible, expectant, all too intelligent eyes, as though she could save him when she couldn't even save herself.

"By the time someone will do it, it's going to be too late," she murmured in defeat.

"Too late for what?"

"For everything…"

"Laura, do you want me to get you some more help? There's this psychiatrist who—"

"No," she harshly interrupted. "No more of those. I'm tired of talking about my feelings. And I've been prescribed so many meds that I should start my own goddamned cartel. Unless you can give me the number of someone who will fix him, you can't help me."

"Laura—"

"I'm going home."

He stood with her. "You'll call me if you're feeling too bad?"

"Yes," she lied.

A numbness settled over her after she started her car. She let the vehicle idle for a few moments before backing out of the parking lot and turning onto the city streets, the sunshine bright and the skies blue. As a swing set and slide became visible, she turned into the lot of the familiar park and braked. For nearly thirty minutes, she sat with the air conditioning blowing over her, watching several children run around the playground, two redheaded boys and a little brunette girl. They tackled each other and then raced up the stairs to the plastic slide, giggling. Dust stained their hands and cheeks.

It took every ounce of energy that she had to leave and drive home. The three-story brick prison loomed over her as she walked up the driveway, black high heels clicking on the concrete. From the corner of her eye, she could see one of her neighbors staring at her. They hadn't talked in years, not since *that* day.

Congratulations! Oh, Laura, you have to let me see your new baby. Well, why did you cover his face with a blanket? It's not that cold outside.

Please don't ask. I can't discuss it right now.

What's wrong? You look so tired. I just wanted to see him.

Please, Katie. Leave me alone. I'll call you later.

Then the stupid woman had reached a manicured hand into the stroller and pulled the quilt back. With a wounded yelp, Katie had whirled around and vomited right in the middle of the sidewalk. And then she'd frantically apologized several times, backing away with beads of sweat running down her face. Katie had never asked to see the baby again, nor had she ever asked Laura back to one of her famous Tupperware parties.

Laura opened the heavy door and walked inside her home, wishing the high ceilings would form a vortex and swallow her up.

Her husband immediately met her in the doorway, his green eyes always full of unspoken accusations. He was over six feet tall and more handsome than she was beautiful, which made his cruelty all the more painful. He was also smarter than she was, an engineer for a multibillion dollar aerospace corporation. She had nothing like that. She felt like a pathetic little mouse in his presence.

"Where is he?" she asked, looking down as she pulled off her heels.

"In his room. Where else would he be?"

"I was just asking." She sniffed. "What would you like for dinner? I think there's some steak in the freezer, so I could—"

"I'm going out." He walked past her toward the door, car keys jingling in his hand.

"Please don't leave me here all alone tonight," she begged, her cold demeanor disintegrating into desperation. "Please. You don't even have to talk to me. Just please don't leave me alone."

"I've been here alone for four hours! Hell, I stayed here for an entire month with him while you had your little meltdown last year. Deal with it, Laura. Take your pills, and learn to deal. You're such an emotional mess that I don't even know what to do with you anymore." He shrugged her off of him as she grabbed his shoulder. "I'll be back before dark."

"You're going out to fuck some slut, aren't you?"

He laughed coldly. "Ha! Yeah. You know me. All I need is another woman screaming in my ear."

"I hate you!"

He didn't respond. The car started with a roar.

In stocking clad feet, she stood in the middle of the entranceway. The clock ticked steadily on the wall, its gold pendulum swinging back and forth. As seven o' clock approached, Laura felt something crumble deep within her mind. *Hopelessness.* A soft, melodious laugh escaped her throat. There was freedom in hopelessness.

Snap!

She ascended two flights of plushy carpeted stairs. Laura sang a ballad to herself, a love song that was currently playing on the radio. That was why he'd married her. Both her speaking and singing voice had always been described as delightful when she was a little girl and then seductive as she'd reached adulthood. Her talent combined with timeless beauty had snatched her a four-star husband.

And he hated her.

She felt strangely calm now. At peace even. Slowly raising her right hand, she knocked on the door of the bedroom on the third floor, right below the attic. The cool air crept down and brushed against her arms, creating rows of goose bumps on her skin.

The door opened, and her son looked up at her expectantly.

"Come with me. We're going for a drive."

***

2034

Christine knew she couldn't stay in the room forever. She'd die.

She'd already stuck her face underneath the bathroom sink twice when the dryness in her mouth became too much to bear. By the dull ache forming in her head and stomach, she also knew that hunger was going to set in soon.

The door didn't lock, and so there was no real safety in being in there. It just felt more secure.

Despite her sheltered life, she wasn't completely naïve to what strange men could do. At age five, her mother had given her a very brief description after the "Where do babies come from?" question. The education was furthered when one of her friends in first grade had triumphantly claimed at a slumber party: "You guys, my older sister told me what *sex* is!" Amongst giggles and whispers, they'd flopped onto their sleeping bags as she'd described the mechanics of it.

Now, *it* was something that unmarried girls never did, something done only after you were married to make children. Under any other circumstances, it was a grave sin, and young women had been confined to isolation for even minor acts of flirtation, batting their eyes too much or puckering their lips. She had never gotten into trouble for any of those acts. The Spirit had become her sole focus as she approached adulthood, and

Christine forgot any sinful little crushes she might have had on younger men.

But now that she knew the truth about the Spirit, she became well aware of the possible dangers. Still, the shadowy man stayed out of the room, only asking every several hours if she was in need of anything. She was at his mercy, but he had done nothing yet.

Yet.

Christine placed her head in her hands and rubbed her temples with her palms. Her head was becoming foggy, and there was nothing in the room to distract her. All she had were a billion questions and fears tumbling through her mind. If he wasn't a real Spirit, then what was all this? Who was he? Was there a Spirit somewhere else? What did Cameron know? Was this all some type of cruel test to assess her purity?

She finally gathered her shattered nerves and left the room again, still having no idea as to what time of day it was. What kind of home had no windows? As before, Christine didn't see him upon first emerging. Her gaze wandered to the locked doors, and she wondered which one led to the exit. And, if she did manage to get out, where were they? Somewhere on the Outside? Somewhere scary?

Hugging her arms to her chest despite the pleasant temperature of the home, Christine walked back to the closet with the collections. There was something calming about that room, as though she might be able to escape into it, into the stories and the music. Before she could explore it further, she saw him come out from behind one of the doors. He closed it behind him, causing the lock to click into place again, and nodded at her. "Ah. You have decided to come out. That is good. You must eat something, or you will become weak."

She stared at him for a moment, warily taking in his appearance. "How long will I have to stay here?"

"It depends on how fast you acquire the necessary knowledge. It depends on *you.*"

"But we're on the Outside?"

"In a sense."

Even if she were to escape, she'd have no idea where to go. Unless…*Raoul.* Her old friend's name chimed like a bell in her mind. Raoul was on the outside. A lump formed in her throat as she wondered if he had been right about everything. "*I don't want you to be hurt if you ever find out that your Spirit isn't what you think it is. Like if it's Cameron manipulating you.*"

Before she had another panic attack, Christine quickly cleared her mind and tried to stay calm, which was very difficult under the shadow man's constant gaze. He never seemed to blink. "I want to go in there." She pointed to the closet.

"Then do so. You may have a day or two to do as you like before we officially begin. Still, I will fetch you a small snack to take in with you."

Turning away from him without another word, she closed the door to the little room halfway and, after checking to make sure that he wasn't following her, began to play with the blue screen. Despite her limited technological knowledge, it wasn't too difficult to figure out. Going through the lists of genres and artists, she sampled one song from each category, all the while waiting for him to come in and scold her. Christine was testing the boundaries and rules, wondering if he would really allow her to see and listen to anything she wanted. Surely, he would tell her she was being sinful at some point.

At some level, she wanted him to become angry at her—to show that his new rules were nothing but a lie—to show that the Spirit was a big lie. She secretly wanted a confrontation where every question was answered and every truth was revealed.

But he never came in.

Or wait. He had come in, she noticed, and left a white glass plate with crackers, cheddar cheese, and green apple slices by the door.

Christine shuddered at how silently he moved. Feeling her stomach churn, she picked up one of the cheese slices, studied it to make sure nothing appeared strange, and then took a bite. Her fear took away most of the flavor, but her mind and stomach were soothed as she swallowed the food. She could think more clearly now at least. She sat on the carpet and ate everything.

Once in a while, she would recognize a song from long ago. Listening to some of the music from the 1960's category, she recalled a tune that her now deceased grandfather would often play in the car, a nostalgic smile on his wrinkled face. *"They don't make 'em like this anymore, kiddo."* The harmony was kind of pretty, and she closed her eyes and listened to the song a couple of times.

Finally, the door opened all the way, and the shadow man stood in the entrance. She flinched out of her daydream and nearly crawled away from the black shoes. Would he yell at her now? Ask how she could be taking pleasure from the sinful music? Reveal this all to be Cameron's test of morals?

"Are you enjoying yourself?" he asked. There was no anger in the question.

"There's so much of it," she replied, forcing herself to stand.

"Yes. Music has survived all of mankind's struggles over the centuries, ever evolving, sometimes for the worse."

"Aren't you mad?" she couldn't help but ask.

For the first time, she saw him blink. "Why would I ever be angry with you, my beauty?"

"Because I *want* to listen to all of this. And I like some of it. I like some of the songs that have sinful words."

"I expected you would. There is a wide assortment, and you should hear all of it."

A cascade of frustration overtook her. He was completely calm. After years of being told what a disobedient girl she was because of her yearnings for the outside, the Spirit shadow man didn't care in the slightest.

Christine shivered as she realized that, in the back of her mind, she'd always been waiting for the Spirit to save her from the normal requirements of women in Cameron's sect. She'd partly walked into this odd situation because the thought of being married off at twenty-one and forced to bear ten children, of being trapped forever, had been terrifying. *More terrifying than this, though—than being imprisoned in a home with a shadow man who was going to do God knew what?*

"Which door goes outside?" she asked. "I just want to stick my head out for air. Please. Just for fresh air. I promise."

"There is no door."

"What do you mean?" She couldn't stop the anger from creeping into her voice.

"The exit is through the ceiling, and I will not show you the mechanics of that yet."

"That can't be true! I bet it's behind one of the locked doors."

"No. Those are my offices."

"I'm going to lose my mind," she told him, hands curling into fists. "If you don't let me get air, I'm going to lose my mind."

"You will be fine for a little while longer."

"Why are you doing this to me?" she whispered. "Why?!"

"I have told you. We have a destiny. You and your Spirit."

You are not my Spirit. She didn't know if she was ready for that confrontation yet, though. Instead, she asked, "What's the quickest way I can get out? What can I do right now so that you'll let me out, even for a moment?"

"I suppose if we begin your voice lessons. That is where we will start."

Jaw clenched, she nodded. "Fine. Then let's start."

She saw a glint of delight within the yellow eyes. "Yes? Very well, then. We will begin today if you are so eager." He walked to the piano and sat down at the bench. She noticed that he removed his gloves to play and was startled by the sight of his bare hands. They were bony and pale, his spidery fingers long enough to reach all across the black and white keys. "Warm ups?" She forced herself to stop staring at them. Her voice shook with fear and anger as she sang the familiar scales.

After only a minute in, he stopped playing and stared at her. "You are not even trying."

"Yes, I am."

"No. You are screaming rather than singing. It is the worst I've ever heard you."

"Maybe I'm not as good as you think I am."

"Of course you are! I have listened to you for two years. Your voice is divine, my dear. In a different time, you would have been a star. Maybe you are still tired?"

"No," she murmured.

"Thirsty?"

She hesitated. "Maybe a little."

"Then I will get you water. You should have really asked, Christine. You are always welcome to these things in my home." He slipped his gloves back on and rushed away. With slumped shoulders, she followed him into the kitchen. Once again, the room was more like the one in Raoul's home, modern with a microwave and several other metallic complex cooking devices. It was also spotless.

"Don't you eat or drink?" she asked. He watched her as she put the glass to her lips, and it made her nervous. Why was he always staring? He had also set another plate of cheese and crackers in front of her.

"Only when this mortal body requires it. Which is very rarely."

"So Spirits don't need food?"

"Of course not."

She couldn't stand the charade any longer. "Can you disappear?"

He tilted his head. "You wish me to go away while you drink your water?"

"*No.* I mean really magically disappear in front of me. You used to just be a voice from heaven. And now I can see you. It would seem like a simple thing for you to vanish and reappear again."

He stared at her so long and hard that she grew frightened and looked away.

"Maybe another time. The mortal body limits me," he finally replied. "I can do other tricks for you." He was holding a fork in his hand, and, with a flick of his wrist, it suddenly vanished. His eyes glimmered.

She continued her interrogation, ignoring the silly trick. "What's Mrs. Valerius doing right now?"

"What?"

"Can't you see her? Can't you see everything?"

"When I choose to see. Calm down, dear girl. Why do you make such silly demands?"

"Because I know you're not a Spirit!" she exclaimed, jumping to her feet with a cry of frustration. "A Spirit wouldn't live in a house like this with a kitchen. Or have a television and all that music. Or any of this! And you can't disappear or see what's happening. You can't be the Spirit!"

He sighed and reached a gloved hand out toward her. She drew back, glaring. His hand fell away. "What do you think I am?"

"I don't know," she murmured. "What else could you be besides a-a man?"

He laughed in a way that made her question her safety. "But you are very wrong about that as well. I have *never* been a man."

She squinted. "Then what are you?"

His right index finger drew a slow clockwise circle on the table. "Consider me a spiritual advisor to Cameron Lourdes."

"Is there a Spirit?" she asked, already knowing the answer. "A real Spirit from heaven?"

"No. There is only me."

"Does Cameron know this?"

"Yes."

"*Why?*" she angrily whispered, leaning forward and gripping the table. "Why would you both lie to all of us?"

"You will come to understand that while you are here. I will teach you. "

"Tell me now."

"No. It is not time yet." She slumped into the chair as the truth was laid out before her. There was nothing left to believe in now, nothing left to save her. "I would never intentionally hurt you," he continued. "I want you to learn. And then you will understand the necessity of it all, I promise." She refused to look at him.

He left the kitchen, and she stared blankly at the table, unsure of where to go from there. She wanted to scream at him, but all that would get her was, *"Calm down, my beauty."*

When she escaped, should she warn everyone? Should she find Raoul? All of the options seemed flawed and dangerous. But she could do nothing while she was still trapped down in that strange little home.

"I'm ready to sing again," she said, walking into the living area thirty minutes later. He was already seated at the piano, flipping through a paper book of music."

He glanced up. "Excellent. I was examining possible song choices for you. You will *greatly* please your Spirit with many of these."

"No. I don't want to call you *Spirit* anymore. What's your name?"

He shifted. "The more you know of me, the less happy you will be."

"What's your name?"

"You will not yield, will you? Cameron said that you were once a stubborn little girl, and it seems he was right. You will not speak it to another soul?"

"I won't," she promised.

"You may call me Erik."

"Erik," she repeated. His eyes seemed to soften when she said it, only to reignite when she then asked, "Are you ever going to show me your face?"

"No."

Despite the iciness of his response, she continued, "Why? I know you're not a Spirit now. And I don't think that I could be any less happy than I already am. I'm sure your face won't matter."

Instantly, she regretted saying it. Erik turned around and grabbed her wrist with such speed that Christine again wondered if he did possess magical powers. "Oh, my face wouldn't simply make you unhappy," he said in a soft voice that was so terrible it nearly brought her to her knees. "It would kill you, darling. And you wouldn't be able to fulfill your destiny if you were dead, would you?" She gaped at him, the leather digging hotly into her skin. "*Would you?*"

"No," she whispered, shaking her head back and forth. "Please."

He released her and threw his shoulders back. It had been the first time she'd seen him off balance, and she never wanted to see it again. Ever. When he spoke, his voice was gentle and collected. "Are you ready to start?"

"Yes." Her voice shook. And she sang for her freedom. She sang for her life.

"There," he stated. "*Yes.* There we go. There's that heavenly voice. Now we can finally begin."

Chapter 13

Although Raoul attempted to forget Christine, a slow depression crept over him in the days following her disappearance. It was all starting to seem kind of hopeless. Then again, there was freedom in hopelessness—freedom to get the hell out of there.

Phillip, maybe sensing that Raoul was a little down in the dumps, had dragged him to the mountains while he attended a secret meeting at a supposedly abandoned lodge. Wealthy businessmen and government officials had established havens like this that were somewhat hidden from the rest of the world. Some were on mountain peaks around old ski resorts or in cushy underground basements. While the more hostile activist groups may have been aware of their existence, they didn't know the exact locations. Bodyguards surrounded the perimeter in case any emergencies did come up.

While Phillip was secluded in his meeting, Raoul hiked around the overgrown trails for a bit, taking in the cleaner, crisp air and stretching his muscles. It always felt great to escape the confines of the decaying city. He had to be a little careful because there were survivalists up in these mountains, people who had given up on civilization and were living off the land. He kept an eye out, knowing they wouldn't hesitate to aim a shotgun at him for trespassing.

After surviving his hike, he met Phillip at the front of the lodge. Sara Lee was supposed to be meeting them at any time. Phillip had bought her transportation, along with a couple of bodyguards, thinking they might make a romantic weekend of it. Raoul sort of felt like the third wheel, but it was better than staying at home and sulking.

"Did you have a good day out there?" Phillip asked, stretching his legs out.

"It was cool," Raoul replied. "One with nature and all that. I miss going hiking and camping like we used to do with Dad."

"Yeah. So do I."

"Did you have fun at your meeting?" Raoul asked.

"Tons."

"Anything new and interesting?"

Phillip lowered his voice. "Sixty-four people were killed in Houston last night. Fifty-five in Memphis. No wonder people have been pouring into Cameron's place like it's a refugee camp. I hear he can't build new housing fast enough. Bastard."

"Jesus."

"Yeah. It's all pretty shadowy right now. You don't really know whose side anyone is on. And now that you have these explosions going off every day, there's even more chaos. People blame the current government for not controlling it. Cameron starts to look like some sort of savior. It's bad." Phillip shook his head. "That girl didn't tell you anything useful, did she?"

"Not really," Raoul murmured. "She believed in the Spirit, said it even spoke to her. Weird, huh?"

"She actually interacted with it? First time I've heard of that. Damn. I wish I'd had a chance to talk with her."

"Do you believe in it?" It wasn't that Raoul did, but he was beginning to think Meg had been right about there being a bigger force at play.

"Of course I don't believe in the Spirit," said Phillip with a loud laugh. "Do *you*?"

"Nah. I just—"

"Hey, Sara Baby!" Phillip hopped up and waved.

"Phil. How are you?" she asked, long, wavy blonde hair falling over her shoulders and fluttering in the mountain breeze. As usual, her clothes, a short red dress that fitted tightly around her slender form, weren't appropriate for the setting. Sara had been a fashion model when there were still opportunities for that line of work. Her great-grandfather had started an automobile company decades ago, and so she was well within the world of "old money." Although she was smiling at them, her green eyes seemed dull.

"I'm good," Phillip replied, sounding a little more upbeat. They shared a quick kiss. "How about you?"

"Fine," she replied in a way that made Raoul guess everything was not so fine. "Hey, Raoul. How are you?"

"Couldn't be better," he lied.

Phillip wasn't completely ignorant to her mood either. "Are you sure you're fine, babe? You look kind of tired." She shrugged. "Can I get you something to drink? I don't know if they have much of a cocktail selection, but…"

"No. I won't be here very long."

"I thought you were staying the night."

She took a slow seat next to him. Folding her hands in her lap, she looked up again with a grim frown of determination. "For the last week, my roommates and I have spent most nights huddled in our basement listening to people scream at each other. And gunshots."

Phillip took her limp hand. "Why didn't you tell me? I would have gotten you more security."

"I live in one of the nicest neighborhoods in the city. You can't get much more secure. And it's still terrifying!"

"All right, all right. Let me see if I can bring you to my mom's house. Shouldn't be a problem."

"Your neighborhood was just firebombed," she angrily replied, drawing her hand away. "It's not safe. And I'm…I'm leaving tomorrow. I'm going to Canada, where the rest of my family is. This isn't a place for people like us."

"People like what?"

"You know." She gave up on trying to be nice about it. "Wealthy, intelligent, sane people!"

"That's a crappy attitude," Phil replied. Raoul knew the relationship was about to go up in smoke.

"I don't care!" she shot back. "I don't care if I sound like a snob or a bitch or anything else you want to throw at me. I'm too tired and scared to care. And you're always busy anyway."

"Yeah. I'm busy trying to fix this horror show. You think I enjoy dealing with it? You think I'm having fun?"

"I don't know," she murmured. "I get that it's your mission. But it's not mine. I'm sorry."

"I get it," he replied, looking away.

"I didn't want to hurt you, Phil." He shrugged and stared forward, hiding his pain. "Well, I told my driver to wait here because I figured you'd be angry. My flight leaves tomorrow night. So I guess this is goodbye."

He finally looked at her. "Goodbye, Sara. Good luck. I mean it. I hope everything works out."

She stood, bent down, and kissed his cheek. "If you're ever up north, please call me. And, maybe if there's a miracle, I can come back here someday."

"Yeah. A miracle. Because that's what's going to fix everything."

They both watched her go, red heels clicking down the driveway. Phillip finished his glass of wine in one long swig. "We were never right for each other anyway," he said after five minutes of staring at the spot where Sara had stood. "She's way too high maintenance."

"Maybe she's not so wrong about some stuff," Raoul replied, a heavy feeling in his chest.

"What?"

"Maybe it's time to consider our own exit plan."

Raoul expected Phillip to launch into a tirade about his duties to the country. Instead, Phillip set his glass down and said, "Well, I'll at least make sure Mom can get out if she wants. Might as well be a realist."

They sat in silence for a while, staring off into the thick trees and lost in their own thoughts. A monarch butterfly landed on the arm of his chair, its sunset orange and black wings fluttering every so often.

In silence, they watched as the butterfly moved off the chair, hovered in the air for several seconds, and then flew away.

***

The pieces that Erik chose for her were by far the most challenging songs she'd ever attempted, ten times more difficult than the hymns she'd sung. The vocal ranges and jumps between notes were much wider, and even the rhythms threw her off key. It seemed like Erik interrupted her every other note to make corrections, which created even more frustration.

"Will I actually be singing these for someone?" she asked, exhaustion creeping into her voice. It was the first time she'd spoken to him that afternoon, communicating with nods of her head whenever he corrected her.

"Not in the near future."

"What do you mean by that?"

"There will come a point when the rules change. And then you will sing as you were meant to. For everyone."

"And Cameron won't mind?"

"Cameron will listen to my sage advice." His tone was odd, and she wasn't sure if there was humor in the statement. She yawned against her will. "It is time for you to sleep, I think."

"What time is it?"

"Nighttime."

Christine inwardly rolled her eyes at his vagueness and, without another word, went back to her room. She hadn't wished him *goodnight* because her night was going to be far from pleasant—and it was all his fault. After closing the door, she quickly undressed and pulled out fresh undergarments from the drawers, along with a clean white cotton nightgown. With a sigh, she fell into the bed, pulling the cool sheets and covers around her.

Her sleep was far from restful, her dreams shadowy and haunting. When Christine woke, she groaned to see where she was and placed a hand against her clammy forehead. A cold sweat had soaked into her nightgown and the sheets. It all seemed so hopeless that Christine didn't want to get out of bed.

She took a two-minute shower, all the while listening carefully to her surroundings over the rushing water to make sure the door didn't open. Christine slipped on another modest dress. While in the closet, she noticed for the first time that there were also several pairs of black slacks and one pair of blue jeans, along with a couple of blouses and sweaters. *Great. More new rules to confuse her.* She brushed her tangled hair, pushed it back with a magenta headband, and decided she looked somewhat human again.

"You slept for nearly twelve hours," he said when she came out. "I was rather concerned that you had died."

She blinked. "I'm sorry?"

"Do not be sorry. The last few days have been rather exhausting for you. Come and eat. Today we will begin your other lessons."

"For my voice?" She wasn't sure if she was ready for another day of endless criticism, even if it did earn her freedom.

"Not right now." As he led her into the kitchen and placed a bowl of o-shaped cereal in front of her, she wondered what he was talking about. Her question was answered when he dropped a pile of thick, heavy books on the table with a thud. "You will read these."

She stared down at them. There was biology, anatomy, American history, world history.

"They are not ideal, full of biases and half-truths," he said. "But they are what is left in this country and will do for now."

"It'll take forever to get through all these. I have to read through *all* of this before you'll let me out?" She'd be a grey-haired old woman.

"No. You must only begin to have an understanding."

"Why?" she softly asked, tracing a finger over the cover. "Why?"

"Why do you want me to learn all this? No one else ever did."

"As I have told you dozens of times, you are far superior to them. So long as you are in my company, you will be safe from their restrictions. And I do not want your ignorance." He paused and then asked, "Do you not want to know more? Are you content with the knowledge you have?"

"No," she admitted. "I'd like to know more. I always have."

He left her at the table and, after sitting there bewildered for several more moments, Christine picked up one of the history books. At least she recognized the man on the front cover as the first president of the United States. For the first time in over a decade, she didn't have to look over her shoulder to make sure no one was watching her "learn more than was good for a young lady." She half-relaxed and began the first chapter of each book, reading until her mind couldn't absorb any more facts. She already knew some things but not in as much detail as the books were providing—the colonization of the United States, the systems of the body, the beginning of civilization. Sometimes she could feel Erik watching her. He would dart into different rooms and close the door, always busy with some mysterious task.

She wanted to keep reading both out of a hunger for information and a mental escape from the insanity around her, but her sight became blurry. Christine set the books aside and took a sip of water, staring at the table and feeling a little lost.

"Do you have questions?" he asked.

She looked up, startled that he was even in the room. "What?"

"Questions from your reading?"

"No. I think I understood it all."

"Yes. You are a bright girl."

"Um, thank you." Christine could sense that he was also intelligent by his speech and even by his eyes. Despite her anger and fear, she could feel her curiosity growing. "Did you have a lot of schooling?" she asked.

"Much of my education was non-traditional. But I am well-informed."

"Did you have a job? I mean, before you became Cameron's advisor."

He laughed, and it was a musical sound. "Do not bore yourself with the banal details of my life. Not when there are so many other things to learn."

Again, it was like trying to knock down a brick wall, and she gave up.

That afternoon (she guessed it was afternoon—for all Christine knew, it was midnight) she sang, and it seemed to please him. "Already an improvement," he stated, eyes shining. "Now that you are not confined to that wretched little room, you will progress much faster."

"I liked the little room," she replied, too worn out to be dishonest. "I looked forward to those lessons every week."

"Did you?" He actually seemed a little surprised.

"I miss the Spirit," she murmured, looking down.

"But you knew, didn't you?" he asked in a gentle voice. "That the Spirit was not what they all said it to be. I could always see it in your eyes."

"No." She clenched her jaw. "Well, I-I guess I didn't want to think about it very much. When you spoke to me, you weren't like the rest of them. That alone made you magical. That was enough. And you *were* my friend." She swallowed past the knot in her throat. "I did trust you."

"Are you so unhappy in my home?"

"It has nothing to do with your home. But you lied to me all this time! You won't let me out, even for air, and that makes me sick to my stomach. Half the time, I still wonder if this is some sort of awful test to see whether I'm really a good girl. I guess I don't pass, right? Argh."

"It is no test, Christine. I promise you that."

"If it's not a test, then why don't you tell me what it is?"

"In time," was his only reply.

In anger, she threw up her hands and retreated to the bedroom. As always he left her alone while she sulked, and Christine again emerged on her own time.

A pattern formed. She preferred to read the textbooks after waking up, when her mind was fresh and able to grasp new concepts. After she ate lunch, their vocal lessons would begin. Sometimes he was harsh, and sometimes he was pleased. She was never sure if his moods were truly dependent on her talent or if his personality was volatile.

Sometimes she would hide away in her room for several hours, lying on her stomach with her face buried in the pillow. She would cry, mostly from frustration and the fear of not knowing where this path was going to lead her. She'd cried for similar reasons in Cameron's community at times, feeling trapped and helpless. Really, she'd never felt all that in control of her own life.

Her spare time was spent looking through the fictional books on his shelves, everything from 1800's and 1900's classics to a few more modern novels, or listening to the assortment of music. For some reason, her desire to watch the movies was less strong, although she did occasionally view a few from her youth.

With all of this at her disposal, she began to form a picture of the Outside in her mind. Or at least of what it had been like until the last horrible couple of years. People had gone to school and then gotten jobs of their choices and then some fell in love and got married and had several children. And some preferred not to do those things at all. People danced and sang and went to movies and concerts and sometimes drank too much alcohol. They took their children to zoos and parks and museums. They celebrated holidays and birthdays and played games and watched sports. A government made laws and police ensured people were safe, but, to a large degree, everyone did as they wanted. They had control.

The World didn't sound so terrible. It was mostly the exciting and happy place that she remembered from her youth.

One morning, Christine came out and sat down at the kitchen table. Usually, he greeted her with breakfast and books, but she was alone this time. It was difficult to say when Erik left the home, but he likely went out while she was sleeping or sulking in the bedroom. Christine never saw him jump through a magical hole in the ceiling. It dawned on her that the ceiling exit was probably behind one of the locked doors, making it even more impossible for her to escape.

With a shrug, she opened a book and settled into her normal pattern. He came into the kitchen about an hour later, and she noticed that he seemed agitated, fingers curled and gait less smooth. He sharply glanced at her as though surprised. "I had not intended on taking so long."

"Oh." She started to look back down and then asked, "Erik, how long have I been here?"

"A little over a week," he replied.

Christine winced. "And Mrs. Valerius knows I'm okay?"

"Yes. She knows you are in the care of the Spirit." He seemed distracted as he turned away. "Have you had food?"

"No, but I'm okay."

"You already eat like a little bird. Let's not worsen it." He pulled a carton of eggs from the refrigerator so forcefully that she was afraid he'd broken them all. When he opened it, the eggs were still intact.

"Erik?" She didn't know why she started the conversation that morning, especially when her captor didn't even seem to be in the best of moods. Maybe it was loneliness or curiosity.

"Yes?"

"I noticed that the history book only goes to 2030."

He gave a short laugh. "You're that far already?"

"No. I got curious and looked ahead. But I was wondering where the rest of it was."

"Yes, it is difficult to find later material. At least later material that is of any use and not a bunch of lies. The best books for that time are in foreign languages and awaiting translation."

"Do you speak other languages?"

"Yes." He turned back to the eggs, easily cracking one on the edge of a bowl in a single motion. She'd always made a bit of a mess while doing that, pieces of the shell falling into the yolk. Thankfully, her father found her clumsy cooking skills funny. He'd kept a part of himself, his gentle humor.

"Which languages?" she asked.

"Four fluently. Spanish, French, German, Farsi." He paused. "With less skill, Mandarin."

"Wow. I can only speak one."

"In time, we can change that," he replied.

"So you must have been to other countries?"

"Yes."

"I'd like to see other countries," she murmured. "Goodness. I'd like to see other states." He didn't say anything to this. "Have you been to other times?"

"*What?*" He finally turned away from the stove.

She laughed. "Well, if you were a Spirit, I bet you would travel through time and see everything, right? Like in those stories."

He tilted his head. "I suppose I would. Odd girl." He said the last part gently, though, and so she continued to speak.

"I wish I'd lived, um, in the 1950's, maybe. Or the 1990's. Everything seemed good then."

"Those times were not so perfect," he said. "No era was. No country is. Do not fool yourself with thoughts of escape to some imaginary time or place. Take what you are given and *work* with it. That is the answer."

Christine glanced down and felt her face warm, wondering if he was aware of her secret thoughts of escaping to a foreign country with Raoul. When he didn't give any indication of being angry with her, she cautiously continued, "You can go to different countries and speak all these languages. So why are you here? Why do you work with Cameron, if you don't even believe in half of what he says? I mean, I have *pants* in my closet. Why are you here when you could probably be anywhere else?" She knew it was an intrusive question.

He turned all the way around. "The same reason that you are here."

"What?"

"A destiny. You and I…we were meant to be at this time…this place. I knew it the second that I heard you sing. I finally understood."

"Understood what?"

"The point of *everything*."

He turned away to continue making her breakfast, and she turned back to her books, thinking they would safely return to their normal lukewarm cordiality. When she sang later that day, though, there came a point where he stopped playing the piano and turned all the way around on the bench to stare at her.

"Did I mess up?" she asked, shuffling her feet.

"No. You did quite well."

"Oh."

"You are simply a vision of loveliness, you know?" Erik stood. The intensity in his eyes caused her to take several steps backward. "And you are still frightened of me."

"I'm still your prisoner," she replied, fingers curling. "I don't know what you want."

"I wish you would not feel that way. I do not want a prisoner."

"But you won't let me go anywhere. You won't tell me anything except that I have some destiny." Her lip trembled. "How can I like you, whoever you are?"

"Like me. What a tepid word. I hope you will never *like* me, Christine." He sat at the piano again, fingertips to his forehead and elbows on the keys.

"Erik, if you would just explain this all to me. Why are you keeping me here?"

"You should go to bed."

"Why are you keeping me here?!"

A long pause. A sigh. "Isn't it obvious by now? Because Cameron Lourdes knows you are here. You know the truth of me now. You know

I'm not a Spirit. That makes you dangerous to him. At best, he would banish you. At best."

"Then what do I do? I didn't ask for this. You're the ones who lied to everyone."

"It will be resolved. Cameron will see that you are no threat."

"Are you ever going to let me out?" She couldn't stop the desperation from creeping into her voice. "How long? A month? A year? Please give me something."

She expected him to give her another frustrating and cryptic reply. Instead, Erik said, "We will discuss that tomorrow. Now go to bed."

Her mouth opened to argue, but she realized that his answer held hope. *Tomorrow.* It was good enough. For the first time, she said, "Okay. Goodnight, Erik."

Maybe there were some things she didn't *want* to know yet.

Chapter 14

2006

"Why are we sitting in the garage? This is boring."

"I wanted to spend time with you. I haven't spent much time with you over the years, have I?"

He looked at her. "But why are we sitting in the garage?"

"It's nice and dark," Laura replied, tilting her forehead against the cool glass of the window. "I just thought we could chat." She breathed in deeply, a headache forming in the front of her skull. The exhaust pipe was stuffed with a small embroidered hand towel, a wedding present from the Bakers. Or was it from the Ortegas? She couldn't remember. Neither spoke to her anymore.

"You said we would go on a drive."

"What's your favorite subject, Erik?"

"You know that, Mom."

"Tell me again. I don't remember."

"It's science."

"What sort of science?"

"All science. Animals and weather and electricity and the body and outer space and..." He looked toward the passenger window with wide yellow eyes. "I don't want to be in here anymore! I want to go on a drive like you said. I don't feel well in here."

"We'll go on the longest drive ever in just a bit," she murmured. Nausea set in as her headache worsened, and she swallowed to force the sensation away. "It'll be a beautiful drive. With gold streets and purple clouds. And your face will be all better. Can you imagine that?"

He blinked. "My face will be better? Did you find a new doctor?"

"Yes. You'll wake up, and it'll be all better."

He put two fingers to the bandages on his cheek and hesitated. "Mom, I really want to go back inside now," he whispered.

"Shh, baby. We'll leave in a little while. And then your daddy will be so happy. Don't you want to make Daddy happy?"

"But—"

She continued to take deep breaths. "Erik, I'm sorry I haven't been very nice to you. You were always so complicated. But now it'll be okay. We'll go somewhere where everyone is nice to us." Ignoring her, he managed to pull up the locking device and open the door. She quickly clicked the lock back into place from her side. "Erik, you won't be happy out there. Everyone hates both of us. I tried to fix you, but no one would let me. Mommy tried, baby."

"I want to get out now!" he cried. "I don't want to be here! I don't feel well!" A tear trickled down his mess of a face, and a soft sob emerged from his twisted lips. *"Please!"*

"Erik, stay here with Mommy."

"No!" He pulled the lock up again and pushed the door open with his scrawny arms, scrambling out. She didn't have the strength to reach out and grab him. Erik stumbled toward the entrance of the house with his hands stretched out in front of him.

"Erik! Fine, Erik!" she hoarsely screamed with her last bit of strength. "Go! But you'd better not tell anyone where Mommy is. I'll kill you if you do! I want to be left alone. I don't want to deal with you anymore. I hate you! So go and leave me alone, you hideous little brat!" She paused as the world spun and darkened. "Oh. Oh, Erik. Erik, I'm so tired of it all. I just want to…to sleep."

He glanced back at her from the door, and their eyes locked together for one final moment. Her only child then ran inside, shutting the door behind him. For a second she was afraid he would tell, but the minutes ticked by and no one ever came.

Laura rested her head back against the seat and remembered being on the diving team in high school, that moment on the edge of the board before she sprang up into the air. She stared over the vast blue water, ready to launch toward the rippling mass in perfect form.

She jumped as the beautiful blue became a comforting blackness.

And she flew.

***

2034

Anticipation ruined most of her sleep that night.

Tomorrow, he'd said. Tomorrow finally became today, at least according to her internal clock, and Christine jumped out of bed and ran to the door, still wearing her nightgown. She approached him with resolve, holding her head high and arms straight at her sides.

"Good morning, my beauty," he greeted her with none of the hostility of the previous night.

"Good morning, Erik."

"Do you want breakfast?"

"Not right now."

"Do you want to begin your lessons then?"

She took a deep breath. "Erik, you said *tomorrow.*"

"Pardon me?"

"You said we would talk about me getting to go out."

"I did, didn't I?"

"Erik, all I want is fresh air. That's all I'm eager for." *Please please please please please.*

"I can assure you that the air here is better for you than that polluted mess outside."

She suppressed a cry of frustration. If he didn't grant her this wish, she was going to lose her mind. *"Please."*

He looked her in the eye. "Assuming you prove yourself trustworthy, you will be singing in one week. For Cameron's latest welcoming event."

Her heart jumped. "That sounds wonderful."

"As I said, you must prove yourself trustworthy." Christine knew that she would have to at least pretend to be a completely 'good girl.' "We will focus on your voice for the rest of the week," he continued.

She was nervous that any quiver in her speech might give away her true thoughts. Still, it was very difficult to concentrate on her lessons that day as Christine wondered what she would do when her moment of freedom arrived. Try to run? Try to warn everyone? Both sounded dangerous, but she couldn't just do nothing, right?

During her break, she played pop music from the 1980's in the closet, a fast tune with a fun beat. Vaguely, she remembered her mother playing the song at times, usually when she was doing aerobic exercises. Her dad had shaken his head and laughed as they danced around, a broad smile on his face. Christine never saw that smile again after her mother had passed on.

And now she danced around for the first time in years, *sinfully* lifting her legs, waving her arms and swerving her hips. It probably looked ridiculous, but she suddenly had a ton of energy to expend. There was something liberating about dancing—as though she were finally escaping the life she'd led of restricted movement, thought, and speech. And, soon, maybe she would be completely *free.*

Knowing how much was at stake, she sang her absolute best for Erik that evening, and he said, "You will amaze all of them. There is no doubt of it. You are their beacon. Their light. Even Cameron believes this now."

She looked toward the carpet. "I'm not sure I'm exactly the role model of what Cameron wants. You've seen to that." She wasn't sure whether that was a 'thank you' or an accusation.

"It does not matter. You look the part, and you will learn to play it perfectly."

Christine bit her bottom lip as she realized he wanted her to become part of this lie. Just like the Spirit was a lie. How many lies was Cameron's world built on? And why was it built on deceit? Why did it need to be?

The next day was the same until Erik paused after their final vocal lesson. "I think we should have a preliminary outing before Cameron's event."

"What?"

"I am taking you above ground briefly. Perhaps it *would* be good for your health. It is nearing sunset, an ideal time." She gaped at him. "If you attempt to run, that will be it."

Christine nodded, deciding to not making any decisions until she could see exactly where she was. "All I want is air. I promise, Erik."

"Put on sturdy shoes and then follow me."

As she expected, he took her into one of the locked rooms. Nothing was in the small space except for walls of grey file cabinets along with another mysterious door. She wondered how big his home actually was, how far back it stretched. A soft beep sounded into the air, but she couldn't tell where it originated. Maybe he had a controller in his jacket pocket? Suddenly, a rectangular portion of the ceiling slid back and revealed an opening of the same shape. A metallic staircase unfolded and descended down to the carpet. He hadn't been lying, and the complexity of it all was a little overwhelming. "Follow me," he said.

She ascended the stairs behind him, her footsteps much louder than his, and found herself to be in the middle of a dark tunnel. Walking forward without a glance in either direction, Erik pushed another button, and the silver doors of an elevator opened. The inside was lit with a dim bulb. "What is this place?" she asked, hugging her arms to her chest.

"It is a shelter built some time ago, able to withstand man's deadliest weapons. And it makes for a very secure home, no?"

The floor lifted beneath her feet and then stopped within seconds.

The doors slid open, and she was again looking into darkness. This time, though, there was a square patch of light beneath a short metal staircase that led to an opening.

"Go up," said Erik. "You will have twenty minutes. Watch your step as you walk; I have surveyed the area, but there could still be a rusty nail here and there."

"Are you coming?" she asked, not knowing what she wanted the answer to be.

"In a moment."

She walked up the staircase, blinking in the natural light. Christine heard birds twittering and almost expected to find herself in a forest. But no. When she reached the top, she saw that it was the remains of a large, circular abandoned building. The windows were all shattered, and flowery weeds had begun to creep through the entrances and the floorboards. Decaying wooden balconies were near the ceiling, and a scrawny squirrel was perched on the ledge, watching her. Tattered red seats sat in the middle of the room, and Christine noticed that she was elevated over them. *On a stage.*

There was no sign of civilization, and she found the room eerie as she climbed down a set of steps and looked around. A few yellowed pieces of papers were lying on the floor, along with fragments of wood and plaster. The building had to have been very nice at one time; she could make out gold decorations on the walls and torn ceiling.

"Be careful where you step," said Erik, startling her. She turned. He was standing in the shadows of the stage, under a tattered blue curtain, arms folded.

"What happened to it?" she asked, her voice lost in the vast space.

"It was abandoned."

"But why?"

Erik shrugged. "The city could no longer afford extravagancies. It later served as a shelter for the rich and powerful in case of an emergency. But, at some point, there was no point in keeping it open at all."

She glanced through a space where a semicircle window should have been and saw nothing but grass blowing in a gentle breeze. A heavy melancholy settled over her. "It's sad in here," she murmured. Christine stepped into the rows of seats. A flapping noise startled her, and she jumped back, hand over her heart. Several grey and brown sparrows flew past her and out one of the windows. Silence resumed, and Christine continued to look over the mess, over old statues and ornaments and what appeared to be a woman's pair of blue heels.

"It is time to return inside," Erik finally said.

She didn't argue, hurrying back up to the stage and following him downstairs toward the elevator. The following day, she didn't ask to go back up. The ruins of the Outside were rather depressing, and that sort of setting provided no means of escape. Christine supposed she'd ask to go up again only when she became desperate for a ray of sunshine.

During her time in the closet, she found something that made her smile again. Christine pulled out the board and pieces from beneath a pile of books and brought them into the kitchen. Placing everything out on the table, she set it up within a few minutes and then ate her ham sandwich. When Erik came in, he started and stared.

"I used to play with my dad," she said. "I mean, I was terrible at it because I was seven. But I remember how."

"Checkers," he replied, touching one of the red pieces with the tip of his gloved finger. "It has been a long time."

"Will you?" She felt less hostile toward him now that she was allowed out, and this was another way to continue gaining his trust. Still, Christine hadn't pulled out the game with purely underhanded intentions. It was another relic from her past that she remembered with fondness.

He didn't answer her directly, only sat down at the table and motioned at her to go first. Erik beat her quickly and without effort, and she awkwardly stared down at a board that only had red pieces remaining. "Did you play this a lot?" she asked.

"Several times."

"Several times." She laughed. "Well, then."

"I prefer chess, actually."

"I've never played that," she murmured.

"I can teach you," he replied with a touch of eagerness. "There are *so* many things that I can teach you."

"I'd like that." She swallowed and looked down, hoping he couldn't see any traces of deception on her face. Trying to make the guilty feelings go away, Christine distracted them both by pointing at the front cover of a textbook. "It's funny looking, isn't it?"

"It is a stegosaurus. For its time, I am sure it appeared completely normal." He sounded very annoyed, and so she tried again.

"Erik, how old is the Earth?"

"How old do you think it is?"

"I don't know." Realizing that he wasn't going to answer her, she pulled out a history book and asked, "Do you think women should be able to vote?"

He paused and then chuckled. "It depends on the meaning of your question."

"What?"

"Well, if you are implying that, because men can vote, then women should be able to do so as well, then I would agree. One gender is not superior to the other. But the better question is—should *anyone* be able to vote?"

"I don't understand…"

"Are most people capable and intelligent enough to make their own decisions?"

She eyed him. "Do you think they are?"

He didn't answer. She rubbed her head, tired of the riddles. "Erik, do you want me to believe what Cameron teaches?"

"No." At least that was direct enough.

"But you want me to sing for him?"

"Yes."

"And I'm not supposed to be confused by this at all?" She gave him a desperate look.

"We will return to these more intellectual exercises later. All right?" Erik reached out to touch her hair, and she didn't flinch away. He ran his index finger over a blonde strand. "Christine…" It was more a sigh than a spoken word. Withdrawing his hand, he left her with her thoughts.

She could feel herself growing more nervous by the moment. If possible, the event could be her escape. If she arrived and was surrounded on all sides by Cameron's men, it might at least be another chance to gain Erik's trust until a true opportunity presented itself.

Still, with each passing day in that underground home, Christine felt that she was falling deeper and deeper into something that was far bigger than herself. And she feared that there would eventually be no turning back.

Chapter 15

He took her above ground two more times, and she explored the dead theater, picking up old programs for shows and looking them over. While the words and pictures were very faded, she could tell that they had once been colorful and vibrant, from a time when the world wasn't covered in shadows.

The evening before the big event, Erik said, "You will wear the blue dress on the right side of your closet. It was meant for such an occasion."

"You mean I shouldn't wear the pants?" she joked.

"Only if you would like to see Mr. Lourdes turn a fiery shade of red."

"Maybe I would." That wasn't a joke, and Christine hoped she hadn't crossed the line. She still didn't quite understand the relationship between Erik and Cameron.

But Erik chuckled. "Someday."

She easily found the dress the afternoon of her performance, finding the shiny material flashier than anything she usually saw. There were also matching flat shoes and a bright blue ribbon for her hair. Her reflection was pale but otherwise healthy; Erik certainly saw that she was well-fed. More than anything, her eyes were somehow wiser, less clouded with fantasies.

When she emerged, Erik looked her up and down. "Perfect. Tasteful yet alluring. Cameron may not completely approve, but he certainly will not regret the results."

She shifted at the strange compliment. "Thank you?"

He didn't notice her nervousness. "We have a two hours' journey ahead of us. Cameron will meet with us beforehand, and you will need to play your part."

"My part?"

"Be an actress. Simply be quiet and compliant. None of those interesting questions of yours, as much as I enjoy them. I doubt Cameron likes curious women."

"Probably not." Christine wondered if she should bring any clothing or toiletries, but Erik might grow suspicious. Outside of one clothing change and a plastic hairbrush, she brought nothing else.

When they had climbed the first set of stairs, she started to walk toward their normal elevator. "This way," Erik said with a nod of his head to the left. He turned on a flashlight. "It will take about ten minutes."

She turned to follow and stumbled in the darkness, lightly touching his black jacket to steady herself. He paused in his steps and allowed her to adjust. They continued down the metal pathway, and Christine could see very little throughout the journey, just the occasional pole or some wiring sticking out of the ceiling. Sometimes there was rumbling from above. Erik finally stopped and pushed a button. An elevator door open, and they stepped inside. "How many different elevators are there?" she asked.

"Three."

"Where does the third go?"

He glanced at her but didn't answer. She knew better than to ask again.

The elevator headed upwards, and the door opened. As before, she went up a short flight of stairs, although this time they led to a slanted green door. Erik took a gold key from his pocket and unlocked it, and she was faced with a dirty alleyway. Broken glass bottles and brown puddles covered the cracked asphalt. She could hear the beat of a radio in the distance along with occasional muffled voices.

"Stay close," Erik said, locking the door. "This part of the city is less savory, although far from the worst of it."

She found safety in the shadow of her captor as she gazed over the urban decay. Suddenly, Christine noticed a long, black car with heavily tinted windows waiting along the curbside. Erik walked toward it and opened the door. She took one last glance around, her gaze falling on a man watching her with glazed eyes, his jeans and white shirt dirty and torn. "Get in," murmured Erik.

Christine climbed into the interior and settled into the plush grey seat. Piano music was playing on the speakers, and the air conditioning was blowing over them, a comforting contrast with the world outside. The driver, a bald-headed man with beady eyes and glasses, glanced back at them. She recognized him, usually working right at Cameron's side. "Are you ready?" the man asked, his voice nasally.

"Drive," said Erik with a wave of his hand. Whomever the man was, Erik clearly wasn't intimidated.

She watched as the city turned into abandoned towns and then that morphed into rural land. Eventually, she could sense they were nearing her old home, and she cast a nervous glance toward Erik. He was staring out his own window, the fingers of his left hand tapping impatiently against the seat.

Finally, she recognized the gates and Cameron's looming residence. While still intimidating, the structure seemed smaller now that she knew no Spirit ruled over everything. To her surprise, they didn't stop right inside the gate. Instead, the car turned sharply into a dark garage attached to Cameron's compound. She hadn't known of its existence. The door slid shut, and she couldn't see anything through the window except the outlines of irregular shapes. The vehicle stopped, and the driver got out to open her door. "Remember what I told you," Erik said. "Play your part, my beauty."

She climbed out of the car. The driver remained there, and Erik led her to a door and then a dimly lit corridor. The lights buzzed over her head, and her footsteps echoed on linoleum tiles. Wherever they were, the bland and modern halls greatly contrasted with the parts of Cameron's home that she had seen. They walked up several flights of stairs, and she had to work to keep up with Erik's fast gait, though it seemed he was trying to slow down for her sake. Erik stopped at an inconspicuous white door that blended in with the plaster wall. He turned the white knob and stepped into a room, holding the door open for her behind him. She blinked in the sudden light and gasped. They were now standing in Cameron's office.

"Go in, my dear," murmured Erik, gently pushing her forward with his hand. "You are fine." Still stunned, she stared around the plush room, only having been in there one other time. The bear rug still disturbed her as did the paintings on the walls of what appeared to be bloody battles between heaven and hell.

"Welcome, welcome." Cameron's voice startled her. His smile was partly hidden by his short brown beard. It was difficult not to glare, but she forced a smile in return. "You look divine. Although, it's not quite the dress I would have recommended."

Erik quickly spoke. "She is a beacon after all."

Cameron hesitated and then shrugged. "It's still a fairly modest dress. No harm done." He turned back to her. "Tell me, my dear. Have you learned a great deal while with the Spirit…Erik? Are you learning to be a godly woman?"

"Oh, yes," she whispered. "He teaches me to be a very good girl." The lie tasted bitter.

"Wonderful," said Cameron, clasping his hands together. "And are you ready to sing for us today?"

"Oh, yes."

"She is," said Erik. "She is perfection. Our current situation has only improved her voice."

Cameron continued to smile, his head bobbing up and down. "Excellent. Yes, I think today will be utterly wonderful, especially if you intend on following through with our discussion, Erik?"

"Yes."

"Very good. Very good."

She glanced between them, wondering what they were talking

about but knowing that a godly woman would mind her own business. Maybe if she were lucky Erik would tell her later. *If there were a later…*

"I believe it is time for us to leave," said Erik. "We arrived a bit later than intended. As usual, your driver was sluggish. And my normal methods of transportation would not have suited Christine."

"Yes, Jeremy is a little cautious, probably because he's hard of hearing. Still, he's my most loyal friend." Cameron bowed his head and murmured several words in prayer. Glancing back up, he said, "Let's go."

The three of them took a similar, although not identical, pathway back to the garage. Sometimes she would glance toward Erik, but he always had his eyes forward and his shoulders back in an intimidating posture. Cameron would stare at her and smile, making Christine all the more nervous. When they arrived at the car, she looked at Erik, expecting him to climb inside with her. Instead, he said, "It is time for me to take my leave."

"What?" she whispered, casting a glance toward Cameron. He was conversing with the driver. "But I don't know what to do."

"Cameron will lead you to the stage and direct you when to sing. If he makes irritating statements, simply nod your head in agreement. That is all you must do."

"Where will you be?"

"Taking on other tasks. Do not think on it. Just sing." He vanished.

Feeling nauseous, she climbed inside with Cameron facing her then turned her head to look out the window. The car left the dark garage and drove a couple miles through the well-kept neighborhoods, and she was shocked to see how many more new identical homes and buildings were being constructed, as well as how far it all now stretched.

"Are you ready?" asked Cameron.

"I think so," she whispered, lowering her eyes.

"We are doing the true work of God, Christine. You, me, and Erik. There is no better time to be alive."

"Yes, Mr. Lourdes."

"Have you been content these last weeks?" he asked, studying her closely enough to make her squirm.

"Yes," she repeated.

"Good. I think it will be a superb arrangement once it's made official."

Official? "Yes. It will be."

The car stopped, and she had no more time to think about Cameron's strange statement. As they climbed out and walked forward through the green grass of an open space, guards now surrounding them, she could hear many voices. A crowd. *Her audience.* An enormous stage had been set up with a microphone and a grand piano. She gaped as the mass of people came into view, thousands of them. Men and women and children all in similar clothing and wearing the same strange expression.

"Look at them," Cameron murmured. "What a blessing."

He headed for the stage, and she was left with several guards. People were everywhere. She feared it would be impossible for her to escape unnoticed, especially while wearing that dress. As Christine looked around for possible breaks in the crowd, she was oblivious to what Cameron was saying. He was likely giving the same speech he always did: *Everyone is doomed except us. Blah, blah, blah.*

I wonder where Erik is?

Before she could look for him, Christine glanced up as her surroundings seemed to darken. The early evening sky had been clear moments ago. A grey blanket of fog had now settled over them. The rest of the crowd was murmuring and also gazing upwards.

"Ah, yes!" exclaimed Cameron loudly enough to make her jump. "That is a sign from the Spirit, warning us that there will be dark days ahead, my friends. We must believe him. We must be willing to fight on even during the most perilous times."

To her horror, the ground shook beneath her, not enough to knock her off her feet, but she still grasped onto the nearest pole. Shrieks rang out from the crowd as people grabbed their family members, and parents picked up their youngest children. Yellow lights flashed above and thunder rumbled, also causing the ground to tremble. Christine squeezed her eyes shut and held on.

"Yes!" Cameron's voice rose above the noise. "The Spirit is angry, my friends. The Spirit is furious at the sin of this country, and you had better listen to him. You had better listen well! He will have his justice, and you want to be on his side when that happens." He paused. "Don't you?"

"*Yes!*" the audience screamed. The ground quaked.

Finally, the shaking stopped. Christine opened her eyes as the sun appeared from behind the fog, brightening the scene again.

"For you see," Cameron continued. "Once justice is served—light, love, and righteousness will rule again." The sunset seemed to glow extra brightly, and the people cheered in agreement, smiling faces raised toward the heavens.

Christine felt sick to her stomach.

Erik.

Nothing but a bunch of wonderful magic tricks.

Nothing but a terrible lie.

A deep anger overcame her, heating her hands and face. *This was so wrong, so unfair to all these poor people.*

In her fury, she was aware of Cameron announcing her name. Christine robotically walked to the stage, staring straight forward, almost oblivious to the crowd. The piano played, and she began the song she had rehearsed dozens of time. Her own voice was distant in her ears, hollow and empty. Still, she sang. She sang her heart out. Except—

The last line of her song was supposed to be: *"And only God's love is real!"*

Instead, she sang, or rather yelled, *"And the Spirit is not real!"*

When the words left her mouth, she stepped backward, shocked at what she had just done. Christine stared down at the sea of confused faces. But before she could celebrate any sort of victory, her voice suddenly continued the song for one more line, only it wasn't really her singing. It was some kind of recording of her, and it flawlessly sang, *"Unless you truly believe!"*

"No," she whispered as the confused murmurs of the audience turned to cheers and applause. "No!" she yelled into the microphone. "Listen to me. It—Please listen!" But no one could hear her. Her microphone was disconnected. She backed away from the front of the stage, shivering in terror.

Cameron quickly stepped up to the microphone, casting a confused glance toward her as though he wasn't quite sure what had happened. The speakers turned back on. "Let's give a hand to Christine."

As salty tears pooled at the corners of her mouth, Christine turned around and ran off the stage. She raced through the grass and toward an aimless target. She would just run and run and run—until she got to the very end of the earth.

Of course, she knew deep down that she wouldn't actually get anywhere. Of course not. A hand grabbed her upper arm as she passed through the shadows of a building. Christine gasped and tried to struggle away, but it was useless. She gave up, shoulders slumping in defeat.

A cold familiar voice said, "Such a shame; I had actually begun to trust you. But did you truly believe I wouldn't prepare for such a trick? Although, I am glad you were creative enough to add the line to your song. Bravo! Bravo, my intelligent beauty."

She closed her eyes as Erik roughly pulled her away.

Now she would never see daylight again.

Chapter 16

Light raindrops tapped against the windows of Raoul's living room, and the air was warm and sticky. While the weather created a more putrid odor than usual, the rain was also a good thing. More people stayed inside, keeping the crime rates and violence lower. Raoul and his two friends were sitting on the couches with glasses of lime soda, all leaning forward as he described the latest news.

"Wait, wait," said Anthony. He spilled a little of his soda on the coffee table. "Sorry. So there was actually some kind of magic show?"

"That's the rumor," said Raoul. "And now some people are saying that Cameron might have at least thirty percent of the state's support. Thirty frikin' percent!"

Meg wrinkled her nose. "How did that stuff even happen?"

"I'm sure it's not so hard to fake an earthquake," Raoul replied, although he wasn't certain. Still, how the hell was a nut like Cameron Lourdes getting away with this? The guy didn't even seem that bright.

The only positive aspect was that Christine supposedly sang at the event, but the rumors hadn't given much description concerning her performance. At least she was alive and healthy. And probably still believing in the stupid Spirit.

"Chandler? Earth to Chandler?"

"Sorry," murmured Raoul. "Just thinking about stuff."

Anthony chuckled. "So what's next?"

"Well, a bunch of people, including Phil, are going to give uplifting speeches soon."

"That's a nice…err…start," Meg said, looking down at her worn jeans and t-shirt. "Then maybe they could fix everything else, too? At least they're going to try to address Cameron."

"Yeah, but it gives him more legitimacy," Raoul replied.

"He already has legitimacy," Meg argued in a gentle voice. "I don't think they can pretend he doesn't anymore."

"I know," Raoul murmured. "But they're going to have to do more than give a bunch of speeches. It looks pathetic."

"What do you think they should do?" asked Anthony.

Raoul hesitated. "I don't know. Take a bulldozer and a couple of tanks to his home?"

Meg giggled. "Nice to see you want to take a more measured approach."

"Ugh," Raoul muttered. "It's ridiculous. Why do people think this stuff is real? C'mon. A one minute thunderstorm? Someone needs to expose him for the fraud that he is!"

"How?" asked Anthony.

"We could go to one of these events and figure out where all this is coming from. You know, expose the man behind the curtain, right?"

"That sounds dangerous," Meg murmured. "I mean, you got away last time. But things are a little different now."

"What else are we going to do?" Raoul asked.

"Leave?" Anthony softly replied. "That's what I'm doing soon."

"You're right. That's probably what we should do. I told Phillip that the other day. But do you guys really want to look back knowing you never tried?" Both of his friends glanced down and said nothing. "One try, and then we can leave. That's it. Please."

Meg looked at the floor and sighed. "Okay. I can ask my mom if she knows anything else that would be useful."

Anthony shrugged. "I'm a good getaway driver." He paused. "And I think I know how some of those tricks might have been done. It's not too hard to make an earthquake simulator, anyway. But, ya know, these people probably aren't looking for a science lesson, Raoul. What if they don't care if it's fake? They want security. And hope."

Raoul clenched his jaw with determination. "First, we prove Cameron's a fraud. Then we'll give them hope."

Meg's forehead crinkled as she frowned. "I just *hope* these people aren't too far gone already. Christine, she seemed so out of it."

"I know," Raoul replied, glancing at the raindrops sliding down the window like tears. "That's why, if nothing else, I want her to know that the Spirit's not real."

"And, if it doesn't work, we leave?" Meg asked, unable to keep the eagerness from her voice. "The three of us and my mom?"

"And my mom. We leave," Raoul agreed.

Deep down, he knew that's what they would end up doing. But he had to try. He had to be more than a coward. Phillip was right; his dad would have wanted it.

***

No words could describe the terror she felt as the black car pulled up beside them, jolting as it stopped in the grass. The top of her arm was still clasped in Erik's long, thin fingers, and she was too frightened to look up into those angry yellow eyes. She desperately searched for an escape that didn't exist.

"Get in," Erik commanded, throwing the door open.

She stood there frozen, mind combing through her few options.

"I will sedate you. Is that what you want?"

"No," she whispered. She didn't want to lose consciousness and become completely vulnerable. Christine climbed into the car, praying for a miracle.

"Leaving a little earlier than thought?" the driver asked.

"Yes," Erik replied. "She is tired."

"Ah, yes. Women do get tired easily. My wife always needs her afternoon nap." He smiled and then turned back around.

Erik would tell the driver that she was being hysterical if she begged for help, and Christine was sure the driver would be on his side. And that would also give Erik an excuse to drug her just as he had done when kidnapping her from Raoul's home. *I should have believed you, old friend. God, I was so stupid and naïve.*

Hugging her arms to her chest, Christine practically curled into a ball in the backseat. At least with the driver present, she didn't think anything too horrible would happen to her. But then what? She glanced at Erik, but his masked face was turned toward the window. Was Erik capable of hurting her? Even killing her? *No, she couldn't think like that right now. She had to survive.*

The long drive went by faster than she would have liked, and she could see the buildings come into view in the darkness. Erik said nothing the entire time, not even sparing her a glance. A shudder traveled through her when the vehicle came to a sudden stop.

"Have a pleasant evening," said the driver with another smile.

"You, too," Christine whispered before climbing out of the car. Without a word, Erik walked behind her as they traveled through the back alleyway. Christine glanced around for any sign of help, but there was only one other man leaning against a building. One of his eyes was missing, and he was holding a translucent green bottle to his lips. Her odds with him wouldn't have been any better, if not worse.

The elevator ride was silent. When the doors slid open, she made no move to escape into the tunnels. They climbed down the ceiling stairs to Erik's home. Erik shut the door and locked it with a sharp click. She held her breath, backed against the nearest wall, and waited.

She prepared herself for anything, screaming…objects crashing against the walls…pain. Her thoughts wavered between yelling back at him in a final confrontation or falling to her knees and begging for her life. Slowly, he turned toward her, fingers curled at his sides.

I don't want to die. As she stared up into those yellow eyes, Christine realized with certainty that she wanted to live. Even though the world was falling apart, she wasn't ready to let go of it yet. And so she fully prepared herself to beg and plead for mercy, if that's what it took to survive the night.

But, after staring down at her for several seconds, Erik only said, "Perhaps it is time for you to go to bed."

Her mouth fell open. Realizing that she was going to be spared for at least a little while longer, though, Christine ran into the room without a glance back. She shut the door and then flung herself onto the bed. A soft sob of both horror and relief escaped her lips as she clutched the covers and buried her face in the pillows. She had tried to save those people in the only way she knew how. Really, it had been more of an impulse than a conscious decision. A very stupid impulse that had fixed nothing.

Throughout that night she heard creaking noises and prepared for him to come in and do…whatever punishment he had planned. But Erik never did. Then the waiting itself became awful as the hours ticked by.

The familiar sound of the piano reached her ears and caused her to sit up straight, still grasping the covers as though they would protect her. A loud song in a minor key was playing, the staccato notes sounding as though they were yelling at her. She shielded her ears with the pillow, trying to make the noise go away before it made her crazy. Finally, Christine sat up and made her way to the door. The music pushed back against her. Was this her punishment? Insanity by music?

Staring at his back as he pounded his fingers against the keys, she resisted the urge to run back to her room. Erik sharply glanced at her. They stared at each other for several moments before she dared to speak.

"Erik. I…" Her voice still trembled. "I-I know you're very angry with me. I'm sorry for that. And I hope you can understand that I just didn't think it was fair. All those people being lied to by you and Cameron. And I had to be a part of that. I got really angry. But I shouldn't have done *that*. So. I'm sorry." He said nothing. "I know I won't be let out of here for a long time. But I hope…I hope…" *I hope you won't do something worse.*

Erik looked away. When he spoke, his voice was soft. "I had hoped to spare you certain sights, at least until later. But I should not have done so. Then you would have understood."

"What sights?" she nervously asked.

"That boy, Chandler." Erik said the name with clear disgust. "He showed you the World, did he?"

"Y-yes."

"Only the pretty parts, I am sure."

"No. I saw some bad neighborhoods with old buildings."

"Old buildings?" He chuckled. "Darling, you do not know what *bad* is."

She wasn't sure if she wanted to know. "What are you saying?"

"We will go on another drive late this afternoon, my dear."

He was letting her out? Was it some sort of trap?

"Until then," he continued, "resume your academics. We will take a break from your vocal lessons today. I believe we could both use a rest from that troublesome voice of yours." He almost sounded amused. Almost.

Christine nodded as it dawned on her that she wasn't utterly doomed.

As promised, Erik called her later that day as she was reading a sad fictional novel about horses. They hadn't interacted much. "It would be wise for you to put on the pants now," he stated, his eyes calm. "And a very plain shirt. We do not want you to stand out any more than your hygiene and health will already cause you to do."

She didn't argue, returning to the closet and slipping on the jeans. They were a little tight but still comfortable. It made her feel strange to wear them after all these years, the curves of her legs and hips now framed instead of hidden. The button down sky-blue shirt also outlined her body in a way she'd never seen. Christine took a band and wrapped her hair into a ponytail before glancing at herself in the mirror. For the first time, she kind of looked like she was part of the World.

"Christine?" he asked impatiently. "I hope you are not dressing up for this occasion." She rushed out of the room, feeling a little strange to be clothed like this in front of someone, especially a man. But Erik only glanced at her. "As good as possible without pulling some of your teeth." Her stomach turned. *Where on earth were they going?*

They took the same underground walk that they had when meeting the car. This time, though, there was a smaller car waiting, an ugly brown one that wasn't nearly as luxurious. The leather seats were somewhat worn, and the driver was unfamiliar, younger with short, unkempt hair. When they were seated inside, Erik spoke to him in another language. The man glanced at her and then seemed a little upset, his eyes widening as he turned back to Erik and said several frantic sentences. Erik spoke again, though, and the driver calmed. Christine looked between them, sensing that they knew each other from a world that had little to do with Cameron.

"What happened?" she dared to ask.

Erik glanced at her. "Ah? He was confused. That is all."

"Tell me. Please."

"You want to know?" His tone was harsh. "I told him where to take us. He thought I might be abandoning you there and offered to take you off my hands because you are so obviously not from our destination. I explained that it was only a brief visit, that you are my permanent companion."

"Why would he take me in?" she whispered.

"There is very little that can be bought at a high price these days. But there are exceptions."

It took her a second, but then she shivered.

"I wanted to spare you that conversation. But you are right; it is time you understand why things are as they are." Her head drooped, and he must have taken pity. "Still, you are safe with me. Do not doubt that."

When the car stopped, Christine immediately sensed an utter wrongness to their surroundings. There were no streetlights, just the occasional dim porch light or glow from a window. The air smelled like a mixture of garbage and sewer, and even a touch of death made its way through the vents. "Come, Christine." Erik opened his door.

She hesitated.

"Come," he repeated. "You want to understand? Now you will."

Taking a deep breath of awful air, she opened the door. The sounds of crunching and scraping and banging assaulted her ears. The air was too warm, and perspiration gathered on her forehead. "Walk close to me," said Erik. She did as he said without question. "There was quite the riot here yesterday," he continued. Broken glass and metal crunched beneath their feet.

"Over what?"

"Lack of work. Lack of food and security."

"Why don't these people have those things?" she whispered.

"They cease to exist."

"I know, but Cameron says it's because of sin. And Phillip, Raoul's brother, said no one knows why. But what do you—" A moan interrupted her, and Christine glanced toward the other side of the street. A girl in her mid-twenties was lying on the edge of the sidewalk. Her skin was sallow and thinly stretched over her cheekbones, and her teeth were half-rotted. It sounded like she was muttering obscenities. "What happened to her?" Christine asked, walking even closer to Erik.

"She is obviously malnourished. But the people in these areas have also turned to a very cheap methamphetamine market to make the world disappear."

Christine watched in horror as the girl raised her head, her matted blonde hair falling into her vacant eyes. The girl stared right at her, and Christine turned away, a chill running down her spine. "Should we help her?" It seemed like such a natural thing to do. When Christine was a little girl, her mother always nursed her when she was sick. Under Cameron, people brought food over and helped with childcare when someone was ill.

"There are millions like her," Erik replied, continuing to walk without a glance at the girl. "Your father joined the sect because he was depressed. People join now to survive. To avoid turning into that." He looked to the side and gestured with his hand. "Or *that*." Two men with eyes and teeth like the girl were sitting in a cardboard box, a small fire burning in front of them.

No. Not just two. If she squinted in the dim lighting, Christine could see dozens of people throughout the streets and alleyways. Hundreds, maybe. It looked like all the people had attempted to cram into the crumbling apartments and then spilled out onto the steps and sidewalks. A baby cried. Two little boys were huddled beneath a torn quilt, watching her as she walked by, their mother lying next to them with a dirty shirt but no pants. Radios played from here and there, a medley of music that she had learned of over the past weeks. Every so often, someone yelled or a door slammed. Twice, she heard gunshots and screams in the far off distance. Erik never flinched.

"Why won't someone help them?" she shakily whispered. "I don't understand."

"As I have said, there are diminished resources."

"But how about another country? Couldn't they help?"

He chuckled and glanced at her. "You think a foreign invasion to be the solution?"

"Not an invasion. Just help."

"It would turn into an invasion," he replied. "It always does."

Before she could reply with some other solution, Christine heard a soft cry near her feet. She jumped back and looked down, focusing on a black object scuttling around near a cardboard box. A short-haired black kitten with green eyes was staring up at her and pawing at the leg of her pants. After checking to make sure the mother and any siblings were nowhere in sight, she picked the creature up and held it against her chest. It swiped at her several times with a little claw and then settled down in her arms.

Erik glanced at them. "Put that down. It is likely diseased."

"No, it's not," she desperately replied. "Please, Erik. I have to help somehow. We *have* to help!" She spun in a frantic circle, kitten still in her arms. "It doesn't have to be like this. How about Raoul? He doesn't live like this."

"Chandler is a member of the high upper class. And they are fleeing in droves before they are slaughtered for their opulence." She cringed at the thought of Raoul being hurt. "Many sections of the cities are like this now. And it will only become worse in the next year." The kitten mewed as though protesting Erik's words. "Now put that down, and we will return soon. I believe you have nearly seen enough."

"I want to take it home." Christine checked the gender. "I want to take her home." She had to save something—anything.

"I do not think—" Erik suddenly paused as though considering the situation. "You want to take it to *our* home?"

"Yes," she replied before noticing that he'd placed emphasis on a certain word. Still, she bit her lip and held firm.

"Fine. But if it shows any sign of sickness, the creature is gone."

Christine clutched the kitten against her shirt. As she walked forward past an alley, her right foot caught on something, and she tripped. The kitten squealed at the sudden movement and struggled to get away. The second her grip loosened, it clawed her hand and dove out of her arms, jumping onto the street and fleeing with a hiss. Christine glanced down and saw that she had tripped over a leg. With the light from a nearby window, she could also see the face of the leg's owner, and he was definitely not alive. And neither was the child lying next to him.

She started to scream. Erik's hand clamped over her mouth. "Do not draw attention to us," he whispered. "Do you understand?" She nodded, and he removed his hand. "You have seen enough. We will go now."

"But my cat…" Heart breaking, she searched for it, the scratch on her hand bleeding. The black kitten had blended into the night.

"We will find you a new animal companion someday."

"But…" There was nothing she could do. She followed Erik, eyes fixed on the concrete so she couldn't see anything else. Christine climbed into the car as soon as it arrived and didn't say a word throughout the journey. Thoughts of escape vanished. Erik's home was heaven compared to this. Maybe a fast death would have even been better than this slow misery that devoured everyone alive.

"I'm very tired," she explained once they had returned, nearly running toward her bedroom.

She desperately wanted to be alone, and Erik allowed her to go with only, "Wash your hands."

She pressed the thoughts of what she'd witnessed out of her mind. They remained on the outside of her consciousness throughout the night, threatening to overtake her troubled dreams.

The next morning, she grabbed several history books from the closet and flipped through to the end, hoping to find some type of answer. Like all the others, they finished too soon to tell her anything. She searched through magazines and newspapers from years ago, but they gave her no information either. Christine threw everything aside and placed her forehead in her hands.

"Good morning," Erik greeted.

"Morning," she softly replied.

"Do you want breakfast?" He sounded the same as he always did, calm and amiable.

"Not right now."

"Very well. Let me know when you are hungry. We will begin your voice lesson in an hour."

"Okay."

He stared at her. "Unless you are too tired?"

"No," she whispered. "I'm okay."

But she wasn't okay. Christine could barely sing that afternoon, her voice a shaky mess, and Erik noticed immediately. He pounded the piano during warm-ups and looked at her. "This is wretched."

"I'm trying."

"No, you are not. What is wrong with you?" She slowly sunk to her knees and stared down at the spotless carpet. "What is wrong with you?"

he asked again, standing up. "Are you ill?"

"How can you ask me what's wrong?" she replied. "After what you showed me yesterday."

"Ah." His voice softened. "So you understand now."

"It's such a sad mess out there. And the only options are Cameron or *that*? I don't know what to do."

"You will stay right here with me." He crouched beside her. "It will all be fine, my beauty. You will see. This time is the darkest."

"But all those people with Cameron are so empty. I hated it there."

"It is preferable to starve to death in the middle of the street?"

"No," she whispered. "That's the thing. It's not. But isn't there a middle? There has to be a better way than making them believe you're like some sort of God. Can't you and Cameron help them without doing that?"

He shrugged. "Eventually that component will no longer be necessary. I am wary of the role. For now, these people require a supernatural sort of entity."

"But why can't things be like they were before? When I was little?" she asked, looking up at him. "Everything was so wonderful then."

"Yes. So *wonderful*." There was a touch of sarcasm in his voice, and she was confused. Hadn't things been good before? "Those times are gone now, Christine. They will not return, and it is best that you forget them. But there is a better future prepared for you than you can imagine."

"But just for me?"

"The rest will receive what they deserve," he replied. He quickly added, "There will be a middle ground, to some extent. Cameron's zealotry will only take him so far before more practical measures are necessary. And I am very practical, my Christine."

She swallowed and asked the question that was supposed to make everything okay. "So Erik, you're really trying to-to help everyone then?"

"Of course. Why ever else would I be involved in this affair?" He paused. "And you will help everyone, too, won't you?" She nodded, her hair falling into her face.

She didn't know if she believed him. But the last few days had taught her that she couldn't save anyone. She couldn't even save a measly kitten.

Christine still missed that kitten.

If she did ever want to escape, it was going to take weeks or months to gain Erik's trust enough to do so. And so she would be compliant. The path was laid out before her. And there was almost relief in the fact that the answer was wrapped up with a bright red bow and handed to her like a gift.

Late that afternoon, as she curled up with a book, Erik sat in a chair near her scribbling something onto paper with a red pen. "Yes," he murmured to himself. "This piece will be perfect with the necessary adjustments. Cameron will accept it; it is much better than that banal material he requests you to sing."

She hesitated before asking, "Does Cameron know that I tried to reveal you?"

"No. But I will not protect you from his rules if you betray me again."

She fully believed his dark words. Christine gazed down at her book again. Several minutes later, Erik stood over her, and she glanced back up. "A walk to the theater?"

She stood to put on shoes. "Yes, I'd like that."

But, when they were upstairs, instead of allowing her to explore, Erik said, "Follow me."

"Where are we going?" she asked. He pulled back a tattered red curtain and gestured to a set of stairs. "Are they safe?"

"They are," he replied. "I have tested them on numerous occasions."

She followed behind him, watching her step as the old stairs creaked beneath her feet. He motioned for her to come forward, and she saw they were on one of the balconies, looking down over the stage and lower audience. The setting sun shone into the room, lighting it up through the windows like multiple spotlights. "Wow," she murmured, carefully leaning forward. "It would have been so beautiful to be up here back when there were still performances."

"One day, you will look down from a place much higher than this," he whispered beside her ear. She shuddered. "You will sing from high above, and the masses will look upon you with awe." He sang a Spanish aria that he had taught her in the beginning. So close to her ear, the tenor voice from heaven hypnotized her, the stage below blurring in front of her eyes. "Now you, Christine. Sing."

Entranced, she began the song at his order, and then Erik joined her. The duet was painfully beautiful, echoing through the room in all its perfection. And she could suddenly see the theater as it should have been— full plush red seats, a polished stage, a golden chandelier hanging from the ceiling with crystal adornments, women in long, elegant dress and men in black suits. When the song finished, she stood there breathing heavily, the dream fading away with the last note. A hand brushed against her waist and hip. A frenzied warmth in the center of her stomach radiated outward, vibrating through her veins. The sensation made her nervous, and she stepped to the side and away from him.

"Is something wrong?" he asked.

"No." She looked up and outward again, the room tilting. "But Erik. I just don't know about any of this. I *understand*. But I don't know."

"You do not have to know now." She turned to face him, never-ending questions on the tip of her tongue. His right gloved hand cautiously moved toward her face, and he placed his thumb and index finger around her chin, guiding her gaze upwards so that she stared into his eyes. "Just look at you," he whispered. "You were meant to be a queen."

She turned her head away and stepped back. "Erik, I think we should go back down now."

To her relief, he agreed.

Chapter 17

2007

Evelyn Hartman had been the principal of Franklin Middle School for twenty-three years. Her wrinkled face was drawn, and her blonde hair had long ago turned grey.

She had been through all of it—from notifying protective services when kids showed up with bruises that clearly didn't come from falling off the slide to parents who insisted that their precious angel would never ever bring a cigarette to school. She'd broken up more playground fights than she could count. And she was also well aware that the school had developed a bullying problem within the last five years. The trouble had trickled down from the high schools. It was the type of district where parents held their boys back for one or two years so that they would have a larger build when they played on the champion football team.

That was why she held firm as she stared at the very tall, handsome, dark-haired man across from her desk while he furiously asked, "What do you mean I can't put my son in your school? I pay taxes, damn it!"

Her light green eyes betrayed little emotion. It wasn't that she didn't feel anymore. She hadn't numbed herself to the woes of these kids who were living through things that children their age shouldn't experience. But she had to be very careful or these parents would walk all over her.

"Don't scream at me, Sir. I'm only being honest with you. And I didn't say you can't put him in here. You're right. It is *your* district. What

I said was that I don't know if it's safe given all the psychological trauma he's obviously suffered."

"He's fine. I took him to counseling. The kid is quiet, but he's fine."

"We also have a problem with kids picking on each other here."

"And that's your problem to fix. Not mine. Why don't you discipline these kids anymore?"

"I am trying to fix it," she replied, keeping her voice steady and calm. "If you're sure it's that easy, maybe you'd enjoy attending a school board meeting."

"Look, Ms. Hartman." He clenched his jaw. "My wife homeschooled him, but she's deceased—"

"And I'm very sorry for—"

"No. I don't need you to be sorry. I need you to listen. I work over fifty hours a week; I sure as hell can't teach him. The private schools clearly don't want a kid that looks like that in their precious halls. So I'm here because this is the end of the line. If you don't admit my kid, I will sue you people." He pointed his index finger directly at her.

"What about a tutor?"

"I don't have time to deal with that. Now are you going to admit him, or do I have to call my lawyer? And he is a damned good lawyer." He stared down his nose at her with an air of superiority.

Evelyn removed her glasses and rubbed her temples. "You realize that neither I nor anyone else can keep an eye on him every second of the day."

"Yes."

"Does he wear a mask all the time?"

"Right now, yes." For the first time, the man seemed uncomfortable, his shoulders drooping. "I'm looking into various prosthetic options. The last surgery was very damaging, and it's taken time for the flesh to heal. But I can promise you that the kids will take to the mask better than what's underneath. So will you. So do I."

Evelyn felt a tug at her heart. The boy had already been through so much. "You realize the other children will at least ask questions? I mean, that's what kids do."

"Don't you people teach tolerance? Isn't that the American way now?"

"It's supposed to be," she replied. Evelyn sighed and stood. "I guess we'll see Erik in one week, won't we?"

He also rose to his feet, standing over a foot above her. She could see the creases of exhaustion around his eyes. "Yes, you will. Thank you for resolving this quickly. I didn't want it to become complicated. God knows, my life has been complicated enough lately."

She imagined that he was the sort of man who had expected everything to come easy.

The boy was one of the brightest she'd ever encountered throughout all her years in education. They administered an exam to test his aptitude, and he nearly had a perfect score. In fact, it only wasn't perfect because the grader said the written portion was incomplete. Either his dead mother had been a brilliant teacher or the boy was practically a genius. Evelyn somehow suspected the latter. Despite her conversation with his father, she attempted to keep a steady eye on him throughout the first days, noticing as the other boys side-glanced him in the halls while the little girls only looked on with wary curiosity. He kept to himself, sitting alone at lunch or quietly at the back of the classroom. When teachers asked him questions, his answers were barely audible but always correct.

No, this wasn't going to go well.

Evelyn considered trying to move him up several grades but knew that could worsen the situation; high school could be especially harsh as kids tried to figure out their identities. She researched gifted programs and online education institutions that his father had been too busy to consider. It became a sort of private project of hers, and she told no one else. After all, no educator was supposed to ever become too involved with these children, right? Unfortunately, the flu hit her hard several days later, and she was confined to her house for two long weeks. With her laptop on her stomach and a white cat on her legs, Evelyn reclined on the couch and continued to click through various possibilities.

The children must have pounced during her absence.

It was around lunchtime of her first day back. She'd spent the morning playing catch up on various administrative issues, a dull throb still in the front of her head. Two seventh graders had been caught with marijuana outside the building, and she'd already received three phone messages from parents wanting to know if the school had a drug problem. Needing to escape the office, she stepped out to do one of her walks around the school, just a general checkup to make sure everything was functional. As she strolled past the cafeteria, a girl with straight black hair and dimples came running up to her. Sally Jane, probably the smartest girl in the sixth grade. "Ms. Hartman! Ms. Hartman! Ms. Hartman!"

"What? What? What?" she asked, momentarily amused until she saw the concern on the child's face.

"Thomas is going to *die*!"

"Thomas is going to *what*?" She knew better than to ask more questions. Time could be everything in these situations. "Sally, show me what's going on now."

Evelyn's heart nearly stopped as she turned a corner of the hall and looked down. Erik was sitting on the stomach of the brunet boy, leaning forward and holding two ends of a shoelace across each other and tightly around Thomas's neck. Thomas's face was turning blue as he sputtered and choked. "Oh my God!" She bent down and grabbed Erik's cold hands, trying to release his grip from the string, but he held tight. "Erik, let go!" she screamed once she found her voice. "Let him go!"

Her voice seemed to shock him out of it. Dropping the string, he turned to stare up at her with those haunting yellow eyes, and Evelyn nearly felt hypnotized. His flesh-colored mask was askew, and she could see a small glimpse of the tragedy beneath it. "Erik, go to the office right now. Right now!"

He stood and backed up, watching her with his head slightly tilted to the side. "You're going to get rid of me now, aren't you?" he whispered. Then he turned and ran.

Evelyn would have been lying if she said she wasn't slightly afraid of that boy in those seconds. The intelligence and pain and *anger* in those strange eyes was gripping, and he clearly had physical strength to match. If he ever reached the height of his father… She swallowed and looked back down at the other boy. "Thomas, are you hurt?" He rubbed the red markings on his neck, tears forming in his eyes. His breathing was normalizing, though, and there was no blood. She took his hand and helped him off the ground. He coughed several times. "I want you to go to the nurse's office and stay there until I come, understand?" He sniffled. She watched to make sure he obeyed her.

Sally Jane was still standing there and also watching, her face a little pale. All the other children scattered, afraid of being associated with the scuffle.

"Sally? Can you tell me what happened?"

"I think Thomas and his friends were going to put his head in the toilet again. They saw his face one day and said it was so ugly that it belonged in the toilet. And then…then today he didn't let them…"

"How long has this been going on?"

"I dunno. Maybe a week? I told my math teacher, but she said that sixth grade was too old to be a tattletale."

"Thank you, Sally. You're not a tattletale. You can go to lunch now. I'll call you out of class if I need you again." She hoped that little girl was successful in life. A doctor or president or something.

Thomas was the youngest son of the coach of a high school basketball team, and she'd already had meetings with his father regarding discipline problems concerning his two older children. It was a useless battle. *Boys would be boys.* She wrote up the incident as a silly fight and not what it appeared to be. Evelyn told Thomas's father that both children were responsible, and wasn't it so funny how boys already needed to be macho and prove themselves at this young age? He'd finally laughed heartily and agreed. *Boys will be boys!* Probably not wanting to look like a weakling in front of his dad, Thomas kept quiet. That whole situation was a mess in itself. Still, at least she could keep Erik out of a juvenile detention center. But she couldn't keep him in that school.

"What the hell am I supposed to do?" Erik's father asked.

"I don't know." She looked down. "He's smart enough to be in an older grade, but I could never recommend you putting him in the high school. Like I said, why don't you hire a tutor? That combined with online courses would be a good bet."

"You wouldn't spew that at me if you didn't know my income."

"Well, I don't know your income. But, yes, I know you're a man of means and…well…What do you want me to say?" Evelyn stood to shut her door and lowered her voice. "I don't want to be the one to teach him that he can't defend himself. But I can't allow what almost happened yesterday to happen again. Either he's going to be hurt, or he's going to badly injure someone else." She looked down at her wrinkled hands. "If you want to take legal actions, I will be prepared to claim that Erik is a threat to the other children. Do you really want that on his record?"

"Why don't you kick that Thomas kid out? He's the threat!"

"Because Thomas is typical and someone else would just take his place. Erik is different. He's a walking target. And you know that."

"You're completely powerless!" he spat at her. "You're pathetic!"

"You're right," she replied. "I can't fix the system. Please. Get your son a tutor. For his sake. Give him a chance."

With a final glare and an obscenity, he left and took Erik with him. She never saw them again.

Later that week, Evelyn checked the files and pulled out the aptitude test, flipping through to the writing section. The prompt was: *"Describe a time when you and your friends worked together as a team. What was your part in the project? Did you and your friends succeed? What did you learn about teamwork?"*

Erik's response was one sentence.

"I have no friends."

The next day, Evelyn Hartman notified her superiors that she would be retiring.

***

2034

"Erik, do you have any yarn?"

After everything, it almost seemed like a silly question. Christine missed some of her handcrafts. The motions of knitting or crocheting always helped her relax when she was tense. And she had good reason to be on edge these days.

He glanced at her as he passed. "I can certainly obtain some for you."

"Thank you. And some knitting needles and crochet hooks, too, please." She glanced back at the television where a movie was playing. It had been made in the 1990's but kept having flashbacks to the 1960's and 70's, so she found it somewhat helpful in figuring out parts of the past.

"We can get some tonight. I am going out this evening on simple business, to an area that is not too terrible. Middle class, you might say. You may accompany me."

"Yes, I'd like that." She often wanted to go outside but didn't know what the destination should be outside of the theater. She felt no sense of belonging now, except in Erik's home. That made her sad.

As they journeyed to the surface and toward the simple brown car, she asked, "Do you drive?"

"Of course." He sounded amused. "But it is wiser to focus my attention on my surroundings and allow someone else to steer."

"I've never driven." She frowned at her inadequacy. "But I guess a lot of people don't have cars now."

"When they did, it was wretched. Lines and lines of idiots every morning and afternoon, chomping on fast food and honking their horns as they waited to go home to their insignificant lives."

"At least they had jobs."

"I suppose. If you could call them that. Paper pushers."

Bright lights soon distracted her, and she remembered driving through this section on her way to the police station. A small smile formed on her lips as she glanced around, no longer as naïve as she had been the first time. At least this placed showed some life and semblance of the past. They drove past that area and to a slightly more rundown section, stopping in a parking lot alongside some brick shops.

"I will return in ten minutes," said Erik.

Her face fell. "Can't I get out?"

"It is still not entirely safe here. I would prefer you remain in the car."

"Please, Erik. Can't I at least open my window? I swear I won't run."

He waved his hand to the side. "Fine. Open the window, if you must."

She eagerly let the warm breeze wash over her and clear her head. The noises were refreshing, people talking as they passed, some with children and others with dogs on leashes. There was life here. What was left of it anyway.

Something moved in the corner of her vision, and Christine glanced toward it. Leaning out the window, she could see that it was a woman in her fifties or sixties, her tattered grey coat and matted grey hair making it obvious that she was homeless. The woman didn't appear as sick as the people in the other place, but she was heading in that direction. A white plastic spoon was clasped in her right hand as she devoured brown beans from a dented tin can. The woman grunted when they were gone, tossing the can aside with a dismayed expression and a soft, *"Dammit."* She slumped against a broken streetlamp, licking her lips.

Head half out the window, Christine watched her with growing discomfort. The woman glanced at her. "What are you staring at?" Her voice was hoarse. "What do you want? I can be here. This ain't anyone's property."

"No. I know. I wasn't staring. You're fine," Christine replied, feeling her face warm. "I-I know where you could find shelter."

The woman laughed crudely. "Where the hell are you from? Mars? Shelters are overflowing into the streets."

Christine wasn't used to this sort of verbal abuse. Still, she tried again. "You could go with Cameron Lourdes. They give *everyone* food and shelter."

The woman stared at her and then laughed loudly, her body shaking with the sound. "Thanks, kid," she said between snorts. "I needed a good laugh tonight."

"Why is it funny?" she asked. "It's the truth, and—"

"Christine!?"

Startled, she turned toward the familiar voice. Her eyes widened. Raoul Chandler was standing there, very out of place in a pressed pair of brown slacks and white dress shirt.

The driver glanced up suspiciously. "I think you'd better close the window."

"Please give me a moment," she frantically replied, turning back to her old friend.

"I didn't think I'd see you again!" he exclaimed, bending down to her level. "What are you doing out here? Are you okay?"

"I'm fine. I'm…" She searched for an explanation. "Helping."

"I didn't think they let anyone out." He glanced to both sides as though checking to see if she was alone. "I didn't know what had happened to you that night. I was really worried!"

"It's been a strange couple of weeks," she murmured, tucking her hair behind her ear. "But I'm okay."

"She wants us all to join Cameron," said the woman, staring at them with amusement. "Won't that be a barrel of giggles?"

Christine glared. "I was just telling her where she could find food and shelter. That's all."

Raoul discreetly pulled a twenty dollar bill from his pocket and handed it to the woman. "Could you give us a moment?"

"I'll give you twenty moments," she replied with a smile, her teeth yellow. "Thanks kid." She looked at Christine. "And thank you for the laughs, Peaches." The woman sauntered off down the street.

"So you're recruiting now," muttered Raoul, turning back to her. "I mean, I knew you were singing."

A part of her wanted to tell him everything, to make him understand the truth, but she knew there wasn't time. Erik wasn't going to be happy about this as it was. "It's very complicated," was all she said. "But Cameron can help people."

He shook his head. "You are so brainwashed."

"I'm not! I don't have time to explain it, but—"

"Does the Spirit still talk to you? Or does he just do earthquakes now?"

"That all doesn't matter now. It's about helping people." A change in the air and a shift in the shadows made her sense Erik nearby; the driver had probably alerted him. "I have to go. Please be careful!"

"Christine, I wish…" Her window automatically rolled up before he could finish. Raoul gaped, probably thinking she was responsible. Then, after throwing up his hands in frustration, he stomped away.

With a soft moan, she faced forward, feeling more isolated than ever. Erik climbed in beside her within seconds. Christine quickly spoke. "I had no idea he'd be around."

"I am aware of that." He sounded only mildly annoyed. "Did you enjoy your little conversation?"

"He doesn't understand."

"Of course he does not. He does not know desperation. Not yet." Erik paused. "And as noble as it was, I would prefer you not speak to vagrants. Some of them are rather unstable."

"Well, she spoke to me first. And, Erik, I just feel so helpless. I sit in your home and read and listen to music, and then sometimes I get to sing. And it seems so silly when everyone is out here starving to death. I feel silly."

"You are not helpless nor silly. Do not be ridiculous. These people are privileged to have you working in their favor at all." She didn't reply. After they'd driven only a short ways, he ordered the driver to stop. Christine glanced up in surprise. "Here. Let us get out."

"Where are we going?" She looked out the window to make sure they weren't in another scary place.

"A surprise for you," he replied. With a swallow, she climbed out of the car and walked beside him in the shadows, glancing into the windows of the stores. He stopped beside a little shop and gestured with a hand. "Go in and pick out whatever you like for yourself. I attempted to create a preliminary wardrobe for you, but it is time for you to make your own decisions on the matter."

"Are you sure?" she asked. "I don't really need—"

"Go. I insist. I will pay for whatever you desire."

The store was smaller but had a beautiful selection. Christine chose three colorful dresses. She bought black slacks and several knee-length skirts, a matching necklace and bracelet with gold hearts, a few shiny barrettes and a silky green and black scarf to wear around her neck. "This will feed me for a week," the store owner said with a grin as Christine placed the items on the glass counter. "And don't worry, pretty lady. I've charged it to an account."

"Thank you, Erik," she said, stepping out with two brown bags.

"Did you enjoy yourself?" he asked as they climbed into the car.

"It was fun." She paused and thought back nostalgically. "My mom used to take me shopping when I was a little girl, and we'd always get milkshakes afterwards. She was always so happy and lighthearted. If she'd lived, I think she would be my best friend." Christine waited for him to take up the conversation, but Erik was silent. "What was your mom like?"

"She was to die for." He continued before she could ask more questions. "One day, we will dress you much more lavishly. For now, subtleness is better."

"I don't really need that much, Erik."

"You do not need much, but I will give you everything."

When they returned to his home, Erik played a soft song on the piano, and she listened to it, peacefully curled up on the couch with a cup of warm tea. It ended, and she rose to put her empty cup in the kitchen. As she returned and walked past him, he spoke to her. "Cameron will request that you sing again soon. He is fast realizing the benefits of advertising. I trust we will not see a repeat of the last performance?"

"No," she murmured. "I promise. I just want to help."

"Good." She started to go to her room. "Christine?" His voice was so soft that she barely heard him.

"Yes?" She turned.

His gaze was fixed on the floor. "I have a request of you. You may refuse; it will affect nothing. It is not a demand."

"What is it?"

"My skin is like ice," he began, nodding his head toward his bare hands on the piano keys. "I am not ill; it has always been that way. But you must be warned."

"I'm sorry," she replied, not understanding what this had to do with her. "Maybe a doctor could help?"

"Doctors can do *nothing*. They are the most useless creatures on the planet."

"Oh."

His voice shook. "I want nothing more than to touch your hand. But I do not want you to cry out—"

"*What?*"

He turned away. "Never mind. Forget this. I am tired, and my mind is not right. The air in this country cannot be good for one's head, can it?

No, it will drive us all mad. Completely mad, Christine. Never mind. Go to bed."

She stared at him. Hesitantly and keeping a distance, she held out her hand as though waiting for a handshake. Maybe she should have run, but he seemed so lost. Maybe they were both lost.

He stared at her offering for several seconds; she almost gave up and ran away from the strangeness of it. Finally, he lifted a long, bony hand from the piano. After another hesitation, he clasped her fingers with his own. His skin was freezing, and his warning made it only slightly less shocking. The chill seemed to travel up through her palm and into her wrist. Her heart jumped.

"You are so warm," he murmured. He closed his eyes. "Thank you, Christine."

He released her, and she stepped backward with only a nod, so confused that she thought her mind might explode. The world around them was in flames and all he wanted was to touch her hand?

As she went to bed, the coldness of his skin still burned her flesh.

Chapter 18

2007

The spotless house was so quiet that it made him a bit nervous, and Farrokh clenched and unclenched his hands several times. Where was the life that came with a child—the noise and mess and a healthy dose of spontaneity? A photograph of a beautiful couple on their wedding day hung upon the wall, along with a headshot of the woman in a shiny black frame. There were no pictures of a little boy, no signs of youth. *Please tell me that I haven't walked into some sort of serial killer's trap. It's not as though I found this job online.* The thought almost made him laugh out loud.

"Can I get you anything to drink?" asked his host and perhaps future employer.

He politely smiled. "No, I'm just fine."

"Please take a seat then," said the tall man, gesturing with a hand. He did so, and the large armchair was extremely soft and comfortable. "It's great to have you here, Dr. Nabavi."

"Please. Call me Farrokh."

"Farr-*okh*." His host gave a short laugh. "I hope I pronounce that right. I also hope you don't mind me asking why a man with your background is tutoring children now."

"Only highly gifted children. And, well, several reasons. I grew tired of university bureaucracy. And of being up past midnight writing grants and trying to get funding. And then when I did get funding, it was often from the Department of Defense. I wondered whether my research was being used for good or—Ah, don't get me wrong; that life was good to me. But it wasn't how I wanted to spend my last decades."

"I can understand. If I still have the same job when I'm sixty, I won't be happy."

"Hm. Well, I have to admit that I am very eager to meet Erik. From your e-mail correspondence, he sounds like a very bright child."

All traces of happiness disappeared from the man's face at the mention of his son. Farrokh had the feeling that his host would have preferred to talk about any other topic for the entire afternoon. "Erik is smart. The phrase 'too smart for his own good' would probably apply." Farrokh chuckled at this. "He is incredibly awkward, though. Quiet and not all that…err…polite when he does speak. I hope that isn't a problem for you."

"I don't believe so. Very intelligent children sometimes have a difficult time fitting in. Erik even more so, I'm sure. I'm no psychologist, but I do understand these challenges." He paused before cautiously adding, "Very sorry to hear about his mother."

"Yes." Erik's father glanced down and rubbed the bridge of his nose. "That certainly didn't help things. Don't get me wrong; my wife had good intentions but zero coping skills. It probably wasn't in either of their best interests for me to leave the boy alone with her day after day."

"I'm sure you did your best." They awkwardly sat in silence for several seconds before Farrokh said, "Well, I know we have a lot to talk about, but I think it would be best if I met him."

"Ready to jump in with the sharks?" he replied with a morose chuckle. "That's fine. Let me see if we can get that kid out of his room."

From the moment that Farrokh saw the boy, he knew that this wasn't going to be like any other mentorship he'd had in the past. And it wasn't just because of the hidden disfigurement or the obvious intelligence. There was something less definable; maybe it was the strange blend of curiosity and indifference in the boy's eyes. The simultaneous apathy and desire for something more.

He smiled, bent forward, and held out a hand. "Hello, Erik. I'm Farrokh."

Erik only stared. "Where are you from?"

After recovering from his surprise at the startling timbre of the child's voice, Farrokh replied, "I was born in Iran, but I left to go to school in the U.S. when I was about nineteen. I've lived in New England since then." He received no response. "Your father tells me you're very smart."

The boy shrugged. "I am."

He heard Erik's father sigh behind them. While Farrokh wasn't offended in the slightest by the boy's mannerisms, his dad was obviously annoyed.

"The great thing about learning at home is that we can go as quickly as you want," continued Farrokh. "You will never get bored."

"What are your qualifications?" Erik asked, looking him up and down like a scientific specimen.

Farrokh started and then chuckled. "Didn't you know? I stayed at a Holiday Inn Express last night." Erik's father guffawed at this, but the boy looked at him as though he were the lowliest creature on earth. Farrokh's smile disappeared, and he truthfully answered, "For starters, I was a tenured physics professor for twenty-five years."

"What was your focus?"

"Recently, laser technology and quantum optics. You're welcome to read the papers I published if you want to know more."

"I would like to read them." Erik glanced away and returned to his book.

"Wow," stated his father as the two men stepped back into the hall. He shut the door behind them.

"Didn't go so well?" asked Farrokh, smoothing out a pants leg. "I may need a little more time to—"

"Are you kidding? I can't believe how much he tolerated you. The last woman left in tears. If you want the job, you're hired. We can work out the details right now."

Call him crazy, but he wanted the job.

It took some time to set up the perfect curriculum, but Farrokh took great pleasure in the new project. He researched various books and online programs that he thought would suit a child of Erik's aptitude, even choosing several college texts. Per the arrangement, he was required to be at the house from morning to afternoon on the weekdays, but Erik was very adept at teaching himself. Farrokh would explain more complex concepts in science and math. To his surprise, he would also have to clarify human interaction in novels when Erik became agitated.

"Why does that girl always cry?" he once asked after reading a chapter from a book that Farrokh had believed would be good for literature studies.

"Well, she misses her lover and is worried he'll die in the war," Farrokh replied, thinking it was pretty obvious.

"Why doesn't she find someone else?"

The older man scratched the back of his head. "Because she loves *him*. It's not that easy to just find another lover." Erik's eyes were still filled with exasperation. Farrokh tossed the book aside. "Let's leave that for when you're a little older."

Their favorite shared times were the science experiments, usually completed in the kitchen or the spacious backyard. Farrokh would bring in all sorts of equipment and supplies that couldn't be found in any public school. Erik loved nothing better than to stare into the beakers of combined chemicals, waiting to see how they would react with each other. He would shift from foot to foot, bouncing up and down with excitement. It warmed Farrokh's heart to meet someone so young who loved science so much.

Their relationship remained professional throughout the first year. Erik was quiet and aloof but polite, although there were occasional days when he refused to leave his room and told Farrokh in no uncertain terms to "Go away."

"Erik, you will learn to show people some goddamned respect!" his father had shouted the first time this happened. "Now get out here, or you will be punished." Erik had opened the door and glared up at them both. "Tell Farrokh that you're sorry." Erik glowered. His father roughly grabbed him by the shoulder. "Tell him you're sorry!"

"I am sorry!" Erik spit out the words. He turned around and slammed the door.

"Maybe we'll have a day of rest," said Farrokh, somewhat disturbed. "He's worked hard and deserves one."

"Ugh," his father muttered as they walked down the hall. "Kid gets into these moods, and nothing can be done with him. All because I brought a woman over last night."

"A woman?"

Erik's father shrugged and glanced down. "Getting back in the game is hard with a kid like that. But, you know, I'm only forty-one years old. I've gotta live a little, right? Not going to roll over and die. Do you have someone?"

"Oh. No. My wife passed away three years ago of illness, and I haven't really felt the desire."

"Oh. Sorry to hear that." He gave Farrokh a friendly pat on the back. "Good luck with the kid today. I'll be home a little late but will of course increase your pay."

"That will be fine."

Erik was quiet for the rest of the week. As Farrokh had said on his first day, he was no psychologist, but he wondered if Erik was still suffering from the effects of some sort of attachment disorder. His father wasn't affectionate, and his mother obviously had had problems. Who knew what sort of trauma he had gone through as an infant or toddler? Still, Farrokh decided to keep his focus on academics and not be a busybody.

That is, until a day arrived when he was directly asked to do otherwise. It was nearly two years into their arrangement. As Farrokh walked into the entryway, he heard an argument upstairs and leaned in to eavesdrop. *So much for not being a busybody...*

"Why do you have to be so weird at these things?" his father harshly asked. "Just talk to people!"

"They stare at me," the boy replied in a softer voice. "They hate me. And I have nothing to say to them."

"They don't hate you! Make conversation. Don't stand in a corner with your arms crossed the whole time like some sort of freak. That sort of attitude is not going to make life easier for you! Grow the fuck up!" A door slammed, and the walls vibrated. His father stomped down the stairs, shaking his head and muttering beneath his breath. He started when he noticed that Farrokh was standing there. "Jesus Christ," he said as he headed toward the door. "If you can teach that kid some social skills, I will give you a million dollars."

"What happened?" asked Farrokh, now that he'd been invited into the fray.

"A shrink said he needed to get out more. So my colleague had a birthday party for his kid, and I figured I might as well take Erik. All that boy did was linger in the corner like some sort of ghost. If he acts like that his whole life, of course people are going to be afraid of him. Of course no one will like him. Ugh!" He rubbed both his large hands over his face. "I'm at a loss. I've never understood that boy. I doubt I ever will."

Farrokh shrugged. "Well, he hasn't been out much. It must be hard for him. But I'll see what I can do."

Several days later, when they were finished with a smoke producing experiment involving household chemicals that put Erik in a relatively good mood, Farrokh brought him into the living room. Once they were comfortably seated on the couch, he asked, "Erik, do you know how to talk to people?"

The boy tilted his head. "That is a stupid question. I'm talking to you right now."

"All right, sure. We talk about your schoolwork. But sometimes you have to make friendly chitchat with people."

"Why?"

"Well, for example, when you're looking for a job. You need to learn how to make connections. You have a meal and talk about silly things like sports or the weather…anything. Or, you know, making friends is important. When you go to college in several years, one of your peers might say, 'Hey, Erik. How about we go out for a drink after class?' Or—" Farrokh grinned. "Girls, Erik."

The boy sharply looked down at the ground. "I don't understand *them* at all. They scare easily and whine and cry over the stupidest things."

Farrokh laughed and lightly touched him on the shoulder. "No one really does. But you need to have the right lines. 'Hi. How are you? You look nice. Of course I'll help you clean the house.'"

"I sincerely doubt they will ever want anything to do with me."

"As you get older, people will understand your…" Farrokh gestured to his own face. "You'll always be smarter than most people. And that can be isolating at times. But, well, let's give it a quick try." Farrokh cleared his throat. "Hello, Erik. How are you today?"

"Fine."

Farrokh waited and then smiled. "So now it's your turn to ask me how *I* am."

"How are you?" he stiffly asked.

"I'm doing great, thank you. So, Erik, have you seen any good movies lately?"

"No. They've all been terrible." Farrokh chuckled, and Erik glared and asked, "Why is that so amusing to you?"

"It's not. It's a perfectly valid response. How about music? What are your favorite genres?"

"Classical or modern instrumentals. I prefer no voices."

"You don't like songs where people sing?"

Erik hesitated and seemed to think deeply about this. "I have never heard a voice that I truly enjoy. They are all off. I can't explain it exactly."

Farrokh nodded "That's fair. To be honest, I can't stand most music these days. But then I'm an old, grouchy man."

They sat in silence for several minutes. Erik glanced at him and seemed to be judging whether to trust him. He then said in a soft voice, "People hate me because I'm ugly. But I am smarter than all of them. I'm better than all of them at nearly *everything*. So why should I care if they hate me?"

"Well. Because life can get very, very lonely without people. No matter how smart you are, what you've accomplished, there's something…something very wonderful about coming home to a warm pair of arms."

Erik stared at him. And then, for the first time since he had known the boy, Erik genuinely laughed. It was really a beautiful sound. "You are a strange, sentimental sap, Farrokh. Still, you are more intelligent than most people in this stupid country. So I guess I'll overlook it."

Farrokh smiled sadly as Erik soon returned to one of his beloved science books.

***

2034

They asked her to sing at a smaller event that celebrated the opening of a new shopping district under Cameron's control. Millions of dollars had gone into the project, as the number of his followers had continued to grow.

This time, when Christine finished her song, she only smiled. Maybe it wasn't a completely genuine smile. Maybe she had the lingering feeling that something was wrong. But she still beamed down at the audience. She could feel Erik watching her from somewhere unseen. To her relief, there were no magic tricks at this event. When she left the stage, Cameron stepped back up to take her place.

She half listened to what their leader was saying. Her mind was in other places, but then Christine became aware of a conversation behind her.

"But I want to play tag!" cried a little girl. "I want to play tag with the boys!"

"Little girls do not play tag," replied the stern voice of her father. "You will stand here and listen to our savior and be right with the Lord."

"But I wanna play!"

"If you do not behave, you will be placed into the closet for the rest of the day to think about your sin. Is that what you want?"

"No," she replied. "Please don't put me in there. It's so scary in there."

"Ask for forgiveness."

She sniffled. "Please forgive me for disobeying my parents."

"Again."

"Please forgive me for disobeying my parents."

Christine inwardly shuddered as memories of her own childhood return to her. Yet wouldn't it have been worse for the girl to starve in an alleyway? Christine remembered the dead little boy and shivered again. Yes, this suffocating lifestyle was better.

"Now there is a godly woman," said the father, nodding at Christine as she walked past them to find Erik. "I bet she does not want to run around with the boys."

"Never," Christine murmured. With a hidden smile, she recalled chasing Raoul around the backyard, in her swimming suit no less, after he'd dabbed pink cake icing on her nose.

Erik met her within the shadows of the stage. Although she couldn't see his mouth, his eyes seemed to smile at her. "You did beautifully," he stated.

"Thank you. Everyone seemed to enjoy it." During the drive home, she recalled the little girl and asked, "Erik? I still don't understand why the strictness is necessary? We could help these people without making them follow all these rules."

"We could not. The outside is chaotic, and these people require, no *crave*, order and discipline. And while I do not necessarily agree with the philosophy that is stressed, that is Cameron's matter. He operates under certain beliefs."

"Cameron is in charge," she said almost to herself. That fact still hadn't cemented itself in her mind. "I know you do all this because you want to help people. But why aren't you the one in charge? Then you could do things in a better way than Cameron, right? Why does he get to decide everything?"

Erik stared down at her, finger drumming on the seat. "Truthfully, I had not planned on remaining here so long. I meant to give temporary assistance to Cameron and then leave for other projects. Circumstances have changed within the last year, and so your question is valid." She smiled slightly at the acknowledgement. "For now, it is best to think of it as a partnership."

"A partnership?"

"Yes. You see, for the moment, Cameron Lourdes and I have a common goal. And we work toward that goal well together—establishing a better society for all these poor, poor people." Christine nodded in agreement. "Later, when Cameron has more power, we will focus on who is in charge of what. Does that make sense to you, my dear?"

It did make sense.

The next couple of weeks passed similarly. She had her academic lessons and her voice lessons, growing more proficient in both. Christine could be nothing but eternally grateful of the fact that Erik had allowed her such an education. His breadth of knowledge was amazing. Now that he trusted her, he would often take her to the surface in the evenings and allow her to explore the few remaining shopping centers and parks. One time, she asked for cheese pizza, and he laughed and immediately agreed to the excursion.

She became comfortable. Maybe *too* comfortable in this strange existence.

Yes, she became far too comfortable.

It was early June, and the air was warm and humid. Cicadas buzzed in the evening, and she occasionally swatted away a fly or mosquito. They were in the abandoned theater, and Erik had made her go to the balcony to work on projecting her voice. At the end of their lesson, he had sung again, and so Christine felt lightheaded and breathless as she stared over the edge.

Invigorated, she started to carefully make her way back down the stairs.

"Christine."

She turned. "Yes, Erik?"

She was startled to see that he had turned away from her, his gloved hands resting on the edge of the balcony. His shoulders rose and fell. "Cameron is willing to allow you to do more on his behalf, if you so wish. Beyond singing."

"I would like that, depending on what he wants. You know I want to help however I can."

"There is a condition." He still refused to look at her.

Several nervous butterflies found their way into her stomach. *Why was he acting so strangely?* "What is it?" He was silent for a very long time. "Erik, what is the condition?"

"I want a…a companion."

"We are kind of companions, though, aren't we?" She didn't know what else their strange relationship might be called.

"Yes. And there are things I will never ask of you. *Never.* I only ask that you remain at my side and in my company. So long as I live, you will never belong to another. That is all I will ask." His voice was soft and distant.

"What are you saying?" she whispered.

"Because, so long as you stay at my side, I will give you the world." He finally turned toward her in one fast motion, reaching out toward her with both hands. His eyes were so intense that she stepped backward. "Clothing, jewelry, books, anything. And perhaps someday I will take you to another country on vacation, and we will walk the streets of London or Paris at night. You would adore it, Christine. And I will ask so very little of you. Only that you are *mine.*"

"I still don't understand."

"If you want to take an active part, if you want more freedom, then Cameron Lourdes insists that we wed."

She couldn't stop the soft gasp that escaped her lips. "I d-don't…"

"And I want you, Christine. As my wife. There will never be another for me but you." He turned back around to stare over the balcony. "As I said, you will not be forced to do anything abhorrent. I swear that to you."

A cold sweat formed on her forehead as she stared at his back, and the room swayed back and forth. She grabbed the wall to keep from fainting, a billion thoughts swirling through her panicked mind.

For years, before the Spirit had spoken to her, she'd sickly anticipated an arranged marriage to someone she barely knew. This was true. Still, Erik was a thousand times more imposing and complex than any of the younger boys. *And she hadn't even seen this man's face!* In fact, all she'd viewed of him were his ice-cold hands. While he fascinated her, she still feared him, still would shiver when he walked too near. He confused her and seemed miles beyond her comprehension, still more Spirit than man in some ways.

On the other hand, at least she wasn't confined to a small home with some simple boy and expected to raise ten children. At least she could have an education and hold onto many pieces of the past, books and music and movies. She could go places and sing. Wasn't the life being handed to her much better than the one she had anticipated?

But some part of her mind still wanted to believe that marriage was about that vague concept of *love*. Not practical arrangements. Not bribes. Not desperation. She remembered how her mother and father had been—the way they'd looked at each other…the smiles and joyous laughter. Yes, *love*. Shouldn't marriage come from love?

Or were such thoughts naïve in this cold, hopeless world? Would marrying Erik be her best chance for survival?

Despite the heat, a chill traveled through her entire body. Christine did the only thing she knew to do—delayed the decision, delayed upsetting him for as long as possible. "I think that I need time," she choked out.

"How much time?" he hoarsely asked.

"I d-don't know. Until the end of the year?"

"You will marry me in December?" His voice shook as he turned to face her. That wasn't how she had wanted him to interpret her words. Christine had meant that she would decide by December. But Erik continued before she could protest. "Yes. Yes, a winter wedding for a white angel. December it is, my beauty. We will have everything. The world! It will be perfection." As she stood frozen against the wall, he rapidly approached her, holding something in his right hand. "You will wear this." He took her limp left hand and slid a gold band onto the ring finger; it fit tightly, strangling her. "Never remove it," he commanded, clasping her hand with his own. "It is a sign of your devotion."

She stared down at the simple piece of jewelry in shock, her stomach turning in fear. "Erik, I don't know if…" Her words were weak and garbled.

"No more words are necessary," he whispered, touching her hair. "You have made me gloriously happy, my beauty. You don't even know what you have done."

She didn't know. She knew nothing.

He took her back downstairs, a bounce in his smooth steps and his yellow eyes shining with joy. As soon as they returned, she told him that the excitement had made her very tired.

"Of course. Of course," he replied, ushering her toward her bedroom. "Sleep. We will speak more tomorrow."

As Christine lay in bed that night, she tried to stop herself from having a panic attack. *Okay, I still have a long time. Six or seven months.* That was plenty of time to think and decide…or escape.

To her dismay, that didn't turn out to be true. While her timeline had pleased Erik, it did not please Cameron Lourdes when they visited him the following day.

"December?" he asked when Erik told him the month. "No, no, no. That is over six months away. And there will be far too much happening at that time."

"But I have to plan my wedding," she whispered.

Cameron frowned. "There will hardly be any guests, silly girl. This will be a very private affair. People will only know that you are married to a favored member. Nothing more."

"A dress..."

"You do not need six months to find a dress. Vanity is not becoming or godly, young lady. You may have three months. That is more than enough time."

"But...I..." She could think of no excuse that would be good enough for Cameron. The pleased gleam in his eyes told her he would marry them that very second if Christine wasn't careful, if she gave him reason to believe she might try to get out of this. Her shoulders slouched in defeat. She hung her head and waited for Erik to speak in her interest. But he didn't. His eyes settled on her and stayed there throughout the meeting.

Cameron folded his hands together. "It is really excellent news. I'm absolutely ecstatic. You both don't know how much you have pleased me and the Lord."

She refused to look at Erik when they were driven home, angry that he hadn't fought for more time. And terrified at what all this would mean for her. Toward the end of the drive, he touched the top of her hand. Christine faced him.

"What does three months matter?" he softly asked. "If you wish for an elaborate wedding, I will still give it to you. There is plenty of time. Although there will be few guests, I will give you the wedding of a princess. You will practically be a princess, so why not?" He paused. "And Cameron is for once correct. After September, there may be chaos?"

"Chaos?" she asked.

"Yes. Things are getting worse out there. For the whole country. Many more people will join Cameron. They won't have a choice. You do not want to hear explosions on your wedding day, do you? Not unless they are glorious fireworks!"

"No." She glanced away.

That night, she did have a panic attack. In the darkness, she clutched the covers and sobbed and gasped, muffling the horrible noise with her pillow. If she didn't stop this now, she would suffocate under the weight of it. Christine knew she couldn't face this, not in a mere three months. If she had to, she would fall to her knees and beg for more time. Throwing the covers off of her, she jumped out of bed and went to the door, not having any idea as to what time it might be. She prepared herself for a horrible confrontation.

As soon as Christine opened the door, she heard the rush of water running. The kitchen faucet. To her relief, the sound covered her footsteps. Heart pounding, she tiptoed to the kitchen and glanced inside.

Erik's narrow back was turned toward her. His black jacket was gone, and he was only wearing a white shirt and black pants. Both hung loosely from his body, nearly engulfing his thin frame. He wore no gloves and no hat, revealing a pale head covered with sparse dark hair. Water was running. And his face had to be bare—because the black mask was resting face up on the counter beside him.

Perhaps in his joy he had been careless, figuring she would sleep through the entire night.

She didn't know.

At that moment, she didn't care. She only wanted to finally *see*.

Before he could turn off the water, she strode into the kitchen and grabbed his left shoulder with her right hand, turning him around and forcing him to look directly at her.

And then, of course, there was no turning back from her fate.

"Nothing changes, my beauty. My fiancée. My darling. Except now you will unfortunately know the face of your husband. But that is your loss. Not mine. I will finally have what is mine!"

Chapter 19

2009 - 2014

Farrokh put several weeks' worth of effort into developing Erik's social skills, but the boy never quite caught on. Finally, Erik said, "I am done with these little chats. If you want to have fake dialogs, let's at least rehearse Shakespeare. I think *Richard the III* would be ideal."

While always helpful when people needed him, Farrokh had never been a social butterfly, usually immersed in his books and research. Maybe he just wasn't the one for this job. He suggested to Erik's father that they find a therapist who excelled at helping children communicate. Farrokh never knew if the man did so, but he returned his focus back to academics during the following years. Amidst science experiments and lessons, as Erik began to completely teach himself, Farrokh ignored the darkening clouds on the horizon until a day came when they could no longer be overlooked.

The air was particularly icy that day, and Farrokh could feel the chill seep through his leather coat and gloves. Sometimes he wondered if he should take his twenty-five-year-old daughter up on her offer to move him out to California. No, he needed to see this project out to its end. He'd already invested so much time into Erik, and he would not feel satisfied until the boy was on his way to college, free from the irritated gaze of his father and from the house that held little warmth.

The home was quiet as Farrokh walked inside that afternoon. He'd been asked to come later in the day and didn't question the reason. Erik's father was sitting at the kitchen table, leaning forward with his right hand over his mouth. A green wine bottle and a clear glass sat beside him. "I probably should have let you have the entire day off," he murmured, briefly glancing up and lowering his hand. He didn't look drunk, but there was a troubled glint in his eyes.

"Is everything okay?" Farrokh asked, removing his coat and sitting in the chair beside him.

"Eh." Erik's father turned to face him. "I took him to an appointment. Well, a consultation. To assess surgical possibilities."

"Any good news?"

"Not especially. Erik's immune system is highly sensitive. They think a transplant wouldn't be in his best interests, at least not any time soon. The drugs he'd have to take for the rest of his life, assuming they even worked, would destroy his health within ten years. And I'm sure they're terrified of more lawsuits after..." He shook his head. "Laura made this more of a mess than it ever needed to be."

"What a shame," Farrokh murmured.

"It seems like we keep making it worse." He took a drink of wine. "They want to wait until he's at least twenty-one. Even then, there aren't any guarantees."

"Well, you know," Farrokh began. "It's a modern world. People are more tolerant."

He grunted. "Maybe I can at least get him a false nose. It's amazing, some of the things they have these days. You can get a fake face made that attaches to the bone with magnets, you know that?"

"You mean he doesn't have a nose?" Farrokh reflexively scratched his own.

"That's right. You've never even seen his face. If he lets you, take a look. When he was a baby, people went into hysterics when they saw him. One lady even called 9-11 and reported that Laura was pushing around a corpse in a stroller. No wonder she went insane."

"I am so sorry," said Farrokh, having no other words. They sat in silence for a couple more moments before he excused himself and went upstairs. Of course, the door to Erik's room was closed. He knocked. "It's Farrokh."

"I don't want to see you."

At least that was better than: *Go away.*

"I just thought we could have a chat." He thought fast. "I have an interesting scientific article to show you."

After several seconds, the door opened. Farrokh walked inside, noting how tall Erik was—and still growing. The boy stared him directly in the eye. "Well?"

Farrokh pulled out a magazine from his briefcase. "Look at this. The government has been designing miniature robots that look like insects for weapons and spy devices. They're deadly and undetectable."

"That is what you want to show me? That's old news." Still, he took the magazine, sat on his bed, and quickly read through the article. "They have made more advances. Except…"

"Except what?"

"They still use very ugly insects. Like mosquitoes. People will want them to go away. If they were beautiful, like butterflies, people would want them to stay, right? They would be more effective spying devices."

"Well, maybe. But, if they were more colorful, people would notice them. Mosquitoes blend in. But people might look more closely at a butterfly and see that it's not real."

"That is why you have to make them perfect. So that they appear to be real butterflies even if they are inches away from your face."

Farrokh scratched the back of his head and chuckled. "Perfection is hard to obtain."

"But not impossible, Farrokh."

"I guess not." He hesitated and then placed a cautious hand on the boy's narrow shoulder. "Erik, I'm very sorry about what you learned today. Don't give up hope, though."

Erik flinched away from Farrokh's touch. "Hope? It's a ridiculous concept. There is action, and there is no action. Any idiot who sits around *hoping* for something is wasting his miserable life."

Farrokh winced. The resentment in Erik was building with each passing year. "Sometimes hope is all one has."

"Then they have nothing."

It was worth a try. "Erik, would you mind letting me see your face? I'm not a doctor, well not a medical doctor, but maybe I could help find a solution. There are hospitals all over the world, each with their own specialties. I could research it for you, once I know what we're dealing with."

Erik glared, quickly jumping to his feet and backing up into the wall like a cornered animal. "I don't need you vomiting on my carpet. The stench would never come out."

"I have seen many, many things in my lifetime. Wounds from war even. While I know your face hasn't made life easy for you, I'm sure that I can look. I only want to help."

"Yes, Farrokh always wants to help, doesn't he? But I know you're curious. Everyone always is. Still, I don't expect you to scream or faint like a woman. No. What *will* you do?" The yellow eyes challenged him.

Farrokh held firm. "I only want to help you."

"Of course you do." Slowly, Erik took his bony fingers and peeled back the flesh-colored material that encased his entire face. As his hand dropped to the side with the mask, he continued to look Farrokh in the eye.

It took him a couple of seconds to take it all in. Farrokh suddenly felt woozy, and his breath caught in his throat. A cold sweat formed on his forehead. He didn't want to vomit, but it took all of his willpower not to do so. He turned around and placed one hand against the wall to support himself. "I'm sorry. Just give me a moment, Erik," he managed to whisper. "I will be fine in a second. I promise."

But, with a heavy heart, he knew he had failed. Silence engulfed the room.

Erik spoke again first. "You, Farrokh. You are the most intelligent, reasonable person I have encountered. And it made you sick. You cannot even look at me. Where is your stupid hope now?"

Farrokh turned back around and was shamefully relieved that Erik had replaced the mask. "I'm sorry. I'm so sorry. But we'll figure something out," he said, forcing a smile. "I'll start researching medical facilities this very afternoon."

Erik laughed, and it sent a shiver down his spine. "You think I *want* to look like everyone else?! I *hate* everyone. So why the hell would I want to look like them? I'm smarter and better at everything than everyone! And I *hate* them! I hate them! *And I don't want to look like them!*" He brought his arm down against a nearby lamp and sent it crashing to the floor.

Farrokh stepped backward. "Erik…"

"Get out!" he rasped. "Get out now! And don't ever come back. I don't need you anymore. I never needed you! You've been nothing but a fucking babysitter the entire time. So don't come back!"

"Erik…"

"*Get out!*"

A tear found its way down Farrokh's wrinkled cheek as he turned and left the room. Probably hearing the commotion, Erik's father immediately met him in the living room. With one glance at Farrokh's expression, he asked, "Did that kid give you problems?"

"No. Not at all." He hesitated, rubbed his arm, and then softly said, "But I'm not sure that I can continue this job. I think Erik is old enough to be by himself, to teach himself. He already has the knowledge of a college junior, probably even higher when it comes to the sciences. The online college classes will be enough. And then he can choose a university and start his life."

Erik's father gaped. "What? No. You're the only person in that kid's life. What the hell did he say to you? I'll make him apologize."

"No. Look. He was right. I am nothing but a babysitter now. I'd hoped to remain his friend. I have enjoyed teaching him. It's been a unique experience that I'm very grateful for. But all things must end."

The man's head drooped, and he appeared extremely lost. "I'm really sorry to hear this. You're right. He is old enough. But Jesus; you've been more of a father to him than me these last years. You know that?"

Farrokh rested a hand on his arm. "I'll contact you if I find any medical breakthroughs that might help Erik. You both are always free to call me if I can be of any help. Otherwise, make sure he goes to college. Make sure he finds his place in the world." *Or I fear he might destroy it.*

Guilt tugged at his conscience as he left Erik's father standing in the middle of the living room. But Farrokh suddenly felt a dire need to escape the despair in that house. It was toxic and infectious, and it was taking a toll on his sleep and health.

The next afternoon, while he was watching a documentary about the Middle Ages and trying to forget the previous day, his cell phone rang. Farrokh glanced at the name on the screen. *Zari Nabavi.* The sound of her voice brought him a needed feeling of peace. "Hi there, Dad! What are you up to? Freezing your butt off, I bet."

"Yes, well, at least I can build a snowman. What do you build? A sandman?"

She laughed. "You're so weird."

"I am. Why don't you ever come visit me?"

"At this time of year? Why don't you visit me?" Her voice softened. "And you know how hard it is for me. To be up there. It always reminds me of Mom."

"I know. Don't worry about it." He watched the snowflakes brush against the window glass.

"Please, please come down here. You'll love it; I promise. It'll be so much better for your health now that you're—"

"Old?" He chuckled. "Do you still have that hippy boyfriend of yours?"

"Dave is very nice, Dad. And he likes you a lot."

"Well…" He hesitated, picturing a bright sun and a peaceful ocean. "Maybe I will come down there for a vacation. I need it." Farrokh had to move the phone as she squealed into his ear.

He needed simplistic joy in his life again. Zari was a painter, and her colorful work reflected her personality. She'd once said, "I don't think I'm edgy enough for some of the other artists. But I don't care. I'm not going to paint stuff that depresses me." That was Zari; that was whom he needed right now. It was odd, but he'd never spoken to Erik of her. Maybe he'd subconsciously wanted to keep those two worlds apart.

They were the best three months he'd experienced in a while, tucked away in a quaint condo a couple miles away from the ocean. Farrokh often relaxed on the beach and drank ice tea, wearing a tacky straw hat and watching the sun rise and set. Zari took him on tours of all the major cities: San Francisco, Los Angeles, and San Diego. Dave was still the same, but Farrokh ignored him. Although he did once tell Zari, "Your neighbor is a dentist, you know? And not terrible looking."

"Oh, Dad."

"You can't blame an old man for trying."

When he returned to the Northeast, still unsure as to whether he would stay or go back to California, Farrokh warily made the phone call he had been dreading. Erik's father didn't answer. No one did. Farrokh didn't leave a message, not even to say, "I just wanted to check up on him."

It was none of his business now, Farrokh told himself. Erik had ordered him to go away, and he had. Maybe everything was fine. One month later, Farrokh put his home up for sale and permanently headed out toward California. He only glanced back twice.

A couple years passed. He didn't regret his decision to leave, although his former pupil would sneak into his thoughts now and then. Farrokh would see some scientific article and think: *Erik would have enjoyed that.* Or: *Erik would have thought that was stupid.*

It was New Year's Day of 2014 when he received a call from an unfamiliar number.

And that voice, ever more beautiful with age, immediately spoke: "I need your help, Farrokh. What I said to you last time…it was not…I was not right of mind."

"Erik?" he whispered. He'd been having lunch with a visiting old colleague and quickly excused himself from the room. "Don't worry about that. What do you mean you need my help?"

"My father won't help." His voice was low and soft. "He's engaged now. He said he won't allow me to ruin what's left of his miserable life."

"What do you need, Erik?"

"I need to leave."

"Why?"

"I'm in trouble, Farrokh."

His heart skipped a beat. "Why? What did you do?" *Theft? Drugs?* A long silence passed. "I have…"

"You have what?"

"Killed someone."

***

2034

Take several sheets of translucent yellow tissue paper. And then a few brown or tan ones. Some have little tears and jagged edges. Some have holes.

Now take a skinless human skull.

Sew the pieces of paper together, taking no care with the seams, and then hastily glue them to the bone. Some pieces stick better than others.

It was a patchwork quilt of horror.

That was Erik's face.

And it was now inches away from hers.

Mouth hanging open, Christine looked away and dizzily sunk to her knees. She sucked in air, trying to prevent herself from blacking out. She was underwater. He raged at her, but she could only make out certain words. *Vile. Ugly. Handsome, aren't I? Idiot girl! Surprised. My dear? Happy? My Beauty! Husband? Never! Forever!*

Slowly…slowly, she looked back up. *"Keep looking, Christine!"* he screamed. "Look until your eyes melt out of their little sockets!"

The mask hadn't been replaced, and she felt the color drain from her face as she took in the horrible visage again. Erik lurched forward as though to grab her hair or strike her, and she lurched backward onto her hands. Shaking violently, she scooted herself under the kitchen table as though that would protect her from the storm. "Please," she whispered.

"Please?" he mimicked. "Please save you from Erik? Oh, my precious darling, no one can be saved from Erik. Not even Erik himself." There was a moment of silence during which she continued to breathe heavily beneath the table, wrapping her arms around her knees and curling into a ball.

"They tried to eradicate ugly," he continued. "But they did not eradicate me! You see, there are people who believe they are masters of the world. That they will solve all problems. Poverty. Hunger. Ugliness. But they fail, Christine. Like a virus, the more you try to fight it, the more it mutates. Until it explodes into a nightmare a thousand times worse than the original!"

She couldn't comprehend what he was saying. Christine remained silent, willing herself to become nothingness, to disappear and cease to exist.

"Get off the floor," he ordered. She hesitated. "The mask is replaced. Get off the floor!" His tone was too frightening not to obey.

She swallowed the bile in her mouth, climbed out from beneath the table, and stood onto wobbly legs. Christine still refused to look him in the eye, too afraid of what she would see in his gaze.

"Nothing changes, my beauty. My fiancée. My darling. Except now you will unfortunately know the face of your husband. But that is your loss. Not mine. I will finally have what is mine!" His cold hand moved beneath her chin and tilted her head upwards so that she was forced to look at him. "Still," he softly said. "I would prefer you didn't hate me. I want you to be happy. But that is your choice now." He paused. "I would never have to let you out again, you know? I would simply tell Cameron that you are being a very disobedient wife. And he would not question it, you know?"

"Yes," she whispered, feeling physically sick. "I know. Erik, I-I need to go back to bed now."

"Yes. Sleep. Have happy dreams. Perhaps you will forget this nightmare."

She ran. As soon as she closed her bedroom door, she dove into the bathroom and vomited. It wasn't solely a reaction to his terrible face, more to the entire situation, to her upcoming fate and his cruel words. She would soon be forced to marry a terrifying, crazy man with the face of a corpse. How would she even get out of bed in the morning?

Sitting hunched over on the bathroom rug, sweat-soaked hair plastered against her cheeks, Christine knew that the worst scenario would be if Erik never let her out again. Even in her despair and panic, she understood that she couldn't let everything fall apart. Not now. They had come so far with trust in the past few weeks.

Erik wanted her to be an actress? *Fine.* She would be.

Sleep never came that night. She rested her head on the pillow and squeezed her eyes shut but remained wide awake, visions of his face and his voice replaying in her mind. Hours later, she gave up and emerged from her room, head held high. Her heart throbbed, and her hands shook. Still, Christine walked forward. He was sitting at the kitchen table. His shoulders tensed as she approached.

"Erik." Her voice was weak. She inhaled and made it stronger. "I wanted to tell you that you're so smart that your face doesn't matter. You're a genius! You're talented. And you've taught me so many new things. And that's what matters."

"Ha! Didn't Cameron tell you that the Lord does not approve of liars?"

"I'm not lying. You're the smartest person I've ever met. The best musician, too. And that's more important than your face. I'm sorry I acted the way I did. I was just surprised. And then you yelled at me."

He sighed. "Lying or not, you are so lovely. The fact that you will have such a hideous husband must be a disappointment."

"No. Nothing's changed. I just wanted to see who I was marrying."

"And you did, didn't you, my little night owl? You saw me. And you will never see me again."

Christine tiptoed away, still unsure as to whether she would have freedom. Asking directly would make her appear eager to leave. After reading the same sentence over and over from a textbook, she put it down. She then went to the closet and took out the game board, only this time bringing a bag with more varied pieces. She didn't know how to set this one up. When Erik came back into the kitchen and glanced down, she said, "I want to learn how to play chess today."

There was slight surprise in his eyes. "I cannot teach you everything in a day. Certainly the basic moves. But it is all much more complex than that."

"Well, we'll have more than a day to learn, right?"

"Right," he whispered, slowly sitting down. He took the pieces and arranged them on the board.

"I like the horses."

"Those are knights, dear girl. And they have very special qualities."

It worked. He seemed to relax as he taught her the strategies involved and how the pieces moved. He became more animated and less guarded, the glint of hostility fading from his eyes. Whatever her intentions, she began to understand the game, even if she doubted that she'd ever be much good at it. Christine was learning to adapt to this new world, to survive and manipulate when she had to do so.

Still, her heart wasn't yet frozen. She didn't hate Erik. In fact, his horrible face made her feel very bad for him. The rest of him was still completely beyond her comprehension, yet she didn't even dislike him. She didn't know what she felt, except overwhelmed and exhausted.

Two days later, Erik announced they had business with Cameron and told her to dress appropriately for the occasion. It wasn't her choice destination, but the thought of sunlight was enough to make her dash to the closet. At least he trusted her enough to let her out, although he kept a very close eye on her throughout the trip.

When they arrived, Cameron smiled in a way that made her very uncomfortable. "Now that you are officially engaged, I need a small favor, Christine."

"What, Mr. Lourdes?" She regretted telling Erik that she wanted to do more to help.

"I have a man, Sampson, scheduled to come in with a television camera. Lines will appear on that white screen over there." He pointed. "And you will read them while he records you. Smile, of course. It may take several times to get it right. Do you understand?"

She looked at Erik. He only said, "Do you have concerns, my dear?"

"I just, um, I don't know if I'll be good at reading lines."

"With that voice and face, you will be perfect," Cameron replied with a laugh. "Silly woman. Let's at least give it a try. For the Lord."

"All right," she murmured.

Erik stepped out, and Sampson came in. He resembled a younger version of Cameron with his short, brown beard. To her discomfort, she missed Erik being in the room. The men were intimidating, and they stared at her as though she were insignificant. Sampson situated her in front of one of the paintings and adjusted the lighting. Once everything was set up and the camera was focused on her, Cameron said, "Begin."

"Good morning," she started, reading the lines and folding her hands in front of her modest dress. "I'm Christine Dachelet. And I'm here to t-talk to you about the...our organization. To set some...some facts straight. To give you...h-*hope*."

"No, no," said Cameron, signaling for Sampson to stop. "Put your arms at your side. You're also stuttering. Be modest but confident. As you are when you sing. Start over."

"It would have helped to have seen the lines first," she muttered so that no one could hear her. With a sigh, Christine reread them. He didn't stop her, so she continued on. "To give you hope. You see, my dear friends, we operate under the principle that all will be provided to us if we obey the rules of God. Cameron Lourdes is extending his blessings and this message to everyone and…"

He interrupted her a couple more times to make corrections. It was nothing but an advertisement. She felt tired as she ended the message with a soft, "God bless you all."

"Perfect!" exclaimed Cameron, clapping his hands together so loudly that she jumped into the air. "Yes, this will do very nicely, won't it, Sampson?" The other man nodded once in agreement; he hadn't smiled throughout the ordeal. Cameron turned back to her. "You may go out and get some sunshine. You are kind of pale. Doesn't he ever let you outside? Haha. Well, he will return in thirty minutes or so, and you can stay in my yard until then."

She did as he said, blinking in the warm light. The grass was bright green, and flowers were blooming all around her. Glancing around, she wondered if this would be the time to run away. *To where?* They were in the middle of nowhere, surrounded by Cameron's guards. Before she could think about it any longer, the door opened behind her and Cameron stepped out, holding the hand of a cute little girl. "This is my granddaughter. Abigail or Abby. She wanted to meet you," he explained, releasing her hand.

"Hi there," Christine said as the girl walked toward her. She'd seen her several times at events. Very little was known about Cameron's family.

"Um, you sing pretty," Abby said with a smile. "And you're pretty."

Christine smiled back. "Well, thank you. You're very pretty, too."

"You will watch her. Sampson and I have some business to work out." Without a word, Cameron turned around and left them there.

Although she was slightly irked that he had forced the job on her, the feeling was replaced with some warmth at being around a child again. "I helped plant these!" Abby exclaimed, proudly pointing to several roses.

"They're beautiful," murmured Christine.

"Oh, a butterfly!" Abby exclaimed, pointing at a monarch that was fluttering nearby. "Poppy says they're very good and to never, ever hurt them. They are gifts from God."

"That's right," Christine agreed. "We definitely shouldn't hurt butterflies." She watched it closely and then frowned. She couldn't explain it, but there was something *off* about the creature. It seemed a little jerky in its movements. With her index finger, Christine touched the insect and, instead of gracefully fluttering and floating away, it almost seemed to *zoom* upwards and out of her reach.

"Aw. You scared it away," said Abby, skipping around the lawn. "That's okay. Lots more are here."

After staring in bewilderment, Christine shrugged. *Maybe I really am starting to lose my mind.*

"My hair is all messed up," said Abby, stopping and touching her tousled braid. "Poppy says girls shouldn't be messy. I hope I don't get in trouble."

"I'll re-braid it for you," said Christine. "How about that?"

With a giant grin, the girl sat cross-legged in front of her. "I can't wait to tell everyone that Christine braided my hair!"

Christine felt a little sick. She was becoming a role model for these girls. Yet she was nothing but an actress. *I really have become a lie. But it's all for a good cause, right?*

She finished braiding Abby's hair and then they both sat in the grass and enjoyed the sun on their faces. Abby told her about a beloved pet pony that she'd recently received. It wasn't surprising that Cameron's granddaughter had privileges that the other little girls didn't. Eventually, after what felt like longer than thirty minutes, Cameron opened the door with a smile. "All done?" he asked. Both girls stood up, brushed themselves off, and headed for the entrance. Ushering Abby inside, he whispered to Christine, "Erik is outside the usual door, ready to take you home."

He was. "Were you waiting for me long?" she asked.

"I merely watched you. You seemed to be enjoying yourself."

"It was nice to be outside," she admitted. "Abby is sweet."

"She is Cameron's granddaughter."

"I know. But she's not Cameron."

Erik paused. "You really do like them, don't you? Like people."

"Well, yes. I do. Good people. Why wouldn't I?"

He shrugged, and they walked in silence.

Her brain finally made a connection as she stared at Erik from the corner of her eye. He stayed away from people, not only because of his status as the Spirit, but because of his face. Had people been cruel to him because of it? And then...

If people hadn't been nice to him, why would he want to help them so much?

Chapter 20

When she awoke and stepped out of her room the next morning, Christine gasped. Arranged upon the coffee table were a wide assortment of colorful yarns, threads, fabrics and other craft material. He'd given her several balls of yarn and some knitting needles weeks ago, but nothing like this. There were also several plants and flowers situated about the room— English ivies, peace lilies, and bamboo palms among others. They added a fresh scent to the stale underground home. Erik walked up beside her.

"This is amazing," she murmured, touching one of the plant leaves. "Thank you."

"I want you to be happy," he stated. "You will be my wife. But I do not want your hatred."

Picking up a black ball of yarn off the table, she turned it over in her hands and asked, "Would you like a scarf?"

He laughed. "Make yourself a very warm blanket. Something to keep you safe and happy during this dark, cold winter—when your dear husband will be very busy." He sat nearby and watched her work, unmistakable contentment in his eyes.

It was days later when Erik gave her what she initially thought was good news. She'd already begun two knitting projects, a scarlet blanket and a black scarf. At first she'd wondered if Erik would be annoyed that her materials were spread out all across his living room. But he hadn't said a word. Again, maybe she made herself too comfortable. It was so easy to do down there in Erik's strange little world.

"You will be permitted a visit with Mrs. Valerius," he stated one morning. "I know you have wanted that."

She glanced up from her knitting in delighted surprise. "Thank you! That means a lot to me."

"It will be at the house of another person. Cameron is still very cautious about leaving you alone with anyone. You know too much."

She frowned, puzzled. "He left me alone with his granddaughter." Erik only stared. She shrugged and said, "All right. I understand."

"You will join her at the Robinsons' house."

"Oh, I know them. Mrs. Robinson does beautiful dressing-making, usually for…" Christine felt her stomach drop.

"Yes. So you will also begin designing your elegant dress. You were worried about it. I did not want you to be."

She showed no outward reaction to the news. At least she would still get to see her friend, even if she could no longer deny the inevitable path her life was going to take.

Mrs. Valerius was waiting outside the home for her when she arrived, and they tightly hugged, displaying more emotion than was usually considered appropriate. Christine was far past caring, though.

"I was so worried about you!" exclaimed Mrs. Valerius, wiping a teary eye. "But then I was reassured that the Spirit was protecting you. They promised me you were okay, and I heard that you sang, so I didn't worry as much." She paused. "Are you…okay?"

Christine answered with a half-truth, "Yes. I'm fine."

"You look good. And you're engaged! That's wonderful. I'm sure he's a good man. Cameron wouldn't allow the marriage to take place otherwise, so he must be a very godly man."

She didn't even know what to say, so she changed the subject. "How have you been feeling?"

"Just fine! A little lonely without you around, but my health has been good."

Mrs. Robinson soon greeted them with a smile, her blonde and grey hair folded into a bun that revealed her high cheekbones. It was rumored that she had once been an actress in movies but had given it all up because Hollywood was full of sin. "I have several photographs of popular designs," she said, ushering them to her sofa. "Why don't you look over them and see what you like? Then I'll take your measurements, and we can talk about all the little details." She left them there and headed into her kitchen. The fresh scent of baked bread wafted outward.

"He'll be the luckiest man in the world," said Mrs. Valerius, fondly looking over the pictures. Christine noticed that the young women in them weren't smiling. They looked resigned. "Which one do you like?"

"I don't know," Christine whispered, touching the album. "That one is nice." It was a little more ornate than the others, the sleeves were puffier and the lacy skirt flowed outwards in all directions.

"That is beautiful." They flipped through a few more photographs. Mrs. Valerius glanced at her and then, in a whisper, said, "They won't tell me about your husband. I promised I wouldn't ask you. So I won't. But please let me know if you have any questions about what will be expected of you as a wife." Christine shifted uncomfortably and nodded, keeping her eyes on the album. "I know the past shouldn't be discussed here, but I turned your age around 1990. And I spent several years after college doing what a lot of women did at that time. You know, you would have relationships, if you could call them that, with a lot of different men. I had my heart broken more than a few times. The arrangement here is better."

Christine furrowed her brow. "I'm so sorry you were hurt. But at least you had choices, even if you didn't always make the right one."

"That's the thing, Christine. Women are very emotional beings. We *never* make good decisions about men. I was lucky with my last husband. And then even more fortunate to find Cameron. You're lucky to be here as well, to have a husband picked out for you."

"I think I'm smart enough to make my own decisions," she nearly snapped.

Mrs. Valerius glanced down. "I'm sorry. This was supposed to be a happy occasion. I didn't mean to make you upset."

"No, I'm sorry," Christine murmured, turning red and looking away. "You don't know…"

"Don't know what?"

"Nothing. Here. Everything is great." She flipped back to the previous dress. "I want this basic design. Let's call Mrs. Robinson back here."

No, these people couldn't be her friends. Erik was right; she knew too much now. After letting Mrs. Robinson decide most of the details, such as flowers and her style of veil, and take her measurements, Christine quickly got up to meet the car outside. As Mrs. Valerius hugged her one last time, she asked, "Are you sure everything is okay, Christine? If something's wrong, I could always try to speak with Cameron. I know he cares about your best interests."

"I'm sure he does," Christine replied with a touch of sarcasm. But she knew nothing good would come of getting this poor woman involved in the potentially dangerous situation. "Everything is fine. I promise. I'll keep in touch with you."

"Make sure you do."

***

Before she knew it, July had arrived. The air was hot, sticky, and uncomfortable, and Christine was grateful for the shorter skirts and light tops that Erik had included in her wardrobe. Unfortunately, she couldn't wear them that day. She was briefly needed at the Robinsons' home for another measurement and to choose shoes and a few other minor accessories.

While she was there, Mrs. Robinson also placed a long veil on her head and smoothed it over her shoulders, clasping her hands together in delight. "When the dress is finished, I'll have to take a photo of you for my album!" she exclaimed. "You're perfect. Your husband and the Lord will be so pleased!" The girl in the mirror appeared extremely lost under the white material; she didn't recognize herself.

Christine swallowed back the panic in her throat. *Only two months left.*

"Cameron has a request of you," Erik began when they met in the car. The driver wasn't there yet. "Within the week, you will attend two dinners with him and several other men. You will not need to say much. Simply be pleasant. They are men who..." Erik hesitated, "must be thoroughly persuaded that Cameron's way is correct. They must be convinced that he is not a zealot."

She grimaced at the thought. "I'm not very good at persuading. Especially because I don't believe in most of what he says."

"You don't have to believe in it. You believe in helping people, as you said."

"So why can't I do that? Why can't I help make food for people or teach them?" Maybe the hot weather killed her patience. Or maybe the veil had pushed her over the edge. Or maybe she finally just wanted to have some control of her life again. She gritted her teeth. "I don't want to do this. I'll care for children. I'll distribute food or clothes or help people in any way I can. But I am not going to lie to these-these high-powered people who treat me like I'm five. It makes me nervous and uncomfortable. I hate it." She folded her arms in defiance but secretly prayed he wouldn't become too angry.

He asked, "Will you still sing?"

"Yes," she replied. "I'll do that. As long as I don't have to give any speeches."

"There is an event coming toward the end of August. An enormous assembly for all members. Right before our wedding. And before what is predicted to be a very tumultuous autumn."

"Will you be doing magic?"

"Yes."

She sighed in disappointment. "I'll sing. But that's all I want to do."

"I had best resolve this right now. Wait here." Within a second, Erik was out of the car, disappearing into the darkness like a ghost. She nervously waited for his return. Surely Cameron couldn't *do* anything to Erik, right? It was surprising how much the thought upset her.

He returned about ten minutes later.

"What did he say?" she asked.

Erik shrugged. "He is not happy. But you will not have to go to the meeting."

"Did you get into trouble?"

Erik laughed. "Trouble?" He lowered his voice. "My dear, I cannot get into trouble. Mr. Lourdes either has my services or he does not. And, trust me, he cannot function without the Spirit. You will sing, and that is enough."

"Thank you, Erik." He cared more about her than he did about appeasing Cameron. That meant something, didn't it?

They drove down the normal route as the sun set. Christine felt drowsy and somewhat calmer now that she'd been relieved of that hellish duty. As they neared their destination, Erik spoke, a hesitance in his voice. "It is growing dark. As always, you may refuse the request. But, I was wondering if you would take a walk with me? Our time together has been so limited lately."

Surprised, she glanced up. "Yes, that sounds nice."

He leaned in and gave directions to the driver. "It used to be a public park and trail," said Erik, turning back to her when they arrived. "The area is a bit overgrown now, but, if you watch your step, you will be fine. And I will guide you."

She walked beside him through the tall grass, enjoying the fresh air and leafy scents of nature. Nighttime and a gentle breeze cooled the air, and she lifted her head so that the wind would brush against her warm cheeks. Erik's hands were behind his back and his head was tilted downward, as though he were lost in thought. Apparently, he was still very aware of their surroundings, though, because he suddenly grabbed the top of her arm. "Do not walk into a hole. You will break your ankle."

She looked down and laughed, stepping to the side. "Thanks. That wouldn't have been fun. I can barely see."

He released her, his hand dropping and brushing against her arm and wrist as it fell. A light tingle trailed down her skin with it. After a moment's hesitation, she took his gloved hand, continuing to stare forward as they walked. Christine was slightly jolted as he paused in his steps and glanced down. A shaky sigh blended in with the breeze, swirling around her. They continued forward, walking so long that her feet and legs ached. She glanced up and saw so much happiness in those yellow eyes that she knew Erik would allow the walk to last forever if he could.

Maybe they should keep walking and walking. Away from all of this. Away from Cameron and the horrors of the rest of the country, until they reached the ocean. But then what? Sail away to an island?

She squeezed his hand and said, "I guess it's time to turn around."

"Yes. I suppose so."

When they returned to the car, and to a driver who looked very irritated yet didn't say a word, Erik still seemed reluctant to release her.

"We'll go on more walks," she said. Her cheeks warmed as his thumb gently stroked the back of her hand.

"Yes. We will. Often." Finally, he let go. Of her hand, at least.

He would never let go of her.

And Christine didn't know if or when she would try to run away. She'd have to be very desperate, to risk her freedom and maybe her life— to leave this peace and security for a dangerous and unforgiving world.

But her mind warned her that she needed the truth. And her heart reminded her that such a marriage would always leave her wanting.

So she couldn't just give in. Not yet.

Still, she couldn't run. Not yet.

And so she was left floating in limbo, waiting for that magical, terrible moment that would decide everything.

Chapter 21

2014

"Killed someone."

"What?" A thousand questions swirled through Farrokh's mind with those two words. "Was it an accident?"

"Not exactly. But it was not premeditated, as they call it."

"What?" He was a man of patience and knew this wasn't the type of conversation to continue over the phone. "Where are you? I'm in California right now. It will take me a day or two to get up there."

"I am in hiding. I won't say where. But I will call you again in thirty-six hours."

"I'll try to be there by then."

He packed lightly and bought a high-priced plane ticket at the last minute, feeling as though an ulcer were forming in his stomach. Guilt plagued him. *Did my leaving send him off the edge? Could I have stopped this? Erik, what the hell have you done?*

"Where are you going now?" Zari asked when he called her. "I thought you were retired."

"Some unfinished business with work. Final experiments to help someone with their thesis. I shouldn't be too long."

"All right. But don't work yourself to death."

"I won't. I'll be back before you know it."

His daughter must have heard something wrong in his voice. "Is everything really okay?"

"Just business, sweetheart. I'll be back soon. I promise." He hung up, suddenly resenting Erik for forcing him to lie to what little family he had left.

Erik called at the very minute he said he would. Farrokh had just settled into a three-star hotel room and hung up his dress shirts. At least the flight had been peaceful now that holiday travel had died down, and he'd had an entire row to himself. Still, once he'd stepped out into the cold wind, Farrokh had nearly turned back around. It was as though two invisible hands had pressed against his back and pushed him forward, forcing him down a predestined path.

"Where are you?" Farrokh asked, turning up the heat in his room and staring out the window. *Charming view of the highway.*

"I told you," Erik snapped. "I will not give you that information over the phone."

For once, Farrokh took a firm hand. He was no longer dealing with an innocent boy. "I'm here to help you. I can just as easily leave. You will be respectful."

A pause. "Do you know where Laura is buried?"

"Your father mentioned it once."

"That idiot is no longer my father. But I will meet you there. Make sure you are not followed."

Farrokh shook his head as he climbed into his rented black Toyota. *I can't believe I am meeting someone at a cemetery.* He continuously glanced at the rearview mirror, but there were few other cars on the road. The sky was partly cloudy, and the air was crisp, bare branches rocking back and forth in the breeze. After parking to the side of the road, Farrokh stepped out of his car, shielded his eyes and glanced around. The brown grass crunched beneath his feet.

Within a minute, Erik came out from behind a metal shed that was used to store equipment for the maintenance of the graveyard. He wore a black turtleneck, loose pants, and gloves. A black scarf was wrapped around the lower half of his masked face. His eyes were different, alarmed and aware.

Farrokh shivered. "Can we speak in my car?"

"Yes."

They climbed inside, and Farrokh turned up the heater. He put both hands on the steering wheel and stared forward. "Before I help you with anything, you will tell me exactly what happened. The truth with no omissions."

"It's a very strange story." Erik stared straight forward as well.

"If someone is dead, then it must be very strange. What happened?"

"A while after you left, that fool began to see this woman. She was very stupid, Farrokh. Completely vapid. And she talked to my father as though I could not hear. 'He can't be normal, being up in his room all the time. He doesn't talk very much, does he? What's wrong with him?'" Erik's voice became high-pitched as he mocked her, growing angrier with each word. "I hated her."

Farrokh felt the color drain from his face. "Did you…?"

Erik turned and stared at him. He laughed. "Your opinion of me is that horrible? You think I killed that stupid woman just because she was a screeching idiot? No, Farrokh."

"I'm sorry. You said you killed someone."

"I suppose I should work on my story introductions? To get away from both of them, I began to leave after dark. I would go to restaurants, theaters…bars, if I could go in undetected. I usually could. Then I would simply watch people. I would watch them talk and interact. I did it because…" He seemed to struggle with the explanation.

"You wanted to understand people a little better?"

"I don't know." Erik glanced down as though ashamed. "At one of the establishments, a sort of bar and restaurant combined, there were these three people who would sit on the patio and listen to the live music every Saturday night. It wasn't good music, usually an amateur guitarist. But they still came to listen, two men and a woman, always at the same table. I went every Saturday to watch them. The bigger male was loud and annoying, but he also didn't want to be seen. He was not ugly like me, so I didn't understand why he wanted to keep his face hidden. Now I do, Farrokh."

"Why?" Farrokh asked, having no idea as to where this might go.

"I'll get there soon." Erik folded his arms across his chest as though shielding himself from something. "One night, the girl saw me. I had been less cautious. She said, 'Hey, kid. Stop being creepy over there. Come out and say something.' I should have run away then. I should have never come back. But she-she was kind of erm... lovely. Unusual but lovely." He awkwardly mumbled the last sentences.

Farrokh smiled despite the circumstances, realizing that Erik had probably experienced a first taste of attraction. "I see."

"She had long, black hair and very symmetrical bangs. All of her was very symmetrical. Large black eyes. And a very perfect little nose. Except she had put a white diamond in it. I wondered, why would someone fortunate enough to have a nose put a hole in it? Still, she was...I...I wanted to see her."

"That's understandable," Farrokh assured him.

"Her name was Liz; she was eighteen. The louder, older idiot was Tyler. And he was involved with her. Marvin was smaller, quieter. I sat nearer to them, ready to run at any moment. But they didn't say a word about my face. She only said, 'Do you know how many days I'd have to go without eating to get as skinny as you?' I told her it would probably take about seventeen to nineteen days depending on her energy expenditure." Erik paused. "Then they laughed, but it was not mean laughter. And then they let me stay."

"I told you. People are more accepting with age."

"They were. I met with them at the same place. They didn't ask questions. Not many. Liz always said things that made everyone laugh. Tyler talked too; he was obnoxious and not very kind to her. But it was all fine until..." Erik paused and stared into the distance.

"Until what?" Farrokh prodded.

"Marvin invited me over to his apartment with the rest of them. I think they only were friends with him because he had an impressive electronics system. His home was practically a theater. I shouldn't have. Bu *she* was going to be there. So I went."

"And what happened there?"

"We only talked. And then we…relaxed. And sometimes, when we did so, the entire world would change. I would think of things I'd never thought of before. And the colors were more vibrant. And sometimes the music, I could nearly see it and smell it. It was all very odd. But rather beautiful."

Farrokh raised an eyebrow. "Erik, did you take drugs?"

"Do not be annoying, Farrokh. I finally was not tense and angry out of my mind. I had friends. You can't even imagine what it was like."

"I'm sorry. Go on. Please."

"Tyler also introduced me to people who would give me money if I did simple things for them. Marvin refused, and Tyler called him a puss— well, a coward. But I am not that term, Farrokh. So I did it. I delivered their stupid packages. And then I did not have to depend upon my idiot father for money."

"You were doing something illegal. Probably transporting drugs." He now wondered if Erik had killed someone in some sort of deal gone bad. It happened often enough.

"I know. But what else would I do? You think they would hire me anywhere? I doubt I have the face that corporate America wants representing them. "

Farrokh slapped his hand to his forehead. "Why didn't you stick with your studies? Why didn't you go to college?! You could have found something!"

"Because it was the only time I was happy! She smiled at me. Do you know what it's like to have a female smile at you?" Erik waved his hand dismissively. "Of course *you* do. So you would not understand! You would not understand what it was like to feel something so good. Why would I give that up to be imprisoned in a dorm with a thousand other individuals who stare at me like I am from the zoo?"

Farrokh felt his heart break. He was running out of words and advice. "You know I just wanted something better for you."

Erik shrugged. "I would secretly buy her things with my new money, little candy or jewelry items. She would laugh when I did so; I don't understand why. But she never told Tyler. That was how it was for several weeks. And then, one night, Marvin and Tyler left to buy beer. I hate the taste of that beverage, but they enjoyed it. So it was only me and her. That is the first time it was only me and her."

"But she was still involved with Tyler?"

"He was not nice to her. He called her stupid often. I don't think he deserved her."

"I see." Farrokh shifted. The dark cloud of this story was slowly becoming visible on the horizon.

"We had taken something to make the evening more amusing." Farrokh rolled his eyes, but Erik didn't notice. "She sat very close to me and told me she was bored with her life. Bored with Tyler and going out to the same places every night. She wanted the whole world, she said, to see it and experience it. And I told her I would give it to her. And then she told me that *I* wasn't boring. She said I was the strangest looking person she'd ever seen. But that was okay. And then…" Erik choked and turned toward the passenger window.

"What happened?" He put a hand on Erik's bony shoulder.

"She wanted to see my face. She said that if I took my mask off, she would take *everything* off in return. It'd be a fun secret, she said. I told her 'no' at first, but she kept asking. She removed her red dress. And I suddenly wanted to see the rest of her. I wanted to see her so badly. Because she was so pretty. All of her had to be just as beautiful."

"Oh, God," Farrokh whispered.

"My mind became very jumbled. The walls were literally moving, Farrokh. So I did as she asked. I did it." He leaned forward and buried his masked face in his hands. "And then I just wanted her to stop screaming. It wouldn't stop, Farrokh! I screamed back and shook her by the shoulders, trying to get her to stop. But she would not stop."

"I am so sorry."

"Marvin came in first. He started yelling. She was wearing very little, so I am sure it did not look right. But I *never* would have, well… And then Tyler ran in. And he had a very large knife. He was screaming." Erik paused. "It is hard for me to remember all that happened next. But, when I regained my senses, she was lying on the bed sobbing hysterically. Marvin was holding the sides of his head. And Tyler. His head was only…half-attached to his body. And my hands and clothes were red and sticky. I ran, Farrokh. I ran and hid and have stayed hidden since."

Farrokh released the breath that he'd been holding. "Oh my God. That is…" He paused and gave himself a moment to take it all in. "But it may have been self-defense, then? If he had the knife first?"

Erik stared down. "You know why Tyler did not want people to see him?"

"Why?"

"He was the lieutenant governor's son. In the daytime, he was a golden boy. In the night time, he was himself."

"Oh." He vaguely remembered a news story stating that some important person's child was found dead under suspect circumstances. He knew Erik would have no chance in court. The state government was already known to be somewhat corrupt. "Why didn't you just concentrate on your studies, Erik?" he moaned.

"Can you imagine what they will do to me in prison?"

"Yes," Farrokh whispered. "But what do you want from me?"

"To get me out of this awful place. Surely you know how."

"I know ways. To get you documents. Did those kids know your last name?"

"No. I did not ever tell her. Even when we were at our happiest."

"If you think I will save you from this mess so that you can become a street corner junky, you are very mistaken."

"No," Erik murmured. "I will never touch those substances again. I want to be right of mind even if I am miserable. I want control. I *need* control. It is all I will ever have in a world that despises me. Control and intelligence." He paused. "I hate them all. You are the exception, if you help me."

"You even hate her?" Farrokh softly asked, trying to make sure the boy's humanity wasn't completely buried.

Erik traced a finger against the window glass. "I want to forget *her*. I want to forget females altogether. They will never be able to stand the sight of me. Women and drugs destroy my control. And I will never allow it to happen again." He turned to Farrokh. "Please get me out of here. I will disappear, and then you can forget me. You can pretend I never existed."

Farrokh silently stared forward for a long time before sighing in resignation. "I want you to promise me you will do something with your life. Promise me I won't regret this. That is what I want to hear."

Without a pause, Erik replied, "I promise."

***

2034

Her dress was nearly finished by the end of July. Because no one would be attending her wedding, Mrs. Robinson and Mrs. Valerius planned a small party for her, inviting about a dozen other women. Most of them had lived there for at least as long as Christine; the newer members were kept at a distance until trust could be established. There was a hierarchy.

Muffins, coffee cakes, and pies were sitting in decorative glass containers on a long table that was situated on the front lawn. White plastic chairs were placed in a circle to allow for discussion, and a tent had been set up in case anyone needed to escape the hot rays of the sun. The garden was especially well-maintained with roses, violets, and sunflowers all brightly blooming. Butterflies and hummingbirds drank the nectar.

It would be the most important day of her life, they told her. She would be a woman now. But Christine didn't feel like a woman. She didn't feel like a child either—more like an autumn leaf that had fallen from its branch and was now floating aimlessly through space.

She sat in the middle of the circle with her hands folded, smiling and nodding as they gave her bits of advice. *Don't ask too many questions of him. Don't argue. Smile and be cheerful. Make sure everything is always kept clean. Make sure dinner is ready at a sensible hour.*

"I hope you have many children," said one woman with a big smile.

The thought of having kids in all of this seemed so far off that it nearly made her laugh. She couldn't even think of the concept in a logical way.

Mrs. Valerius gave her one piece of good news before the party was over. "The night before your wedding, you'll stay with me. Cameron thought that would be more traditional. Won't we have fun? It'll be just like old times!"

After all the other guests were gone, Christine tried on the dress in Mrs. Robinson's home. It fit her perfectly, lightly clinging to her hips and waist then falling out in an enormous white cascade over her legs. The color made her appear even paler. Her blue eyes stared back at her with uncertainty. She was going to be a wife in one month. *His wife.*

The night after her small party, as they walked through the middle of the pine woods, Erik seemed slightly agitated. His steps were faster than normal, and his fingers twitched beneath her hand. "We must discuss something," he finally began. "I have business away for two nights."

"Will I go with you?" she asked, glancing up. She was always eager to see more of the country.

"No. It is nowhere you could travel."

She frowned. "You're not going to make me stay down in your home by myself for all that time, right?"

"I do not know if there is any choice."

"But I'll go crazy." The thought was already making her claustrophobic. "Couldn't you at least teach me how to go to the surface?

Just for fresh air?"

"It is not always safe. There are animals out there."

"Squirrels?" She rolled her eyes. "You don't trust me, do you? I won't run, Erik. Are you going to monitor my every movement forever? Am I going to stay down there every time you have to leave?"

"Of course not. Eventually we will move to a home that is more suitable for my wife. It is just a temporary arrangement."

"Please?" she whispered. "Please let me prove to you that you can trust me. I'll only go where it's safe. The theater. I won't run."

He stared at the dirt ground, his grip tightening on her hand. "You do not know what it would do to me to lose you."

She squeezed his fingers. "I'll be there when you get back. I promise."

"We will see."

She reluctantly let the issue go for that moment, and they continued their silent walk.

When she arose the next morning, uncertain as to what the day would bring, Erik approached her. He held a strange rectangular black object in his gloved hand. "While there may appear to be only squirrels, there is always the chance... I do not want you to be completely unarmed if you choose to go up. Push this red button. Right here. And then say: *Fire.* Your opponent, be it an animal or person, will receive quite the shock. Literally."

She stared down at it. "Will it kill them?"

"Not on the setting that I have programmed for your voice alone. Although if your life were in danger, their possible demise would not be your main concern."

Slowly, she took the device, feeling its coolness in her palm. And then the realization hit her. "You're letting me out?"

"The stairs and closest elevator are all programmed to your voice. I trust you did not want to go to the alleyway alone?"

"No. The theater is fine."

"Good." Erik showed her what she could eat and where all medical necessities were, along with how to gain access to the top by herself. The stairs and nearest elevator would somehow react to her voice; all other exits were locked for her safety. Erik also handed her a small black phone. "Unless you are in danger, it is best if you do not contact me. My circumstances are complicated. If you are in trouble, though, do not hesitate for even a second."

"Will you be in danger?" she asked.

"No. It is all just silly business."

"That's good." She was feeling a little overwhelmed, a taste of freedom within her grasp.

He touched her hair. "I am sure I will see you when I return?"

"You don't have to worry." She looked him in the eye. "I'll be here."

"Good. I will see you in two days then." He stroked her cheek with his index finger before disappearing to the surface.

And then there was a stillness that made her stomach turn with anxiety. The home was too silent. Christine waited for an hour and then decided to see if he'd really given her access.

She held her chin high and spoke to the ceiling in the dark, little room. "Open," she said in a loud voice. With a soft click and a bang, the stairs descended. Christine climbed them and was faced with the middle elevator. "Open." The doors obeyed, and she stepped inside. When she exited at the top, she headed for the stairs. The birds twittered above her.

For the first time, she was alone. It was almost strange not to feel Erik's constant gaze on her. The air was still, and the late morning sun was bright. She made her way outside the theater building to look at her surroundings. She gazed over what used to be a parking lot but was now covered with high, thick weeds. In the distance, she could see more trees and other rusted rectangular structures. The populated city had to be nearby, but her sense of direction was somewhat disoriented.

Unaware of her own intentions, Christine walked forward and

continued to explore her environment. She almost expected an alarm to sound, alerting the world that she'd gone too far. As she walked by an old dumpster area, her foot landed against something that crackled beneath her step. It was a brochure, and she expected to see another advertisement for a show.

But no. This one was different. The folded brochure was dated 2015 and stated in bold blue letters at the top: *Let Hamilton Genetics help you with your most precious gift.* Christine squinted as she picked it up and flipped through the material. The company promised that babies would have no defects, physical or mental, when they were born.

Christine didn't know what to make of it. The sound of nearby male voices startled her, and she ducked behind the nearest tree trunk, suddenly alarmed at how far she'd walked from the theater. She pressed her back against the rough bark, aware of the weapon in her pocket. She held her breath. Two middle-aged men with long beards and torn jeans and t-shirts were passing and talking, both carrying sacks over their shoulder. She could barely hear their conversation.

"Should we stop here?"

"Nah. There's nothing in there but rubble. Let's get farther in." He groaned. "Haven't had a beer in months. Haven't had a woman in longer. Someone shoot me."

"You're telling me. I heard there might be a camp ten miles out. Maybe we'll find both there."

"There's always some goddamned rumored camp. Always a bunch of BS. There's nothing. We'll be lucky to rob a store out of ten bucks."

She huddled there even after they had passed, releasing a sigh of relief when the men were completely out of sight. She made her way back to the theater and down into Erik's home, checking to make sure that all the doors were shut tightly behind her. Christine stayed there the rest of the day, making herself a cold turkey sandwich on white bread and reading over her books. She didn't venture outside again until early the next morning. With the birds and the chattering squirrels, she watched the sunrise and took in the fresh air for an hour.

She knew it before she thought it. She wasn't leaving. She wasn't running away.

But…Christine glanced to the side of the tunnel. There was one curiosity that still bothered her. *What was the third elevator? Maybe she could take a quick look.* She hesitantly headed in the direction opposite the alleyway, fingers curled at her side as her footsteps echoed in her ears. Christine walked for so long that she wondered if Erik had been lying and nearly turned around. But then she saw two doors that looked a little shinier than the others. After staring at them for several seconds, she commanded, "Open."

Of course, they didn't obey. She pushed the button. A down arrow lit up in yellow, and a robotic female voice said, "Password?"

"Open," Christine repeated with more confidence.

"Voice unrecognized. Please retry."

With a frown, she knew she'd never get in. It wanted Erik's voice and the correct password. Christine started to turn around. But then she heard something, a soft murmuring far below her feet. Kneeling down to her knees, she bent at the waist and put her right ear to the floor, hands flat at her sides. Faint voices tickled her auditory canal. There were many of them, and they made no sense.

"Did you hear that Kristen is expecting her seventh…?"

"Thank goodness my flowers…"

"Stock prices have fallen down to their lowest levels since…"

"How many eggs do you…?"

"I really don't think the President has a prayer at…"

Dozens of voices talking about dozens of different things.

Were there people down there? No, it didn't sound like that. Or televisions?

After listening for nearly ten minutes, Christine rose to her feet. Unnerved, she walked back to Erik's home. Pulling the ingredients out of the drawers and cabinets for an apple pie, she continued to think about the voices but could come up with no explanation. She listened to music while knitting for several hours, the smell of her dessert floating through the rooms. The phrase "idle hands are the devil's playthings" was common in Cameron's world, which explained why she was used to keeping busy. In the middle of her work, Christine glanced up as a passing thought startled her. She missed the sound of the piano.

The realization made her so uncomfortable that she soon went to bed, even though it was only seven in the evening.

In the morning, she went outside and enjoyed the sunlight again. As before, she went back down. Christine ended up baking oatmeal raisin cookies and finishing half the blanket before he came home. Erik entered silently, appearing in the living room and staring down at her with his head tilted.

"Did you have a nice time?" Christine asked after she recovered from her surprise.

He chuckled. "I would have greatly preferred to have been with you." She gave him a close-lipped smile. "Why are you bright red?"

"I um…missed the sun, I guess."

"I will give you lotion so that you are not miserable." He glanced around. "You have made the house smell interesting."

"Thanks. Feel free to have anything from the kitchen, if you actually ever eat."

"I eat. I simply spare you the sight."

"You don't have to do that." She wasn't sure how she'd react to his face again, but the thought of him being unable to eat in his own home made her sad.

"What matters is that you are here. You are still here."

"I told you I would be."

"Yes. You are a good girl."

She turned to go back to the couch and then remembered something. "I didn't use this," she murmured, pulling the device from her pocket. Christine held it out to him.

"Keep it, my dear. My wife should not be completely unarmed in this sort of world."

Christine was unsure if she wanted to keep it. As she settled back onto the sofa, she briefly remembered the voices and wondered if she'd ever be able to ask about them. But if Erik knew she went in that direction, it might make him angry. And she wasn't about to shatter the fragile trust for a third time. And maybe the sound had really come from high above. Or what if it had been her imagination? She had managed to believe in a magical Spirit, after all...

She forgot about it as the beautiful legato music from the piano soared throughout the room, wrapping her in a soft and comfortable cocoon.

Chapter 22

2014

Farrokh had always lived within the law, but that didn't mean he hadn't occasionally operated within the fuzzy grey area—the same area where the government often functioned. He was from a country that didn't have the most amiable relationship with the United States. He had also worked on grants sponsored by the Department of Defense and been involved with laser technology that was now used to create weapons. And, in the 1980's, he had been of assistance when the U.S. was trying to smuggle an important scientist out of his home country. All of this combined had given him a variety of interesting connections. And also resulted in a few people owing him favors that he never intended to pursue.

Until now.

The man sitting across from him in the small diner had sandy blond hair with slight streaks of grey. He had a large build, muscular shoulders, and a permanent twinkle in his green eyes. His jaw was strong, and his smile was genuine. "Farrokh, I haven't heard from you in ages. How the heck are you?"

"I'm good. How are you, Peter?"

"Getting old. I still feel like we just celebrated the millennium. Still partying, right?"

"You know me. Always partying, although probably more like it's 1899 these days."

He laughed and took a drink of black coffee. "I hear you. We're all slowing down. So what can I do ya for? I'm guessing you didn't want to meet just to see my handsome face?"

"Ah. Nothing good, I'm afraid."

"What's up?"

"I need to get someone out of the country."

"I…see. They in trouble?"

"Yes. You could say that."

He leaned in and lowered his voice. "Well, let's cut through all the BS. Even if I can't help you, I'm not going to blab unless there's an imminent threat. You know me, Farrokh. But I have to know what I'm dealing with. Is it a threat to the country? Someone with terrorist connections?"

"No, no." Farrokh was relieved that he assumed the worst. It would make the truth more palatable. "Nothing related to international affairs. Not a threat to the country or anything like that. He was born in the U.S., and I don't think his parents had international ties. But he's still committed a severe crime."

"I see." He put a hand over his mouth and studied Farrokh with an intensity that probably came from over twenty-five years of interrogations. "So why are you saving the bastard?"

"That's a great question. And I guess my only answer is because he is my friend," Farrokh answered honestly. "He's young. I don't think he knew what he was doing. The crime was committed in self-defense; it just can't be proven. But I believe he can do great things in time. I don't think he deserves to rot in a prison cell for the rest of his life."

"All right. Anything else I should know?"

"He does have a very severe facial deformity. He wears a mask to cover it."

"That's great!"

Farrokh stared at Peter as though he'd lost his mind. "What?"

"It's a great excuse to get him out. Medical reasons. No one would look twice at it."

Farrokh suppressed a smile, not wanting to appear overeager in this delicate situation. "So you're going to do this for me, Pete?"

He laughed. "I trust you. You've always helped when you felt it was right and refused when you didn't. You're so goddamned ethical, it's annoying sometimes. We'll make it work."

"Thank you." Farrokh stared down into his cup of tea. "I think we're doing the right thing."

From out of a bureaucracy whose gears usually turned so slowly, a passport and other travel documents were soon ready. The police were still investigating the murder of Tyler, but Erik had done a decent job of keeping his identity a secret around those kids. And while Erik's father certainly wasn't eager to help, he hadn't turned his son in to the authorities either. Farrokh knew, though, that it was just a matter of time before some neighbor would wonder if the strange, rarely-seen masked boy next door was the one being described to police. Peter would be of some help if Erik were arrested at the last moment, but all of them had worked quickly enough to make sure it didn't get to that level. The media would go crazy with conspiracy theories.

Several states away from where Erik and he had once lived, Farrokh waited in a small coffee shop for a last visit with his former pupil. At just past 10 p.m., Erik entered wearing a long black coat and hood. Cold yellow eyes shone from behind a flesh-colored mask. Farrokh wouldn't have wanted to run into him on a dark street corner. And he wondered if he had done the right thing by releasing this young man upon the world. "Hello," Farrokh greeted.

Erik sat in the chair with his shoulder to the door, so that he could keep his face away from the entrance while still keeping one eye on it. "Good evening, Farrokh." He sounded resigned and tired.

"Is it all figured out?"

"Yes. To Canada first. Then Europe. It will be a grand adventure, won't it?"

"Did you say goodbye to Zachary?"

"I know no one by that name," Erik stated in an icy tone.

"I understand." He let it go. "Any idea what you'll do? Navigating a foreign country by yourself is no easy task. Trust me; I've been there."

"I will be fine. I have various talents. Thanks to you, I have a full education."

"But no degree."

"Those are overrated, *Dr.* Nabavi."

Farrokh sensed him smiling behind the mask. "Let me know that you've made it out safely. I trust Peter, but he is one of the men in black, if you know what I mean. And then…"

"Then I will leave you in peace," Erik whispered. "Do not worry. You have done enough."

Both men soon stood; he had stopped thinking of Erik as a boy. Farrokh held out a hand, and Erik slowly shook it. "Do good things, Erik. Please do good things."

"We do what we do," Erik replied. And seconds later, he was gone.

Farrokh sat at the table by himself for nearly an hour. A heavy feeling settled over him, the weight of his conscience telling him that he'd just done something very, very wrong. The sensation followed him as he left the café and returned to his hotel room. His head ached, and his stomach hurt even more. For some reason, he wasn't ready to return to California and face his daughter. So he waited a week, taking long walks of solitude and wondering when his physical ailments would subside.

Finally, his stomach hurt so badly one night that he drove himself to the nearest hospital. The day before, he had vomited up blood. They kept him under observation for several days and ran tests, including a gastroscopy, during which a tube was inserted into his mouth and down into his stomach. Then they took a biopsy. When the results came back, he knew instantly, by the expression on the doctor's face, that it wasn't good news.

"You have a malignant tumor. Gastric cancer, I'm afraid. Somewhat advanced."

It didn't completely sink in at that moment. "That'll teach me to dump hot chili on my burrito, won't it?" he softly joked.

"You have lots of options, Dr. Nabavi. Surgery, radiation, chemotherapy. And then homeopathic remedies are very popular these days. Depending on where you want to receive treatment, I can tell you the best facilities."

He could tell by the doctor's voice that it was all a matter of prolonging his life, not saving it. And Farrokh was more about quality than quantity these days. "How long?" he asked.

"You never know with these things."

"How long?"

"You should tell your family."

"How long?"

The doctor sighed. "If you act quickly, with treatment, maybe a year. Maybe two."

"Thank you."

He didn't cry. And he didn't call his daughter. Not yet. A numbness settled over him. And while Farrokh hadn't thought of Erik often during the last week, too caught up in his own trauma, a guilt still tugged at the back of his mind. The weight of his recent actions and his illness pressed against him, and there were brief moments when it almost became too much. But no. There were still precious loose ends remaining. After being released from the hospital, Farrokh booked a plane ticket back to California.

As Farrokh departed and drove six miles away from the hospital, he was hit by a cold rainstorm. The water drops pounded against his window, and he squinted to see as the glass fogged up. He hoped the roads wouldn't turn to ice.

A grey car in front of him spun out of control, its back right tire completely blowing out. Farrokh held his breath and gripped his steering wheel, watching as the vehicle finally came to a peaceful rest at the side of the road. He squealed to a stop behind it, checked back to make sure no one was coming, and jumped out of his car. The cold wind and rain penetrated through his clothes and coat.

A young, thin man with blond hair climbed out of the other car seconds later, clutching the sides of his head. "Oh, God. Oh, God," he repeated over and over. Rain dripped down his face as he opened the back door and spoke to someone, frantically waving his hands toward the tire. Farrokh ran over to the man's side and glanced into the vehicle. A pretty young woman was gasping in the backseat, her red face drenched in sweat and scrunched up in pain. At first, Farrokh thought she'd been hurt. But then he gazed lower and saw the true cause of her distress. She was very, very pregnant.

"If you can get her into my car, I'll take you to the hospital," Farrokh said once he found his voice. "Otherwise, I'll call an ambulance."

The man rapidly nodded. "I think I can get her in. That would be faster, right? Oh, God. Thank you! Thank you, Sir!" They managed to half-lead, half-carry the young woman to Farrokh's car, both taking one of her arms. As Farrokh climbed into the driver's seat, the couple sat in the back. Farrokh completed an illegal U-turn over the grassy median and sped to the hospital through the rainstorm.

Over the pattering on the windshield, he could hear the man and woman murmuring words of love and reassurance to each other. Occasionally, she would moan or gasp, and Farrokh would speed up. He certainly did not want to deliver a baby. At the lit up entrance to the emergency area, he pulled up to the curb and helped them through the glass doors.

"Boy or girl?" Farrokh asked before the man walked away to his wife and arriving child.

"Girl," he replied with a tired smile, rubbing one hand through the back of his wet hair. "We didn't think it was possible. And she wasn't even supposed to come for another month. But here we are, thanks to you."

"Congratulations. I have a daughter myself."

"Please let me know if I can ever do anything for you. God bless you, Mr...?"

"Just Farrokh," he murmured. "You take care." Farrokh headed back to the car.

For the first time in a long time, a strange sense of peace settled over him. *Release. Catharsis.*

As he drove to the airport, the rain stopped and the clouds parted. Rays of sunlight streaked through the window, and the water droplets shimmered.

Farrokh silently wept.

It was time to go be with Zari.

02/15/2014 12:25AM
From: deathstalkingabroad66 (Unknown)
To: fnabav21 (Farrokh Nabavi)
I am safe. Goodbye, my friend.

Chapter 23

2034

A strange quiet had settled in along with the warm weather. Maybe Raoul should have been grateful for it, but the stillness was almost uncomfortable. He felt as though he were waiting for something, and the anxiety was making him increasingly restless.

There were no new rumors concerning the Spirit. Cameron gave a few more speeches, and Christine sang. People continued to join, although the growth had slowed somewhat.

Phillip was still worried that far too many of Cameron's people were going to be elected. Some candidates from the mainstream parties were also voicing support for him, saying that he was providing security and adequate resources. Raoul was helping to fight this type of thinking where he could, making phone calls and having dinner meetings.

That was what he had been doing before running into Christine that eerie night. The encounter had left Raoul depressed and also a little spooked. It was as though they were being watched the entire time, a sinister and invisible presence hovering around them in the darkness. *Fantastic. Now you believe in the Spirit, too?* Still, he'd never quite shaken the feeling.

"Well, what are we going to do?" Anthony had asked a week ago as they rode around in Raoul's car. "Wait for nothing?"

"I don't know," Raoul admitted. "Maybe see if things get better on their own now. If they do, no one will want to join Cameron."

Suddenly, a commercial on the radio interrupted them. *"I'm Christine Dachelet. And I'm here to talk to you about our organization. To set some facts straight. To give you hope."* A chorus sang in the background.

Raoul's mouth fell open. His hands clenched, and his face grew warm with anger. "What the hell?!" he asked when it was over. "What the hell was that?"

Anthony had shrugged. "You know she's a part of it."

"But that was complete propaganda! It's sick. It's so messed up. How could she be a part of that? How could she do that?" He rubbed both hands over his face. "They have completely messed up her mind."

It had made him even more determined to put an end to this.

He had dinner with his brother and mother on a Saturday night. Judy turned to Phillip. "I'm glad that you could come to dinner tonight. You've been so busy."

"I know, Mom. I have. We're getting so close, though. I've got to give it a hundred and fifty percent."

"I know. Just be careful. I worry."

"I've got great bodyguards. Don't worry. I'm fine." His phone rang, the high-pitched tone startling them all. "I better take this." Phillip answered and hopped up from his chair. "Yeah? You're kidding, I can't even—" His deep voice faded away as he strode out of the room.

Judy shook her head. "I wish he'd turn the volume on that thing down." They ate in silence for several minutes. She set down her fork and stared at him. "You keep an eye on your brother."

Raoul chuckled. "He's the older one. Maybe he should keep an eye on me."

"He always has to be in the spotlight. Just like your father. It's dangerous, especially in these times. People see him as wealthy and part of the government, so they scapegoat him for everything." She paused. "If only they knew how much he did on their behalf."

Raoul sensed that the last sentence was more in reference to his father. "I know. But Phil will be okay. He knows what he's doing."

"What am I doing?" Phillip smirked as he came back into the kitchen.

"Being the best son ever," Judy replied.

"Hey!" Raoul playfully glared at her. He turned back to Phillip. "Anything interesting?"

"Yes, actually." Phillip sat down and faced forward; he did love being the center of attention. "So first, John dropped out of the race."

"*What?*" Raoul knew what that meant. It was now Phillip running only against Cameron's man, Xavier, with no other party to challenge them. "Isn't that really good for you? You should blow that guy out of the water."

"Yeah. Sort of too good to be true."

"That's wonderful," said Judy, clasping her hands together. "You won't have to run around giving as many speeches, right?"

"Let's not rush to conclusions, Mom. This is still a little weird. Also, Cameron is going to have some final event at the end of this month. Like their version of a convention."

Raoul dropped his fork onto his plate. It clattered loudly, startling his mom and brother. "Sorry. Um, wow. Do-do you think the Spirit will make a showing? Heh."

Phillip shrugged. "Maybe. It sounds like it's going to be big. But it's not going to be televised live, so anything with the Spirit will probably be edited out."

"When is this thing?" Raoul asked.

"About three weeks. Why?"

"Nothing. Just curious."

The conversation drifted away from politics as Judy discussed some changes she wanted to make to the house, pulling out old carpet and adding a stronger fence to the backyard. Raoul half-listened, his mind in other places. After dinner, he said goodbye to his family and crept back to his apartment. He locked the door behind him. Taking a deep breath, he dialed a number.

"Hey, Chandler," answered Anthony. "What's up?"

"We're on."

***

"You have such nice, thick hair," Mrs. Robinson murmured, styling it with her slender hands in front of the mirror. Christine winced as she tugged on it. "We'll sweep it up for the wedding. Unless your fiancé would like it down?"

"I don't know," Christine replied, eyeing herself again in the white dress. It was the final fitting. This would be what she would look like on her wedding day. The girl in the mirror still appeared kind of lost. "I haven't asked."

"You should learn these things," she chided. "How else would you please him?"

Christine frowned, annoyed at these conversations that all the women wanted to have. There were more important things to think about than how Erik wanted her hair.

"Will you be singing at the next event?" Mrs. Robinson finally released her blonde locks.

"Yes," Christine replied. "One song." Her voice lessons had been intense over the last few weeks. She wrung her hands, and her reflection did the same.

"Very good." After glancing to the side, Mrs. Robinson leaned in beside her left ear. "I bet I know who your husband is going to be." She smiled slyly.

Christine paled. "Who?" she whispered.

"The chorus conductor. It explains why you get to sing. Cameron keeps it a secret because people might frown over the age difference. But I think it will be just fine."

Christine inwardly laughed. The man was at least seventy, a grouchy widower. She smiled at the older woman in the mirror. "It's a secret."

"I knew it," said Mrs. Robinson, giving her shoulders a gentle squeeze. "But I won't tell."

About twenty minutes later, she joined Erik outside in a waiting car, grateful to escape that woman and her advice. All details of her wedding had been decided, right up to the type of flowers that would decorate the altar.

"Is everything to your liking?" he asked once she was seated. "Did you have enough time?"

"Yes." She looked up into the yellow eyes and saw gentleness. "The dress is very beautiful."

"I am sure you will look like a queen. I wish I could give you something grander. I wish the entire world could witness your beauty, and they will under different circumstances. But I am afraid I can never be in the spotlight."

"It's fine, Erik. It'll still be a very nice wedding."

Before they left, he took her to the stage where she soon would be performing. The event would be outdoors in a new concrete structure, very similar to a circular stadium. Tens of thousands of people would fit in the seating area. The bright green grass was cut short, and golden and silver banners with religious symbols hung on the grey walls. Two large screens stood at the sides of the stage. "You will have to project your voice very far," he stated as they stood on the stage together in the evening light and looked outwards. "But I know you will be able to do so."

As they walked away, she took his hand. "Erik, where will our wedding be?"

"In the chapel attached to Cameron's compound. He has insisted on officiating. You do not mind?"

"No. I was just wondering." She wanted to prepare herself for every detail of that day and avoid going into shock.

On the night before her performance, he played the piano while she crocheted. The song suddenly stopped. The music always seemed to entwine itself with her handcrafts, and she was thrown off when he stopped playing. Christine frowned and undid several bad stitches. She glanced up and saw that he was staring at her. When their eyes met, Erik sharply turned away and stared down at the keys. Silence followed. And then… "Are you happy?" he asked in a barely audible voice.

"What?"

"Are you happy?" he repeated.

She hesitated. "I'm…" She honestly didn't know what she was. "I still feel like there's so much I don't know."

He tilted his head. "Why must you know everything to be happy? Ignorance can be bliss, you know?"

"I don't need to know everything. But some things would be nice."

"Like?"

"Well, about you." She started with something simple, as opposed to: *Why are there weird voices in your basement?* She still wasn't sure if that had been her imagination, and Erik hadn't left her alone again. "Your family. Where are they?"

"I have no family."

Christine eyed him. "So did they pass away when you were a baby? Is that what you mean? Please tell me something about you. Otherwise I feel like I'm marrying a Spirit."

"*Fine.* If only to satiate your curiosity. My mother killed herself when I was a child. She was a miserable woman. The idiot who was once my father wanted little to do with me. So I left. There is only one individual from my youth whom I have any respect for, and he is long deceased."

"I'm so sorry," she murmured with a swallow. "But I'm glad you told me."

"It was long ago. It does not matter."

She looked down, wanting to give him the truth but still not understanding what that was. "Erik, I always felt kind of doomed after my father brought me to that cult. I felt so trapped, and my future didn't seem like it could ever be happy. But you've given me a lot more. The chance to learn so many things. And to sing. And I love talking to you." She paused and pulled at a loose piece of yarn. "And so I-I'll be your wife. And I think that maybe…maybe we could be…be okay. But Erik…"

"Yes?" he rasped.

"Maybe someday we should leave here. If things don't change. And go somewhere else. Somewhere without Cameron Lourdes."

"Don't you want to be a queen?" he asked. "I can give you so much here."

"A queen? I don't even understand what you mean by that. And there are so many lies. And Cameron, I don't know if I trust him." Despite her apprehension, it felt good to admit these things to Erik.

He hesitated and ran his fingers along the keys. "Let us get through this dark winter. And, then, we will think of other things. And maybe you will learn to be happy here. You will have everything you could ever want." The pale skin on his neck twitched as he swallowed. "It may not mean very much, coming from an ugly creature like myself. But that is why I offer you the world as well. Does having the world at your fingertips balance out marriage to a freak? I had always hoped so."

Her chest hurt as she heard him say these things. And she was disturbed that he seemed to see this as some sort of bargain. Christine got up and walked over to him. She sat down beside him on the piano bench. His shoulders tensed as she rested a hand on his arm, but he didn't look at her. "Erik, you're not a freak. All I want is honesty. And kindness. You don't have to give me anything else."

"But I do," he replied, glancing at her. "I must." He sighed. "Look at you," he whispered. "From the second I heard you sing, I knew there was no other in the world for me. It was you or nothing." He turned slightly so that he could rest both hands on her shoulders and then trailed them down her limbs. Both of his long, thin arms were nearly wrapped around her as his hands came to rest at her wrists. Their legs touched. "If you want me to stop touching you, say so." His voice brushed against her ear. "You allow me to get so close to you as it is, yet I always want more. I'll never get enough of you, my beauty. So you will have to tell me when to stop. Tell me, and I will do no more." He held her close to him, eyelids shutting. She shivered, her head leaning against his shoulder. "I love you," he whispered.

"I…I know," was her hoarse response. As her heart raced, his hands released her wrists and moved to her warm stomach. She gasped as they traveled upwards.

Erik took the sound to be fear and quickly released her. "Forgive me," he rasped, withdrawing his hands and jumping up from the bench. "Please forgive me."

"No. Don't be… I just…*slowly*." She could barely get the words out of her dry mouth.

"Slowly?" His arms hung limply at his sides.

She took a shuddery breath. "Everything has moved so fast, that I just need other things to move slowly. Please."

"Slowly." She took his repetition of the word to be disappointment. Until he said, "Not never. But slowly."

"Yes," she whispered. "That's right, Erik. Slowly. Not never." She quickly wished him goodnight and went to her bedroom.

He didn't speak of their interaction the following day, jovially focusing on her performance instead. Christine was grateful for this, still needing time to process all her confused feelings. That evening, she wore a velvet burgundy dress that would shimmer under the lights of the stage. Her hair was clipped up in a golden barrette. Christine wished she could sing for something other than Cameron's stupid events. They took the usual path to the top and met the black car. By now, Christine was so familiar with the trip that she could have probably made it by herself.

As they drove closer, she noticed a dark green vehicle out of the corner of her eye. It was stopped by the side of the road, almost hidden beneath the shadows of several tall trees, and a younger man was standing next to it. He was of East Asian descent and unfamiliar, dressed in the attire of Cameron's people. A blond head in the passenger's seat caught her attention as the car whizzed by them.

She felt her heart skip a beat.

Raoul?

She side-glanced Erik. He was looking out the opposite window. Christine said nothing, swallowing the lump in her throat.

It couldn't have been. He wouldn't put himself in danger again, right?

"Are you nervous?" Erik asked, turning and watching as she folded her arms across her chest.

"A little," she admitted.

"You will do fine, my love. We have been practicing for weeks."

"I know."

It couldn't have been Raoul.

After Erik disappeared to wherever he went during these events, she was driven to the assembly. Thousands of people had gathered throughout the structure, standing right below the stage and sprawled out through the other seating areas. Christine waited in the back shadows as Cameron gave a long speech about how the time of God's victory would soon be upon them. She half expected Erik's magic tricks to come next and cringed at the thought.

When he was finished speaking, Cameron announced that it was time for her to sing. The audience applauded, but she could feel Cameron frowning at her beneath his beard. Ignoring him and gathering herself together, Christine went up to the front of the stage. Her stomach turned as she stared at the sea of smiling, hopeful faces. To her relief, she started strongly, voice soaring throughout the gaping space. Her confidence increased; Erik had prepared her well.

Toward the middle, Christine sensed that something wasn't quite right. A tension hung in the air. Still singing, she glanced to the side. Cameron had disappeared. Except for her, the stage was empty. The audience was glancing behind her with puzzled frowns, and guardians were running toward the back. Over the sound of her own voice, she heard men yelling.

Her mouth closed before she finished the song, and Christine turned around in alarm. As she did so, a gunshot rang into the air behind her. Another. *Bang.*

With a soft cry, she dropped to her knees and covered her head with her arms. People screamed from down below and footsteps pattered across the stage. Her eardrums echoed with the disharmony around her. Within several seconds, someone roughly shook her shoulders. She looked up. A guard stood over her with a grim expression. "Get up and get off the stage," he said. "You're fine. Just get off the stage. You're not in danger." She shakily stood, looking around for Erik or another explanation. The crowd had started to run away from the stage area.

Slowly, though, the people turned and looked toward the front again, their brows furrowed with fearful curiosity. Some people murmured, and others gasped.

Once she was on the ground, Christine noticed their faces and glanced back as well.

She gaped in horror.

Cameron and three guards were holding a young man by the arms and shoulders. *Raoul.* He struggled to get away, nearly punching one of the men in the mouth. They held fast and roughly forced him down to his knees, facing the audience.

"Here we are," said Cameron into the microphone. "Here we are. There is no danger. Everyone calm down." The crowd quieted and waited. Christine froze.

"Here we meet in peace, my friends," Cameron continued. "Here we come to praise God and celebrate in utter peace. We harm no one. We operate within the law and follow the democratic process. Yet do you think the sinful, evil Outside will allow us peace? *No.* Instead they send in two *boys* with their guns to hurt us. They bring in violence!" The crowd booed. Cameron pressed his palms down against the air to quiet them. "Do you know who this is, my friends?" he asked, gesturing toward Raoul. "This is the wealthy and privileged son of Senator Ethan Chandler. He is the brother of candidate Phillip Chandler. He comes from a long line of powerful men in Washington. As many of you may remember, Ethan was tragically murdered. But did this young man learn anything from that horrible act? No. No, of course not. He now comes here to put a bullet in *my* head all for political gain! That is the Outside for you, my friends. Brutal! Merciless! Hungry for power and control! And that is why they will fail!"

The audience roared in agreement.

"You're a goddamned lying murderer!" Raoul shouted, his face bright red. She could only hear him because of her proximity to the stage. "I didn't—" One of the men clamped a hand over his mouth and whispered what was likely a terrible threat. Raoul glared hotly but was quiet. She tried to determine a course of action. *Where was this going to go?*

"So now what are we going to do?" asked Cameron to the crowd.

"Hang him!"

"Kill him!"

Raoul's face turned ghost white as the mob cried out for justice. Christine prepared to sprint forward and beg for her friend's life in front of the bloodthirsty audience. She gathered her energy and adrenaline, unwilling to think of what could happen to her once she was up there. Cameron's next words spared her.

"No," Cameron whispered into the microphone. "No. We are going to grant forgiveness. That is what we do here. That is what God wants us to do. Unfortunately, the young man who accompanied Mr. Chandler this evening is no longer with us. He tried to kill one of our own, one of our godly women, and we had no choice but to defend her. We were unable to revive the young man, and my heart breaks over this. As should yours. But, with Mr. Chandler, we will return him to the Outside. And we will pray for his soul, won't we?"

"Yes," the crowd murmured in agreement.

"Pray for him!"

"Save him!"

Christine stared at the hypnotized crowd as though she were in a strange dream. She could see the clear agony on Raoul's face even as it looked as though his life was going to be spared. His friend was probably dead, she realized. Had that other boy really tried to kill an innocent woman? Raoul would never be part of something like that, right?

"Good luck out there, Mr. Chandler," said Cameron Lourdes as the guards dragged him away. "Let's hope the authorities in your sinful world are as merciful as I am."

For no reason at all, the crowd cheered at this. Christine felt like the only sane person there. And sanity hadn't exactly been her most loyal friend these last few months…

After glancing over both shoulders, wondering if Erik was watching her, she followed the guards that were dragging her old friend away. She wanted to make sure he was truly safe. And she wanted answers. Because, even in the chaos, Christine knew that one of two things had happened.

Either Raoul's hatred was so strong that he and his friend had come there that day to commit a senseless act of murder.

Or Cameron Lourdes had just overseen the execution of an innocent person.

Chapter 24

Maybe he should have noted the size of the crowds and realized just how popular Cameron had become within those last months. Or perhaps he should have listened more closely as Phillip complained that Mr. Lourdes now had connections within the government and police force. By the time Raoul realized he was dealing with far more than a little fringe cult, it was too late. These thoughts would haunt him for months to come.

Anthony had been hesitant on the phone. "I don't know, man. Things have been quiet. What if we disrupt the peace?"

"We're just doing a little spying," Raoul insisted. "If we get caught, we'll get kicked out. Like I was last time. No big deal. Don't you want to know what the Spirit really is? Don't you want to expose it for a giant fraud?"

"I'm curious, I guess. All right. I'll figure something out. Is Meg helping?"

Raoul hesitated. "Nah. Probably better to keep this one between you and me."

"Sounds good."

Anthony brought equipment that could detect where sounds and vibrations were originating and measure the strength of them. If the *Spirit* tried another earthquake or thunderstorm, they wanted to determine how the realistic noises were produced. While Anthony had ideas as to how the visuals were created, he said that would be harder to track. "We could be dealing with holograms or some other kind of 3D projection technology." A deep frowned crinkled his forehead as he thought it over.

"What's wrong?"

"I'm weirded out, I guess. The people or person creating this stuff has to be really smart. If it's holography, you're dealing with lasers. If it's digital, someone knows a lot about computer graphics. I only know the very basics from college. Why would someone so intelligent be helping this nutcase?"

Raoul considered this for several seconds and then said, "Power maybe? Cameron can excite the crowds. The other people can do the illusions. If they work together, they both win."

"Could be," Anthony replied. "Even creepier, what if Cameron is someone's puppet?"

The thought made Raoul shudder. At least Cameron was a tangible enemy. But what if there really were something darker involved? "Nah," he finally said, trying to reassure both of them. "I think Cameron is in charge. But you're right; he must have some smart friends."

Their first disturbing signs that this mission was going to be unsuccessful were the massive crowds and the size of the venue. He watched thousands of members migrate toward the front gates.

"Do you still want to do this?" Anthony asked.

"Do *you*?"

His friend laughed nervously and shrugged. "Yeah. Let's do it. We're here. What's the worst that could happen? I'll be Shaggy, and you can be Fred."

Raoul also laughed. "We're going to need a dog then. And Daphne is part of the cult. I don't think the Scooby gang is doing so hot."

The humor helped their nerves a little bit. Clothed in their attire, white long-sleeved dress shirts and black pants, Anthony emerged from the car first. They both wore miniature headsets with microphones that would allow them to communicate with each other over a two-way radio. To make it less suspicious and because someone might recognize Raoul's face, Anthony would go in first. He would begin the investigation and let Raoul know when it was safe to follow.

"Good luck," Raoul said as Anthony climbed out.

"You, too," Anthony replied with a half-smile.

Stomach flip-flopping, Raoul waited for Anthony to start talking. Twenty-five minutes ticked by. Finally, he heard, "I'm in. Trying not to look like I'm talking to myself."

"You're around the craziest people in the country," Raoul replied. "I wouldn't worry."

"Heh. All righty. Give me some time to look around. It's really crowded."

"K." Raoul tapped his foot as he waited.

"Wow," he heard Anthony murmur.

"What's up?"

"It's insanely busy. So behind the stage area, kind of connected to it, there's this building. It's got three or four floors; I'm on the second. I told them I needed to repair sound equipment, and they let me in. I can see the entire arena from the window. I'm wondering if some of the tricks happen in here. There's a lot of wires."

"Any sign of our Spirit?"

"Not yet. Just one long, terrible speech, dude. But you should be able to get in. Go up the right side of the stone wall, and there's this entrance with only one security guard. Cameron is speaking, so everyone is paying attention to him."

"Got ya. I'll take a look."

After glancing over both shoulders, Raoul left the car and headed in the right direction, footsteps softly crunching over the dry grass. The arena was a fair distance from the front, and it took some time to walk up there. Soon, he could hear Cameron's voice and the cheers of the audience. The entrance Anthony had mentioned was now guarded by two stern men, but Raoul found another opening where the guards were speaking to each other in low voices. Their backs were toward him. As he approached, static crackled in his ear. "Hey. What the hell?"

Raoul stopped walking. "What happened?"

"There's this butterfly…"

"A butterfly? Wow. Thanks for letting me know." Raoul chuckled.

"No. It's not what you think. It's…holy shit." A pause. "Someone's coming!" he exclaimed in a whisper.

Raoul's eyes widened. "Give me a second. I'll get there." He tried to creep through the entrance, sensing for the first time that this had been a truly bad idea. He needed to get them both out of there. *Now.*

"Hey!" one of the guards exclaimed. "You can't come this way! Authorized personnel only. Go through the front and get your name checked, kid!" Before they could grab him, Raoul dove into the crowds who were now focused on…*Christine.* He heard her beautiful voice singing. There was no time to think about that. On Anthony's side, people were yelling.

"What's going on?" Raoul frantically asked. "Who's there? Tell them I'm coming. And that this is my fault!"

"What are you people doing?" Anthony was speaking to someone on the other side. "Hey, let go of me! Get your damned hands off me!" A pause. And then Anthony spoke as though he just noticed someone else in the room. His voice quivered with pure terror. "Who the hell *are* you?! *Please!*"

Raoul heard another voice that made his blood run cold. It was nearly supernatural, beautiful and horrible. And it rasped, *"He knows what he should not know…"*

Cameron's voice came next. "Oh dear."

"Quiet," said the terrible voice. "The boy is wired."

They must have discovered the microphone because there was only loud static and then silence. Ignoring everyone around him, including the men who were chasing him, Raoul shoved past people and forced his way into the building that Anthony had described. The rooms on the first floor had plush white carpet and expensive black leather furniture; it was a ritzy location to watch the assembly. He found a set of polished wooden stairs and climbed toward the top. Rapid footsteps echoed behind him. "Where are you?" he hollered, staring at four different closed black doors on the second floor. "Anthony? Where the hell are you!?"

Raoul was given his answer by the sound of two gunshots behind the closest door on his right. "No!" He threw it open, just in time to see Anthony slump to the carpet, two bright red stains forming on the front of his white shirt, one on his chest and one on his stomach. He cast Raoul a look of apology as he hit the ground with a thud. Raoul choked in horror and reached out toward him. *"No!"*

"Get out of here," Anthony rasped, the light fading from his eyes. "The Spirit…it's *real*…" Blood trickled from the corners of his mouth.

"No!" Raoul choked out again. He cursed and knelt down beside his friend. "God, no, no, no. *Please no.*" He touched the stains as though his hands might stop the bleeding, knowing deep down that it was too late. There was far too much blood; the shots were intended to kill quickly.

Before he could even try to help in any way, Raoul heard a sharp *click.* Two revolvers were pointed directly at him. Still crouched down beside his friend on his knees, he put both red stained hands up in the air, squeezing his eyes shut and preparing to die. "Please." A final plea for life.

"Stop!" exclaimed Cameron. Raoul glanced up as he entered the room. "We cannot kill *him.*" Cameron turned to one of his guards and whispered something into the man's ear, gesturing toward Anthony's body. The guard shook his head. Mr. Lourdes glanced at Raoul. Raoul glared back, the sight of his dead friend bringing him near tears. "Yes, you're very lucky today," Cameron murmured.

"Get away from me!" Raoul snapped. "You shot him! You killed him, you evil bastard! We have to get him to a hospital."

Cameron clicked his tongue. "If he is dead, a hospital will do little good. He must face God's judgment now." Raoul's pleas were ignored as he was dragged away from the lifeless body.

Seconds later, he was certain that he was going to be publicly executed in front of an angry, screaming crowd. With fear and fury, he listened to Cameron's horrible lies, unable to stop himself from finally speaking out. A guard had then whispered in his ear, "If you don't shut up, I will slit your throat right here." A cold chill of fear ran through him, but he was quiet. Only his powerful family had saved him that day. *But not Anthony.* As Raoul was dragged off the stage, as the realization of what just happened completely sunk in, silent tears ran down his cheeks.

They brought him to a black car, and he stared at it with renewed terror, wondering if that was where the deed would be done.

Then Raoul heard a voice behind him. A beautiful voice.

A last hope.

"Raoul!" A gasp and a cry. "Please! Just give me a second. He's my-my cousin!"

He spun around to see Christine trying to wrestle away from several of Cameron's men.

"Christine! You have to believe me!" he desperately yelled in a choked voice, pushing away his own captors. "We weren't going to hurt anyone! I promise! He's a liar!"

"Shut up!" the guard snapped, forcing his head down to make him get inside the vehicle.

"No!" Christine yelled, elbowing one of the men in the chest. "I want to make sure he's okay! Let me go!"

Someone was playing a soothing piano melody on stage, probably trying to lull the audience back into a peaceful state of mind. Some people appeared as though they were trying to leave, but the guards refused to let them out yet. Raoul blanched as Cameron left the stage and approached them. The vile man's eyes were focused on Christine, his stare filled with anger and alarm. Even hatred. Raoul realized that she could be in danger. He forced himself to calm down and stop struggling for her sake. "I'll be okay," he called, mustering all the confidence he could under those circumstances. "I'll be fine, Chris. Don't worry."

"Calm down, you stupid girl! He'll be taken to the police," added Cameron in a steady voice. His hands were curled into fists. "They'll decide what to do with him. I'm done with the matter. Now get back to the stage!"

Christine appeared to stop struggling, turning in the opposite direction. Hoping she would be safe, Raoul reluctantly started to climb into the car, again praying for his own life. To everyone's surprise, she whirled back around, easily breaking free of the guards and dashing toward him, dress flying out behind her.

"I don't know what to believe," she whispered, grabbing his left hand as the guards pursued her. She was so warm. Her eyes held an awareness that he hadn't noticed before. No longer did she look like a brainwashed porcelain doll.

"The butterflies," he said through gritted teeth.

"Butterflies?"

They were both grabbed and pulled in opposite directions. He held her right hand tightly, long enough to whisper into her ear, "Something about them. Anthony found one, and something was wrong with it. They *killed* him for knowing. You have to believe me. We didn't hurt anyone." With one last desperate glance, he released her.

"That's enough of you!" Cameron snapped as the guards grabbed Christine and practically carried her away. "You are an ungodly devil of a woman!"

Sirens wailed in the distance. The police were here.

"I'll be okay," he called to her, feeling more certain of it now. She looked back at him, fear and confusion in her pretty eyes.

For the first time since they had seen each other as adults, Raoul felt as though he might be able to reach her. But now it was too late. It was all too late. With a groan of resignation, he climbed into the back of the dark car.

"The police are sure slow these days," muttered one of the men as they were driven to the front.

"Soon there won't be any police, right, kid?" One of the other men roughly nudged him. "You'll have nothing left to protect you. You and your rich family. Maybe they'll bring back the guillotine." He sneered.

Raoul said nothing, jaw clenched as he focused toward the front. When he saw an angry Phillip waiting out front with several police officers, relief hit him so strongly that he let out a sound between a laugh and a sob. He glanced back once, hoping that Cameron wouldn't hurt Christine. But Anthony's last words returned to him.

"The Spirit...it's real..."

Something told him that Cameron wasn't completely in charge. Something else was out there.

Watching.

Waiting.

Plotting.

He and Anthony never had a chance.

***

She wasn't sure what would happen to her as she waited in the shadows by the stage with four men surrounding her as though she were a threat. As the piano played, people were finally allowed to leave. Police came in, but she was unable to see what they were doing. In the corner, Cameron spoke in whispers to several of them. She eyed the group suspiciously, feeling her stomach turn.

When she saw Erik's form emerge in the darkness, a tower of black with two windows of yellow, Christine moved to approach him. One of the guards blocked her, but then Cameron called to him, "It's fine. Let her go now. Someone else can deal with her."

Casting a quick glare toward the guards, she walked toward her fiancé. They stared at each other. "Let us go," said Erik.

Once they were in the car, Erik took out a small black phone and dialed. In a low voice, he spoke to someone. "Yes. No. No, I am leaving with her. No. It is all taken care of. *All* of it. Do not be an idiot. I will see you soon." Christine stared at him expectantly as he hung up, wishing he would offer answers so that she didn't have to start begging for them. He said, "I am simply resolving matters with Cameron." He didn't seem angry.

Christine stared down at her hands, not wanting to start the conversation with the driver present, even if he couldn't hear well. She waited until they were home, wondering if that was where Erik would reveal the happenings of that day or whether he was as furious with her as Cameron was. But he only said, "I imagine you are tired. You have had a very long day."

"I am tired. But I-I'd like to know what happened there. When I was singing. I'm so confused, Erik."

"You heard Cameron." His tone had an edge now. "Chandler and the other boy were out for blood. They were attempting an assassination and received exactly what they deserved."

"But I don't think Raoul would hurt anyone like that. He doesn't like Cameron, but—"

Erik laughed, and it made her shiver. "This new world makes people act in terrible, terrible ways, my dear. Their true natures come out. So your friend, whom you so *desperately* chased after today, has turned into a cold-blooded killer. Astounding, isn't it?"

"I followed him because I thought they were going to kill him! He is okay, right?"

"Why do you care? I just told you what he tried to do."

"Because he was my friend. And I think Cameron is wrong. I don't think Raoul—"

"Are you accusing me of lying?" Erik whispered, now towering over her.

She was afraid again. Because if it ever came down to physical power, she would have no chance. Christine stepped backwards. "N-no."

He must have realized the awful effect he was having. He reached out a pale hand toward her. "My love. That wretched boy is safe. He has been returned to the Outside, and they will deal with his crimes in their own way. Now I want you to forget today. Our wedding is very soon. Think only of that! Think only of our happiness."

The desperation in his tone made her uncomfortable. "Erik…"

He knelt down to his knees and took her hands. "I will make you so happy. Forget that boy. Forget Cameron. It is only us, in the end. Everyone else could fall off the face of this godforsaken planet, and it wouldn't matter. We will be married very soon, right? You will be my wife?"

But you said you wanted to help people. Staring down at him, she could see it in his eyes at that moment. Along with the desperation and adoration, there was something else.

Guilt.

Erik, what did you do today?

And Christine knew that she could no longer ignore that persistent feeling of utter wrongness. She gave him one last chance to be honest. "Is there anything I should know? About today? About Raoul? About Cameron?" *About the butterflies?*

He gripped her hands tightly, clearly panicked. "My love, please let us forget these silly matters. It is all boring politics, you know? Just silly games men play because they have nothing better to do. Let me sing for you," he begged. "Will you forget this horrible day and let me sing for you?" She nodded in resignation, knowing he would give her nothing. Erik stood, sat at the piano, played, and sang in a foreign language. And, as always, it was beautiful. It was perfection. And it warmed her in indescribable ways.

But it didn't make her forget. Her mind had become too strong, and it fought against the music. After he ushered her off to bed, her mind raged at her all night, throughout all her shadow-covered dreams.

There was one place that might give her answers.

In the morning, Christine returned to her textbooks as though all were normal. She smiled at him when he came into the kitchen and thanked him when he made her a waffle covered with sweet blueberries. She asked him about a math word problem involving a car and a canoe, and he explained it.

Right before her voice lesson, as Erik eagerly poised his fingers over the keys of the piano, she approached him. With a bright smile that told him she'd forgotten the previous day, Christine asked, "You know what I think would help me sing even better?"

He glanced at her. "What is that?"

"To have a recording of my voice. Then I could hear myself singing and know where I need to improve."

"That's an excellent idea," he replied to her relief. "I had thought of it before, but, ah, you know how busy these days are. But yes. We will do so!" Erik jumped up, went into the closet, and brought out a small, circular device. He flipped it on with his thumb. The little green light indicated that it was recording. "It's of extremely high quality. You will be able to hear yourself perfectly."

"Thank you!" she said as he placed it on top of the piano. And then she sang her heart out. The fear and anxiety that she was unable to show on the outside came through her voice, so much so that even Erik noticed.

He stared at her at the end of the first song. "Something is different," he murmured. "There is so much emotion in your singing. I have never heard anything quite like it."

"Is that bad?"

"Not at all," he murmured. "It is rather brilliant. Do not lose it." He turned back around.

"Erik, will you sing at our wedding?" she asked toward the middle of the lesson. She prayed he couldn't hear the tremble of deception in her voice.

He tilted his head. "I had not planned on it."

"What about this song?" She reached into her pocket and handed him a piece of folded notebook paper where she'd scribbled the title. His eyes narrowed. "Can you read it? My handwriting is kind of messy sometimes. I'd always get in trouble for that. Because girls should have pretty handwriting." Christine giggled.

He read the title aloud. Then he laughed. "Are you really serious? Christine, that is a terrible song from the 1980's. It would kill me to sing it."

She also laughed, always keeping an eye on the recorder to make sure it was running. "That was my parents' song." Another lie. "I'm kidding, Erik! You can sing something else. Or nothing. We can just be together that day."

"You're such an odd girl, you know? I will consider singing something. Not *this* but something. For our wedding." There was such delight in his eyes that she began to feel horrible. But the path was set now. There was no turning back.

Now that she had the recording, all she needed was the opportunity. Christine realized with dismay that she could be married before it arrived. How could she betray the man who was legally her husband? She knew that divorce and separation were common on the Outside, but it still would feel awful to be so deceptive after the vows had been read.

Fortunately, she was spared the heart wrenching confusion of that terrible situation.

The opportunity arrived two days before her wedding. She'd done well in her acting; Erik didn't seem to suspect anything. They hadn't talked about that awful day with Raoul again, although it still replayed like an endless loop within her thoughts.

"I will be gone for about five hours," he said one afternoon, sounding very irritated about the trip. "To meet with Cameron before our marriage and to attend to other issues."

"Will I still have access to the theater? I kind of need some sunlight."

"Yes," he replied after a moment. "I will see you when I return?"

"Yep! I'll make dinner. Chicken or pot roast?"

He chuckled. "Whatever you prefer, my love."

"And maybe blueberry pie for dessert?"

"Yes, that sounds delightful."

"I hope it's a nice day," she chattered. "I'd like to bring up some bread and feed the squirrels."

"I wish I could join you," he murmured, touching her hair.

"Me, too. Maybe another day."

Each fib rolled off her tongue until lying almost became second nature. She was an actress. She played the part she'd learned for years. *The perfect wife.* And it was going to come back to haunt every one of them.

Her heart pounded during the hour that she waited in the underground home to make sure Erik was really gone. If he caught her in the act, she was doomed. Christine slipped on a pair of jeans and a simple purple blouse that would allow for easy movement. She tied her tennis shoes tightly. And she grabbed two objects, the electric weapon and the little recorder.

Christine went up the stairs, each footstep creaking loudly. All her movements made far too much noise; she wondered how Erik learned to silently dart from one place to the next. How had he become so much like the Spirit he pretended to be? *Maybe she would find out today.*

Holding her breath, she walked the long journey toward the mysterious third elevator. It waited there for her like Pandora's Box. She'd already rewound the recorder to the correct place while in her bathroom, turning on the shower so Erik couldn't hear the noise.

Please let this work. She pushed the elevator button. She pushed "play."

"Password?" asked the elevator.

"Open," said Erik's voice.

Christine waited, clutching the recorder so tightly that her fingers turned white.

"Password incorrect," said the elevator.

Her heart dropped. "Open" wasn't the password. She should have known Erik wouldn't make it that simple. Of course he'd be smarter than that.

Christine let the recorder play to see if he'd said any other password possibilities. *"Are you really serious? Christine, that is a terrible song from the 1980's. It would kill me to sing it."*

Could it be "song"? *Erik loved music, right?* She rewound the device to that word and gave it a try.

"Password incorrect. One try remaining before system closes."

Only three tries? That made the situation even more desperate. Was it "music"? Did he say that word anywhere on the recorder? Christine groaned in utter frustration. But then, suddenly, she knew what her last best guess would be. What did Erik love more than music? She ran the recording to the word she wanted.

"Password?" asked the elevator.

"Christine," said Erik's voice.

The elevator hummed. "Please repeat password."

Christine squinted and quickly tried again.

"Christine."

"Questionable voice interference. Please repeat."

No, no, no! The password seemed right! Now what was wrong? What did "questionable voice interference" mean? She tried again. "Christine." Erik's beautiful voice rang into the air.

"Questionable voice interference. Please repeat."

Christine pounded her right fist twice against the metal doors and groaned in despair. She knew that the elevator system detected that Erik's voice was a recording or sensed that something was off. Erik *had* thought of everything. She would never know the truth. She would never know if the man she married was being honest with her.

And then she thought of one last possibility.

How much time was left? At least three hours probably.

Christine raced back to Erik's home, climbed down the stairs, and found the phone on top of her dresser. Then she jogged back up, completely out of breath by the time she'd reached the doors. She stared down at the phone in her hands. She dialed the one number Erik had given her and placed her hand over the receiver so that he couldn't hear what was happening on her side. She pushed the elevator button. It lit up in yellow as she held the phone up to the doors.

After one ring, Erik answered exactly how she wanted him to answer. "Christine?"

She squeezed her eyes shut.

"Questionable voice interference. Please repeat."

"Damn it," she whispered. No hope. No hope at all.

"Christine? Are you in danger?" Erik's voice was panicked.

She spoke into the receiver. "I'm sorry, Erik. I just got scared. But I'm okay now."

"Are you sure? I am showing that you are still underground."

"Yes, it was just a-a shadow. I'm jumpy. But I'm fine."

"I told you to only use this phone in an emergency."

"I'm sorry. I just got so scared," she whimpered. Her fear wasn't an act. She turned around and walked away from that stupid elevator.

"It is fine. I will see you soon?" To her alarm, he did sound slightly suspicious.

God help me. "Yep. I'll be here."

"Very good. I will be home in several hours."

"Sounds great."

Tears dripped from her eyes as she hung up. No hope.

Erik returned an hour or so later. "All is well?" he asked, looking back and forth.

"Yes. I'm almost done with dinner." She cut into the roast, watching as the juices streamed out of the tender meat and into the black pan.

"Thank you, my love." He watched her for a moment. "Tomorrow night, the night before our wedding, you will stay with your former guardian. Cameron wants to uphold the tradition, and I know you will want to see your friend." He sounded tired. "The next day, they will help you dress. And then I will come for you." Erik gazed at her gently.

"All right. That sounds nice." She had no plans to run and was utterly out of ideas.

It looked like Erik was going to say something else, but he didn't.

Chapter 25

"What the hell were you thinking?! Do you know what you've done?"

The words bounced off Raoul. The pain he had experienced the previous day was far worse than anything Phillip could throw at him as they stood in the living room of his mother's house. Judy sat to the side with her arms folded, several tear streaks still visible on her cheeks.

"What were you thinking?" Phillip asked again.

Raoul swallowed and stared at the rug. "We wanted to know how the Spirit worked, how all the illusions were done. That's it. We didn't go there to hurt anyone. They killed him, Phillip. For no reason. They're the criminals. Why am I the one in trouble?"

"Because you were in *there*!" Phillip snapped. "Don't you know how bad that looks? My brother snooping around there? With guns!"

"That's a lie! We didn't have guns!"

"Well, they said you did!" Phillip continued to shout. "They said you were trying to assassinate Cameron! Do you know what that looks like? Do you know how dangerous that is now? We're the good guys, Raoul! You just made us look like the bad ones!"

"Phillip," his mother softly interrupted. "He's been through enough. And I believe him. I don't think he went there to hurt anyone." Raoul cast his mother a grateful glance. He knew he'd put her through a lot that day, too.

Phillip shook his head. "It's not about believing him. I believe him, too. It's about what it looks like. It looks like we're using violence to keep them out of power. That's the kind of thing that starts riots."

"Can't we prove that Anthony was innocent?" Raoul asked. "They killed him in cold blood. Cameron should be in prison!"

"It's not that simple. You were the ones who went in there. I don't know what Cameron did to the crime scene, but the police are saying it looked like Anthony was trying to kill someone. His fingerprints were all over a gun."

"Are the police in on it?" he asked, feeling sick inside.

"I don't know," Phillip admitted. "Not all of them. Probably some."

"I can't stand this!" Raoul exclaimed, pounding his fist against the wall. "That man is a psycho, and people still take him seriously enough to give him power. You should have seen the crowds there, Phil. It was terrifying! This country has gone insane!"

"Is Raoul in trouble?" Judy asked, looking at Phillip. "Will he go to jail?"

Phillip hesitated. "It was a possibility. But I told everyone that he would be leaving the country soon. No one wants a circus of a trial right before the elections. Both Cameron and our allies want to sweep this incident under the rug." He paused and looked down as though ashamed. "In other words, we don't go after them for Anthony. They don't go after us over Raoul's trespassing and…apparent attempted murder. I hate agreeing to under-the-table deals like that. But I didn't want my little brother to face court in this corrupt system. These times call for tough choices."

"Oh my God," she murmured. "What a mess."

"I want you to leave, too, Mom," Phillip added.

She sharply glanced at him and frowned. "What about you?"

"I'm staying here. I have to. Fighting on until November. And maybe then things will get better. But I want you guys to be safe."

Judy shook her head. "No. I'm staying with you."

"Mom—"

"Get Raoul out, but I'm staying with you." Her voice became

panicked. "I'm not going through that again. I'm not going to spend day after day waiting and wondering if my son is okay. If you're here, I'm staying."

Phillip ran a hand through his hair. "We'll talk about this later." He glanced at Raoul. "So little bro. You're leaving within the next two weeks. Probably to England. We have cousins there." Raoul remained silent, staring at the ground. Phillip came over and put a hand on his shoulder. "Raoul? I know it sucks. But, right now, this is what needs to happen. To get people off our backs. And for your safety."

Raoul shrugged and said, "Fine. Get me out of here. I can't do anything anyway. That's obvious." He paused. "Can you help me get Meg and her mom out, too? I promised them."

"I'll see what I can do. It shouldn't be too hard to arrange travel. But what will they do once they're somewhere else? It's not that easy to find work."

"I'll take care of them. I'm not going to lose any more friends."

"I really am sorry about Anthony. Don't blame yourself. No one could have seen that coming."

Raoul felt his stomach clench at the mention of his friend's name. Of course he blamed himself.

And he was finally ready to leave this horrible place. He was finally ready to let go.

But, that night, he got a phone call.

***

The evening before her wedding, a driver dropped Christine off at Mrs. Valerius' front door. Each step felt heavy. Her heart ached with the knowledge that there would be no turning back tomorrow. A light summer breeze rustled the grass and the leaves. Otherwise, there was silence. With a small overnight bag slung over her shoulder, Christine raised her hand to knock. She did so three times. No answer. She tried again. "Hello? Mrs. Valerius? It's Christine!"

Why weren't any lights on?

A hand clamped down on her shoulder. Another one fell over her mouth, preventing her from screaming. Someone yanked her backward. "Don't make a sound, or you're going to be in big trouble," rasped an unfamiliar voice. Her eyes widened in terror. The bag fell from her arm and landed on the pavement.

Hands shoved her into a car, a different one. Her tormentor had been one of the guards, a middle-aged man with black hair and cold dark eyes. He climbed in beside her.

"Where are we going?" she whispered.

"A little meeting with Cameron," he replied. "No more questions, woman."

She shook her head in disbelief. "Why couldn't he just tell me to come? Why'd it have to be like this?"

He didn't answer her. She gave up, her stomach sinking further. When they arrived, the frightening man grabbed her arm and escorted her into Cameron's darkened complex. Was something horrible going to happen to her? Would Erik really let it? Their footsteps clicked hollowly against the tiles.

She thought they'd go to Cameron's office for this meeting. Instead, she found herself in a small, cold room. It looked like it was used for storage; cardboard boxes and plastic crates were stacked along the walls. Two wooden chairs had been placed in the middle of the room, contrasting with the mess around them. A single lightbulb hung from the concrete ceiling. She shivered. Nothing good could happen here.

"Sit," said the guardian, gesturing to the chair on the left. It wasn't cushioned. The other one was. She obeyed. "Cameron will be here soon. Don't you dare try to run."

She wrung her freezing hands together and stared at the boxes. They were labeled with mundane titles. *Books. Financials, 2030.* Finally, the bearded leader entered. One of Cameron's lips twitched upward as she sat there pathetically. "Welcome, Christine. So glad you could come."

"I didn't have that much of a choice," she replied, unable to keep her voice brave. Yet, she also couldn't pretend like she didn't know anything.

"Can I offer you anything to drink? Water? Tea?"

"No."

"All right, then." He took a slow seat across from her. He folded his hands and leaned forward. "How are you tonight?"

"Fine."

"Ready for your wedding?" There was a nastiness to the question.

"Yes."

"But you're not really, are you?" he asked. She didn't answer, her hands squeezed into fists. "We have a problem, don't we?" he asked with a sigh, leaning back. "You don't want to be here, do you? You don't want to be married to him. And I can't say I blame you. He looks like something that lives in my attic crawlspace, doesn't he?" Christine glanced up, horrified that he would actually say that. "I thought the idea was far-fetched. But I was willing to try. Maybe you'd be attracted to his position of power? Or you're both musical. Whatever." Cameron shrugged. "I thought having a little wife might calm him down. He's so frenetic. Too high energy. Angry."

"What do you want?" she whispered.

"Haven't you heard my speeches? I tell everyone what I want every day. I want peace. Truth. Goodness. Godliness." He glared. "And I don't want *you* here, distracting Erik from his duties. A disobedient wife is the worst kind of disruption. I know you're that type. First, you wouldn't go to the meeting. And then that business with you running after Chandler. I can see it in your eyes. Stubbornness," he hissed.

"Did you kill Anthony?" she asked. "Or was that Erik's idea?"

Cameron tilted his head. "The boy was a spy."

"Did you?"

He rolled his eyes. "Call it a joint decision."

"Why?" she growled.

"He was dangerous to us. That is all I will tell you."

"What does Erik do for you? What is all this?!"

"That is all I will tell you," he repeated. "You have no more business here."

"What are you going to do to me? Can you at least tell me that? Are you going to kill me?"

"What do you want me to do to you?" asked Cameron. She shuddered. "You don't want to be here, do you?" She stared down. "Do you?" She gave in and shook her head. "I didn't think so." He shrugged. "I can't permanently make you disappear. Erik would know. So that saves you, doesn't it, you lucky woman? But I can say that you ran away. With Chandler. That it's illegal to keep you here against your will. That I let you leave, so that everyone can be happy."

"What are you talking about?" she whispered, seesawing between terror and hope.

"You leave tonight. Go wherever you want as long as it's far away from here. I don't want you near my beautiful community. I don't want you near Erik." Cameron leaned so closely that she could smell his garlicky breath. "But if you tell anyone what you know, anything about Erik or what you've learned, I will make the lives of your friends here miserable. The Valerius woman? She'll wish she wasn't born."

Christine paled and jumped up. "What did you do to her?!"

"Nothing. Yet." Cameron smiled. "Everyone will be perfectly fine if you go and forget this place. Go and leave us alone. You could never appreciate my vision, anyway."

It sounded almost too good to be true. But they hadn't even discussed the most important barrier. "He'll be furious, Cameron. At me. At you!"

"He will be. At first. But he'll get over you. You're nothing but a silly, stupid girl. And I can use his anger. Anger can be very, very useful under certain circumstances. God's anger, for example."

"What do you mean?"

"That information doesn't concern you. None of this does. Just. Get. Out."

Her mind swirled with a hundred thoughts. Oh, how she wanted to leave. She knew there'd have to be consequences, but she wanted out of this mess so badly. Something was so very wrong about this whole place, and Erik refused to give her any answers. *Oh, God. Erik. He'd be devastated. What was the right thing to do?*

"I don't have all night. Yes or no? I think the answer's easy. Don't cut off your nose just to spite your face, just to annoy me. We're talking about the rest of your life. Do you really want to stay here? Married to him? You want to feel his hands all over you every night as you do your wifely duties?" He stared at her face. *"Well?!"*

"I want to go," she whispered. Both relief and anguish washed over her as the words left her lips. "I want to go."

"I thought so." She saw the gleam of victory in his eyes. It made her sick to her stomach.

She still thought it was a horrible trick, that she'd be taken outside and gruesomely executed. Just like Raoul's friend. They led her to the front of the complex, the light from the building shining down upon her. The air was sticky, and she was sweating from terror. A car pulled up. Blinding headlights. She stepped backwards, fearing the worst.

A door opened with a grunt. Someone stepped out. She squinted. She cried out. Christine ran toward the figure and threw her arms around his shoulders. "Raoul!" Warm arms embraced her. He kissed the side of her head. "Raoul! Oh, God!"

"Christine. It's so great to see you," her old friend whispered in her ear. "Do you want to leave with me?"

A choice. She finally had a choice.

"Get me out of here," she replied. "Please!"

"Thank God," Raoul murmured.

Cameron spoke from above. "You'll leave the country tonight. As we agreed. If I ever see or hear from either of you again, the consequences will be beyond anything you ever imagined."

"We're gone," said Raoul, gripping her tightly. "You'll never see us again. I swear to God."

"You don't know anything about God," Cameron replied.

"Let's go," she whispered, fearing their time was short. Surely, *he* wouldn't really let her get away.

Raoul took her into the car, and they clutched to each other in the backseat. With fear and relief, she wept into his shoulder. He stroked her hair, promising it would all be okay now.

They would keep their word to Cameron.

They were done trying to be heroes.

Chapter 26

It was anger that fueled her escape more than anything. Not disgust, as Cameron thought. But anger at the way Erik had pretended to be a Spirit during the first few years that she might have been able to escape. And then, once Erik had revealed himself, he'd taken all her choices from her. And then he'd lied, probably more times than she even knew. *How many had he killed?*

But maybe she was angrier at herself than anything else—for believing the lies and letting him control her with them for so long. For nearly coming to…*No. She couldn't think about these things now. It would make her crazy.*

The car sped forward. She couldn't see the driver very well. Christine leaned forward to make sure he wasn't wearing a mask. It was just an older man with white hair, eyes concentrated on the road. He didn't look like he worked for Cameron. "Where are we going?" she whispered, her cheek pressed back against Raoul's shoulder.

"We have a flight out of here tonight. To England. I have relatives there. They're good people."

"Oh," she whispered. "So far."

"They said they'd turn you over to me if I left fast. There was never a second thought. Phillip got me ready to go. I hugged him and my mom goodbye." Raoul swallowed. "I hope they'll follow us soon."

"I'm so sorry you had to leave them because of me."

"I had to leave anyway. After Anthony. It wasn't because of you. But, even if it was, I would have done it. I had to get you out. Are you okay?"

"I don't know." Another sob escaped her throat. "Please just hold me."

"I've got you. We're out of there."

"I didn't bring clothing," she murmured, silly little thoughts entering her mind.

"We'll get whatever you need, Christine. Don't even worry about it. We're going to be political refugees, so your documents are taken care of."

She didn't even know what he was talking about. She trusted him, though. Raoul was the only person in the world whom she did trust.

Her body ached to slumber, but her mind remained alert as she continued to cast nervous glances out the back window. "Almost there," Raoul eventually said with relief as they passed a faded green sign that alerted them to the smaller airport. Tall lights came into view, and a small concrete building sat out front. A wide-open space marked the landing field.

"When does the plane leave?" she asked, checking the time.

"Ten minutes, I think. We're leaving with some envoys." The car came to a rough stop. Raoul grabbed a manila folder and his white duffel bag, and they raced forward to the lighted aircraft. On the front of the white jet, in yellow cursive letters, was the word *Apollo*, maybe the name of a company. The pilot, a middle-aged man with a short black beard, met them out front. He wore a white name tag on the front of his navy blue suit and appeared to be some type of government official. "Morning," said Raoul, his voice casual and friendly. "Or is it night still? Sorry we kept you waiting. Heh."

"Forget all the political mumbo jumbo; I bet you two are eloping," he said with a deep voice and a knowing smile. "Is that why we're up so damn late? Young love?"

"Hah. Something like that."

"Well, all right then. You got all your documents? Something been arranged for you once you get there?"

"We got 'em." He started to open the folder.

"No, I know who you are. Spoke to your brother hours ago. And you look like your father. We're good, Chandler. Let's get out of here. Just waiting for our first officer to get out of the bathroom."

Raoul maintained a calm outward appearance as they entered. Three other men sat in plush red seats, all dressed in black suits and solid-colored ties. Thankfully, Raoul seemed to be used to these kinds of people and greeted them with handshakes.

"There's Raoul," said a man with a blond handlebar moustache and sparse hair of the same color. "I read about what you did. I was damned happy to wait for you, too." He leaned in and whispered, "Too bad you couldn't shoot the bastard. All of us would have cheered." He made his index finger and thumb into a gun and pretended to fire it. "*Pow.* Am I right?"

"Eh," said Raoul with a shrug, obviously a little uncomfortable. "We do what we can."

The same man glanced at her. "This your lady?"

"Um, yeah. This is my girlfriend." Christine was glad Raoul didn't give out her name.

"Nice to meet you." He winked at her.

"Nice to meet you, too." Christine weakly smiled. She sat in the nearest empty seat, clutching Raoul's hand as he sat beside her. "Go, go, go. Please *go*," she whispered to herself. Raoul's jaw was clenched, and she could tell that he was thinking the exact same thing.

When the younger first officer came out of the bathroom, pushing the door a little too hard so that it loudly crashed into the wall, she nearly flew out of her seat. It made her sick when she thought of the possible consequences of all her actions that evening— and she was now sitting next to Raoul and clutching his hand as though it were the only thing keeping her alive.

"Ugh. Thanks everyone for keeping me up these hours," said the first officer, stretching his arms over his head. "Especially you, kid," he joked to Raoul.

"We're giving you work," the man with the moustache replied. "Not something to be taken for granted these days."

"True. Well, I've had coffee, so I'll get you there in one piece." He chuckled. "Not sure about Bill in there, though. He's trying to kick his caffeine addiction, so watch out!" They all laughed.

She wished they would *shut up* and *go*.

But soon the engines started with a loud whir. She gripped his hand even more tightly, squeezing her eyes shut as the aircraft moved forward. When the jet finally took off, Christine released a soft sob. Looking down one last time, she thought she saw the outline of a tall, eerie shadow in the darkness far below. But it was probably her paranoid imagination.

She could hear Raoul exhale. The men chatted with each other, and he chimed in every so often. But Christine only rested her head on his shoulder in a daze. The last hours were beyond her comprehension. She was in a dream. And she was desperately trying to stop it from becoming a nightmare.

"You can sleep," Raoul murmured to her. "We're safe, I think."

Even now, she didn't think she could. Every time she closed her eyes, she saw *his* eyes. She felt his pain and his rage. *You didn't give me a choice, Erik. Or the truth. About anything. You know that. You know why I'm gone.*

***

Safe over a vast ocean, she eventually calmed down. Someone offered her a couple of pills to help her sleep, and she took them, too exhausted to even be suspicious. Raoul gave her hand reassuring squeezes. They didn't talk much; there were too many people around. And Cameron had warned her to keep quiet.

She finally nodded off for a long time. The next thing Christine felt was Raoul shaking her shoulder. "We're almost there, sweetheart."

She sat up with a soft gasp. The jet landed with a thud, jolting them. But it wasn't until they were both standing in an international airport, preparing to follow a woman to a customs and immigration desk, that it hit them both. The lights were bright, and the few people they could see had healthy glows to their faces and life in their eyes. It was a new world. "We made it!" Raoul exclaimed with a grin, raising his fist in the air. "Woohoo! *Yes!* We did it!"

She weakly laughed, tears falling down her cheeks. "I can't believe it!" Her voice was hoarse, a far cry from the finely tuned instrument that Erik had molded. "I can't believe it! I can't believe it!"

Raoul picked her up and hugged her. During that moment of elated relief, Christine received her first real kiss. He leaned forward with his hand still on her waist, her head tilted upward, and their lips touched for several seconds. The woman glanced at them and smirked. An unsure grin formed on Raoul's face, and he laughed and scratched his head. "Heh. I'm sorry. I'm just so damn happy right now."

Honestly, she wasn't even sure what *happy* meant anymore. But the certainty in Raoul's eyes made her heartbeat almost return to normal again. She couldn't have asked for a better friend that night. She owed him everything.

He noticed her expression. "Is something wrong? Are you still afraid?"

She rubbed her palm against her temple. "Raoul, I'm so grateful to you. I just… It's all so much right now. It's all so much, and I'm exhausted. My head is going crazy. I literally feel crazy."

"You've been through a lot. It'll take time." She nodded, staring toward the nearest window. Outside, the sun was in the sky. A new day. A new country. *A new life.* "Is there anything I can do?" he asked.

"You've already done so much. So, right now, just hug me," she whispered. "Hold me and say we'll be safe forever. Maybe someday I'll believe you."

"We'll be safe forever. I promise."

But she didn't believe him yet.

Her paranoia had followed her across the Atlantic Ocean. She always looked over her shoulder when they rounded a corner. She second glanced people, especially if their faces were turned or in the shadows. They spent most of the first day making sure their paperwork was in order, and she tried to leave behind as few traces as possible. Everyone had been nice enough throughout the process. At least they believed Raoul to be behind the strange circumstances—a political fugitive.

"Will our names be in the computers?" she asked an older, stern-looking woman who was going through their file one last time. She seemed to have some authority.

"Yes. Of course. Why?"

"Could you put it all in a paper file? At least for a little while?"

The woman stared over her thick glasses, annoyed. "Not without getting into trouble. If you're worried about someone seeing it, don't be. This is a highly secure system."

"Nothing is perfect," Christine murmured.

"What she means," said Raoul with a nervous sideways glance, "is that nothing is really secure these days, right? Supposedly secure systems are always getting hacked."

The woman sighed. "All right. I'll try to keep things discreet." She looked between them. "What did you people do? Try to kill…" She stared longer at Raoul. "*Oh.* I saw you in the papers. You tried to stop that son of a bitch who wants to take away my right to vote. Yes. Yes, I'll help you."

"Looks like we're good to go" said Raoul, sounding amused as they walked out.

"In the papers!" she frantically exclaimed, turning toward him. "We're in the papers! Raoul!"

"I couldn't help it," he murmured, turning a little red. "People think I tried to kill Cameron, and I don't want to disappoint them, I guess."

"I don't care what they think! Everyone knows where we are! Oh my God. Oh my God." She almost had a panic attack.

He placed his hands on both her shoulders. "Woah. I don't understand why you're so upset. Cameron let us go. He was glad we were leaving. You think he'll change his mind?"

"He might."

"Why? He wanted us both out of there. Are you not telling me everything?"

"I can't yet," she murmured. "I just want to feel safe. Please don't ask me yet."

"All right. But I have to understand sometime."

They had permission to move freely around the country. Raoul could use his driver's license for identification until they decided whether they wanted to be permanent residents. Phillip had given him a large sum of cash, and so they completed a quick currency exchange. Luckily, they were now in a place with a vast public transportation system, so driving wouldn't be an issue. Raoul continued to use his credit card.

"Can you be traced through that card?" she asked. She was still so new to the world.

"Sort of. We're safe, though." He insisted this over and over. He didn't understand.

Raoul's cousin, Michael, was about ten years older than him. His shoulders were broader, like Phillip's, and he wore glasses. Raoul said that he was involved in the banking industry and doing well for himself. His wife, Brooke, was a shorter woman with hair that curled cutely beneath her chin. She worked as a nurse. They welcomed Christine and Raoul into their two-story grey brick home, just outside of London.

"So you'll each have your own room," explained Brooke, guiding them into the first bedroom. It had a yellow and lavender striped bedspread and some colorful abstract art on the wall. Triangles on top of squares on top of circles. There was one small dresser with three stacked drawers. Brooke placed some fluffy pink towels on the dresser. "This can be

Christine's. You let me know if you need anything."

"Thank you very much." She actually needed everything, from underwear to a toothbrush.

Raoul's room was a little bigger with a solid blue bedspread and its own bathroom. He set his bag down.

"You two want something to eat?" asked Brooke. "You must be exhausted." Christine found her accent calming and charming. She did feel a little safer there.

"I think we're good," said Raoul. "Thanks for letting us stay. Hopefully, we'll find our own place soon."

"Just take your time. I know it's a mess over there. We were very happy to help, especially after what you did."

Raoul looked completely wiped out, and Christine knew he needed to sleep before they did anything else. Poor Raoul fell onto the bed and was out within minutes. He didn't even take off his shoes.

What *were* they going to do? It had happened so fast that the farthest she'd gotten in planning was escaping. That had seemed so insurmountable that she didn't dream further. And now that they were actually there…

She hadn't eaten anything since lunch in Erik's home the previous day. A ham sandwich and some grapes. Her stomach growled at her. She looked in Raoul's luggage for a package of peanuts that he'd gotten on the plane. The salt tasted good on her tongue. She glanced out the window and saw an older woman walking her Dalmatian. A little boy riding a bike. *I can't believe I'm actually standing here.* A short, strange laugh escaped her lips.

She was tired but didn't want to be alone. With a sigh, she went to the other side of the bed and tried to sleep, fatigue and paranoia in a constant battle over her mind and body. Fatigue finally won. The creaking bed awoke her sometime later.

"Hey. How are you doing over there?" Raoul was propped up on his arms and looking at her.

"I'm okay."

Raoul yawned loudly and looked at the clock. "Wow. Guess I really needed that."

"You were up all night for some reason," she joked.

"Oh, yeah." He was very cute when he smiled. "Well, I guess we'd better have dinner and figure out a long-term plan. Get an apartment. I guess? Or is it a flat here? Then find work. Welcome to adulthood, right?"

"I know what you mean." She had started to feel safe in that house and almost didn't want to leave it. But surely they had to be okay for at least a little while, right? They were in an entirely different country. Michael recommended a Japanese restaurant within walking distance. Christine stayed close to Raoul's side and held his hand, keeping herself half-hidden by his shoulder. They sat at the bar. She liked the dark interior of the restaurant, and they were obscured from the doors and front windows by an aquarium with colorful fish. A fountain bubbled nearby.

"K. Give it a try. This is good stuff once you get used to it."

"Who eats raw fish?"

"The taste is covered up by other stuff; you won't even notice the fish. That's going to taste like avocado."

"All right." A pause. A mouthful. "Raoul, I noticed the fish! Ah! I need a drink of something."

He quickly pushed her soda toward her, chuckling. "It takes a few times to get used to sushi."

"I'm getting some teriyaki chicken. That's good, right?"

"Yeah. You'll like that, I think." He took out a pen and yellow notepad. "All right. So we need to get us both some clothes and basic things."

"A toothbrush would be nice," she agreed.

"I also need to call my brother."

"Right. To let him know you're okay. Don't say anything about me. Please."

"Sure."

She hesitated. "Maybe you should make a quick call from here right before we leave. So we're not traced. Is there another phone you could use?"

Raoul stared at her. "Christine, I wish you'd tell me what's on your mind." She buried her face into her hands, elbows on the table. "Sweetheart, it can't be that bad. Did Cameron threaten you?" She didn't answer. "Is that it?"

"Yes," she finally whispered.

"What'd he say? He can't hurt you here."

She swallowed. "He said if I told anyone about…everything, he'd hurt my friends. The woman who took care of me after my father died. I believe him."

Raoul placed his hand over hers. "He won't find out. I'm just trying to understand why you're so worried. Is Cameron really that powerful? Is he really that smart? Maybe you were there so long that you've built him up in your head. Because I don't think—"

"You're right," she said, her hands dropping. "Cameron isn't that powerful. It's who he has working for him."

"What—"

"I'll tell you later," she whispered. "Not here. Not in public."

"All right. Please, though. Later. Because if we are in danger, then I need to know about it. So that I can act." She didn't tell him that there was nothing he could do. Raoul changed to a lighter subject. "Now you should try this one."

"What's in it?" She eyed the roll suspiciously.

"Octopus." He grinned. She threw a napkin at him, but it landed in the middle of the table. They both laughed, the tension melting away into nervous optimism.

That night, the sound of him softly snoring from the other room was comforting enough to put her to sleep. The gentle patter of the shower greeted her ears as she dressed the next morning. After dinner the previous evening, she had bought a couple of pairs of pants and t-shirts. A package of underwear and another bra. Basic hygiene supplies. It was sort of strange, having to take care of herself again.

A knock at her door. "Come in," she murmured, trying not to be paranoid.

Raoul was brushing his teeth. "Morning. Did you sleep okay?"

"Yes, thanks." As she stretched out her arms, Christine noticed the ring on her finger.

They had survived a night.

And they'd survived her entire wedding day.

Raoul took a slow seat on her bed. "So. I'm still waiting to hear what's going on. No one's around now." She looked down. "You don't have to tell me. But I think it'd be easier for me to understand where you're coming from. You're so scared all the time."

After glancing outside the room, making sure no one was listening, Christine shut the door. She sat back on the bed.

"You want to know about the Spirit," she began.

"The Spirit," he muttered. "That again. What do you mean exactly? Do you mean just like a voice? Or a light? What exactly *is* the Spirit?"

"So you actually believe in it now?" she asked, her lip twitching upwards.

He shrugged. "Anthony saw something that day. I don't know what to believe anymore."

"He's a man," she said.

"What?"

"The Spirit is a man named Erik."

"Okay. And this one *man* does all the creepy illusions?"

"Yes."

Raoul laughed, and his shoulders relaxed. "One man? Christine, that's great! That's no big deal. Here I was starting to believe that some supernatural thing was really going on. Something awful." He chuckled again. "But just one guy."

She moved away from him. "No. No, you don't understand. He's a man, but he's not like anyone else. I can't explain it. Sometimes he seems more like a spirit. And he's very, very dangerous. I still can't believe I got away that night."

"This is still one guy, though. You can tell us where he's at. Phillip can try to stop this!"

"You want to know where he's at? He's probably looking for me!"

Raoul frowned. "Wait. Why is he looking so hard for you? Isn't this Cameron's guy? Does he think you're going to rat him out?" She shook her head. "Christine, what is it?"

"He loves me," she whispered. "More than you could ever imagine." With a soft moan, she thrust her left hand out. "Raoul, I was supposed to...*marry* him."

"*What?*" Mouth falling open, he stared at the ring in near horror. His next words came out jumbled. "Was—was it like an arranged c-cult thing?"

"No. *Yes.* I don't know!" She threw up her hands. "It doesn't matter because there's no way I can do that now! Right? I can't do that, right?"

He grabbed her hand. "We both know that whatever happened to you in that stupid cult wasn't right. Forced marriage? That's like medieval. But how'd you get caught up in all that?"

"I don't even know where to begin."

"The beginning? Whatever you can, Chris. I'm still confused."

"I wanted out so badly, and I plotted my escape for when I turned eighteen. Sometimes I even thought about finding you. All I thought about was getting away."

"I thought about you, too," he said with a small smile.

"A couple years ago, I sang for Cameron's assembly. I think my father thought it would help me find a husband or something; he was sick and worried about me. I wasn't exactly the perfect daughter. After that assembly, Cameron told me that the Spirit wanted to speak with me. And so I went into this little room and heard the most beautiful voice in the world..." She paused. "So I talked to it and sang for it, thinking the Spirit had really come from God. I thought maybe everything Cameron said was true, that his people were chosen by the Spirit for some higher calling. Imagine that? Thinking you're actually chosen by God for something big." She shook her head in self-disgust.

"You didn't think anything seemed wrong with that situation?" he gently asked.

"Deep down, I did. I wasn't stupid. But it really felt like some powerful presence was there watching me all the time. And then his voice, Raoul. I can't explain it, but it didn't sound mortal."

"Actually, I think I heard it."

She glanced at him in surprise. "Really? When?"

He looked a little forlorn. "The day Anthony was killed. Just for a second. It was pretty horrifying at the time. I can understand why you didn't think it came from a human."

"I think I also wanted to be saved from that place. And the Spirit didn't treat me like all the other men there. The Spirit treated me like I was important, like I was worth something. But the night that I disappeared from your house, that's when everything changed."

"What happened?"

"I woke up in *his* house." With a heavy heart, Christine told him of her initial captivity and her mind numbing fear in those first days.

"That twisted mother fu—"

"Please."

"Did he ever hurt you?"

"No," she murmured. "Even if we'd..." She gulped. "Gotten married. Um, he said he wouldn't ask anything of me that I didn't want. It was like he only wanted me there. With him."

"Yeah. I'm sure this guy just wanted to hold your hand."

"Raoul."

"Sorry. I'm so angry right now. If I would have known this, I would have brought the army to Cameron's door. I mean it. I still might."

Hoping to calm Raoul down a little bit, she talked about how Erik had educated her, adding, "I'm not sure if I would have gotten away from Cameron if not for that. I think that's why being with Erik seemed liberating in certain ways."

"That is weird. Is he a religious fundamentalist?"

"No. Not at all."

"What about Cameron? Is that an act, too?"

"I think Cameron believes what he says," she said after a moment. "He really thinks this is what God wants."

"So Erik is helping because why? Power? Money?"

"That's a good question. I don't know. Except…" She hesitated, not sure if she wanted to share this part.

"What?"

It was too late to go back now. "Erik wears a mask. I wasn't sure why at first. Just for a disguise, I thought." She swallowed. "But his face is, well, it looks like a skeleton face. It looks like someone sewed pieces of paper on a skull. He doesn't even have a nose."

"*Really?*"

"Yes. I'd never seen anything like it."

"That's horrifying. But what does it have to do with him helping Cameron?"

The answer taunted her from the edge of her mind, but she couldn't quite grasp it. "I don't know." Suddenly something hurt so badly in her chest that Christine could say nothing except, "I think I've said all I can for now. I'm tired. But now you know why I don't feel safe. It's not Cameron. It's him. It's Erik."

"You really think he'll try to find you?" Raoul's face was a little white. "We went so far. Maybe he'll just, you know, forget."

"Maybe. Or maybe he'll tear up the whole world."

Chapter 27

The nanny was ill with some sort of virus, and so Cameron had been watching over Abby for the past couple of days. She had a plastic child's kitchen to play in, and that kept her busy and out of trouble. That night, she slept in a bedroom down the hall from his, clutching onto a stuffed brown bear. He'd been trying to rid her of the plush toy, thinking it juvenile, but didn't feel like dealing with her tears.

Cameron had settled into his bed, head comfortably situated on the goose feather pillow, and tried to forget the concern that had plagued him that day. His decision had been a dangerous one, even if it had been the right call. Still, he knew there would be damage control.

He was waiting for it.

Suddenly, he felt a chill in the air. Before he could dwell on it, the sound of pattering footsteps approached his room. "Poppy!"

He sat up. "What is it, Abby?" His first thought was that she might be sick. Despite her healthy appearance, she was not always well. Cameron blamed her origins, a so-called designer child. God created imperfections in the human body that kept it alive. Man would pay for destroying them.

"Poppy, there's a ghost!"

He laughed and shook his head. "You silly girl. There's no ghosts. Did you say your prayers?"

"Yes."

"Then that will keep away all the demons."

"But I did say them, and there's still a ghost!"

"There aren't ghosts. Let's go back to bed." He led her to her room and pulled back the covers.

Face still scrunched up with worry, she slowly climbed inside them. "I'm scared…"

"There's no need to be. The Lord will keep all the bad things away because you're a very good girl." She nodded but didn't appear convinced. "Goodnight, Abby."

"Goodnight, Poppy."

He frowned as he returned to his room and hoped no one was spreading unholy ghost stories. He'd have to give a speech regarding pure conversations, especially around young minds. Cameron settled back into his bed. He closed his eyes.

"Eeeaaaaah!"

The child's scream ripped through the hallways. Cameron jumped out of bed, tripping as the sheets wrapped around his legs. He reached her closed door; the screaming stopped.

But then he heard singing. A lullaby in a foreign language. Maybe French? The sound was so beautiful that Cameron felt the melody creeping into his mind, making him want to fall asleep right there in the hallway. He shook his head to clear the cobwebs. With a nervous swallow, he threw open the door.

The sight nearly gave him a heart attack.

"Erik, what the *hell* are you doing with my granddaughter?" He turned on the nearest light, but the room was still dim. Yellow eyes glowed.

Erik stared at him but continued to sing, cradling her unconscious form, one arm supporting her back while her legs dangled over the other bony limb.

"Give me Abby," Cameron whispered.

The singing didn't stop.

"Give me Abby!"

The singing ceased.

A pause.

A whisper. "What have you done, Mr. Lourdes?"

Cameron felt a shiver overtake his entire body. A cold perspiration formed on his brow. Still, he managed to threaten, "Give me my granddaughter. Or I will call every single guard into this room. How'd you even get in here?" Anticipating something like this, Cameron had hired extra men to watch over them. Apparently, that hadn't worked. He should have guarded Abby more carefully. "I'll scream for help."

Erik's head tilted to the left side. "That would be a senseless way to destroy your security team. The cleanup would be horrendous."

"You couldn't take them all on!"

"I think I could. In fact, do call them here. I think I might *enjoy* it, Mr. Lourdes. One needs a thrill every now and then."

Threats were getting him nowhere. Panicking inside, Cameron softened his voice and tried reason. "Erik, give me my granddaughter. What in the world are you doing with her?"

Erik shrugged. "I was merely putting her back to sleep. She said she saw a ghost; you did not believe her. You really should have. I see ghosts all the time." He looked down at the child and brushed her hair from her face. "What have you done, Cameron?"

"Give me her, and we will talk. Do you understand me? Give me Abby. Please! She hasn't done anything!" Erik finally held out the little girl. Cameron grabbed her into his arms, relaxing as he saw that she was breathing and uninjured, only in a deep sleep probably brought about by Erik's unholy voice. Or she had fainted from fright. "I am going to put Abby back to bed. And then we will speak outside. Do you understand?"

Daring to turn his back on the masked shadow, Cameron placed Abby into bed and pulled the covers over her, checking once more to make sure her breathing was steady. "Now we will leave *this* room and talk." To his relief, Erik followed him into the empty hall.

Cameron kept his voice steady. "I did what was for the best. The girl came to me and pleaded to leave. She cried and wept, begging for the boy. So I did what was best that night. For me. For her. And God. And my followers. And for you! She was a wicked girl. I made her promise not to give away our secrets. And then I let her go."

Erik took a step toward him. "You—"

"She flew into that boy's arms faster than one of your butterflies. She knew too much! Because of you! You told her too much, educated her! She was dangerous! I spared her life, but she is gone."

Erik's hands curled. Cameron prepared to call for security. "I hate you," Erik whispered. "I will rip you—"

Cameron pointed his index finger directly at his chest. "I warned you many times that she was going to cause problems. Let this be a lesson. I'll find someone else for you. A well-behaved and obedient girl. A Godly girl. It will be easy. But that little—but Christine cannot come back." The yellow eyes were hot with rage. "Women can't be trusted. They're manipulative creatures, always ready to betray you when something better comes along. That's why my way is best. That's why they don't need to know everything."

Erik whirled around with a growl, burying his face into his gloved hands. "He's a spoiled little boy! He's a child! He's a nothing! Why would she want him? You're lying! She can't want him! Not when I can give her so much more! I can give her everything!"

"You can watch the video for yourself. Watch her run toward him."

"You're lying! You're lying!" Erik screamed and moaned. "You're lying, and I will kill you for it!"

"Let her go. Direct your efforts back to where they belong. Use your new knowledge and your anger to build my new world. We're so very close. I can feel it in my blood. All you've done for me. You'll forget her. God will help you forget her."

"If I find out you're lying, I'll rip your head off!"

"Watch the tape of her leaving. Watch her face when she sees the Chandler boy."

With a last snarl, Erik left him standing there. Cameron knew that Erik would watch the tape. Erik would tear it apart, examining it for any manipulation. But the video of her leaving was real.

Sensing her growing disobedience, Cameron had created a situation where Christine would be alone. And then taken advantage of that situation. He'd forced her into a room where no one could overhear them. She'd told him the truth. She'd wanted to leave.

So, really, Cameron's decision had been entirely ethical. It had been a Godly decision, one he didn't regret.

Erik disappeared for a while, which greatly disturbed Cameron.

But then Erik returned. And he was ready to go back to work, which greatly pleased Cameron.

* * *

Surviving the first day, her wedding day, had felt like a miracle.

As the next weeks passed, Christine wondered if she had a guardian angel. Maybe her father, looking down from heaven, realized the fate he had handed his daughter and was now helping her escape.

The days blended together. No one ever sprang out of the shadows to grab her. No yellow eyes glowed from the darkness. She walked freely through the streets, blonde hair waving wildly in the late summer breeze. She rode the double-decker buses and the cabs. She went with Raoul's cousin to get fish and chips at a pub. They took her to a few museums and music venues. She could be okay here.

"How is Phillip?" Christine asked one day at lunch as she picked apart a creamy lobster roll. She was still getting used to the food there. Jeans, sneakers, and t-shirts with silly designs had become her uniform as she attempted to take on a more casual and relaxed appearance. Today, her yellow shirt featured a smiling orange sun.

"Good," replied Raoul. His forehead was wrinkled, and he was looking to the side.

"Are you sure? Is anything wrong?"

"No." He glanced at her and smiled. "Everything is good. We had a three minute conversation, and then the static got really bad. We could hardly hear each other. So we hung up."

"That's weird."

"Probably just bad service down there. No big deal. I'll call him again in a few days." He quickly changed the subject. "I found out that my cousin may be able to help me get a job. It'll be kind of clerical, but I can work my way up."

"That's wonderful! So we're really going to make this place home?"

"Is that okay?"

"Yeah."

They had gotten to know each other better in those weeks, chatting a little bit about their former lives. Raoul had grown up normally, continuing to go through the public school system. He'd done well academically and been on the track and tennis team. The death of his father had of course shaken him up. After high school, he'd attended a private college in the northeast for two years until it closed its doors because of financial problems and nearby violence. Phillip had offered to send him to a foreign school, but Raoul declined.

"It wasn't a big deal," he said to her with a shrug as he took a bite of cheese pizza. "I still wasn't sure what I wanted to do. I come from a long line of politicians and lawyers, but I never quite fit in there. I always thought owning a restaurant would be cool. But the economy is such a mess that I wouldn't have been able to start a business in the states anyway."

"I didn't get to dream of being anything," she murmured. "I was lucky to not be married off sooner."

"What about now?" Raoul asked. "You're a great singer."

She shifted, all thoughts of music leading to one place. "I may do that again." *Or maybe she would never, ever sing again. Her voice had been nothing but trouble.* "But I really think I'd like to be a teacher someday. Maybe for nine or ten year olds."

Raoul nodded enthusiastically. "Yeah? I always thought coaching kids would be fun. You should go for it."

While they finished their dinner, she asked, "Raoul, why do you think things got so bad back home?"

"I don't really know. Countries rise and fall all the time, I guess."

"Yeah."

"Hey, Chris. Can I ask you something? About what happened to you?"

"Go ahead." Christine wasn't exactly ready to talk about it again, but, without Raoul, she wouldn't have escaped at all.

"So after you were kidnapped, you had to have been let out again, right? I saw you that one night, and I know that you sang for some assemblies. And then that advertisement for Cameron."

"You saw that stupid thing?"

"Yeah. I heard it."

Christine grimaced. "Yes, Erik trusted me enough to let me go out eventually. I would sing for Cameron's ceremonies, and then they wanted me to help him recruit. I don't know why," she muttered. "I definitely wasn't enthusiastic about it."

"Probably because you softened their image."

She grunted. "I told Erik I hated doing those things, and he did get me out of it. I said I would still sing. And I only agreed to do that because, one night, Erik showed me this terrible part of the city. He said that he and Cameron were helping to save people. And these poor people definitely looked like they needed to be saved. They were starving and sick. I even saw a dead child."

"Yeah," Raoul murmured. "I know what you're talking about. So what made you finally want to leave? The arranged marriage?"

"That and Anthony," she admitted. "That was the final straw."

"How'd you know I was telling the truth?"

"I just knew that you hadn't gone there to kill anyone. I knew it was a lie. And Cameron confirmed it. I think he wanted to scare me away from there."

"Did you ever find out about the butterflies?"

"No. But I did hear...it's hard to describe, like lots of voices at once. Coming from down below Erik's home. Maybe they spy on people?"

"I knew they had to be something like that!" Raoul sat up straight, his expression half-victorious and half-angry. "Where did Erik live anyway?"

She lowered her gaze. "Why are you asking me that?"

"Because it'd help."

"You want to tell someone where he is, don't you? That's why you want to know."

"It could be our chance to stop them," Raoul replied, trying to get her to look into his eyes again. "I could tell Phil, and he could lead the authorities right there."

"You can't lead *anyone* there. They'd get killed!"

"Not if we send enough people!"

"It'd make it obvious that I'm with you if you told Phillip over the phone. What if someone heard?"

"We'd be careful. I'd find a way to…" He rubbed the back of his head. "Christine, you have information we couldn't get from anywhere else." Suddenly, Raoul's mouth dropped open, and he appeared wounded. "You still feel some sort of loyalty to him. You're protecting him. That's it, isn't it?"

Her face flushed. "It's not loyalty! I'm finally free. Don't you understand? I want to forget all of it. And every time we involve ourselves, we're in danger again."

"I'm trying to put a stop to some really terrible stuff. All those people being manipulated and lied to! What happened to you is unforgivable! We won't go back. But at least Phillip should know where this psycho is hiding." She frowned at him. "Fine. I get it," he muttered.

They didn't speak to each other for several hours. It was their first real fight since the start of their journey.

Not wanting to feel like she was losing the only person she had left in the world, Christine approached him that afternoon while he was watching the news. "Raoul," she softly began. "You can tell your brother about the propaganda. But the location of Erik…so much could go wrong."

She couldn't give him that. All of the consequences would be on her shoulders.

He sighed. "You're right that it'd be dangerous to bring attention to ourselves here. And we can't do much anyway. Creepy butterflies? One mysterious man is the Spirit? They'll think we're crazy. They didn't even believe me about Anthony. It's useless."

"But *we're* free," she said, sitting down beside him. "I still can't believe we made it."

He took her hand and squeezed it. "Me neither. You're right. Screw it!"

They had both been forced to grow up too fast in some ways, Christine supposed. And so, for a while, they were like two teenagers. They had dinner at a fancy Italian restaurant and then went to an ice cream parlor. Christine chose chocolate, and Raoul bought apricot. He took her to a silly movie, and she laughed until tears formed in her eyes. And then she did cry for a couple of moments in the dark theater, overwhelmed by all the sudden changes in her life. They went into a novelty shop, and she tried on a funny straw hat with three large white feathers on the top. Despite her protests, Raoul bought it for her, saying, "We should get something to remember this evening."

They sat on a plastic bench beside a fountain with a mermaid statue on top. No one else was around. As the air became colder, they leaned into each other for warmth. They kissed. It quickly deepened, and the rest of the world blessedly faded away as she closed her eyes.

"Are you okay?" he asked, pulling back so that his face was inches from hers. His hands cupped the sides of her head. "I know you've been through hell and back. Not trying to rush you into anything."

She opened her lids, feeling her face warm. "Yeah. I'm great. I just don't have a lot of experience…"

"Oh. You're absolutely fantastic, Christine." He leaned in again, soon moving to her cheek and ear. They kissed until they were breathless.

When they both drew back, she looked down shyly. "So."

"Heh. Um…"

They sat there several minutes until she asked, "Have you had a lot of girlfriends?"

"Heh." Raoul seemed kind of uncomfortable. "I had two that were about as serious as you get for college and high school. One just didn't work out. We were only sixteen. The other left college when things started getting bad. But I'm not sure we would have stayed together. It'd take her four hours to get ready for a date." Christine giggled at this. "She wanted me to come with her to Australia. But I thought things would get better, so I stayed with my mom and brother." He shrugged. "So that's my exciting love life."

"It was better than mine. Dating was forbidden. You had a courtship with the person you were supposed to marry. Sometimes they didn't work out, but the families were shunned for months if that happened. So it usually *had* to work out."

"Is that what you had with…?"

Christine hesitated. "No. That was different. More like a bargain."

"What do you mean?"

"Nothing. It doesn't matter now."

He shuffled his feet and cleared his throat. "Well, Chris. We could just date. It doesn't mean marriage or any weird promises. If it works out, that would be awesome. If it doesn't, we'll still be friends who survived this whole mess together. We can help each other out here."

She smiled at the simplicity of it. "That sounds good. Date. I've never done that before." His eyes lit up, and he kissed her lips again, the fountain bubbling behind them.

She wrapped her arms around the neck of her boyfriend. Yes, she had a boyfriend now. And his blue eyes were so warm and full of hope. And they were safe.

Even in these wonderful moments, she couldn't stop her mind from drifting backwards, from feeling *his* rage as though he could see this entire scene. *You can't control me anymore. I'm done!* After that evening, she took off the ring and put it in a little cardboard box. She shoved it in the back of a drawer that held her socks and underwear. The spot where the ring had once been burned as though to frantically alert her that something was missing.

She should hate him for all he had done.

Yet she couldn't. And maybe that was more frustrating than anything. Erik had made her feel more things than she ever thought possible across the entire spectrum of human emotion, but hatred wasn't one of them. Raoul had been right; she was still protecting him on some level.

All she could do regarding Erik was *hurt* and cry and wonder what had made him like that.

Chapter 28

Raoul was a little alarmed at how difficult it had become to reach his family. Along with the phone calls, he'd now sent three unanswered e-mails. Still, he didn't want to upset Christine any more than necessary. She was already glancing over her shoulder every five seconds.

He tried again. The phone rang three times, and then Raoul heard the faded voice of his older brother. "Phil?" he asked.

"Raoul? Is that you? I can barely hear you?" The static grew even louder.

"Yeah. It's me. I just—" The line went dead, and he was left with a cold dial tone.

Frustrated, Raoul rubbed his temples. Had the infrastructure really deteriorated so much that he couldn't even make a stupid phone call? He didn't try again.

At least we're safe here. He contented himself with warm thoughts of his new girlfriend. He'd loved her for so long, and it was fantastic to have his feelings almost reciprocated. He hoped that he could be what she needed right now and nothing like the nightmare she'd escaped from. Christine was still distant, staring into space with her brow furrowed or not responding when Raoul spoke to her, but that was to be expected after everything she'd been through. In time, maybe Raoul would suggest counseling.

For a while, they ignored the news from back home. When Michael informed him of a riot or a bombing, Raoul let the information bounce off of him. There was nothing they could do. Until a day came when it was impossible to disregard their former home.

For lunch, he and Christine went into a sandwich shop with several televisions mounted on the wall, the sort of place where sporting events were often broadcasted. It must have been a slow day in sports because the news was on. Ignoring the TV altogether, Raoul and Christine were sitting next to each other in a booth, having an enthusiastic conversation about travel. "I'd love to go to Japan," he said. "I hear you can't believe the technology they have now. Robots that do everything, even prescribe medicine. Probably why they have one of the top economies."

"That would be neat. But I'm still dying to see all of Europe."

"We should take some tours then!"

"Yeah. The old castles and churches. I've read so much about it, and—"

Suddenly, a breaking news report flashed onto the nearest television screen. They both glanced up at the sound of the grim voice.

Raoul tried to ignore it again. "Yeah, it sounds really—"

"Hold on!" She shushed him.

A grey-haired anchorman with glasses spoke urgently into the camera. "More bad news out of the U.S. last night. Two explosions rocked major cities, one near Atlanta and one in Dallas, causing severe damage to financial districts. No injuries have been reported so far, but authorities say a lot of data may have been lost. Authorities are again focusing on Citizens Against Classism, or CAC, although so far there have been no claims of responsibility. Let's go to Ryan for more information."

A younger man flashed onto the screen, his expression also gloomy. "Right now, we're only beginning to get details. Our reporters down there have to exercise extreme caution in these situations."

"Yes, we all remember the three journalists from Germany who were killed in last year's riots. Very tragic."

"Indeed. We know right now that there have been explosions in at least three buildings, and that authorities and emergency personnel are responding to the situation. The blasts happened at night, which may minimize casualties. Still, it had been quieter this summer, with many hoping that we were seeing an end to the violence. Unfortunately, that doesn't appear to be the case. If anything, the situation has worsened within the last week."

"Do we have a statement from the Prime Minister or other officials?"

"No. But we've been assured multiple times that England has secured itself against the rapid decline of the United States. If this continues, there will of course be ripple effects felt all across the world. There will be economic and security issues to resolve. But most developed countries have made sure that basic commerce, travel, safety, and general operations will continue even under a worst-case scenario. During the emergency talks held last October in London, world leaders were able to work through many of these important details."

"Thank you, Ryan. I'm going to bring up a map here to remind everyone where this all stands right now. All right. Larissa, you've been following this situation for several years. Go ahead and take us through this map."

A petite brunette woman in a black pantsuit came into view. "Thank you, James. Okay. Over here in this green-shaded area, you have the somewhat more stable northern and western areas of the U.S. The state and local governments have remained functional and continue daily operations. Unemployment is lower, and there has been less unrest and violence. If you're still in the country, this is where you'd want to be. The Northeast, which contains many of the bigger cities and financial districts, was doing adequately until about a year ago. But now they're having a lot of economic problems and a lot of growing discontent as people become more and more desperate for food and basic necessities. So far, the violence hasn't been quite as bad here, but, in another year, who knows how bad conditions might be? As we head downwards, toward what many are describing as an increasingly hardline culture—"

"Cameron Country," said James, urging her along.

"Yes," she replied with less enthusiasm. "The support for him in this purple area is very strong. It's not hard to understand why, given the terrible violence and poverty in these major cities. His men are still expected to do very well in the upcoming elections, and he may become governor of his state. Even in the northeast, his supporters could do much better than expected. We're still following the polls, although it's been very difficult to get a reliable sampling."

"And if Cameron Lourdes does gain an upper hand in the U.S. politically, what will the outcome be? If any?"

"There is still so much we don't know, James. How much influence will he really have? What happens to those down there who express dissent? Will the U.S. Constitution be upheld? Will the country divide itself? How will the military react? These questions have a lot of people very concerned."

James shook his head. "It's strange to think about the rise of Cameron Lourdes, isn't it? Ten years ago, he was completely unknown. A couple thousand members at most. Within the last few years, his support has multiplied exponentially."

"That's true," she agreed. "But, once again, it's really not so hard to see why. While most other countries climbed out of the severe recession that gripped the world during the 2020's, the United States continued to decline. Economics and historians will continue to puzzle over…"

"So this is what it looks like from the *real* outside," Christine whispered, eyes still glued to the television.

"Yeah. Strange, isn't it?" Raoul murmured.

They soon left the restaurant, but Raoul noticed that her eyes remained distant. He could feel the rigidness in her body whenever he hugged her. Christine remained that way over the next few days as Raoul frantically tried to contact his brother. The phone call was always the same, nothing but static and frustrating noise. All of this combined was making him extremely nervous, as though something were creeping up behind him, readying itself to strike.

Christine started to watch the news for long periods of time, staring at the screen with wide eyes. "There's nothing we can do," Raoul told her, cautiously touching her back. "I know it's sad. But…"

"It started getting bad again five years ago," she whispered. "Right? *Right?*"

"Yeah. I guess so. Why?"

"That's when Cameron said the…Spirit had come."

"Oh. Huh."

She pointed. "Look at how things are the worst in the states that are closest to Cameron. And then it creeps outwards, spreading like a stain," she murmured. "Look at it. Look at how it's spread. Almost a perfect circle."

"Yeah. They explained that on the news. People are joining him because of all the problems down there."

"What if it's upside down?" she whispered.

"What? What are you saying?" She didn't answer. By late that afternoon, Raoul was ready to drag her away from the television. They needed to take a walk or something, escape the house and find some fresh air. As he approached her, he saw that both hands were now clutching the sides of her head.

A reporter was speaking about new riots; orange flames jumped out behind him. Christine was rocking back and forth.

"Christine, you have got to turn off the television!" Raoul snapped. "We can't do anything! It's making you crazy!"

She jumped up and faced him, her face crumpling. "He lied!" she gasped. "He lied! About *everything*! Why?! He lied! It was always him! It's all him!" She was convulsing, shaking and sobbing, barely able to breathe. "No, no, no. I can't believe it. I can't believe it!"

Afraid she was going to go into shock, Raoul embraced her, trying to quiet her. "Calm down, baby. He can't hurt you anymore. Everything's going to be okay."

But she continued to whisper, "How could you? *Erik, how could you?* Oh my God. Oh my God. *Oh my God!*" Her voice grew louder until it reached a shrill scream.

"What's happening? I don't understand!" He was glad that Michael and Brooke weren't home as they probably would have wanted to call an ambulance.

Christine muttered to herself with wide eyes. Raoul took her to his bedroom and held her the rest of the night, asking no more questions. Christine clung to him tightly, her fully-clothed body melding against his beneath the covers. Raoul murmured reassurances to her, wishing he knew what was going on in her head.

The stress of the day must have taken a toll on him. Raoul didn't feel or hear her leave the bed. When he awoke, Christine was sitting in a chair by the window. Her knees were pulled up to her chest, and her arms were wrapped around them.

"Christine?" he softly asked, sitting up. His jeans and long-sleeved shirt were wrinkled from sleep. "Are you okay?"

Without turning around, she spoke, her voice strained and broken. "I'll tell you everything. Even where *he* lives. And you…" She swallowed. "You have to tell Phillip. Maybe there's still time to save some of it."

"What's going on?"

"We'll be in so much trouble if anyone ever finds out. Maybe it's too late. And maybe nothing can be done now."

"What are you talking about?"

"It's all been planned. All of it. I see now. I can't believe it. But I know it has."

"What's been planned?" he desperately asked.

"All of it, Raoul. *All* of it." She looked at him. "And because I've left, it's going to be even worse."

***

The glint of madness had been replaced with the familiar coldness. Only if Cameron looked very closely could he see the subtle twitch or spasm in Erik's smooth movements that indicated all was not well with his prized mercenary.

Without a word, Erik walked into Cameron's office, pointed a small black device at the table, and pushed a button. A white light flashed, and then a digital three dimensional map of the United States popped up onto the smooth surface. He zoomed into the eastern half of the country. The background was yellow, but various locations were marked with stars of different colors. All stars were marked with dates.

"A change of plans, Cameron."

"What do you mean?" He slowly stood and glanced toward the doorway, making certain that one of his bodyguards was in earshot.

"We're going to do this quickly. We're going to do this my way. Because your way has been ineffective and, more importantly, very boring."

"Explain," Cameron whispered, wondering what he was getting into now. Still, his hands tingled with excitement. This was the focused Erik he had missed these last months. That stupid girl had destroyed Erik's concentration. Even the security systems and spying devices were performing more poorly, likely due to that little blonde distraction.

Erik pointed to two locations. His voice was calm; only the most astute listener might have noticed a tremble. "The beginning," he stated as though starting a bedtime story. "Smaller. Enough to destabilize and renew panic, now that you have made your political connections." A pause. "Now here and here. Much more significant. Afterwards, riots and looting are probable. The authorities will want more control, and martial law may begin in those cities. Your numbers will grow as people search for food and security. This will occur in several cycles." Another pause. "But all of that is merely a bit of *fun* before this climactic day in October. First, you see, this one…this little orange star…this one will obviously create very explosive chaos. You will then give a speech that night. A very welcoming and uplifting speech. In fact, I will write this speech because I do not want you to make any idiotic errors. And then—" He pointed to the final event, a blue star, with one bony index finger. The finger curled, as if the hand of the Grim Reaper were claiming the entire location.

"You cannot be serious," whispered Cameron, trailing his finger to the star as well. His skin changed colors.

"It will be perfect."

"But it's…"

"A false flag. There will be indisputable proof that it was the work of the federal government."

Cameron swallowed. "There will be very high casualties on that day, won't there? For my people. You know I like to avoid those."

"We will limit it to the highest needed for the reaction we desire. Certainly not enough to damage your numbers in the slightest. Even without my electronic manipulations, you will win every election in which you have a candidate."

"Marvelous."

"Where your support is strongest, the violence will soon calm. It will be a sort of conditioning process. Support Cameron Lourdes, and you will be safe. You will be fed and comfortable and happy. That is the message they will all receive."

"And the west?" Cameron's voice had a touch of eagerness. "The north?"

"We used few resources there for now. First, see if you can manage what I do give you, Cameron. See if you are as capable as you believe you are. Do you agree to it?" Erik widely gestured toward the map.

"Yes. It makes sense, reluctant as I am for that last part. It makes sense. And our hands will be clean?"

"We will look like the only bright shining beacon of hope in all the frenzied horror. My greatest triumph."

"It is God's triumph," Cameron admonished him. "We are merely God's soldiers. But yes. Only possible through your hard work." Cameron turned away, heart pounding from the information that Erik had just given him. *So close, Lord. We are so close to Your country. All will soon be right and just and good.* "Erik, thank you for this. It is truly amazing."

Erik clicked off the map. He started to turn around.

"How have you been faring?" Cameron dared to ask before he could leave. "Anything I can do for you? Do you want me to introduce you to a good girl? I have one in mind. Dianna—"

"I don't want her!" Erik snapped. "Keep out of my personal affairs, and I will keep out of yours. I will speak to you only concerning matters of business. Understand?"

"I just don't want you to be unhappy," said Cameron with a shrug. "After all you have done. Aren't you tired of thinking of that little witch?"

"I said to keep out of my affairs!" Within seconds, he was gone.

Erik seemed to be in control of himself again. Still, Cameron hoped he hadn't made a mistake in allowing Christine to live. He hoped Erik wouldn't go after her.

There was no one who could do what Erik did. He possessed qualities that Cameron didn't know could exist in a single man— intelligence in dozens of disciplines, speed, cunning...an almost supernatural ability to be everywhere at once.

That's why Cameron had hired him.

But Cameron always had that disturbing feeling that he was using the Devil to do the work of God. It made him uneasy, but he saw little way out of it at this point.

Still, the Spirit was the single individual who had the power to destroy everything that Cameron Lourdes had so desperately worked for.

Chapter 29

Erik and Cameron had not simply taken advantage of an awful situation, of a collapsing economy and a crumbling country.

They had *created* the terrible situation.

All of the madness and destruction in these last several years—it was them. As this revelation descended upon her, something inside Christine snapped. She could barely hear Raoul trying to calm her down as the cold wave of horror threatened her very sanity. Only sleep had somewhat dulled the panicked despair. A bitter resolve overtook her as she stared out the window in the morning. She liked the anger; it was better than the anguish, than the utter feeling of betrayal she felt at all Erik's lies.

Raoul didn't even believe her at first. She scooted to make room for him and rested her head on his firm shoulder. "I don't see how one man could be responsible for all of that. The complete collapse of almost half the nation? Seriously?"

"I've told you he's not an ordinary man."

"But–" He rubbed his forehead. "We're talking about a single man destroying an entire country." Maybe remembering a history lesson or two, he added, "I mean, it's not impossible. But…"

"It's the timing; this all started when he came. And the way that Erik knew bad things were going to happen in the fall. It's the way Erik spoke. As though he were on a mission or something. I would be queen. Oh my God." *All the lies about wanting to help people.*

Raoul slowly nodded after thinking it over for several minutes. "Cameron's been making people so terrified of the world that they'll join his stupid cult just to stay safe. It makes sense, now that I think about it. The random violence and craziness. It was the only way someone like him could get power."

They were both too shocked to speak, perhaps searching for some simple solution that didn't exist. They were barely old enough to vote in elections. How would they help to save an entire country? She felt so very small and insignificant.

"Is there a place to read more about this?" she asked. "Maybe about Cameron?"

"There's the Internet."

"Oh, yeah." She realized that, while Erik had provided her with more books than she'd ever imagined, he had denied her access to a computer with networking capabilities. Because she'd grown up without such things, Christine had never thought to ask. And maybe Erik never wanted her to discover certain information.

They got on Michael's laptop. Raoul searched for informative articles and then sat behind her as she browsed through them.

Cameron Lourdes, third and youngest child of Edward Lourdes. Edward Lourdes owned a group of successful financial service firms. His eldest child, Paul Lourdes, enjoyed investing in startup biotech companies and other organizations that were involved in cutting edge scientific research. While sailing in 2025, Paul was killed when he accidentally fell overboard. The middle child of Edward, Courtney Lourdes, is a surgeon who currently resides in Ireland with her family. She has been an outspoken critic of Cameron...When Edward died in 2026, the billion dollar inheritance was split in Cameron's favor after a legal battle over the terms of the will.

"I wonder if Paul's death was really an accident," Raoul muttered, looking over her shoulder. Christine grunted in agreement and continued to read.

Cameron married Alanna Williams in 2000, and they had one son, Matthew Lourdes. It is reported that, unlike his father and brother,

Cameron was unsuccessful in his business ventures. He was forced to declare bankruptcy in 2008. In 2014, Cameron reportedly had a vision during a trip to Jerusalem in which God spoke to him and told him to "give up all worldly goals and possessions and create the perfect holy society." This began the small fringe group who followed very stringent and antiquated rules…Cameron's wife died of breast cancer in 2018…Matthew later disagreed with his father's beliefs, and the two became estranged. Matthew married a successful lawyer and had one child, Abigail. He committed suicide after his daughter's birth for undisclosed reasons…His wife died soon after in a car accident.

Christine scrolled down. It was interesting and suspicious but not helpful. The end of the article was annoyingly vague.

Their membership increased somewhat during the 2020's as the entire world suffered through a severe financial recession. But it wasn't until the 2030's that membership exploded, coinciding with Cameron's inheritance as well as the unanticipated deterioration of the United States…Supernatural phenomena. Unproven. Mysterious disappearances. Also unproven.

She glanced through the other articles. At best, all they mentioned were rumors of disembodied voices or similar occurrences. "It's like I'm the only one who knows. And now you."

"Do we go to the press? The authorities here? Who do we tell? How do we stop it?"

"I don't even know if anyone would believe us," she murmured. "And we'd draw a lot of attention to ourselves."

"I've got to tell Phillip somehow. He has good connections. People might believe him, especially if you tell us…"

"Where Erik lives," she whispered even though no one was around. She tried to ignore the unbearable ache that surrounded her heart. *Did you think I'd never find out, Erik? Or did you think I wouldn't care?*

"Maybe I'll finally be able to reach Phil without static today."

She frowned. "I'm not sure if you should keep calling and e-mailing him. Something isn't right."

"Then what should I do?"

"I don't know."

He squeezed her hand. "We'll figure something out. I still can't believe this."

With a shaky breath, Christine revealed the location of Erik's hideaway, feeling sick to her stomach the entire time. Raoul unsteadily jotted down notes on a white paper pad they'd found in the room. "But don't let Phillip go down by himself," she finished. "He has to get help."

They stayed together that night for mutual comfort. He had one arm around her as she rested her head on his shoulder and placed one hand on his chest. "This is all so effed' up beyond anything."

"I know. I never dreamed it was this horrible. If I had—"

But Christine didn't even know the answer to that. If she'd known the extent of what was happening, what would she have done? Begged Erik? Screamed at him? Tried to hurt him? Or offered him anything he wanted if he just stopped this madness?

Lying in each other's arms, she doubted either of them slept that night. When she woke up, Raoul was gone. She looked around nervously, still afraid that they were being watched by hidden eyes in the shadows. Just as she climbed out of bed, Raoul entered, grinning.

"Guess what?" He reached out toward her.

"What?" she whispered, taking both his hands. Even positive excitement made her nervous.

"I finally reached Phillip. He's going to fly here in a couple of days. Then we can tell him everything in person!"

She gasped. "Will he make sure he's not followed?"

"I told him to be careful. He'll probably jump on a government flight at the last minute. Like we did. I know it's scary, but this is our best shot. He's the only one who might be able to do something. He has good connections."

"If it works, it would be the best thing ever." Goosebumps ran up and down her arms.

"We'll make it," he said, giving her a long kiss. "We'll get this figured out!"

She tried to believe him, blocking out all thoughts of betrayal. She wouldn't allow herself to think anymore. If Raoul could safely lead them out of this nightmare, then she would hold his hand the entire way. There was nothing else that could be done, no other path or light to guide her.

Despite Raoul's brave words, she could sense that he was a little anxious as they waited for Phillip. There were times when he still couldn't reach his brother. The morning before Phillip was supposed to arrive, Raoul called three times without success, trying to organize final plans. Finally, he got a hold of him. "Hey, Phil? Okay. Yeah, I can hear you. I've been trying to…What? What? Yeah. Okay. Sounds good." Raoul hung up. "He said he'll call back in ten minutes. He's in a meeting."

But Phillip didn't call back in ten minutes. After a half hour, Raoul tried again and couldn't get anyone. "Maybe you should just wait till he gets here," she said.

"I don't even know where his plane is landing."

"He'll call you when he arrives."

"I guess."

Raoul was gone for about four hours that day as he started his new job. A paper pusher, in his words. She stayed at home, looking online at nearby educational institutions and trying to figure out the equivalent of a U.S. high school diploma. It seemed kind of complicated. Equivalencies. Exams. It was impossible to concentrate now that she knew what was happening back home. She wanted so badly to feel normal, and now that was beyond reach. How could she ever forget?

When Raoul returned, they started making dinner plans for when Phillip arrived. Some sort of fish restaurant. He should have been landing at any time. Raoul's phone finally rang. "I told you he'd call," she said, nudging his shoulder with her arm.

Raoul answered with a smile. "Hey! How—?" His smile disappeared. "Who the hell is this?" Christine leaned into listen.

"I believe you have something of mine, Mr. Chandler." A pause. "And so I have acquired something of yours."

The color drained from her face and the air left her lungs. Her stomach dropped as though the floor had fallen out from underneath her feet. Somehow, her hand found Raoul's arm, and she clutched it, untrimmed fingernails digging into his skin. "No." The silent word escaped her lips.

"Who the hell is this?" Raoul asked, the volume of his voice rising. "Where's Phillip?"

"It will be somewhat of a loss on my end if you do not make the exchange," Erik continued calmly. "You are obviously quite content with my sweet bride. But a Senate candidate is something that I have little use for."

"You—"

"Return her to me, and your brother will be fine. Otherwise, he will not be, and we will try this game again with someone whom you hopefully value a bit more. Your mother, maybe?"

"You evil son of a bitch! Leave my family alone! I'll fucking kill you! I'll— You...you..." Raoul sputtered as his face turned red, features twisted more by terror than anger. "I'll kill you!"

Christine grabbed the phone from Raoul's hand before he made things even worse. "Erik!" she yelled into the receiver, her voice catching. If they'd been face to masked face, Christine doubted that she could have been as brave as she was in that moment. "Stop this! I'll come back! Leave Phillip alone! You can't do this!"

A long, uncomfortable pause followed. "My beauty. It is *so* good to hear your voice again. I have missed it so dearly. I really have. I have missed you very much." His tone was softer and gentler, almost hypnotic. "And you missed your wedding, didn't you? Ah. These last weeks have been unpleasant for your poor Erik. All because of that wretched boy."

"It was my choice to go! Because of what you've done! Everything you've done, Erik! How could you? How could you?! You—" She was about to launch into a long and angry tirade, but now wasn't the time for that. Raoul's brother was in mortal danger. She attempted to regain her composure. "Leave Phillip alone. If you want to hurt someone, hurt me!"

"Why would I ever harm you?" He sounded genuinely horrified. "I *love* and adore you. These are his sins, and you merely became caught up in his child's games. Yes, this is a transaction between Mr. Chandler and myself. So let him decide, my love. Say twenty-four hours to consider it? That is fair, I think. More fair than he has been to me."

Tears ran down her cheeks. "Why are you doing this?! I told you it was my decision! Erik, stop this. Stop all of it…"

"I miss you, my beauty. I hope that I will see you very soon. He has twenty-four hours to inform me of his decision."

The line went dead.

"No," she whispered. The phone dropped from her hand with a clatter. "Oh no. No, no, no."

Raoul's face was buried in his hands, the tips of his fingers rubbing his forehead. "I'll kill him," he muttered.

"This is all my fault. We should have taken your family with us. I was so stupid not to see that. So stupid!"

"You're not," he weakly replied, leaning against the wall for support. "You know that." Raoul picked up the phone again, dialing the numbers with a shaking finger. Christine leaned into listen again. It rang twice, and then a woman's voice answered.

"Hi, Mom," Raoul began, pain in his voice. "It's me."

"Raoul?! Are you okay?"

"I'm fine. Don't worry." He hesitantly asked, "How about you?"

"I'm okay, but I'm not sure what to do. It's getting so scary here again."

"Is there any way for you to get out of the country?" Raoul asked.

"I might be able to find a flight, but I'm afraid to leave our neighborhood. It's hard to know what to do."

"That's why I had Phillip bring Meg and Caroline there. So you'd have some company. Are they still there?"

"Yeah. They're very nice. Cari is a little strange sometimes."

He let out a broken laugh. "I know, Mom. She is. Hey, do you remember what Phillip keeps in the bottom left drawer of his office desk there?"

"Yes," she whispered. "But I can't use a gun. I haven't tried since Ethan took me to a range when we started dating. I don't remember very much."

"Get it out anyway. If anyone tries to break in there, you might have to use it. Understand? You have to protect yourselves. Then, I want you all to pack your things and start calling some of Phil's and Dad's friends. You know, all the well-connected people. Tell them you're scared. The second someone offers to get you out, take it. Okay?"

"What are you going to do?"

"Don't worry about that right now. I'll meet you somewhere later."

"I'm so scared. I wish you or Phillip or…your father were here."

"I know, but it'll be okay. Phil and I will be okay. I have to go now, all right? Protect yourself."

"I love you, Raoul. Please stay safe. And let me know if you hear from Phillip."

"I will. I'll call you again when I can." He thickly swallowed. "I love you, too, Mom."

Chapter 30

He placed the phone down with a heavy sigh, his shoulders slumping. Christine rested a hand on his arm and gently squeezed it. Her heart ached as she felt the burden of responsibility for all of Judy's pain. Raoul's entire family was in danger because of her. They were silent for several minutes, both staring off into space. She then said, "We have to go back. Or I do."

"We can't." Raoul looked nauseated.

"You know we have to. Your family, Raoul! I'm not letting them die because of me!"

"I can't just deliver you into that monster's hands. No. I won't!" He pounded a fist against the plaster of the wall, sending white particles to the floor.

"What about your brother?"

"I'll figure something else out. Anything. I'm not taking you back there!"

She tried to keep her voice steady, despite the panic welling up inside her chest. One of them had to be reasonable. "What you need to do is get Phillip back by any means. You should tell him everything that I told you. You two can try to stop all this!" Christine reached for the phone. "I'm calling *him* now to say we're coming."

He grabbed her hand to stop her. "Please, Chris. The bastard gave us twenty-four hours, right? Let's try to think of something."

Her arm dropped back down to her side. Erik had won even without following them. Christine couldn't dwell on where she might be in one or two days, what her final fate might be. All that mattered was making sure Raoul and his family were safe.

But you know now. At least you know everything. Yes, at least she wouldn't be a naïve child when it came to the truth. And she'd also learned about how romance could be. Laughter and teasing smiles and soft touches and stolen kisses. Whatever happened, Christine would keep the memories close to her heart. Maybe it wasn't all for nothing.

Christine placed her hand against his cheek and guided his face so that he was looking into her eyes. "Raoul."

"I wanted to help you escape so badly," he said, meeting her gaze.

She smiled sadly at him. "We have to go back and make things right." He frowned and said nothing, glancing at the floor again. Leaning forward, she kissed him on the corner of his mouth. "Whatever happens, I'll be okay."

Placing his hand behind her head, Raoul pulled her forward and pressed his lips directly against hers. Reclining on the soft bed, they continued to kiss, long and slow at some points and frantic and desperate at others. She could feel the warm skin of his back beneath his shirt and his rapidly beating pulse. His hands raked through her tangled hair. And then he moved so that he was atop her, his lips trailing over her cheek, throat, and neck. His hands skimmed against her chest.

Finally, he drew back and stared down at her, and she was barely able to see his face in the dim light. Christine hesitated as her breath caught in her throat. She gently pressed against his chest to put him on his back and lay atop him once more, her head on his shoulder. Her hand rested on his cheek, and she stroked it with her fingertips. She whispered, "I want my first to be when there's hope and happiness to look forward to in the morning. Not all this fear and sadness; it's too painful. It's too fast and desperate. I don't want that memory."

"Me neither," he murmured. He tucked a blonde strand behind her ear and continued to run his fingers through her hair.

Christine wondered if, after he fell asleep, she should sneak out and return to the United States by herself. She could call Erik and tell him she was coming back alone—but only if Phillip were released to his family. Surely, Erik would arrange all transportation. And Raoul would be out of danger.

She pretended to only be rolling off of Raoul and to the other side of the bed. He murmured her name. When he seemed to be soundly asleep again, Christine stood up and found her suitcase. She crept into her room and began throwing in the few items she'd accumulated, clothing and toiletries. She grabbed the hat that Raoul had bought her.

She hesitated in the doorway. She should leave him a note, telling him to stay where it was safe until Phillip was released, to not follow her. Finding a black pen and white pad on the desk, she began to write. A hand touched her shoulder, and she turned to see Raoul staring at her with confusion. Apparently, she wasn't very good at being quiet. "What are you doing?"

"I…" She swallowed. "I think I should go back alone."

"No," he protested. "You can't do that."

"I don't want to put you in danger." She bit her lip to keep from crying again. "It might be safer this way."

"I'm at least coming back to the country with you. Okay? You don't have to take this on all alone."

"But—"

"Let me go as far as I can with you. Please."

Pressing her lips together, she nodded. "Okay. But we have to go back."

"I know."

She allowed him to lead her back to the bed, maybe knowing deep down inside that it wasn't the best decision. Christine supposed she could have been cruel, told him she didn't want him around any longer and wished to break up their relationship. But Raoul wouldn't have believed her at that point anyway. He was determined that they be doomed together, it seemed, holding her against his chest the rest of the night. Neither of them really slept.

She sat up in the early morning hours, before there was light in the sky, unready to embrace what the day held. "It's time to make the call," she said. "I don't want to wait anymore."

"All right," he reluctantly muttered. Raoul took out his cell phone and stared down as though it might bite off his hand.

"Do you want me to c-call?" She fumbled over her words. "Maybe he'll be more patient with me."

"I'll make it."

"Okay. But just be direct," she pled. "Don't make him angrier. We have to make sure your family is safe."

"I know." He dialed his brother's number, grimly staring forward as he held the phone to his ear. Christine leaned in to listen.

"Good morning, Mr. Chandler." Erik answered after two rings. There was a clear note of victory in his voice. "Have you considered the terms of the transaction?"

"Yes." Raoul spit out the poisoned word.

"And?"

"We're coming back. So don't touch my brother. Got it?"

"A wise decision, boy. Very wise. You will go far in this intricate world." The sarcasm in the statement was painfully evident. "Now listen carefully to my instructions. I am sending the details of your flight. All is paid for and arranged. I have made this very convenient for you, Mr. Chandler. Nothing in your pathetic little life has ever been more straightforward. After your flight arrives, you will take a cab to your next destination. That has also been arranged; you needn't give the driver any information. And then a black car will deliver you from there. Am I clear? Any attempt to diverge from these instructions will not be good for anyone's health, so I suggest you follow them closely."

She clenched her jaw and spoke. "Just me, Erik. *I'll* take the black car. And then you have to let Phillip go." Raoul shot her a distressed glance.

"The black car is only for you." Once again, his voice softened. "It will ensure you a comfortable drive to your home."

"And Raoul will be safe?" she pressed.

"All will go as arranged."

"Erik, you're not answering my question. If I come back, tell me that Raoul and Phillip will be safe!"

"Be calm, my love. Despite the boy's treacherous actions these last weeks, they will live. Once you are here, all will be as it should be again. We are agreed?"

"Yes," she whispered.

"Excellent. I will see you very soon, Christine."

"Go to hell!" Raoul hung up and flung the phone to the side where it bounced once on the mattress. She was too shaken to reprimand him. The inevitable path continued to unwind, and there was no turning back now.

True to his word, Erik electronically sent Raoul the necessary information to get them there as fast as possible. With a bitter expression, Raoul clicked through it. "Is it all there?" she asked.

"Yes." She didn't take offense at his clipped answer, unable to imagine how Raoul must be feeling right now.

They said little to each other as they headed for their flight late that morning, unable to admit that this was their final defeat. Still, they held hands throughout the journey, giving each other a reassuring squeeze. Very few people were on the plane to the United States. Who would want to go back to that madness? "You guys trying to get relatives out, too?" asked one older man seated behind them.

"Something like that," Raoul muttered. He stared forward, jaw clenched and eyes narrowed.

The man continued speaking. "I've got my brother and niece down there. Hoping to get everyone into Canada. The paperwork has been a nightmare but better that than to hide there illegally, right? Never thought I'd see the day when it all fell apart." He tsked three times.

Her fear worsened as her stomach turned, but she tried not to show her fright on the outside. If Raoul knew she was terrified, he'd be even more hesitant to save his brother. Christine took several deep breaths. *Find hope. Find something to hold onto or you will lose your mind.*

Music. Yes, the music was always beautiful. There was nothing comparable to Erik's singing or the piano; she had often become lost in the notes. She remembered contentedly sitting on the sofa and knitting as he played. And reading at the kitchen table as he cooked her breakfast. And the walks. And the chats about everything from world history to the origin of languages to biology to every other possible topic as they'd strolled along holding hands. Everything he said was new and fascinating. Her kind words to him, that she'd forced herself to forget until now, had not been empty lies.

But the horrible problem was that, as Erik taught her and met most of her requests, he was also making other people's lives utterly miserable. That was the true horror. He placed her upon the highest golden pedestal, showering her with gifts and affection, while he simultaneously stomped on the rest of the world. With all his magnificent genius, which in the hands of another might have brought such good to humanity, Erik chose to bring an entire country to its knees. He could kill without hesitation, devastate an entire family. And she could never, ever forget these things now. They were forever burned into her memory.

Was there any possibility of influencing Erik once she returned? Did she have any chance if she begged him to stop this madness? Christine closed her eyes, overwhelmed by the thought of confronting him about all his terrible crimes. Because, if Erik didn't listen to her, then she would have to hope that Raoul and Phillip figured out a way to stop the destruction of the country. And that would result in even more violence and death.

She must have fallen asleep. When she opened her lids, she realized with dread that they were almost there. The plane landed, and they grabbed their bags and walked out with the few other people. The airport was half empty; many of the shops and restaurants that had once been there were now dark. "I'll take the taxi with you," he muttered as they headed in the direction of the escalator for ground transportation. It wasn't functional; they would have to walk down.

"But not the black car."

"We'll see."

She turned to him and stopped walking. "No, Raoul. You have to let me go by myself at that point. I'll be fine."

He stared at her with an intensity that made her squirm. "Will you? Will you be fine, Christine? What will happen to you if you go back there? Seriously?"

"It doesn't matt—"

"Yes, it does! What will happen to you?"

"I'll just be stuck in a basement house for a while. That's all." Her voice again caught in her throat, and it didn't come out very reassuring.

"Will you be forced into marriage?"

"I don't know." He could likely hear the answer in her tone. Grabbing her hand, Raoul led her to the escalator, and they walked down it to the next level. Instead of heading toward the area for taxis and buses, though, he strode quickly in the opposite direction, pulling her behind him. "What are you doing?" she asked in a hushed voice.

"I'm not doing it."

"Raoul—"

"*I'm not fucking doing it!*" He looked angrier than she'd ever seen him. "Phillip wouldn't want it. Him being used as a pawn to turn you over to some evil—"

"Raoul, calm down." She stopped walking and jerked him backwards. "Your brother! We have to think about this."

"I have thought about it. I thought about it the entire flight. And I'm not doing it."

***

The thoughts had haunted him throughout the plane ride. And then Christine had just unintentionally given him the final answer. The decision was made, and there was no going back.

Forced marriage.

What exactly did that mean for her?

No. No way in hell.

The hate he would feel toward himself for delivering her, his childhood friend and the girl he loved, into that sort of horror would be just as bad as the guilt he'd feel if his brother died. There was no good option now. And so he took her hand and marched forward. Raoul would still try to save his brother. He would try with all his being and with Christine beside him.

"You're insane!" she snapped at him, eyes darting back and forth. Still, he heard a note of confused gratitude intermingled with the anger, which further cemented his decision. He was tired of her attempting to put on a brave face when it was so easy to tell that she was crumbling inside. Someone had to save her. "Phillip will die. Don't you understand? He'll die! Just like Anthony!"

"I'm going to try to stop it," he replied. "But Phil wouldn't want me to give into those goddamned terrorists. I know it. So we are going to try to save him. And no matter what happens, this was the right thing to do. Okay? I know it is."

"You're so stupid," she said in a choked voice. "You're going to get hurt! You're going to get hurt all because of me!" She stood there looking utterly lost. "I don't know. I don't know what to do."

"Stay with me. I'm in this till the end. I love you, for God's sake. Okay? I love you. I'm not leaving you." She moaned. He glanced around. "We need a car. It'll be nice to be in control of our transportation again."

"Where are we going?"

"To an old friend of my dad's. He's a good guy, and people really liked him when he was in office. I think he can help. He has the same connections that Phillip has."

"What are you going to say to him?"

"First, that Phil has been kidnapped. And then I'm telling him everything."

"We're in so, so much danger." She looked around frantically. "I don't think we'll make it."

"We will. Just need a car. Right?" He gave her a lopsided smile.

"Oh, God. Raoul, you're so..."

"Insane and stupid. I know." With her hand in his, he began to walk again. "Do you still hate peanut butter, Christine Dachelet?"

"Yes. It's sticky and icky." She laughed at the memory. And, after one last glance behind her, Christine warily allowed him to lead her forward.

He was able to rent a midsized car without a surcharge for his young age. Like every other place, car rental agencies were struggling for business and just happy to see a customer. As there was already a paper trail behind them indicating they'd arrived at the airport, one last transaction didn't seem to matter. Raoul chose a midnight blue vehicle, hoping to blend into their surroundings at night. After looking up the address of his father's friend, he grabbed Christine's hand and they again made their escape. She gripped the sides of the leather seat until her fingers turned white.

"It'll be okay," he constantly reassured her. Raoul switched the radio to a soft rock station and held the steering wheel tightly. It was about an hour later, as the sun started to set, that he knew he was a little lost. From barbeques and family gatherings, he vaguely remembered the enormous home of his father's friend. It was a magnificent house, made of dark grey stone and with a balcony in every bedroom. Raoul also knew that the man still resided in the United States. Although he was no longer in office, he would still attend conferences with Phillip.

"All right," he murmured, pulling over to a gas station. "My GPS is messed up. I need to stop and look at the map again."

"I need to use the bathroom."

They both climbed out and went into their respective restrooms. Raoul waited for her outside, browsing over a paper map to find the location. He waited and waited. Disturbed, he poked his head into the girls' bathroom, hoping not to upset any other women. "Christine?" One glance told him that the cracked stalls were all empty. Had she gone back to the car by herself?

Raoul raced outside and glanced at the dark vehicle. No one was in the front or backseat.

Frantic now, Raoul looked around, finally seeing her down the street, blonde hair glinting in the moonlight. They were on the edge of a wooded area, and she was limply standing beside a large pine tree, staring outward into the pitch blackness. "Christine? What the heck?" He ran toward her and grabbed her arm. "What are you doing?" When she didn't respond, he turned her around to face him. Her eyes were half-closed, and an eerie closed-lipped smile played across her face, even more distorted by the shadows. "Christine?"

"The Spirit," she mumbled. "He asked me to help him."

Raoul swallowed nervously. "There is no Spirit. Remember? Let's get back inside the car, baby."

"Mm? But the Spirit said I should help. There's so much to do before…"

He grabbed her shoulders and shook her. "Christine! Wake up! There is no Spirit! It's not real!"

The jolting movements seemed to awaken her. A grunt emerged from her throat, and she stared up at him with wide, confused eyes. "Raoul, what are we doing over here?"

He sighed in relief. "You were sleepwalking or something. It was weird. Maybe you need some rest."

Christine shivered. "I felt so strange. Right before I went into the bathroom, I remember looking in this direction. A voice started calling me—" Christine seemed to sense something. She twitched and then turned back toward the forest. Her face became white. "No," she whispered.

Raoul looked in that direction. At first he thought it was just a tall shadow, a swaying tree or something out of nature. But it moved toward them, floating forward like a ghost. Two yellow lights accompanied it.

Eyes. Yellow eyes. He was certain that his heart stopped for several seconds. "Is that—?"

"Yes." Her little voice was carried away in the breeze. He cursed beneath his breath, watching the figure descend upon them, frozen as though hypnotized. Christine snapped out of her stupor first and turned to him. "Raoul, get out of here!" She grabbed his shoulders and tried to push him backwards. "Run! Go! Get in the car and go! Please go! Go! *Go!*"

"No. No, I'm not going anywhere." He wasn't a coward. Trying to ignore his terror, Raoul stepped in front of her, blocking her from the path of the wraith.

"No," she whispered. "Raoul. No…"

The figure stopped about ten feet in front of them. "Mr. Chandler, I presume?" The voice sent shivers down Raoul's spine. Again, he could understand why Christine once thought that the source had been supernatural. "I am utterly delighted to finally make your acquaintance. The pleasure is truly all mine."

He forced the unnatural echoes from his mind. "You're not laying a damned hand on her."

"Raoul," she continued to whisper in his ear. "No! Get back! Get behind me!" Then Christine spoke to *him* in a raspy, choked voice. "Erik, I'm here now. So leave him alone. Give him his brother and leave them alone. I'll come with you!"

"Yes, I will take you home, my beauty," Erik said in a strangely gentler voice. "You must be very tired from your long journey. Did you enjoy yourself?"

"Where's Phillip?" she snapped.

"Unfortunately, the younger Mr. Chandler didn't follow my instructions." Raoul's heart plunged. "Yet the elder Chandler brother is alive. But I am making some necessary modifications to this already broken transaction. They will both remain in my custody for reasons I have deemed necessary."

"No!" Christine yelled, poking her head out from behind Raoul's back. "You leave them alone, and I'll come with you. That was our deal, Erik!"

"The boy invalidated the agreement with his recent actions." Erik took a step toward them.

"No," Christine moaned. "No. Leave him alone! Raoul, get back! Run! *Run!*"

"Get away from her, you fucking monster!" Raoul growled, intense anger overcoming all of his fear. He reached down and grabbed a large chunk of cement that had broken off from the sidewalk. Even if he could stun the bastard just long enough for them both to run back to the car, that would be enough…

Erik softly chuckled. "I have nothing more to say to you. You are so entirely insignificant that I will not waste any more words." He walked toward them with quick easy strides. With all the force he could muster, Raoul hurled the cement directly toward Erik's head. In one smooth movement, Erik deflected the heavy object with the back of his gloved hand, sending it to the dirt ground with a loud thud. A blinding flash of white light illuminated the trees and street. And then there was only pure and unrelenting pain as scorching electric fire surged through Raoul's body, burning into his veins and throughout his limbs. He groaned and fell to his knees, jerking and twitching in utter agony. It was beyond belief, threatening to take away his consciousness and control. When the pain ceased, he was on his back and staring up at the night sky, at the twinkling stars and milk-white moon.

Christine was screaming. *No! No, he had to save her!* Still half-paralyzed from literal shock, he moved his head to search for her. She was unharmed and still standing. Raoul realized that she was only shouting on his behalf.

"Stop!" she shrieked, now shielding Raoul with her arms spread out at her sides. Erik loomed over her, mere feet away. "Stop it! Don't hurt him anymore! Please! Please! I'll do anything! Just leave him alone! Take me, and leave him alone!"

"Run," Raoul whispered, struggling to sit up onto his elbows. But he doubted that she heard him.

Erik spoke. "Now we will return home. To our home. Yes, my love?"

"Yes! I told you I was coming!" She was sobbing violently now. "Just leave him alone, Erik! Stop! Please stop!"

"Calm yourself, my dear. You need to rest. You appear tired and very unwell. I do not think he has taken good care of you during your little escapade, has he? But I will. I will take very good care of my wife, despite this minor setback. All will be as it should be once again."

Erik walked forward and stood over them both. The masked figure leaned down, and Raoul stared in horror as those hate-filled yellow eyes came closer and closer. Christine shrieked again. "No! Leave him alone!"

Something cold pricked his arm. "No," Raoul groaned as he faded from consciousness. "Leave her—"

When he awoke, he was on a thin, metal cot and surrounded by four dismal concrete walls. There were no windows, only one dim overhead bulb. He could physically move again, but he could go nowhere. The door was locked; there was no way out.

They had lost.

They had lost everything.

Chapter 31

Twigs and leaves crunched beneath her dirty tennis shoes; *his* footsteps were silent. Dark and twisted trees surrounded Christine on all sides; he stayed just slightly behind her. His voice guided her, controlled her because her mind was too exhausted to resist. And what else would she do? Run? That had worked so well…

"Forward, my love. Simply go forward. Now slightly to the left. We will be there soon. Are you cold? There is a blanket in the car."

Behind them, she heard a soft rustling and whispers. Her head jerked around, and she watched as two indiscernible figures in black grabbed Raoul's unconscious body beneath the arms and dragged him away. She gasped. And she couldn't help but ask, "What will happen to him? Where are they taking him?"

"He will live. That is all you must know." Erik's voice was cool.

"Will he be hurt?"

"He will be ignored because he is utterly insignificant. I suggest you push him from your mind immediately. The less you think or talk of him, the better his health."

I should have come back here by myself. I never should have brought Raoul. Stupid, Christine. He'll probably end up dead, all because of you. What did you think would happen? Did you think Raoul and Erik would calmly shake hands and make the exchange? Stupid, Christine.

A monarch butterfly flitted around them in a circle, its wings gliding in the cold night air as it celebrated the capture of the runaways. For whatever reason, she suddenly longed for her mother. Although it had been over a decade since her death, she was whom Christine wanted right now. Maybe it was because the men that had touched her life—her father, Cameron, Erik, and even poor, dear Raoul—had each made decisions that had led her to this moment. And so Christine longed for the serene and thoughtful smile of a woman she barely knew.

Butterfly garden. That was why she thought of her mother.

"First, we'll dig holes to plant the flowers. Try not to get too much dirt on you. Aw! Well, there goes that shirt. Oh, well."

Another frightened glance backward. Where did they take Raoul?

"Give me your hand now. I'll put seeds in there. Oops. Don't drop them. There you go."

She was in a black car now with a cotton blanket spread over her legs. Erik was beside her. It was so dark that she could barely see her trembling hands in her lap. The man who glanced back at her from the driver's seat wore sunglasses despite the nighttime and a black handkerchief over his mouth.

"There. We planted a butterfly garden. Very good job. You'll come take care of it for me next spring? I knew you would."

"Go," commanded Erik. She was jerked forward with the car.

"I'm proud of you, Christine. You're so smart and talented. I want you to promise me that you'll stay in school and follow all your dreams. And then, if you want, you can find someone who you love and want to spend your life with. Oh, sweetheart—sweetheart, don't cry. I'll watch over you. Whatever you decide, I know you'll do wonderful things. I love you so much."

Christine choked back tears.

I'm sorry, Mom. But Dad took me out of school; I think he kind of lost his mind after you died. We left, and I never took care of the garden. And Cameron wouldn't let me have any dreams. And love—I think I'm too exhausted to love anyone ever again. I wish you were here. Maybe you'd know what to do. Because I don't. I don't anymore…

Christine refused to look at him for most of the drive, staring out the window with her arms crossed against her chest. Weak, helpless—and positively furious. She did glance at him once, only to see that Erik was staring directly at her, forever watching. Christine flinched and looked away again.

"Your room is ready for you," he said as they neared the city. "I have barely touched it. I knew you would return soon. I always knew you would return after your child's adventure was over."

She didn't acknowledge him. She would either start crying again, making herself even more vulnerable, or she would blow up into a hysterical and angry mess, thereby dooming Raoul and Phillip. So she was a statue. It was safest to be a statue.

They passed the normal alleyway where she thought they would enter Erik's underground abode. He must have seen her glance back in surprise. "I do not know how discreet you have been with our secrets," he murmured. "In your excitement during your little journey, you might have said things you shouldn't have. I forgive you of course, but I also must take the necessary precautions. But, my dear, will you tell me how many individuals now know our secrets?"

Our secrets? She glared. She wanted to tell him that the entire army would now show up, but spiteful lies might make things worse. And so she told a protective lie. "I didn't tell anyone."

"Do not lie to me. I know you told that boy. Look into my eyes, and tell me the truth."

She gritted her teeth and turned toward Erik. "Just Raoul," she muttered before turning away again.

The name seemed to make him momentarily tense, but then Erik nodded. "Very good. That is what I thought. Still, precautions are necessary. We will go through the theater entrance." The car stopped with a jolt, and she was staring at a field. The grass swayed back and forth, whispering and rustling in the wind.

Erik again walked behind her through the dark grasslands, the vegetation crunching beneath her feet. But something was wrong.

She stared at the field, trying to determine whether she was completely disoriented. "Where's the theater?" she whispered. Had Erik knocked the entire thing down in mere weeks?

He laughed softly. "Still there. It is a mere illusion. Step forward. Step forward, my love. You will see!" In front of her now, Erik made a strange motion in the air with his hand, as though he were grabbing and pulling something that was invisible.

Christine continued to walk in that direction, and, in the time it took her to blink, she was suddenly standing inside the familiar crumbling building. But she hadn't seen the entrance right in front of her! Gasping, she stepped backward. She was outside again, but the theater wasn't there. All she saw was an empty field. She stepped forward and was in the building once more. "H-how?"

"Old tricks of bending light. A few new tricks with quantum optics. Merely an illusion."

"But it's a whole b-building," she stuttered. "You made a whole building disappear?"

"Yes, it is one of the largest objects I have tried. Imperfect. If one looks closely in the daytime, there are flaws. At night, it is nearly ideal." Erik sounded very impressed with himself. "It is a temporary adjustment until I determine where our new home will be as husband and wife."

My God. He was impenetrable. She had never had a chance.

There were more doors, locks, and passwords than she remembered throughout their journey downward. The underground world would be her home for as long as Erik desired. When Christine was finally back down below, she stood there staring at her familiar surroundings. The sight was almost too much; it signified the utter futility of all her actions. She closed her eyes and breathed in and out, trying not to dissolve into panic. Erik watched her. "Do you require anything, my love? Now that you are home again, we can attend to all your needs. Whatever you desire will be yours."

"I think I want to go to bed," she said in a dull tone. She couldn't converse rationally with him right now.

"That is for the best. You look exhausted."

As relieved as possible under the circumstances, Christine escaped those intense yellow eyes. Something brushed against her arm as she entered her room. Her head snapped up, and she saw that the wedding dress hung on the door. The veil dangled nearby from a nail in the wall where a picture had once been. Christine backed away from the items. She paced back and forth across the room, through the bathroom and into the closet and then retraced that path all over again. She felt pathetic, like a dimwitted bunny trapped in a cage.

Finally, she gave up and collapsed onto the bed. For another night, she barely slept. She wanted to stay in the room all the following day and maybe forever, to not face the looming conversation. But she couldn't delay any longer. Raoul's and Phillip's lives were on the line, and time was running out for the country.

Her clothes were dirty and wrinkled from running from place to place with Raoul. She didn't want to put on one of the more elegant outfits from the closet, but, if she came out looking like a mess, Erik wouldn't take anything she said seriously. She put on a plain pair of black slacks and a grey sweater.

"Erik?" Her voice was soft as she approached him at the kitchen table. He seemed to be waiting for her there with his gloved hands folded together.

"Good morning, my love." He paused and studied her. "You did not sleep well, did you? I can tell. I can give you something, if it is a problem. You must have your rest." His voice was soft and calm. Yet there was an edge that told her to be extremely careful.

She decided to wait until he was more relaxed. "I want some water."

"Of course. You must be very hungry and thirsty." He retrieved it, and she shakily took the cold glass. Next he set out a thick loaf of French bread and a block of white cheese on the counter. With a large, silver knife, he sliced them into perfectly even pieces on the cutting board. *Chop. Chop. Chop.* "Your books are there if you wish to resume your lessons," he continued. "If you wish to wait until after you rest, that is also very understandable. Where were you in your history lesson?"

"Um. I don't remem—the explorers," she said. How strange that she did remember. But history had become her favorite subject. "Cortés."

"Ah. The *conquistadors.*" He sounded so delighted with that word that she wanted to scream at him. "Yes, you must return to them later."

"Later," she parroted. Christine soon sat in the living room holding a slice of bread with mild cheese on top, rigid even as he played a soothing melody on the piano. The food tasted salty. Erik would constantly ask her if she needed anything. Outside of the edge in his voice, he acted as though nothing had happened, as though he didn't have Raoul and Phillip locked up somewhere. As though she had never tried to escape.

Finally, late that afternoon, she could no longer keep up the bizarre charade. Had he blown up more buildings before making her breakfast that morning? It took yet another hour to gather courage. Christine waited until he was situated at the piano, seemingly serene and no longer on guard. And then she approached. Her voice betrayed her terror. "Erik."

He glanced at her. "Yes, my love. Did you want to sing now? I have missed your voice so dearly."

"I don't want to sing right now." She gulped. "I want to talk."

He continued to play. "Talk? Of what? It would be wise to wait until you have had time to rest. Then you will be in a better state of mind to discuss matters of importance. I have made you dinner. A chicken and rice soup that you will greatly enjoy."

"I want to talk now."

"Go on, if you are very troubled."

"I-I know you helped kill Anthony." She waited for him to deny it. Maybe Cameron had lied.

He didn't. His voice was colder. "The boy was an intruder. He chose his fate. Although perhaps the younger Chandler is to blame for the entire affair."

"But he wasn't armed! They weren't trying to hurt anyone! Why didn't you and Cameron just turn him over to the police?" No response. "No one would have believed him about the butterflies. And the butterflies! Erik, that's…very creepy. You can hear everyone, can't you? Can you see them, too?" Still no response. "But Anthony didn't deserve to die. That's why I left. I left because I was terrified! And I accepted Raoul's help because he was my friend. So please don't blame him."

He still refused to look at her, and it made her all the more nervous. Erik played on and on, the melody becoming faster, louder, and more complex. "You do not comprehend the mechanics that go into creating this sort of infrastructure," he finally said as though discussing how a car operated. "How one loose screw can topple the entire system? One error can destroy years of careful preparation? You have no idea, my beauty. And you do not need to know the multifaceted details. The boy chose his fate. The day is regrettable, but ultimately his fault."

"Erik, that is so *cold*," she whispered.

"Then all nations are *cold*," he snapped. "Do you know of a government that does not execute or severely punish spies? No, you do not know. You do not know enough to make these judgments."

She was frustrated and dangerously close to losing control. Christine decided to jump in for the kill—for the true act that Erik could never hope to justify. "Well, I do know now! I know everything! It's not supposed to be like this! The country isn't supposed to be this awful!"

"What are you talking about?"

"Things have been terrible for the last five years, since you first came here! It's worst in the cities near Cameron. And the way you talked about me being queen. And things getting really bad in the autumn. You did all of this!"

"Ridiculous."

But Christine heard him hit a wrong key as he played the song. Erik never erred. *Ever.* He had not expected her to know this. While she had the slightest upper hand, Christine quickly continued. "I know it's true! All this terror. It's been you, hasn't it?" Her voice cracked again. Maybe she sounded weak, but at least the pain-ridden words were finally coming out in one long, unstoppable stream. "This was your plan, wasn't it? You were making the country poor and frightening all this time just to help Cameron get power, weren't you? So that you could have power, too? Is that it? Or was it something else? Erik, what have you done?" She was about to cry now. "Why have you done this?!"

Erik stopped playing. His hands dropped to his lap. He slowly stood and half-turned, looming over her now like a dark cloud. Christine stepped backwards but met his eyes. "I suggest you take a nap and try to calm yourself," he stated. "You are not well. You are imagining things. You are hysterical."

"I'm not! I know it! Why have you done this?! Why won't you answer me?"

"Go to bed, Christine. You are not well. You are saying very irrational things. And my patience is waning."

She should have obeyed at that moment when she heard the tremor in Erik's voice that signified he was losing control. But she wasn't exactly at her sanest either, and so Christine made the mistake of continuing the confrontation. "It's the most horrible thing in the world! Why?! All those poor people…"

"Go to bed."

"How could you do this?"

"Leave me."

"Erik, you're a monster!"

And that did it.

"That little idiot has completely poisoned your mind against me!" Erik exploded. His rage was far more terrifying than hers. His yellow eyes turned orange as he rounded on her. His arms were out and his hands were clenched into bony fists, his sharp knuckles sticking out like protruding nails. "He has ruined everything with his lies!"

She hunched down but continued to speak. "Raoul doesn't have anything to do with it!" Her voice lost its strength. Raoul's name sent Erik over the edge. A lamp smashed as it flew from the nearest table and onto the carpet. The bulb flashed out, and the room darkened. Terrified, Christine turned and ran toward her bedroom, hoping he would leave her alone and allow her to hide forever. But, to her horror, Erik was following. He was ten times as fast as her, footsteps silent. She didn't even bother to close the door and threw herself up against the farthest wall with a thud. "Erik," she whispered. "Please. Please. I just wanted—"

She just wanted what? Erik to fall to his knees and beg for forgiveness for all his terrible crimes? Had she really thought that would happen? Maybe in her most beautiful dreams. But real life, it seemed, was determined to be a nightmare.

He stood in the doorway, shoulders heaving up and down. "I had hoped to give you a day of recovery," he said, his voice softer again. "I had hoped to be gentle even after you allowed that boy to lead you astray. But it is now time for you to finally accept your destiny, Christine. No more childish games. No more delays." A pause, and she wondered in horror what he would ask of her. "You will put that dress on, do you understand? You will put it on now."

"Erik—"

"Put on the dress." He removed it from the door and thrust it out toward her.

Her shoulder blades dug painfully into the wall. "Erik, I can't—"

"*Now, or I'll kill him! I will drag him from his cell and kill him!* Do you understand? I have waited long enough for a wife, and I will have her! I will have her now!" Erik flung the gown on the bed. "So put on your dress so that we can be married. And then perhaps you will forget that detestable Chandler boy." He slammed the door behind him. The walls and pictures vibrated.

After staring at the closed door in shock for several seconds, Christine screamed and pounded her fists against the wall. "No! No! No!" She paced, but there was no escape. Her gaze fell on the dress. *What choice did she have? Let Raoul die? Did she really think this wouldn't happen anyway? It was her fate. Erik was right. He had made it her fate.*

I tried... I tried!

She grabbed the dress off the bed, digging her fingers so deeply into it that she nearly poked holes in the delicate fabric. Going into the bathroom for a false sense of security, Christine peeled off her clothes. Before the coolness of the air against her naked skin could produce any dreaded sense of vulnerability, she climbed into the dress. She refused to look at herself in the mirror until completely covered by the glossy white material. Her hair was wild and tangled, and her eyes and cheeks were red. Her face was pale and bordering on too thin. The loveliness of the dress added a macabre touch to the entire picture. To her horror, she couldn't zip it up all the way in the back. Christine threw her long hair over the opening and prayed to God it wasn't noticeable.

For some reason, she couldn't get herself to put on the veil. It sealed everything. Slowly, she slipped on white flat dress shoes with no stockings. And then she sat on the bed and stared at the ground.

"Have you put on your dress, Christine?" he asked twenty minutes later.

"Yes," was her hoarse response.

"Then come out, my dear. Come out."

She stood and made her way to the door, still clutching the veil in her right hand. Opening it, she stared up. The look in his eyes made her want to run away again.

"Yes," he whispered although it nearly sounded like a hiss, reaching a hand outwards. "Yes, that is perfect." He took several steps toward her. "More beautiful than I ever imagined. You will be the loveliest wife in the world." She refused to look at him. He held out a hand to cup her chin; she turned her head away. "You may only do this now to save insignificant lives. But, eventually, you will understand where you belong. You will be a queen, Christine. No matter what you have seen, what you have heard or what poisonous thoughts that vile boy has put into your mind, this is how it is supposed to be." Erik gently pried the veil from her closed hand. She shut her eyes as he fitted it atop her head and then smoothed it over her hair and shoulders. "There. Yes. Perfection." A tear ran down her cheek. "Stop crying. Everything will be fine now."

She placed her hands over her face and wept, her shoulders violently shaking. "Why?" she moaned. "Why are you doing this?"

"Stop crying!"

"Why?!"

"Stop crying! I could do anything for you! He can do nothing! He's nothing! *Nothing!*" He grabbed her by the shoulders and shook her. "Why?! Why?! I thought you were different than the rest of them! You're just like the rest of them! This is why I'm here! This is why—" With a growl, he released her and moved away from her. She slumped to her knees. *"This is why this is all mine!"* he roared.

"Erik. What are you talking about?" she whispered, staring up at him.

"I don't want you like this! Get out of the dress." He moved toward the door, limping away like a frightened animal. "Get out of that goddamned dress," he whispered in a dangerous voice. "Get out of it!"

"But I thought—"

"Get out of that dress! You don't want to be my wife? Fine. You can be a slave like the rest of them. You can be a nothing! I could have given you everything. Now you won't have anything!" He slammed the door behind him.

She ran into the bathroom. She threw off the veil and the dress. She peeled off the undergarments. Christine turned the handle for the bathwater to an uncomfortably warm temperature. The whir made it difficult to hear her sobs. She stepped into the bathtub, sat on the porcelain, and folded her arms around her legs. Too tired to weep anymore, she just sat there. For at least an hour. Soaking. Until her skin was wrinkled and flaking. Washing away all of it.

When she got out, she put a soft felt robe over her body. She curled up in the bed. For a while, she lay there in her numb state. But her heart finally fought back and forced her to feel again. Christine cried into her pillow until no more sounds could escape her throat.

It was not marriage that was so truly horrifying. It was not even that she was back here again, possibly trapped underground for the rest of her life.

It was that he wouldn't listen. Horrible things were happening all around them, and he truly didn't care.

Erik was so indifferent to human suffering that she no longer believed he could be reached.

Chapter 32

Christine drank water from the sink as she had done when first kidnapped. The only thing she had for entertainment was a single mystery novel that she had brought in to read many weeks ago. She didn't feel like looking at it.

Although sometimes she would sleep or lie there crying, many hours were spent dashing off into daydreams. Some were of her youth. And some were hilariously practical like her driving a car or teaching a class full of smiling students. She liked the latter the best, even if those dreams were as impossible as going back in time.

Erik was better than her at everything. Maybe Erik was better than the entire world at everything. How do you ever win against such a person, especially one who shows no mercy?

Finally, he asked her if she was hungry.

"No," she replied.

Hunger was present but very distant, a vague gnawing sensation that could easily be ignored. And she didn't want to see him. She didn't even want to talk to him, but Erik might enter her room if she said nothing.

"Fine," he snapped. There was silence after that. Christine buried herself beneath the comforter. She wasn't sure how long she stayed there, but it might have been over forty-eight hours. She seesawed back and forth between depression and dreams.

Her door flew open. She lurched back, the covers pulled up to her chin. "You must eat someday!" he exclaimed, holding a plate of steak and mashed potatoes. He set it on the nightstand with a loud thud. His voice was strange, almost shrill. "I command you to eat now. You are not going to starve to death here!"

"I'm tired and not hungry." She turned away from him.

"If you don't eat, I'll kill that boy. If you die, he dies. Now do you have an appetite?"

She glared. Although her mind told her she wasn't hungry, her body was crying out for nourishment. Christine slowly picked up the fork. She stabbed the steak, twisted off a piece, and nibbled at it. It was flavorless, but her body craved the protein. Erik stood over her, his arms folded.

"Do you want more?" he asked when she was finished. "Let me get you more."

"No. I'm done." She turned away again.

"Why must you hide away in that room when everything of value is out here? You have your crafts. And your books and your music."

"I thought I was a slave," she muttered.

"I did not mean that," he whispered. "I was not right of mind. I don't want that. Please. Please come out."

"I don't want to."

"You will eventually forget him, you know. You will remember what I can give you!"

"I told you," she whispered. "This has nothing to do with him."

"Doesn't it?" Erik asked with a sneer in his voice. "You do not think I am aware of all the affections that were exchanged between you both? The many nights you spent together?" She could feel her face turn red. "I am sure that looking upon such physical flawlessness would make the hideous monster all the more less appealing. I am sure that every disgusting kiss you shared with that idiot was nothing short of perfection!" Erik spat. Then he softened his voice. "I will never ask any of that of you; I am not that cruel. That is one thing Chandler received that I never will, and I can only hate him for it. But I love you still. And you will stay. And you will stay alive. And someday you will understand that I can give you what the boy never can!"

She stared at him, her mind spinning. "Erik, nothing you just said made any sense. You think Raoul's *looks* have anything to do with this? Didn't you hear me at all? It's what you've done! You're destroying thousands of lives. Why won't you listen to me?"

Still, Erik didn't listen. "He made you despise me!"

"You made me despise you!" She hadn't meant to say that. Erik stepped backward. "Erik." She shook her head, not wanting to prolong this torture any longer. "I'm tired. You can leave food by my door; I'll get it there." Christine turned and placed her cheek on her pillow.

She again returned to her daydreams. She lost her perception of time and was unsure how much later Erik again knocked at her door. Startled from an actual dream about a thick, dark forest, she asked, "Yes?"

A pause. "Christine, you must know, the day after tomorrow I am leaving for a few hours."

"Okay." She had no fantasies about escaping.

Her door opened. His eyes were very strange, and Christine was slightly afraid. "You must promise me that you will not *hurt* yourself while I am gone," he said. "You must give me more time to make you understand what I will give you."

After a confused pause, she said, "I won't hurt myself." Although thoughts of taking her own life had brushed against her mind as distant possibilities, she hadn't yet given them serious consideration. Seeing another part of the world, Christine had realized that there was still joy out there. There were still beaches and mountains and cities with lights and smiling faces. Lying there and fantasizing about them still seemed preferable to morbidly thinking up ways to kill herself. In that way, she supposed she had some vague sense of hope.

Erik didn't seem to believe her. "If you try, I will have to restrain you."

"I'm not going to hurt myself. I'll be here lying on this bed *alive* when you get back, okay?"

He hesitated in the doorway. She stared up at the ceiling. "Will you not ever come out?" he whispered. "I will play for you. Sing for you. Any song, no matter how ridiculous. And when the area is secured, I will take you out to see it. You will not be down here forever once I can trust you again."

"You mean, once you and Cameron have destroyed everything, I get to see it? Thanks."

"I told you that is ridiculous! This country has destroyed itself!"

"Erik, stop," she whispered. "I know now. I know everything."

Erik left. Ten minutes later, she stepped outside and found a plate of roast beef, potatoes, and carrots. Christine took the food into her room and devoured it quickly. It was warm and delicious, and her poor body seemed to thank her for finally feeding it again. Like a prisoner, she left the empty plate outside her room.

Would this be the rest of her life? She could take weeks of it. But months? Months of nothing but food and that room and Erik asking her if she was still alive? The realization brought on a feeling of claustrophobia. Erik had mentioned eventually going aboveground…

The thought gave her a moment of hope. And then she was angry because Erik controlled that very same hope.

The bedroom door squeaked open. He was back. She looked down. Erik was carrying a large blue plastic container. He popped opened the lid of the rectangular vessel and hesitated. "You must stay alive," he said. "*She* would not stay alive, but you will."

Christine blinked. "She?"

"Nothing. I misspoke. I am tired, you see. So tired…" He tilted the container onto her bed and shook it twice. To her utter disbelief, the black kitten tumbled out onto her sheets, wriggling and meowing as though highly distressed from the trip. It had grown in the last few months. Her guard dropped for several seconds as she took the fuzzy creature into her hands. "You see, I will not care for the animal. It is not mine, and I have no feelings toward it. So, if you want the cat to live, then you must live. Do you understand? You have to stay alive, or it will starve to death."

What a cruel thing to say; she almost glared at him. And yet Christine took the kitten into her arms because of course she wanted to keep it alive. Of course she'd do everything she could to make it happy and safe. "How did you find it?"

"The same location. Near the gutters." He placed a plastic bag of what she guessed were supplies by her door and left. Gaining some focus, she hopped up and unfolded a small metal cage in the corner of her room. She set up its box, food dish, and water bowl inside, carefully creating a small home for her fellow inmate. She left the door open, deciding she would only lock up the kitten if she had to leave. They both needed as much freedom as they could get.

"Well," she said. "I guess this is better than where you were. I hope you like it. We'll both be here for a very long time. What's your name going to be?" Christine asked as it ran through her hands and pressed up against her. Obviously, the poor baby was starved for affection. "I think I'll just call you Cocoa." It made her think of childhood winters snuggled up in fuzzy blankets with her mother.

She again frowned as she realized that Erik had exploited her weakness. Still, she wasn't going to reject a defenseless animal to be spiteful. The kitten had done no wrong, and Christine didn't play games with the lives of innocents. It didn't take long for her to fall in love with Cocoa once more. At least she had a friend.

Erik pursued her again that evening. "Will you never come out?" he asked. "For an hour. Merely an hour of your company is all I request."

"I'm tired," she replied as usual.

"If you do not come out, I will—"

"What will you do?" she asked, preparing for a threat.

There was no response.

The kitten was sleeping on her stomach. Maybe it was the fact that she suddenly had something to care about again, something real to focus on and stay sane for, but a realization dawned upon her.

The last confrontations had turned out so horribly that she barely wanted to try. And yet. *Christine, what do you have left to lose?*

She set down Cocoa and stood, making her way to the door of the bedroom. He wasn't visible, and so she went to the sofa and sat down into the cushions, preparing for the worst. Immediately, Erik came out. She wondered if his hearing was that good or if he was somehow monitoring her every move. "You emerged from your room." There was such relief in his voice that she knew she had to pounce.

But Christine was not a skilled negotiator yet. And her first mistake was asking for far too much and not giving enough.

Her tone was cold. "Erik, I know what you're doing when you go out. I want you to stop it. Stop all of the disasters. All this horror. And then I'll come out of my room. I'll come out whenever you want."

His shoulder twitched. "I merely go to dull meetings. That is all. Simple appointments for boring matters."

"You're lying." She tried something else. "If not that, then let Raoul and Phillip go."

"Ah. So this is all just another pathetic ruse to save that boy!"

"Think of their mother! She must be so worried about them. "

"I wouldn't know about concerned mothers," he coolly replied. "They can't be released yet. Later, maybe."

"Stop doing this! Stop making people miserable!" Her hands clenched at her sides.

"They are already miserable. They were already doomed long before I ever arrived, and you should not mourn for them. Humankind, especially in this vile country, does not deserve your tears! So do not ask for this!"

Was that an admission?

"Erik—"

"Leave me."

She knew better than to keep pushing this time. "Fine. Then I'm going to my room. And I'm not coming out because I'll know you're killing a bunch of people. And I can't stand that! And you don't care how much you hurt me by trying to make me a part of this!" She turned toward her room, distraught despite her attempt to remain composed.

"It is structural damage!" he snapped in a low voice before she was gone.

She turned to look at him. "What?"

It seemed to take energy for him to explain. As though he had never wanted nor expected to have this conversation with her. "As before, you see. Structural damage. At night. Your precious people will likely not be in the buildings," he spat.

"Then why—" She sighed. "It's still going to cause panic, isn't it? You make people turn on themselves. Or they join Cameron to stay safe."

"That is the nature of man," Erik replied without looking at her. "They easily destroy themselves. They need only a bit of encouragement."

"You've done far more than encourage them."

"Leave me alone, Christine."

"Erik—"

"*Leave me!*"

She obeyed. Again, she had failed, and the weight of that was crushing.

***

Despite gaining nothing, Christine came out of her room without any more provoking. Spite and anger were getting her nowhere. So she forcefully threaded the terrible feelings into her newest project.

"What are you making?" The question was soft and cautious.

Her answer was in the same tone; she kept her eyes on her work. "Gloves. They're a little more challenging, so I thought I'd give them a try."

"Ah." He stood there watching her knit, looking from her face to her hands and then back again. Although his presence made her uncomfortable, Christine would admit to herself that she was grateful not to feel confined to the small space. "Dinner?" he asked after a pause.

"Yes," she replied, setting her project to the side and making sure

Cocoa wasn't going to attack the yarn.

"Will you sing this evening?" Erik asked as he sat at the table and watched her eat the leftover soup.

She nearly responded: *Will you stop killing people?* Gathering self-control, Christine replied, "I would like that."

No, she could no longer come at this from a place of anger. Because while Christine was furious at Erik for many things, she was not as irate as he was. She doubted that she'd ever be angry enough to not care whether people lived or died. When it came to anger, Erik won by a million points.

She would have to try something else.

First, she turned on the news to show him exactly what he was doing. The riots and protests. The broken glass and looting and vandalism. The poverty. And tears. The panic. He glanced at the noisy screen and said, "They were a nation of shallow robotic consumers who had not one intelligent thought in their heads. That is what you are so worried over? They are pathetic. You should only care about us, my dear."

She didn't answer. But, suddenly, something very significant occurred to her. The way Erik spoke.

At its core, where Erik was concerned, maybe this wasn't about power. Or wealth. At its core, this was more like revenge.

At his core, Erik wasn't simply an indifferent and power-hungry force. And he wasn't like Cameron; he didn't believe that this was the 'right' thing to do. She doubted Erik believed in God at all.

No, Erik was angry. Very angry. Nearly insane with rage.

And she wasn't quite sure what this would mean for her. She wasn't sure what it meant for anything. She only wondered if she'd have anything left of herself by the time it was all over.

Chapter 33

To her surprise, Erik displayed mercy earlier than she thought he would. "I think I should take you to the surface for several hours," he stated as she was reading. "For your health." A pause. "I trust you will not attempt to escape?"

"I swear I won't." After she put on her tennis shoes, Erik took her aboveground. Cool fresh air and daylight were precious, and she weakly smiled at the birds and squirrels that had made their homes in the crevices of the abandoned theater. They renewed her energy and brought clarity to her mind. Life. Hope.

"You may always ask if you wish to go above," he said as they departed. "I do not want my flower to wither."

"Thank you for taking me outside, Erik. And thank you for finding Cocoa."

His shoulders relaxed. "Within the next year, I will find us a home aboveground. And perhaps this theater can be renovated. I would like nothing more than to take you to a live performance."

"I'd like that," she replied, playing his game as they went back down. "But don't you think Cameron will forbid most shows once he's in power?" She had to make Erik see the consequences of all this.

"Cameron will do as I say. I wish you would not even consider him."

"Well, he is the leader of—"

"He is a puppet!"

"Your puppet?" He didn't respond.

She let it go. Christine sang again that evening, trying to do her best even though she had no energy. Erik didn't even mention her deteriorating voice.

All he said was, "Perhaps you need to drink more water."

While they had reached a comfortable pause in her lesson, Christine dared to ask another question. Maybe it wasn't the best time, but she was desperate for an answer. "Are both the Chandler brothers still alive?" Her voice quavered. She could see his fingers curl. "I'm not asking you to free them, although I wish with all my heart that you would. But just…just promise me they're alive."

A long moment of silence during which she grew more nervous followed. "They are alive."

She swallowed her fear. "Can I see them? To make sure they're okay?"

"No."

"Please. I'm not asking for their release."

"Why do you care so much?" he snapped.

"Because I feel responsible! You wouldn't have done this to them if not for me."

"Your conscience will be the end of you. I take full responsibility. You are to blame for nothing."

"I still feel responsible."

He said nothing, his back turned stiffly toward her. An impenetrable brick wall.

Slowly, Christine arose from the sofa. Just as she had months ago when she'd told Erik he wasn't a freak, Christine walked to the piano bench and sat down beside him. Erik flinched. "What are you doing now?" he snapped.

"Where did you learn to play?" she asked.

"I taught myself from an early age."

"You're very talented. Probably more so than anyone in the world." He said nothing, his eyes on the keys as though he didn't trust her. "You could do anything you wanted," she continued. "Be anything."

"That is where you are very wrong, my little love."

"Why am I wrong, Erik?"

"I will be nothing else but what I am. I am what the world has made me."

"I don't think that's true. I think you could change everything."

"You're lying." He leaned away from her. "If I had nothing to give you nor take away from you, you would leave me. You would leave *again* in an instant. And then I would be alone forever."

There was that pain in his voice. There was his weakness. And yet she couldn't say what he wanted to hear. He stared at her from the corner of his eye, his masked face inches away from hers. Their breaths were the only sounds in the room. She started to place a hand against the side of his head, just a comfort.

"No. No! *No!*" He wrenched away from her. "Empty words to get your way! *Empty!* You will run away again! You will leave me like all the rest! You cannot trick me!"

"No—"

"You cannot ever see my face!" he roared at her.

She was so startled that she backed off the bench and landed on her knees. Christine gaped up at him from the floor as he towered over her. "Erik," she whispered. "I've already seen your face."

He seemed momentarily confused. "Yes," he murmured. "Yes, you have." He paused. "This is all mine, Christine. You cannot leave me!" Sitting on the floor still, she put her face into her hands and started to weep. It was all becoming far too much for her. "Stop crying," he ordered in a softer voice. "I hate to see you cry."

She pulled her knees up to her chest. She bit her lip and stared forward. "I want you to tell me why," she whispered. "Why are you like this? Because if you're doing all of this for no reason, then…then you are a…"

"You want to know why?" he rasped. "Fine. Then stand up. Stand up, my curious beauty."

She obeyed in an instant. He strode toward the room that held the file cabinets and the descending staircase. Christine could barely keep up with him. The temperature was colder in there, and she shivered. He turned on lights that she hadn't known existed. Then he unlocked the other door in the room, and she followed him through the entryway. More fluorescent lights flashed on. She saw file cabinets and drawers and a smaller computer that was turned off. Finally, Erik stopped in the farthest left corner next to a black cabinet with four drawers stacked on top of each other. His bony fingers entered a code into a white keypad, and all the drawers popped open.

He whirled to face her. "I am not going to stand here and give you my life story. I do not have the time, patience, or sanity for that enticing conversation. But sate your curiosity. Stay up all night, if you like. I hope you find all your exquisite justifications." She stared after him as he retreated in several fast, furious steps.

Christine swallowed, still stunned. Slowly, she turned toward the black cabinet.

She opened the top drawer all the way. It squeaked in the eerie silence. Inside was a small cardboard box with lots of small items and papers haphazardly thrown into it. She grabbed the first item on top.

A photograph in a purple frame. Light and cold in her hand.

With a picture of two blonde women and another with curly black hair, all who were near her age or a little older. All three were very pretty and had silly smiles. Their cheeks were painted with blush, and their eyes were heavily done up with mascara and blue eye shadow. They were clinking champagne glasses together. The picture was dated 12/31/1993. She looked at the label on the back. It said: *Ashley, Heather, and Laura! Happy New Year!!!*

What a strange thing to begin with. A strange thing that didn't help at all.

Happy New Year, indeed.

It was going to be a very, very long night.

Chapter 34

Laura was the important one in the first picture. Laura was the star of the entire first act.

Part of the top drawer was devoted to the girl. Pictures of her hiking in the mountains, tanning on the beach, playing tennis, swimming, out with friends, at a concert, graduating, dressed up in fancy gowns. There were many photos of her with an older, similar-looking woman who had to be her mother. There was also a photograph of her at dinner sitting beside a leaner, well-dressed man with salt and pepper hair. That had to be her father; their dark eyes and small noses were similar. Christine got the impression that her parents had been separated.

Finally, there was a wedding picture, and Laura was very beautiful in her strapless white gown with her hair pinned up and decorated with silver barrettes. Oddly, the man at her side in the picture, her husband, had been cut out. He had been very tall, standing over Laura by at least a foot.

Laura had to be Erik's mother. Why else would she be so prevalent? There was no physical resemblance except maybe in the way she held herself, the way she threw her shoulders back, a certain confidence in her posture. The last picture in the stack was a headshot dated 9/26/2000. Christine noted that Laura looked much less happy in this one. She smiled slightly, but her eyes were tired. Her face even seemed thinner.

Christine's answers came next in a stack of birthday cards. Laura's mother had sent her one ever since her first year of college. Many had floral designs with glitter that stuck to Christine's fingers or pictures of mountainous landscapes. The first cards contained simple messages.

2/22/1989: *Happy Birthday! Caesar misses you. Every time I go riding, I can tell he's looking for you. And Angel still waits for you by the door and whines every afternoon. I guess your pets don't understand the importance of an education. Love, Your Favorite Mother.*

2/22/1990: *Happy Birthday! Hope you're having a great time at school! Don't get into too much trouble up there! Love, Your Favorite Mother.*

2/22/1991: *Happy Birthday! Can't wait to hear about your new guy. Sounds like a catch! Love, Your Favorite Mother.*

Christine enjoyed reading through them. There was such warmth in the messages that she occasionally had to remind herself that she was reading the words of Erik's grandmother.

Then, the clouds arrived. The notes became longer and less lighthearted.

2/22/1994

Happy Birthday, Laura!

Tell Zachary to take you somewhere nice. I still don't know if I forgive him for leaving you alone last New Year's, but I know his job keeps him busy.

Sweetheart, I know you're stressed, but it will all work out. You're still so young, and these fertility treatments are getting better and better. As I said on the phone, please stay away from any of that so-called experimental stuff. You don't need to be the guinea pig when I'm sure there are a bazillion other things you could try first. And there's always adoption. Thousands of kids out there could use a good home. Don't worry. It'll be fine one way or another.

Anyway, call me if you start feeling blue again. Always here to talk.

Love,

Your Favorite Mother

Christine gently closed the card, feeling nervous as she opened the next one. She only had two more to go.

2/22/1995

Happy Birthday, Laura!

How are you feeling? You sounded tired on the phone, but that's pregnancy for you. Tell Zach to make sure you're eating and getting enough rest. I can't wait to come up and see you both. I know you're excited! Can't believe I'm going to be a grandmother soon!

Love,

Your Favorite Mother

And the last.

2/22/1996

Happy Birthday, my sweet daughter.

I'm coming back up as soon as I can. I just have to go to a doctor's appointment this Wednesday. Can't get these stupid headaches to go away.

Laura, I know you think that the world is ending. I'm so sorry that this has happened, but you have to be strong for all of you. That poor baby has a long road of rough surgeries ahead of him, but we will get through this. Doctors can work miracles these days. If you start feeling too bad, please have Zach get you some help until I can get there.

Love you all.

Your Favorite Mother

Christine's hands were shaking. Why were there no more birthday cards?

A newspaper clipping gave her the answer. A short obituary.

Trudy Jean Hollander passed away on June 30th, 1996 at her home in Tampa Bay, Florida. She is survived by one daughter, Laura Rachelle LeBlanc, son-in-law, Zachary LeBlanc, grandson, sister, and...Trudy was born in 1938 in Memphis, TN...

So Laura's mother had died soon after Erik was born. And with her died Christine's most important window into the past.

There wasn't a lot of material over the next ten years, just occasional medical records or scribbled doctors' notes that she could barely read. Erik had been born with a very severe craniofacial disfigurement.

Almost as though he'd been born with no face at all. A medical professional had noted it was a miracle that Erik possessed excellent vision and a functioning mouth. The rest was very, very bad.

And then the next box had more newspaper clippings.

From 2004: "Face Transplant to be Performed On Youngest Known Patient in U.S." It didn't mention Erik's name. None of the articles did. There were various opinions about how young was too young and the major health effects of the operation. The biggest concerns were that the body might reject the transplant and that the child would be required to take immune-suppressive drugs that might damage his long term health. Still, the hospital ethics committee had approved the procedure after "very long discussions and intense conversations with the child's parents."

And then. In 2005.

"Lawsuits Expected in Face Transplant Nightmare."

"Craig Henderson Loses Medical License, Faces Jail Time in Transplant Mishap."

"Hack Job: Did Dr. Henderson Lose His Mind During Surgical Horror?"

Stomach turning, Christine read through the articles. Something had gone very, very wrong during the non-routine surgery. *It was horrible," said a source who wanted to remain anonymous. "I didn't know what he was doing. I said, 'Stop Dr. Henderson. What are you doing? Stop! You're going to kill him if you don't stop!'"*

The details were sparse as the family clearly wanted privacy, but the patient had left the hospital in worse condition than when he'd arrived. That much was clear. Christine pushed the box aside and sat in the silence for several moments. She bravely moved on to the next drawer.

Laura's obituary was on top. She had killed herself, Christine remembered. Now that she had seen a picture of the woman and explored her life, the knowledge was a little more painful.

But not as painful as what Christine saw next. One wrinkled and torn page of an incomplete e-mail exchange:

…believe what you're saying. You really think she tried to take him with her that day? I knew she was depressed, but God that's awful. Zach, you have to get him to tell you what happened. It can't be good for a kid to hold in something like that.

Candace

09/25/2006 7:13AM

Hello Sis,

Believe me, I took him to several of the best shrinks in the state. The kid won't say a word to them except "Leave me alone." But yeah, when I got home that day, I found Erik sitting by himself in a corner. First time I saw the kid cry since he was an infant. My best guess is that she tried to make him stay in the garage with her. I can't believe how far gone she was. I still wonder whether there was something I should have done for her.

I think he'll be ok. I'm going to get him enrolled in school soon. That's going to be a nightmare, but I sure as hell can't stay home. I'll go as crazy as she did. The kid needs to be socialized anyway. Laura kept him way too isolated, and it wasn't good for anyone's health. One shrink even thought Erik showed signs of an attachment disorder. What a goddamned mess.

Don't mean to sound cold. Just stressed and horrified by all this. Hoping it gets better soon. Hope all is well in Tokyo and with your travels. Don't worry about things back here. It's all under control. Hope you can visit for X-mas. Miss you.

Zach

P.S. Damned network went down. Printing this out and faxing it.

Christine read through it several times to make sure she understood. Not only had Laura killed herself. But she had tried to—

The exchange fell out of Christine's hand and onto the floor. And she could say that she now understood why Erik wasn't completely together. Her own father had brought her into a cult, and Christine wasn't sure she'd forgiven him for those years of grief. But having your own mother try to kill you—that was an entirely different horror.

But why the entire country, Erik? There still had to be more.

Unfortunately, the next drawers and boxes didn't help very much.

There were stacks of school papers. She read through some of Erik's writing, and the information was already far over her head. But the brilliance was obvious. Someone had scribbled friendly notes in the corners in black ink. *"Excellent analysis of the chapter, Erik! Can't wait to see what you think of Schrödinger."* These were some of the happiest exchanges that Christine found in the entire file. The handwriting remained the same across the next five or so years. Erik must have been privately tutored.

The last file was disturbing. A murder had occurred at the end of 2013. There were articles about the incident that stretched all the way into 2020, most of them printed off a computer.

"Murder of Lieutenant Governor's Son Rocks State. Female witness possibly on hallucinogenic drugs at time of crime, further complicating investigation."

"Possible Masked Suspect Identified by Second Witness."

"Questions Remain in Murder…"

"Deceased Physics Professor and CIA Involved in Bizarre Cover-up? Government Denies Responsibility."

"Possible Suspect Located in Belgium."

"Person of Interest in Spain?"

The last items in the drawer were mere souvenirs. Some foreign money. A couple folded flags. Blank postcards. Pictures of old buildings and landmarks. And a red hair ribbon. Her hair ribbon, she realized. From the time she'd sung right before the Spirit first spoke to her.

Christine sat there feeling sad, confused, and very, very lost. Now what?

She had a better understanding as to why Erik was so isolated from the world—why he preferred to be a Spirit…why he had reacted so horribly to her seeing his face…and why he had been terrified that Christine would kill herself. And why he didn't want to be left alone. *But, Erik, why the entire country? I still don't understand.*

After glancing at Erik's mother one last time, she got up and left that strange room. Laura had given up; Christine knew she couldn't now.

When she entered the living area, she didn't see Erik at first. Christine went into her room and made sure that Cocoa had food. She took a seat on the couch and picked up her yarn again. When she heard him come in behind her, she didn't react immediately, unsure of what to say. The water ran in the kitchen. He opened and closed a drawer, rattling the silverware inside. Then a cabinet. With a growl of frustration at her own inaction, Christine got up and followed him.

"Erik, I…Erik, nothing I say will be quite right…"

"You need not say anything," he interrupted in a soft voice. "I do not need your pity for events that occurred decades ago."

"It's sympathy," she protested.

"Keep that, too. That is all useless now, and I especially do not want it from you."

"Well, you still have it. For your horrible surgery. And your mother. I can't even imagine. I am so sorry."

"Now that you know, you will quit inquiring."

"But Erik. I don't *know*. I understand why-why you don't like people very much. I understand why you'd be angry with that doctor and your family. I understand some things. But I'm sorry; I don't understand why you're doing this."

"If you do not know, then you never will."

"We've come this far. Maybe I'm too stupid to see it. Maybe you'll just have to tell me."

"You are anything but stupid."

"Obviously I am not."

He said nothing to her. Deciding to leave it alone for at least a few more hours, she sat on the couch and picked up the nearest textbook. She stared at the pages but didn't digest the words. A tense silence hung in the air for nearly five minutes. Christine could feel him watching her from behind. She could almost feel his anger building and building like a massive storm. Her shoulders tensed. But she still wasn't prepared when his voice boomed into the small room: *"How can you not see the systemic failure?!"*

She jumped and turned around to face him. "The wh-what?"

"The total and complete failure of this society," he rasped. "How can you not see it?"

She closed the book and set it to the side. Christine turned around to face him, looking him in the eye. "I don't see it, Erik. I'm sorry. Please explain it to me."

"Let us start with the health system," he began, walking to stand in front of her with his hands behind his back. "My mother could not naturally...she chose experimental treatments to have her *precious blessing.* Whatever vile company it was, they promised that, in addition to conceiving, she would have the perfect child. It was preposterous in that decade. But not impossible these days. Abby is one, you know?"

"Abby is what?"

"A perfect child." He waved his hand to the side. "Like I said, preposterous lies told to my weak-minded mother at the time. She did conceive, but—well, you tell me, my love? Was I born without flaws?"

"Erik," she whispered. Still, she forced herself to stay dry-eyed through this. For both their sakes.

"My poor mother was trapped with me for ten years or so. The first five years of my life were spent in hospitals. I remember very little. Just whiteness and the smell of chemicals. And general pointlessness. The next five years, I was confined to our home. She refused to take me into public, and I do not blame her. Both of us were ruined creatures by that point, and my idiot father was of no help. He worked whenever he could, avoiding his tragedy of a wife and monster of a son."

Erik glanced at the ground. She felt the urge to stand and approach him, to offer some type of comfort. The rage in his eyes as he looked up again stopped her.

"I was the first child in line for a groundbreaking procedure of those decades," he continued. "Along with more intensive surgeries, I was literally going to receive a new face. Oh, my poor mother was absolutely ecstatic! I had never seen her quite so happy in all her life. She would no longer have a freak for a child, after all." Erik chuckled. "I am not of the belief that the procedure would have worked well for me in the first place, but that does not matter. What matters is—" A dangerous pause. "Do you know what the good surgeon said, Christine? As I slipped into sleep?"

"What?" she whispered, fingers curling into the sofa.

"He got right beside me—just like this…" Erik leaned down next to her. Christine shuddered violently as he spoke into her ear. "'Hello, Erik. I'm sorry. I'm sorry. I'm very sorry. But I'm having a bad day today. I'm sorry, but I'm having a bad day. And you will, too.' Then he softly giggled like a drunken madman. And I awoke even more hideous—worse than what you saw that delightful night in the kitchen."

She felt the blood drain from her face. "My God. Did you ever tell anyone that he meant to do that?"

"What good would that have done?" he coldly replied. "Dr. Henderson lost his license and went to jail for a year. He was under the effects of alcohol and out of his mind, just another broken piece of a generally failing system. No surgeon wanted to touch me after that. It would not have mattered anyway. What matters is that my face was further demolished. What matters is that it was yet another massive failure!"

"Why wouldn't it have mattered?"

"To put it simply, my disgusting body has had enough. It rejects anything foreign." It sounded like Erik was gritting his teeth together as he said, "I will never let another doctor touch me anyhow. I am done with them."

"I don't blame you," she replied. "I wouldn't either."

"So let us finish the last part of this chapter. My mother. Falling into hell with no help. Drugged out of her mind. Given a few useless sessions with shrinks. But ultimately left to kill herself inside a running vehicle. But—my dear mother did try to correct her mistake. A shame it was only a suicide instead of a murder-suicide, eh? It would have saved the country lots of trouble, no?"

"Erik, please don't."

"You know that is true, my love, do you not? All the better for everyone, including your lovely self, if I had ceased to exist that day."

"Erik—"

He paced. "But I do exist, Christine. I am here, and this country has only itself to blame. Now that we have established rampant failure with the health system, let us move on. A quick glance at the educational system. So that he could continue to ignore me, my father enrolled me in public school where I was tormented for obvious reasons. And then I was promptly removed when I defended myself. While the idiots who attacked me remained there, and then went on to a university where I am sure they failed out after the first semester. Failure of the education system. Do you see that, Christine?"

"Yes. That was wrong."

"Good," he replied with relief. "Very good, my dear. You are following along very nicely. I remained hidden away for a very long time, under the tutelage of the only man in the country worth anything." Erik glanced at her. "He saved me, and he should not have."

"How did he save you?"

"Patience. It soon became clear to me that I could not remain with my vile father for much longer. He became involved with a repulsive, shrieking woman who wished to send me away simply because I did not think she was worthy enough to converse with. So I began to leave whenever possible. I even searched for work. *Legal* work. But, while my intelligence was well beyond anyone else's, no one wanted to hire a freak. It's not good for business, you know? Economic failure. And that failure followed me wherever I went—until I stepped outside those charming boundaries that society likes to install so that the *right* people are always hired." A pause. "But again, I get ahead of myself. Let us step backwards."

Erik then told her the story of his first murder, but Christine had the feeling he left out some details regarding a young girl he had met. Still, she didn't pry. He gave her enough information to understand why he was angry. "I killed someone in self-defense. Yet he was the son of a powerful man, and I had no chance under this festering system. I looked like a monster; it would have fit their narrative perfectly. Had it not been for my tutor, Dr. Nabavi, I would have been imprisoned for life or sentenced to death. Failure of the justice system."

"I'm so sorry," she began. "But Erik, I—"

"But you want to know of my return, right? I left this country. I would never forgive, but I did attempt to forget. Yet I could not escape my beginnings. I was a strange foreigner with the face and physique of a demon. And my past would creep up on me whenever I attempted to remain legitimate. So I left the world as you know it. And I found places where my talents were celebrated. The cracks and crevices of societies."

"What do you mean by that?"

"I began small. Black market transactions. Messy odd jobs no one else desired. Hell, I did anything to survive, beyond your worst nightmares. People even paid to look at my face. Some would even pay to–" His hands dropped. Her stomach turned. "But then my luck improved. Through no fault of mine, the world economy was abysmal in the 20's. Populations were unemployed, hungry, and crime ridden. The useless governments did not know how to fix it. There were little uprisings of all sorts. I worked for whomever could afford my services, pulling the strings where I was needed."

She paled. "You've...done this before?"

"I assisted," he snapped. "But not like this, no. I merely offered a helping hand, be it building communication devices or weapons. Spying. Hacking. But, mostly, I learned a great deal as to what makes a society tick. Which was very useful when I arrived here."

"You just decided to come back?" she softly asked. "To destroy it?"

"I am not that impractical. The United States started to naturally recover along with the rest of the world. I assume Cameron panicked; he knew his organization would not do well if people were thriving outside of it. So he sought me out. He'd heard through underground channels of my work. After I received a large sum of money, I agreed to meet with him.

"Like most intelligent people, I originally thought Cameron was a raving lunatic with no fighting chance. It seemed a waste of energy to even try. But he *had* done well enough on his own. His sect already boasted tens of thousands of members. He was charismatic, and people were attending his speeches in very high numbers. For a zealot, he was practical."

"You thought he had a chance?"

"Perhaps. But you miss the point, my love. Cameron Lourdes was paying me millions of dollars to uproot a country that I utterly despised. Whether it worked or not, was there ever a better bargain?" She didn't answer. "The Spirit fit perfectly into the design. And the type of people that Cameron initially attracted were easily manipulated. They were desperate. They wanted to be controlled. They were the same people who had scorned me my entire life! Finally, it was *I* who controlled their lives. Finally, they would know what it was like to have no hope." He was silent for a moment. "But then *you*."

"Where did I come in, Erik? Was I just another stupid, gullible person to manipulate?"

"How can you even ask that?" he snarled. "You were everything. You changed everything." He rubbed his temples. "Cameron desired a slow transition, and that was for the best, as a fast fall would have looked suspicious. I started small. An explosion here or there. Events that caused a riot between various communities, rich versus poor, conservative versus liberal, etcetera. It created a world of blame and mistrust. Once I dipped a hand into the economy, though, that was the key. An economy has very little to do with supply and demand and everything to do with complex computerized algorithms that few people understand. They call them flash crashes. Everyone assumed they were glitches, that the system was no longer stable. And slowly, very slowly, it all spiraled downwards. My original intention was to complete the project and then, well, I didn't have much to go home to. Until you."

"What do you mean?"

"When I heard you sing, I knew I needed you. There was no point in having a life without you, Christine Dachelet." He looked at her urgently, but she glanced away. His voice became softer, weaker. "At first, of course—well, why would you ever look twice at a monster? No, you would never want me as I wanted you. But, suddenly, I saw what I could give you. No. I would not hand the broken country over to Cameron Lourdes. My entire existence made sense. I would secure myself a place at the top, and you would be one of the most decorated women in the world. *That* is why you would stay with me."

"I don't want to be a part of this," she whispered. She stood, hands clenched at her sides. "I understand that you've been hurt many, many times. And I know that nothing I say will ever fix it, will ever be good enough. But millions of people are completely innocent. And some of them are good. They don't deserve this!"

"It is too late. From the moment my poor mother conceived me, this has been my path. From the moment your father brought you to Cameron, it has been yours."

"I won't. I'll run! I'll tell someone! I'll do anything!"

"Then you will stay down here forever and never come out!" he growled.

She had cried and begged and screamed. She had been mean and nice. She had genuinely felt for Erik and wanted to take his hand and comfort him. Had he shown any sign of remorse or that he would cease with this madness...

But he was so very far gone.

"I want to *help* you," she murmured. "Let me help you."

He seemed well aware that she did not mean *help* him destroy the country. "You are far, far too late."

Chapter 35

Residential. Business. Assembly centers.

Cameron traced a finger along a penciled drawing that several of his planners had recently created for him. While Erik may have preferred his fancy advanced equipment, Cameron still favored a good old-fashioned paper map.

Over in the isolated eastern areas, that was where the less cooperative individuals would eventually be placed. Those who went against the rules. Those who didn't believe Cameron's words of truth, beauty, and justice. They would have to be reeducated about the ways of God. Or eliminated.

As Cameron worked, he was also listening to the radio and growing increasingly disappointed. Another evening was passing, and there were no major occurrences. Erik's original plan had not proceeded. It wasn't that Cameron really cared how this all came about so long as the elections proved fruitful. He was more concerned about Erik's dependability.

Cameron had recently heard some disturbing news from those in his circle. Apparently, the elder Chandler brother had vanished, leaving his mother worried.

"I bet Chandler said screw it and is living it up in Europe or something," one man had remarked. "Just didn't want to lose face after all those inspiring speeches he made."

But Cameron wasn't so sure. When he received the visit that gave him his answer, he was looking through a series of letters from officials.

The notes were brief, polite and professional but with the slightest edge of alarm.

"They are merely trying to get a feel for your policies," Erik had said many months ago when the first few messages arrived.

Cameron had frowned. "I really don't want to work with any ungodly people."

"You want to cut off trade with the entire world? That should do wonders for your economy. But it is yours, so by all means do as you please."

"God is on my side," Cameron replied. "He will provide no matter what choices I make." He paused. "Still, it's too early to burn bridges. You're right. I should be careful. Unusual allies can be useful." He had thought of Erik as he said this.

Erik had shrugged. "Be vague. Make no promises, and use the language of a politician. Tell them you have no power yet. Tell them that if you were to rise to a higher position, you would take a measured approach to all current issues—"

"Maybe you should write the responses. You're the one who has spent so much time abroad. You know how to deal with this."

"Must I do everything, Mr. Lourdes?" But Erik took the letters and left.

Cameron found himself missing that calm, controlled relationship with Erik. And it was all that girl's fault. She had nearly ruined everything.

Cameron wasn't sure whether to be thankful or afraid when the masked man showed up that evening. "Erik!" He quickly set his drawings and papers to the side and stood, keeping a safe distance. "Good evening. I wasn't expecting you. But I have to say that I'm glad to see you. I thought you'd disappeared on me." The yellow eyes were unreadable. Not insane or resolved. More detached and distant. It unnerved Cameron. With a swallow, he gestured to the radio where a commercial for mouthwash was playing. "I was wondering…I thought more was supposed to be happening by now. More *events.*"

Erik shrugged. "I have changed the operations. Compacted it into a single magnificent night."

"Why?"

"Simplification."

Cameron scratched the back of his head. "Well, I won't question it. I don't really know about those types of things, being a very peaceful man myself. So long as all goes well with the bigger picture."

"It will. The state is destabilized enough for that one night to make all the difference. And so it will all come together without any unnecessary noise. You will give my inspiring speech, and we will proceed from there."

"And I'm certain that my multiple connections will step in. Yes. Well. It sounds like you know what you're doing, Erik. It sounds like a smoother plan, if you ask me. Saner, really. And it'll use fewer resources."

"Yes."

"Are you coming to that dinner party I invited you to? It's really important that you be there. You can't stay invisible forever. Not if you want to be in a legitimate position once the real work begins. I can start by introducing you to a few people at this party."

"It sounds painfully dull, Mr. Lourdes. I don't know yet."

"All right. Well, think about it." Cameron paused and then casually asked, "I've heard some strange news regarding the Chandler family. Do you know anything about that?"

"All matters to do with the Chandlers are my concern now." Cameron started as Erik then said, "I have *her* back. If you interfere this time, I will kill you. I will find another raving extremist to take your place. Is that understood?"

He was about to reply with: *How dare you speak like that to me? Or: How the hell did you get her back?* But Cameron kept calm. "Are you keeping her under control this time?" he asked.

"She poses no threat to you. I think I have made that clear multiple times."

"No threat, eh?" Cameron inhaled. "All right. Let's see, then. You can bring Christine to my little get-together. We'll see how she really behaves. How's that? Lots of other wives will be there."

"I don't trust you near her."

"So you're just going to keep her locked up forever? Surely, you want a wife you can take out in public once in a while. Bring her to my dinner. You'll be with her the whole time."

"We will see."

"I need you to be focused, Erik. There is nothing quite like the Spirit. In fact, I have people asking about your absence. They miss you around here. You and your little miracles. It gives them hope."

Erik looked toward the window. "All tricks and illusions that can be taught to another."

"You know that's not true. There will never be anyone who can do what you do. You can *make* people obey me."

"Can I? What do you wish for, Cameron? Total hypnosis of populations? A torture chamber?"

"That's not what I meant." Cameron continued, "If you want the girl's complete obedience, we can work on that, too."

"I do not want her obedience!" Erik snapped. "I wish for her…happiness." The last word was nearly a whisper.

"Ah. See. You don't understand. An obedient woman is a happy woman. Everyone is much happier with the natural order of things." Cameron grunted. "Don't you know what happened with Abby's mother? She was a defense attorney. Do you remember the Potts murders of 2025?"

"Vaguely," Erik replied with disinterest. "I was in a different country. Some billionaire hacked up his wife and daughter, no?"

"Yes. Well, she was the one who got him off. All because of some technicality about police proceedings while gathering evidence."

"It happens often."

"Not under me, it won't! That disgusting woman destroyed the life of my son. She gave him no attention, practically ignored little Abby when she was born, despite all the money she put into getting the 'perfect' child.

She did as she wanted, slept with whomever she wanted. She was a whore. And my son was a coward for not making her obey. It is just one example of what happens when you do not keep a handle on your wife."

Erik laughed. "Cameron, didn't you learn long ago not to preach to me?"

"Your apathy is getting annoying. What exactly is it that you want? I know you don't believe in what I stand for. I've always known that."

"Then why, pray tell, are you using me to do this?"

Cameron hesitated and looked at his wrinkled hands. "Because let us face it. The most virtuous could, would not do what you do. You are a cold means to a beautifully warm end. I'll give you a high place on my board of advisors. You'll be a very powerful man. What else do you want from me?"

"I want—" Erik paused and stared at the floor for a long moment. "I want to return home."

Cameron eyed him. "And the final night? All will proceed as planned?"

"Of course. Bring champagne, Mr. Lourdes. Or do you not drink? I never remember all your fickle rules." He shrugged. "Ah well. We will celebrate either way. The night will be ours. Five years in the making, right? Yes, five glorious years."

"Come to my dinner, too," said Cameron.

Erik disappeared as quickly as he had arrived.

***

With Cocoa sleeping on her lap, Christine remained in front of the television much of the night. She was waiting to see if the world would end. Every time Erik stepped out, it was a possibility.

At one point, the anchorman announced breaking news, and she nearly had a heart attack. But it was a plane crash in Asia. Cocoa meowed and yawned.

Erik silently entered during the early morning hours, and she glanced up at him as a shadow fell over the living area. He stared down at her with surprise and anger. "Did you stay up all goddamned night? *Why?* "

"Waiting." She gestured at the screen. "For whatever is going to happen next."

He rolled his eyes. "Then you must have been sorely disappointed."

"Where were you, Erik?"

"At a meeting."

"With Cameron?"

"Yes. The idiot has invited us to a dull dinner party."

"Why does he want me there?"

"He wants to see that you won't cause him problems. That you will...Anyhow, you don't have to go. I'd prefer you not be near him. It will be incredibly boring."

"I want to go," she said after a moment.

"Why?" he asked with a note of suspicion.

"To see if there have been any changes there. To see what's happening. Please?" She hesitated and then continued, "I have to leave here sometime. If you're going to be in charge of everything, shouldn't I get to see it, too? Or am I going to be locked away forever?" Erik didn't answer. He turned and began to remove his gloves. "I won't do or say anything. I'll be good, okay? I just want to see."

"I will think about it," Erik replied. She started to turn back to the television, knowing better than to push. "Are you tired?" he asked.

"Not really. Too much, um, adrenaline, I guess."

"If you are not going to bed, I wish to show you something. Enough politics. I *can* do other things, Christine. They are useless little tricks. But you will like this one. Put on shoes and warmer clothing."

She was ready within five minutes. They climbed out of his house, and she was shocked as they headed toward the infamous third elevator. "Seven. Six. Nine. Four. Three." Erik read the numbers to the doors, and they slid open. He then glanced at her. "Do not bother memorizing the code, my love. It now changes every time and is fed to me through another device."

"I figured it was difficult."

He looked as though he were going to affectionately touch her hair. His hand drew back, though, and they walked inside. She was jolted as the elevator moved downward.

The doors slid open, and she found herself in a dark room. It lit up the second she stepped out, illuminated brightly by fluorescent bulbs. She was faced with dozens of computers, monitors, and other complex machines—speakers and knobs and wires and buttons. Some buzzed or hummed, and she could hear a few jumbled voices speaking just as she had when she'd put her ear to the floor. As she walked over sterile linoleum tiles to the middle of the room, trying to decide what to look at first, a bright screen flashed on in front of her.

Erik went to the central computer and typed something on the keyboard. The lights dimmed, and there was a flash as a soft, white glow engulfed the room. Christine blinked and curled her arms up into her chest protectively. Erik's eyes glowed in the dark as he turned toward her. "Choose one, my dear. The ocean. The rainforest. The savannah. The mountains. Choose a place."

"Um, the ocean."

"A perfect choice." Another flash. Then a bluish, wavy light filled the room, giving the appearance of water. She was amused by this but then gaped as a school of orange fish with black eyes swam past her. Holograms. Yellow sea horses and purplish jelly fish bobbed up and down in the water. Colorful coral reef surrounded her on all sides. Christine gasped as a tiger shark swam in circles in the distance. Light from above filtered through the water and rippled on her skin. All of it was an illusion, of course. Still, it was extremely realistic and beautiful. Erik flipped another switch, and there was sound as well. Gentle and distant echoes beneath the ocean. "And then, if you wish to be a bit theatrical—" Very soft and smooth piano music played, accompanying the scene.

She turned around and around, watching the underwater world with fascination. Her stress evaporated, and she almost lost herself in the cool blueness. Finally, Erik pushed a button, and everything disappeared. The lights flashed on. She blinked as the weight of reality fell back heavily on her shoulders. "That was wonderful," she murmured.

"I could show you anything," he explained. "Take you anywhere. That does not mean I will not take you real places one day, of course. I will do that, too." He shrugged. "Anyhow, a simple trick for your amusement. It is nice to see you smile sometimes."

"I knew you could do other things," she eagerly replied. "I mean, you could do anything you wanted. Science. Music. Art. All of it combined. Just like this. People would buy this."

"This is frivolous. There is absolutely no point to it." The room was still somewhat dim, the glow of the various machines casting them both in eerie lights.

"I liked it," she said, rubbing her hands together for warmth. She waited for him to take her above again.

Instead, Erik entered more information into the computer. His hands typed so quickly that they were a blur over the keys. Where was he going to take her this time? She leaned forward. The picture on the screen was far from beautiful. She finally understood. "There," Erik said in a disinterested voice, stepping back. "There is the elder brother. He is mildly sedated for his own well-being."

Phillip was lying on a bed and watching a television in what looked like a dark and dilapidated motel room. There was a plate on the nightstand by his bed that signified he was being fed. A purple bruise was visible on his forearm, but he seemed okay given the circumstances. "He'll be released, right?" she asked.

"Eventually," Erik assured her. "I will not risk it when we are so close."

She waited. Erik only stood there. Finally, Christine asked, "And his brother?"

Erik's shoulders tensed, but he leaned forward and typed. Christine's felt a sharp pain near her heart as the picture appeared. Raoul's room was more like a prison cell than a motel. He was clearly not sedated. He paced back and forth across the concrete with his forehead creased. Every so often, he would put an ear to the door. At least he wasn't severely injured, nor did he look like he was starving. Still, the frantic expression on Raoul's face made her cringe with regret.

"There. He is alive."

"Thank you, Erik," she whispered. "Is he near Cameron?"

"No. I have some of my own people looking after both of them."

"Your own people?"

Without responding, he turned off everything in the room, and they were left in darkness. Christine returned to the surface and immediately headed for bed.

Instead of sulking, she stayed near Erik for those next couple of days, thinking that her presence would do more good than anything else. She sat beside him in the evenings and asked him questions about her textbooks. She made dinner one night, a pasta and vegetable dish with a cream sauce of her own invention. She sang when he requested it, and she even hugged him goodnight. He finally agreed to take her to the dinner party, after reminding her twice that the lives of the Chandler brothers were still in his hands. "And Cameron won't dare try anything now," he quietly added. "Not when he is so close."

Christine knew something very bad was approaching. But getting Erik to tell her more was still like banging her fists against a concrete wall.

"We will leave in two hours," he told her on the night of the party. "I suppose you will want to change. Although I do not care if you wear pink slippers and jeans."

"Only if you wear them with me." She liked the bewildered gleam in his eyes whenever she said something unexpected or teased him. It reminded her of his lingering humanity. She sometimes wondered why he hadn't forced her to marry him yet. Was he still waiting for her to agree to be the Queen of a ruined country?

Christine went to her room to change and stared at the row of longer modest dresses. That entire life seemed so distant now. She put on a long, pine green gown that reached her wrists and ankles. Velvet buttons decorated the front, and the neckline practically hugged her throat. She wrapped her hair up in a bow of the same color. Erik laughed when she emerged. "What?" she half-snapped.

"No. I do not mean to be cruel. I simply forgot how you once used to be, before I pulled you out of there." He gently added, "You look like you did the first time I heard you sing. I was hiding behind the stage, my attention on something more important than Cameron's inane speech. I only heard your voice. And then I nearly ripped the entire curtain down to get a glimpse. You were so small. So frightened. Yet your voice…"

"Well, I was terrified. My dad thought that would be the only way to get someone to notice me. I guess he was right." She looked down. "You must regret it now. Pulling me out of there. Teaching me. I guess Cameron was right about Eve and the apple."

"No. I do not ever regret that. I simply wish you could understand the benefits of being above the rest of them. They are unworthy. We deserve to be above them. You do."

She dared to reply, "I wish you would have taken me out of Cameron's sect and then left the country with me. I wish we were far away from here."

"You would have run from me," he protested. "The instant you saw what I was, you would have fled. I would have had nothing to offer you but a monster's face."

"I might have been frightened at first. But after you explained everything and I was given time, well, I would have been very grateful. You wouldn't have been a monster. You would have been a liberator."

He didn't respond, but she did catch the slightest glint of surprise in the yellow eyes. Again, she didn't push. Each victory had to be quiet and subtle.

As always, it was good to return to the surface. The drive through the city was peaceful, and the world appeared to be generally the same. Not in the middle of an apocalypse, at least. Maybe it wasn't too late.

Cameron's compound eventually loomed over them. It looked as though it had been renovated. The entire community seemed to sparkle, and she could tell that it was thriving and growing. The expansion stretched far back beyond what the eye could see. They took their normal path through the garage and dark passageways. Instead of heading toward Cameron's office, though, Erik led her down another empty hallway. They climbed a set of carpeted stairs, and the lights were bright as they reached the top. She heard the deep voices of many men, along with the occasional softer voice of a woman.

Erik raised a gloved hand and knocked at a polished wooden door. Within several seconds, it opened. Cameron stood there in a more formal suit than she was used to seeing him wear. His beard was neatly trimmed, and he was wearing glasses. "Erik," greeted Cameron with a smile. "So good to have you here." He glanced at her. While he still grinned, the loathing was evident on his face. "Christine," he said with a nod. She tried not to glare.

"We will not be staying long," said Erik. "You wanted an appearance."

"Yes," replied Cameron. "You will remain a Spirit to most people, but you cannot remain that way to everyone. Not when you will be at the head of all meetings that I cannot attend. I told you I would hand you a place at the top. Tonight you will begin to claim that place."

Erik said nothing, but Christine sensed a tension in the air.

Cameron stepped back and gestured toward a large dining area with a long dark wood table and a golden chandelier. Silver dishes covered in ornate lids sat atop the table, and chairs with dark red cushioned seats surrounded it. Many men of different ages were gathered around the feast. They wore black suits and ties, and she didn't recognize any of them. "These men are all lesser versions of you," Cameron said in a soft voice. "Doing a bit of background work for me throughout the country. Some are former congressmen. Some were in the military. The godly wealthy. They are not all true believers. But they have their reasons for supporting me, and they have vast resources. Erik, you have shown me that some compromise is necessary."

"I see," Erik murmured, eyeing them all with disdain. Christine could only stare with a growing sense of dread forming in her stomach.

Cameron walked into the room and cleared his throat. The men glanced up, and their eyes immediately fell upon Erik with fear, fascination, and curiosity. "I'd like to introduce my architect," he began in a loud voice. "My mastermind. As with the rest of you, no names for now. Most of you, of course, are already aware of our little singer here, Christine." One of the men nodded at her and smiled. She looked away. "This man is really responsible for most of my success," continued Cameron. "When he speaks, I suggest that the rest of you listen."

"Why aren't the rest of us wearing masks?" asked an older man.

Cameron grunted. "That is his choice. You'll respect it. And if you want to wear one next time, by all means do so." The man rolled his eyes but stayed silent. Cameron turned to Erik. "The other wives are in the room next door." His voice fell to a whisper, but Christine was still able to hear. "They are already corrupted women. I mean, they haven't been trained in the proper ways. It's something to deal with later. So I guess she can go eat with them."

"Yes," Erik evenly replied.

Cameron turned to her. "Christine, you may go into the door on your right. I think they've already begun." She wanted to stay and listen but headed in the indicated direction.

"Do we all get little wives that look like this?" She heard one of the younger men ask this as she left.

"If you want one," Cameron wryly replied.

Christine shook her head in disgust and glanced at Erik again. He wasn't looking at her, but his eyes appeared highly aggravated. *Good.* He wasn't enjoying himself.

She opened the heavy door and stared at seven women sitting

around a similar dining table. They were also of varying ages. Looking up, they all greeted her with nods and 'hellos.' They were clothed as she was in long dresses that looked more like costumes. There was a deceptiveness to all of it. One of the younger women passed her a china plate, and Christine stared down at her ham and pineapple slices as they continued a conversation about…She squinted and glanced up. A foreign movie?

"Yes, it was a little out there for me," said a middle-aged woman with brown hair that curled at the ends. "What do you call it? A little abstract and just plain weird. But so much better than anything produced here."

"I saw one like that from Italy the other day," replied a slightly younger woman with curly blonde hair. "Oh, what was it called? Darn. I can't remember. I think it translated to *Turn Off the Lights.* Something like that. It was scary but kind of erotic." The other women all hummed in interest. There was silence as they ate, interrupted by the occasional comment about how delicious the food tasted. Christine would steal glimpses of them all, attempting to read their thoughts.

A woman on her right with plump red cheeks spoke. "You're Christine, aren't you? I know we're not giving names. But you're—I know you already. From television."

"Yes," she replied and shifted awkwardly.

"John—err, whoops." She giggled as if this were all a joke. "I mean, my husband says that your husband is very, very important. Next to Cameron, the most important of all. Is he in there now? Is that true?"

"I don't know," she muttered, looking away and wishing to disappear. She wasn't going to reveal that they weren't actually married.

"No politics at the table," an older woman with short curly grey hair chided. "We all get enough of that at home as it is, don't we?" The others nodded in agreement. "Ugh." She rolled her eyes. "We were just talking about movies, Christine. What are your favorites?"

"Oh. Um. I like *The Wizard of Oz,"* she murmured. They all laughed, and her face burned.

"That's fine, sweetie," said the older woman. "Ladies," she said, looking at the other women with a scowl. "Christine was raised inside this place. So please don't be rude."

"Oh," said the middle-aged brunette. "Well, we'll show you some good movies. The best ones are all foreign now."

Christine could no longer suppress her confusion. "Wait. I don't understand." She raised the volume of her voice, and they turned to stare at her. "You're all allowed to see movies?"

The brunette raised an eyebrow. "Well, aren't you now?"

"Yes, but I'm—but doesn't Cameron forbid it?"

The blonde laughed. "Don't be silly. We're not like *them.* Out there. No offense to you."

"I don't understand," said Christine.

"Well, this is how my hubby explained it to me," the blonde continued despite half-hearted protests from some of the others. "Most of the intelligent people fled the country when everything got so bad. There are exceptions. Our husbands, who stayed behind to help Cameron. A few well-meaning powerful families like the Chandlers tried to piece things back together like they used to be, but that was a lost cause." Christine flinched at this statement. "So, anyway, with the smart and rich people all gone—it's the poor and erm…less smart people out there. That's all that's left, right? So they have to be heavily controlled and monitored or else they'll eat each other alive. My husband says that Cameron's rules will be good for them. We on the other hand, well, we'll do as we please."

The brunette laughed. "That's right. Although…" She smirked. "It could have been explained with a little more tact. Anyway, I've warned my husband that if he tries to take my movies from me, I'll move to Europe." They all chuckled and murmured their agreement.

Feeling sick to her stomach, Christine excused herself as they continued their conversation about foreign films. She wandered into the hallway and could hear the voices of the men in the next room. They were talking about alliances. Apparently, one of the men in there was a general.

Christine turned the knob and carefully peeked inside. At first, she didn't even see Erik. Eventually, her eyes focused on the shadows in the farthest corner. He was standing there with his arms crossed.

A hand clamped down roughly upon her shoulder. She jumped and gasped.

"Hello, Christine." Cameron spoke into her ear. "Are you enjoying yourself?"

"Yes," she whispered with a shiver. She had stupidly not noticed that he was no longer in the dining room. Christine braced herself.

His hand tightened around her shoulder to the point of pain. "You listen to me, you disgusting little bitch," he whispered. "I don't know your plans or what you're up to. I don't even know why you're back here, but I'll blame Erik for that one. But I do know women. Whatever evil tricks you're using against Erik with your devil's ways, I will find out. Mark my words, if things don't happen as they're supposed to within the next week, the people you care about will suffer. Do you understand me?" She was frozen. He shook her back and forth. "I said, do you understand?!"

"Yes!" she spat.

"Good girl." Cameron loosened his grip and ran his hand down her arm. She quivered in disgust. "You've already been such an inspiration, you know? I've learned fast how important it is to keep your kind under control." There was a burst of laughter from the dining room with the women. Cameron glanced up and glared toward it. "Lots of work to do. But soon everyone will come around to my way of thinking, right?" She said nothing. He patted her on the head and released her before heading back into the room with the men.

With horror, Christine turned to dash back into the dining room with the women. Just as she put her hand on the knob, another palm fell onto her shoulder. She yelped and turned around.

Erik stared down at her. "What are you doing here?" he inquired. He glanced toward the room where the women were giggling. "Bored with mindless drivel? As am I. We will leave soon and avoid these occasions as often as possible."

She warily stared at him, relieved that he wasn't Cameron and yet so very angry that Erik was a part of all of this. Would he even care that Cameron had just threatened her? Probably—but only because he loved her. Not for the right reasons. Not because all of this was truly evil.

It took her a moment to find her voice. "Erik, will you let me see Mrs. Valerius before we go?" Cameron's words had struck fear into her heart.

"That was not my plan."

"Please," she whispered. "This isn't a trick. I promise. I just…I really want to see her. I miss her."

"Yes," he muttered. "I will take you in a few minutes, to please you."

"Thank you."

Somehow, Erik excused them both. Thankfully, he was as eager to get out of there as she was. Christine said a soft goodbye to the other women, and they enthusiastically waved back. She thought that they were rather naïve, thinking Cameron's laws would never affect them. Then again, maybe there would be a hierarchy where some suffered more than others.

It all disgusted her.

"Be quick," said Erik when their car pulled up by Mrs. Valerius' home.

"I will." She rushed out into the darkness and pounded on the door. *Please let her be okay.* To her relief, the older woman answered. A yellow knitted shawl covered her shoulders, and her grey hair was swept up into a bun.

"Christine!" she exclaimed. "I wasn't expecting to see you tonight." Christine dove forward and embraced her. "Oh my. Well, it's good to see you, too, dear. Are you okay?"

"Yes," Christine whispered.

"Are you married now? I heard strange things."

"I-I don't want to talk about that right now." she quickly replied. "But I'm fine. How are you?"

"Oh, I'm well. About the same as always." Still, there was an odd note in her voice.

"Are you sure?"

"Yes. I'm fine, dear." She paused and then whispered, "But the rules have changed around here. No one is allowed out now."

"Oh no," Christine murmured.

"Yes, it's very dangerous out in the evil world. I guess we're being protected."

"Is that all that's changed? Please tell me. I don't have very long to talk."

"Well, I can't really say right now. It's not safe. But most things are the same."

"Please?" she begged. "You need to tell me what's happening. I might be the only one who can help."

Mrs. Valerius hesitated. Her voice was so soft that she nearly mouthed the words, "Well, this girl… She's a little younger than you. Ellen Mills, I think is her name."

Christine nodded. "Yes, I remember meeting her once."

"Yes, that's right. She tried to run away about a week ago."

"What happened to her?"

"I don't exactly know. But I haven't seen her in a while. I have seen her mother and sister, though, and they look absolutely sick. But they won't talk about it."

"That's all you know?" Christine asked. "You don't know what's happening?"

"That's it. These are very strange times. You never know what to believe, do you?"

Christine hugged her again. "Please take care. Stay safe." They exchanged a last glance before Christine turned around and headed back to the car.

Did he know anything? He was the only one with enough power to stop this. He was her only hope, and that was utterly terrifying. "What is wrong with you now?" he asked. Erik pushed a button that made a glass panel rise up so that their conversation was concealed from the half-deaf driver.

"Erik," she whispered. "I think something very terrible is happening." As they departed, she finally told him about Cameron and Mrs. Valerius. If he didn't believe her or didn't care, well, she was out of ideas anyway. This was it. This was the end.

Of course, Cameron's words and actions set off his temper. "That sniveling little idiot. How dare he touch you! I will—"

"Erik," she interrupted. "I don't care if Cameron insults me or, God, even hurts me. I don't care! I care about what's happening to all of these people. Do you know what's happening to the girls? Don't lie to me. What's going on?"

"I do not know. *You* have taken my attention this last month. You have consumed my thoughts and moments. Cameron does as he pleases."

She didn't know if she believed him. "Are you still going to do this?"

His answer was the only thing that kept her from descending into irreparable despair.

"I do not know." Erik turned to look out the window. His fingers curled, and his thumb and index finger rubbed together.

Her mouth fell open to argue and then slowly closed. It was her first moment of hope.

Chapter 36

When they returned to his home, Erik merely said, "You should change out of that horrific outfit and go to bed. And forget this wretched, pointless day."

When she was finished slipping into a pair of cotton pajamas, Christine opened the door and glanced out. Erik's forearm was bent up against the wall, and he was leaning forward and burying his face into the crook of it. His shoulders moved up and down with each slow breath. A part of her wished to go out and comfort him, but Christine thought it was better that he feel this distress. Maybe he would change his mind, would realize the scope of the human suffering in all this.

Erik made her breakfast, sweet strawberries and whipped cream over waffles. He was unusually quiet, though, asking no questions about her studies or anything else. There was no "my beauty." She could see a slight tremble in his hands as he poured her milk.

She soon braved his temper and asked about the girls again. Precious time was ticking by—time that Cameron could use to do…whatever awful thing he was doing to them. "Erik, is there any way to see what might be happening to those women?"

He glanced at her. "After you went to bed, I checked the surveillance system. I could see nothing. Perhaps the halfwit is only trying to scare you. I will speak to him. He will never threaten nor touch you again."

"But Mrs. Valerius said the girl disappeared."

"Don't they simply put people into closets to dwell on their sins or some nonsense?"

"They did before." She scowled. "But that wasn't so nice either. Being trapped in a dark little hole for hours and hours while a bunch of adults tell you how terrible you are?"

His eyes flickered with regret. "That will not happen to you again."

"No." She was growing increasingly frustrated with his passivity. "I'm trapped in a very nice place, and that probably makes me the luckiest woman in this part of the country. Me and those other ladies at dinner. We'll all be locked away in fancy safe places with lots of foreign movies to watch and books to read, while everyone else is tortured." Immediately, Christine regretted her anger, thinking it would set her back on her mission. But Erik didn't yell. He stared down at the keys with detached eyes, almost as if he hadn't even heard her. "Did you really see nothing on the surveillance videos?"

He shook his head. "No. I suppose Mr. Lourdes has become wise to my setup and learned how to escape detection."

Christine wasn't sure if she made any progress. He was very quiet and very vague, which was preferable to proclamations that taking over half the country was their destiny. She was going to continue her path of persuasion the following day, but Erik wasn't there when she woke up. A bowl of cereal and a cup of fruit had been placed out for her breakfast. A chilled turkey sandwich was in the refrigerator for her lunch.

Christine switched on the television, but nothing new had happened. Her heart calmed, but she still waited on the couch all day, occasionally trying to distract herself with a book or handcraft. Erik returned late that afternoon, appearing in the living room and walking past her without a word toward the kitchen.

She stood. "Where were you?" she asked with a more accusatory tone than she meant to use.

"Out."

She eyed him. "Did you find out anything?"

"I did not go to there."

"Then where did you go?"

"Out," he growled.

She gave up. "I missed you." Christine returned to her book.

"That is so very likely."

He was in a terrible mood. She allowed him to become lost in his piano music for the rest of the evening. Erik closed his eyes as he played, in deep concentration and practically swaying in circles with the soft legato notes. It felt like a lost day.

Tick, tick, tick. Time was ticking away. A warm salty scent greeted her as soon as she opened her bedroom door. He stood in the kitchen cooking ham, eggs, pepper, and onion on an iron skillet.

She knew she couldn't allow his disposition to deter her again. Christine pursued him after she ate half her meal, nearly knocking a glass of orange juice off the table in the process. "Cameron said something important is supposed to happen this week. This is it, isn't it? Something big is coming?" He didn't respond. "Erik, when?"

"Tonight it begins," he whispered.

"What will you do?"

"I do not know."

She wasn't going to let him get away this easily again. "How can you not know? It either happens or it doesn't, right?"

"What happens will happen."

She groaned and rubbed a hand over her face. "You're making me crazy, you know? Please tell me what's going to happen. Can't you at least give me that?"

After a moment, he said, "Sit down."

She did so, right on the edge of the couch, leaning forward. Erik stood in front of her and then half turned away. "Understand that I finalized the details of this plan soon after you-you left me. I had always anticipated a massive occurrence in October, before the elections. But it became worse after you—" He swallowed. "I wanted others to suffer as I was suffering, you see."

"Did you try to stop us?" she asked. "Me and Raoul. When we ran."

"A half-hearted attempt," he murmured.

"Why didn't you?"

"I saw recordings of you. Various surveillance videos. You appeared so relieved and hopeful. Two infuriating faces of youth and hope. I thought I could give you a couple of weeks to play your silly games. But, once you were really gone, I lost my mind."

"I'm sorry I—"

"No, you are not." He glanced back at her, glaring. "If not for my interference, you and that boy would be on the other side of the world."

"That's because it's wrong! But if you stop this—" *Could she really say it? Could she really make that promise?* The images of all those people flew through her mind. All the suffering. "What's going to happen?"

"What was originally supposed to happen…" He paused. "It has not happened. There was supposed to be more chaos by now. More desperation. Before the final day."

"Why hasn't there been?"

"Because you keep looking at me," he dully replied. "And soon there will be nothing but hatred in your pretty eyes. I will not even have your pity. But you will still look at me."

"That's…Erik. What happens on the final day?"

"There is supposed to be an initial explosion in a major city. In a shopping district. A tragedy beyond words. Cameron is then going to make a speech. It will be in front of a very large crowd, at least in the tens of thousands. The speech will call for peace and unity, and it will be incredibly uplifting. I would know; I wrote it. And then—then as the crowds cheer for him, multiple explosions will rock his community."

She gaped in disbelief. "Why would you bomb Cameron's people?"

"The explosions will have all the fingerprints of the federal government." She stared up at him in confusion. "You see, it will look like a desperate attempt by the current administration to defeat Cameron. There will also be smaller explosions at CAC headquarters and other organizations opposed to the current administration. It will ultimately look as though the federal government is attempting to eradicate all its enemies. They will appear as brutal tyrants to the entire world and lose all support. Cameron will be more popular than ever."

"Does Cameron know about this?"

"Of course. He knows he will not be harmed."

"My God. But what if not everyone believed it? What if they fought back?"

"Of course some will." Erik shrugged. "We are prepared for that. Other countries experience such conflicts all the time. Civil wars."

Her hands fell into her lap. She couldn't look at him. It was too horrible. It made her sick.

Erik continued, "But even if Cameron didn't support my plan, well, I am not sure how much longer he will be around. After he took you away from me, his days became numbered. It was… all so much easier before you. I cared about nothing."

"Was it better before me?"

"No. Of course not. You were the first good in my life since Farrokh."

"Farrokh," she repeated and squinted. "Is that Dr. Nabavi?"

"Yes. Farrokh Nabavi," he murmured absentmindedly. The name struck some chord of familiarity in her mind. She couldn't remember specifics, though.

"I want to know what's happening to those girls. Before you make any decision, can't we see that? Can't we go there together and find out?"

He hesitated. "I will find out for you."

"I want to go. I have to."

There was far too much turmoil in his eyes for her to trust him to do the right thing. Too much conflict and rage and pain. For at least twenty years, Erik had worked toward this revenge, not just against the country, but against mankind itself. Each person who had wronged him had added another brick of hatred. She had spent mere weeks trying to break him down and reassemble him. And that was simply not enough time.

"I want to go to there and find out what's happening to those girls," she continued. "I want you to know, too. And then, if you still decide to do it, we'll watch the fireworks together. What are you trying to hide? I know everything now. Pretending that this is all some happy transition to a great new world—those days are all gone, Erik. You can't hide from me anymore. That mask doesn't hide *anything.*"

"What makes you think I will even care?" he aloofly asked, although she still heard a tremor in his voice.

"Maybe you won't. Maybe you won't care about them or the lives you're going to take tonight. Or anything except revenge—"

"If you did not care so much, you would be fine."

"I do care about everyone else! I care about Raoul and Phillip and Meg and Caroline and Mrs. Valerius! I'm not going to stop caring about them!"

"But not about me!" he roared.

"Erik, I do care about you," she whispered.

"No." He backed away and pointed his index finger toward her. "No, everything you do is a manipulation to get your way. A game. A bargain. You only pretend to care to get what you want."

"I care, Erik, despite how hard you sometimes make it." She stood.

"You make me insane!" he growled, walking past her in a black blur. She stepped out of his way to avoid being knocked over. "I cannot think! I do not know. Five years of careful planning. Five years only to be stopped by you?"

Before she could respond, he began playing something very horrible on the piano. At first, she thought he was just banging random keys, but the notes soon formed a very macabre, loud, and unpleasant melody. Placing her hands to her ears, Christine ran out of the room before the sound made her completely crazy. She put her head beneath her pillow as it continued, the notes penetrating the door to her bedroom. She couldn't even think, wrapping the pillow over her ears as tightly as possible.

On and on and on. For hours, it seemed.

Finally, she came out, eyes bloodshot and face drained of color. "Erik!" she screamed. "Stop! *Please stop!*"

He ceased playing and sharply glanced at her. "Why? Because you are beginning to feel as mad as I am? Good. Now you know what you've done to me!"

"What!?" She clenched her jaw. "I didn't ask for you to hear me sing that day. I didn't ask for you to be the Spirit. And I certainly didn't ask you to bring me here! Why do you and Cameron want to blame me for everything?"

"I am not him!"

"Then stop helping him! Stop acting like any of this is my fault! It's not! So stop punishing me!"

There were several seconds of silence. "No, it is not," he whispered. "It is not your fault. You're paying for the sins of everyone else in this horrid world, simply because I love you. And I don't know if I can stop. I—I am so very damned. What does it matter now? What does anything matter? I am damned."

Then Christine knew what she had to do.

Deep down, she'd been waiting for someone to save her still. For Raoul to make a miraculous escape. For someone to fix this. Someone stronger and braver. But only she could now.

"I'll be right back. I promise." She went into her bedroom and closed the door, leaving him staring after her. The veil was still lying in the corner of her bathroom, and she picked it up. She placed it on her head, the comb slipping into her hair, and smoothed it over her shoulders. She glanced into the mirror, resolved. Calm.

Then she found her bag with all the contents she'd brought back from London. She tugged out the little cardboard box and opened it. Slowly, she removed the ring. And slid it onto the proper finger.

She went back out.

Sitting on the piano bench, Erik glanced at her. He gasped and leaned backward.

Christine sat beside him and took both his hands into hers, entwining their fingers together. "Erik," she began. "Stop this. Stop all of this right now. And you know what will happen afterwards? We'll leave this horrible place. We'll get married and be together. We'll start over again. And we'll be just fine." She kept her voice steady. Her words were true.

"It's just another m-m-manipulation," he murmured. Yet his gaze stayed on the veil. "You'll leave the second you get your way. You'll leave me alone and with nothing!"

"I won't. I swear to God. I swear on everything. Stop this nightmare. I'll be your wife. A real wife. I'll forget about all of this." She paused. "But, Erik, if you go through with it, I will want to die. I can't be a part of this. You'll have to tie me up to stop me. So stop this. And give us both a chance at life. Please."

She withdrew her hands and embraced him, hugging him against her. He shivered and closed his eyes, resting his head near her neck and chest. One of his hands fell limply into her lap. A soft moan escaped his lips.

"You are so warm and soft," he murmured after several minutes, nuzzling his face into her shoulder. "So good." She heard him sob, "I don't want to be alone! I don't want to go back to that. To nothing. I don't want to have nothing again."

"You won't. Stop this, and I swear to God that you won't." She untied the strings and removed the mask. He flinched, but she didn't. Christine placed a hand on his tattered cheek, stroking it with her fingertips. She nearly tilted her head against his. "We're going to get married. We'll see the world. We'll do everything together."

His head rose as he looked at her. "You'll stay with me forever? You won't run?"

"Forever. Neither of us will be alone." He raised his head and gazed into her eyes, as though trying to determine whether her words were true. His fingers stroked her cheek. Slowly, she leaned in to—

But Erik stood to his feet suddenly, staring forward. "I will check on the girls. I will see…"

"I'll go with you." Her heart jumped with relief.

"It may be dangerous. I could go. And tell you what I—"

"We're in this together now," she firmly replied, standing beside him, still not trusting him to do the right thing. "I have to go with you tonight. However this ends, I want to be there."

"Wear sturdy shoes," he murmured.

Chapter 37

She grabbed her best tennis shoes, throwing off the veil but leaving the ring on her finger. Christine raced back to the living area to put them on, not wanting Erik to sneak away in her absence. But he didn't even try to do so. He was rubbing his temples, his posture stooped. They left together.

"Where are we going?" she asked as they walked outside through the theater entrance.

"You will see." They quickly strode a long way across the field and then, once they reached the city, through several alleys. Finally, they stopped near an abandoned brick garage. The entrances were all locked, but Erik pressed a handheld device and uttered a sequence of numbers. One of the garage doors rolled up with a deep rumble. A two-door sleek black car sat there, obviously driverless. The windows were tinted, and the color caused it to blend in with the darkness. The doors unlocked, and Erik climbed into the driver's seat. "We have no allies in your little mission," he explained. "No one can know. Not Cameron. Not my men."

She climbed into the passenger's side and stared down at what had to be very expensive black leather seats. The dashboard was lit up with navigating devices and other lights and symbols she didn't understand. His driving was like the rest of his movements as he backed out and headed through the empty streets, fast and smooth. It was all a little surreal. "Why don't you always drive?" she asked.

"It is better for me to have my attention on other matters at all times. Let someone else do this mundane task."

"I think it'd be fun to learn."

Erik laughed. "I am sure that could be arranged." He spoke again. But not to her. "Override event set for today at 3:47 PM."

"Cancel event set for today at 3:47 PM?" asked an automated female's voice.

"Yes."

"Event cancelled."

Christine breathed in deeply. "Where are we going?"

"Exactly where you wished. Cameron's compound. I am supposed to meet with him beforehand, and I will do this so he does not become suspicious. It is the perfect night for spying. All the citizens will be in the stadium to listen to his speech, and the streets will have a lower security presence than normal. As will the compound. We will find your answer, as you requested."

The world passed as it always did. The dirty, impoverished cities. The abandoned towns. The people on the sides of the highways with strange signs. Fields and trees with brown leaves still dangling from the branches. And finally Cameron's deceptively bright and shiny world.

"Climb into the back and stay down," Erik ordered so harshly that she jumped. Christine obeyed. Without rolling the window down, Erik somehow spoke to someone, maybe the security person at the front gate. "You will let me pass without interference." Erik drove through without stopping. Their surroundings darkened, and she knew that they had entered the garage area connected to Cameron's compound. For the first time, she felt that Erik was her ally.

He parked and turned to look at her. "You will stay here while I speak to Cameron. No one can see inside. The doors are locked, but I will be alerted if they open. That means I will also be aware if you make any inane attempt to escape, do you understand?"

"Yes." Did Erik really think she'd run off all by herself? She huddled there in the silence after he left, hoping that nothing went wrong. It would be terrifying if hours passed and he never returned. What would she think? That he'd decided to go through with it? That Cameron had discovered their intentions and had Erik killed?

Christine exhaled in relief when Erik opened the door on the driver's side. "Did you speak to him?" she asked.

"Yes."

"What did you say?"

"That all would proceed as planned, although I have made modifications. He suspects nothing."

"When is Cameron's speech?" she asked.

"Thirty minutes or so. We will need to wait here for some time. It is best to have as few people on the streets as possible."

While she didn't think she could sleep, Christine closed her eyes. After about thirty minutes, she opened her lids, too nervous to slumber. Erik's arms were crossed over the steering wheel, and his face was buried in them. She gently touched his back with her fingertips. He glanced at her. She gave him a closed-lip smile. His head swerved to look at the clock. "We'll have to walk. We will draw too much attention in the vehicle."

"Will someone see us?"

"No. I have learned how to move about without notice. You think I would help build this place without hidden access?"

"You built it?"

"Not the original foundation and structures. That was Cameron's doing. I simply added to it so that the Spirit could be omnipresent. I have put more effort into this project than any other one in my entire life. It is a rather horrific masterpiece, no?"

As he led them forward, Christine was shocked by the intricacies of the path. They went through several dim and winding hallways connected to the garage and emerged in a room toward the front of the compound. She blinked in surprise; it was their old room where she'd come for her voice lessons.

Erik fondly glanced at it as well. "The most secure room. When the doors close, they are impenetrable from the outside. I would never allow someone to interrupt our lessons."

To her surprise, Erik pulled back a square patch of blue carpet and revealed a door engraved into the floors. He opened it, and they descended down a set of concrete stairs and into the darkness. They walked through a cement underground tunnel. Erik held a device that provided just enough light for them to get by. They went back upstairs and passed through cramped spaces between houses and buildings. Then back underground for a bit. Twice, they even went through actual homes. She gaped as they saw Sampson putting on pants through a glass wall.

Erik snorted. "Cameron had me keep an especially close eye on those closest to him. He is highly paranoid."

"Do you think he keeps an eye on you?" she asked with worry.

"Oh, he would absolutely love to do so. If he could."

Cool air brushed against her skin throughout the journey, sending goose bumps up and down her arms. If it weren't for the terrible circumstances, Christine might have found a little thrill in this mission, sneaking around with Erik through back passages and little tunnels. Finally, he said, "This is the closest exit. I will go first. Stay behind me and remain quiet."

They emerged near several small blue duplexes with perfectly trimmed yards and dying gardens. The late afternoon autumn sun cast shadows that concealed them if they remained near the foundations. They soon approached a stoic brick building that contained at least eight stories. It was simple, yet there was something sinister about the structure. "Where are we?"

"The medical facility."

"That's new, isn't it?" He nodded. "How do you know she's here?"

"I pulled a file in Cameron's office. All it said was "Procedure C." I do not know what we will discover. Are you sure you want to find out?"

"Yes." Too nervous to think straight, Christine headed for the front glass doors. Erik spoke, "Do not be ridiculous. You think they will let you march up there?"

"Then how do we get in?"

"The back, of course. But you will have to be very silent. Sometimes your footsteps are like that of stampeding elephants." She glared. "But I love you for it," he said affectionately.

Erik easily manipulated a lock, and they entered through the back. It was cold inside, far too frigid for comfort. They ascended an empty stairwell. She tried to walk quietly on the white tiles, but her footsteps echoed. "Sorry," she murmured. He just made an amused noise. Someone came by, a nurse of some type, and they ducked to the side. "What if someone does see?" she asked.

He shrugged. "They can be neutralized." He probably saw her expression. "Temporarily," he added.

The top floor was quiet. There were no nurses or other employees around. An empty metal desk and metal chair sat in the middle of the room beneath a single, dim fluorescent light. Several grey file cabinets were beside it, all closed and probably locked. Surrounding the desk on all sides were seven white closed doors with silver knobs. It was isolated and dark and creepy. Christine's heart pounded wildly. "Which way?" she asked.

"I am not sure it matters." His tone sent a shiver down her spine. She started to head for the nearest door. Erik grabbed her shoulder. "Christine. I could look for you. I will not lie as to what I discover."

He knew it was bad. They both knew it was bad.

"Erik, I've been through a lot," she whispered. "I'm tired of hiding from things."

Erik manipulated another lock and stepped into the room. A silence passed. Then he said, "The girl is asleep. We will be quick."

Christine's stomach turned as she entered. It looked like a strange combination between a hospital room and a hotel room. There were bandages and silver scissors and a green bottle of pills sitting upon a nightstand, but there was no modern medical equipment. The walls were painted white, and the single window was concealed by grey blinds. Christine stared down at a sleeping dark-haired girl who was a little younger than she was. "I don't understand," she whispered. "She looks okay."

Erik tilted his head and studied the girl. "Either they have done something to her mind, or—" He lifted the white sheets and ugly brown blanket.

Christine stepped back with a gasp of horror.

A foot was missing, chopped off directly above the ankle. White gauze hid the carnage.

"No," she choked, stepping backward again and covering her hand with her mouth. Yet she'd known it would be something like this. Cameron's punishment for her taken out on these poor girls. A missing foot, the perfect penalty for running away. "No, no, no."

"Christine," Erik whispered, touching her shoulders. "It is—"

"No!" She ran out and started to grab the knob of the door to the next room, labeled Room 1, needing to know whether every area held the same sort of horror. Erik grabbed her and held her in place.

"Christine," he said in a soothing voice. "Let me look first. I will not lie to you. We cannot afford to have you break down here, do you understand? Someone will hear."

She stepped back. She was on the verge of a panic attack and knew this would be a very dangerous place to have one. After touching the side of her cheek, Erik entered and closed the door halfway behind him.

First, there was a silence. And then Christine heard a very strange and heartbreaking conversation take place.

"Is someone there?" asked a younger female's voice. "I feel someone. Please. Is someone there?"

Silence.

"I know someone is there!" she continued. "I feel you. Please speak. I'm scared! Please say something!"

And then Erik's voice. "Yes, child. It is the Spirit."

"That voice!" she cried with pained delight. "You are the Spirit!? Please say something else," she begged. "Please. Please don't leave.

Please. Are you there, Spirit? I still feel you."

"I am here, child."

"Your voice is like heaven. Oh, Spirit, I'm sorry I wasn't good. I'm so sorry. Please say you'll forgive me. I'll be good now. I'll be a good example."

Erik weakly whispered, "You are forgiven, child."

"I'll go to heaven?"

"Of course. All is forgiven."

The girl hesitated. "Will you take me there now? Take me to heaven?" A sob escaped her throat. "I don't want to be here anymore. I want to go to heaven with you, Spirit! Please!"

"It is not time yet, my dear," Erik replied, a crack in his voice. "It is not time to go to heaven."

"No, please. Please don't make me be here anymore!" she begged. "Please take me with you!"

"I cannot," he whispered. "I cannot do that now. But you will be fine. You will. Goodnight, child. Goodnight."

When Erik emerged and shut the door behind him, Christine saw something in his eyes that she had never seen before that moment. Disgust—not toward the girl but toward all of this. *Regret.* The girl's sobs were still audible from inside.

"What—?" Christine couldn't even force the question out.

Erik inhaled before softly answering, "Blinded."

Hugging her arms to her chest, Christine cried. She felt Erik pulling her forward by the shoulder and allowed him to have control. "You must be quiet," he said. "You must. Or they will find us."

Somehow she was able to make her sobs less audible. He led her down the stairs and out the back door, through tunnels and passages that blurred before her eyes. She was still too shocked to do anything but be compliant, unable to think or comprehend what was happening. Christine stumbled once underground, but Erik caught her and steadied her. Finally, when they were in the practice room again, she felt some lucidity. Christine stopped walking and was jerked forward as he continued toward the exit. Erik paused and looked down at her.

"What are we doing?" she whispered. "Where are we going?"

"Leaving," he replied. "We are leaving. There will be no explosions. Cameron will give the speech, and nothing will occur. He will not have my services. So he won't last much longer."

Christine nodded as his words warmly washed over her. He was done. He was really, really done. "Thank you," she managed to choke out. He started to turn away. She remembered Cameron's threat. "Erik, he'll hurt them out of revenge," she whispered in a panic. "The other women! He'll hurt them because you went away, and he'll blame that on me!"

"He will not last long without my help," Erik replied. "The economy will improve, and people will thrive outside the sect again. Do you understand?" She nodded but continued to wipe tears away. "This is what you wanted, no?" he angrily asked. "To leave? Did you not promise to me that I just had to stop this and take you away from here, and all would be fine? Did not you say that multiple times?"

"Yes, Erik. I'm incredibly grateful. It is what I wanted. But—"

She was interrupted by a soft ringing. It came from Erik's jacket. His phone. With an angry sigh, he pulled it out and looked at the screen. He pushed the button to answer it but said nothing to the person on the other end. She could hear someone screaming into his ear. Cameron.

"Don't do anything stupid," Erik finally said. "All will still proceed as planned. You'll make a mess of this situation. Wait for me." Christine studied his eyes, trying to tell if Erik was lying. What if he changed his mind again? "Yes. I will be there soon. Do not be an idiot, Cameron. Do not undo all of my hard work!" Erik hung up and stared forward.

"Well?" she whispered, taking his hand and pulling him back from whatever ledge he was standing on. "Erik? What's happening?"

He looked down at her. "Cameron is prepared to go forward with an inferior version of my plan. It won't work, will look entirely too suspicious, but people will still perish." Erik studied her face. "There is a way to completely end this tonight. With that audience present, it would be perfect. But I would have to leave you alone."

"Is it dangerous?" she choked out.

"For you, yes. Not for me. And I will lock you in here. It is your choice. However, if I do this, we will have to leave the country very quickly afterwards. I will take you, and you will never see this place again. Do you understand?" His voice shook.

"What are you going to do?"

"A sort of announcement."

"I–" *Could she trust him to do the right thing?*

"It is your decision, Christine. Be it tonight or within the year, Cameron Lourdes is finished."

"Do it," she whispered with a swallow. "Let's stop this now."

"Fine, then. You will stay here. Be silent. Don't open the door."

"I won't." He turned to leave. "Wait!"

Erik whirled toward her. "Hush! Someone will hear you. What is it now?"

"I-I just wanted to tell you to be safe, Erik. I want you to come back. Okay?" She smiled at him, her first genuine smile in a long time. Erik stared at her a moment longer, and then he left.

Christine slid down against the wall and to the carpet, breathing heavily in the silence. Waiting. Shivering. Several minutes later, she heard someone near the door, loud and unfamiliar footsteps that were not Erik's. She squeezed her eyes shut, hoping no one had heard them talking earlier. The door jiggled but remained locked. They couldn't get to her.

A silence passed. Maybe the person was gone. The wait was agonizing.

Her thoughts were interrupted by a child's high-pitched, agonized scream.

The threats began.

It seemed that yet another girl was about to be punished in her place.

Chapter 38

Christine clutched the sides of her head and stared at the floor, praying that someone would come to the rescue before this horrific decision had to be made. Yet she knew that wasn't going to happen.

"No! Ouch! Ah! No! It hurts! *No! Help!*" The little girl cried out, her voice hoarse from tears. "Help me! Help me!"

"I know you're in there!" hollered a man. "I heard you. And I'll rip her arm off if you don't get out here! Do you understand? I am this close."

She could stay in that room and *live*—and listen to a child be tortured to death. Or she could leave and stop the torment…and maybe die.

"No! Help me!" The girl released an earth-shattering scream.

Please God help me. Surely you're not really on Cameron's side.

Trembling, she stood and made her way to the door. She opened it and looked out. One of Cameron's guards, a short and heavyset man with beady eyes, had Abby's arm twisted behind her back so tightly that the limb looked like it was about to snap in half. The little girl's face was scrunched up in pain as she tried to sink to her knees and escape.

"Stop it!" Christine shouted. "I'm out now! Leave her alone!" Large hands clamped down roughly on her shoulders from behind. A chill raced through her body. *Why hadn't she looked behind her?* Maybe it didn't matter. As soon as she'd stepped out of that safe room, she'd signed her life away.

The first man pushed Abby aside. She fell down to her hands and knees on the ground, sobbing and scrambling away. As the second man held Christine in place and began to tie her hands behind her back with a rough and scratchy material, the first man spoke into a radio. "It worked," he said. "It's Christine Dachelet. And she's definitely all alone."

"You found a girl to use?" asked Cameron. His voice was raspy and angry. "Good. I was worried you wouldn't with the assembly happening right now. Excellent. Excellent. Get her to me right now. You'll both be rewarded. Reinforcement is on the way."

"Reinforcement?" he replied with a snort. "I think the two of us can handle this little gal."

Cameron grunted. "Evil things come in small packages, my friend. I have to go. Get her here. *Now.*"

"Done." The first man turned the radio off.

"When he told you to find a girl, I don't think he wanted you to torture his granddaughter," said the guard holding her with a chuckle. She still couldn't see him, but Christine could sense that he was taller and stronger.

The first man shrugged. "She was the only one around."

"What if Lourdes finds out?"

"Well, I'm not going to tell. And *you* won't tell. And, from what I understand, Mrs. Dachelet here is going to be lucky if she still has a tongue in the morning." Christine shuddered, the visions of the others girls coming back to haunt her. Death wasn't the only thing she had to worry about. "And you—" He looked down at a sniffling Abby. "You're not going to tell, are you, sweetheart?" he asked with clear intimidation. Abby shook her head and wiped her eyes. "Good girl." He turned back to Christine. "It's time to go. I know you'll be a good girl, too."

The one time she tried to struggle, her arms were jerked back with such force that she swore she heard them pop in their sockets. Several other men joined them as they arrived at an awaiting black car. Surrounded on all sides with her hands tied behind her back, Christine was trapped. The men stared at her with an awful mixture of disdain, curiosity, and desire.

"What's she done?" asked a younger one. "I thought she was our spokeswoman. Yeah. She's that singer."

"Who knows? But Cameron says she's the greatest threat we've ever faced."

They all looked her up and down before laughing heartily.

"What'd you do, sweety?" asked the young one directly to her. "Burn your husband's dinner?"

"I bet she left the iron on too long," said another. "Put a big ol' hole right in the middle of his shirt!"

Christine ignored them as they continued to guffaw. From several of them, she sensed more ignorance than evil. They had found security and a sense of belonging here, and now they were simply doing their job. And that's what Cameron had built his entire society upon, wasn't it? Ignorance. How ironic that he had used the most intelligent man in the world to do it.

Erik, where are you? She willed herself not to cry in front of them, to not be as weak as they thought she was. Her hands shook in her lap.

A memory returned.

Her father pulled her up onto his warm lap. "Did I ever tell you about your birth, Christine? No? Well, it was one heck of a crazy day. You were early, and your mother and I didn't know what we were doing. Our car broke down in the rain, spun out of control right in the middle of the highway. A very nice man, an angel right from heaven, put us into his car and drove us straight to the hospital. A Farruke' or something like that. Wish I could have sent him a gift basket. He might have saved your life that day."

She smiled sadly to herself. Farrokh.

Erik was right. They had been set on paths from the beginning of their lives.

The car arrived at the arena, and one of the guards threw open her door. A cool gust of air hit her arms and face. In the distance, she could hear Cameron's voice and the cheers of an enormous audience. She was forced out of the vehicle, and she blinked in the bright, artificial light.

Christine stumbled as she was pushed forward. She looked for a stray shadow or a golden orb, any sign of hope. She saw nothing.

And she knew that no one was coming to save her.

She could hear Cameron's speech when they got out of the car. The cheers of the crowd grew louder and louder until they sounded hysterical in their excitement.

"No matter what happens," said Cameron in a loud voice. "We will have no fear!" The audience roared. "We have God on our side! This is our time!"

Instead of continuing the speech, Cameron paused for a very long moment. Outside of a few murmurs from the audience, there was nothing. "All-all right," Cameron finally continued. "All right. I apologize. I was overcome with such…gratitude to the Lord that I lost myself and forgot my lines." The audience softly chuckled and applauded. "I want to thank you all for your—"

As Cameron spoke, Christine noticed a note of aggravation in his voice. The quality of the speech also seemed to decline in those next minutes, as though Cameron hadn't been prepared for it, as though he'd been expecting something to happen. And it hadn't. Despite her circumstances, she felt satisfaction.

He concluded, "And that is why we have gathered tonight my friends. Our event coordinator will now tell you about our future meetings. A piano solo will conclude the assembly. Goodnight. God bless you all." Applause followed.

Then Cameron found her. Her heart dropped. "Ah. And what do we have here? It looks like our favorite little singer. Christine. Good evening, Christine. So good to see you tonight." His tone was bitter. "Where is Erik, my dear?" he asked, leaning over her and spitting in her face. "Surely he doesn't let his little wife wander alone from place to place? And these clothes." He tsked several times and ran his hands over her arms. "They're not very becoming of a young lady. What on earth have you been up to, my girl?" Christine glared at the ground.

Cameron gestured for them to move forward. The guards followed him, forcing Christine toward the building in back. Was she going to die in the same place Anthony had? The blinds were all drawn, but the sound from outside was still audible. A piano was now playing a gentle melody, signifying the end of the assembly. Cameron stood over Christine as she was forced into a hard chair.

"Where the hell is Erik?" Cameron screamed, leaning right into her face. "He was supposed to be here! This was my night! And you destroyed it, didn't you, you *disgusting* little bitch!? Where is he?"

"I don't know," she muttered, keeping her gaze focused downward. He backhanded her hard across the right cheek. She groaned and turned her head. "Stop! I don't know anything!"

"Well, it looks like he's abandoned you here, doesn't he? He left you in that room all alone." Cameron continued, moving away from her and pacing across the room. "Maybe he's abandoned both of us. Erik is a soulless monster. The Devil, I think. He cares about nothing except himself. Perhaps he's playing us both, my dear? Is that it? He doesn't care about either of us?" He leaned over her again, a demonic leer contorting his flushed face.

"Please," she begged in horror.

"Where's Erik?!" He grabbed her chin with his thumb and index finger, forcing her to look him in the eye.

"I don't know!"

Cameron then said, "Well, now I am going forward with *my* plan. And I'll make sure that the Valerius bitch is the first to go. I'll make sure she's burned alive!"

"No!" she shouted with a sob. "Please don't! Please stop! I don't know anything!"

Cameron ignored her. "Do it," he said to one of his men. "It's ready to go." The man nodded and raced off. Cameron waited there with his arms folded.

"Please," she whispered. "Please don't do this."

"This is my destiny!" he snapped. "With or without that freak of nature, this is my time!"

She waited for an explosion, hunkering down into the chair and bracing herself.

No explosion came. Instead, they all heard something very strange outside. The piano stopped in the middle of the song. A few shouts followed. Then a haunting, echoing voice.

Erik's voice.

Someone ripped open the blinds. Everyone in the room gaped as bright light filled the room, illuminating them all in a ghostly glow. "What the hell are you—?" Cameron started to ask but then looked outwards with the rest of his guards. Every audience member was staring up at the two screens by the stage, hypnotized. The stage itself was empty.

"Oh," Christine whispered.

The haunting voice echoed throughout the entire stadium. "Good evening. Welcome. Allow me to introduce myself. I am…the Spirit."

"Praise God!" shouted several people.

"Save us!"

"Take us with you!"

Others fell to their knees and raised their clasped hands toward the sky. With that perfect voice, his words were very believable.

"What the hell?" roared Cameron, finally able to rip his attention away from the spectacle. "Someone turn on the sound! Someone show me the screens! What the hell is happening?"

One of the other men pushed several buttons on the nearby electronic system. A television screen in the room flashed on, and he flipped through several channels. A tall, dark, faceless silhouette appeared on the screen. No details could be discerned. It was a talking shadow with the voice of an angel.

"Unfortunately," Erik continued. "I am here to clarify a few matters, and I fear that many of you will find yourselves rather disappointed. You see, you have been deceived beyond your wildest dreams. I have taken your lives and made you mere puppets. And perhaps—perhaps since you believe me to be a Spirit, you do not care. You want me to control you, no? Ah. But here-here is where you will be disappointed." A pause. "I am but a man. Or perhaps a monster. But I am no Spirit." A pause as the faces of the audience contorted in confusion. Still, they remained mesmerized. "Now let me tell you, and the rest of this nation, a little tale…"

"No," whispered Cameron, pulling himself away from the voice. He pounded his fists against the glass so hard that Christine feared it would shatter. "No! No! *No!* Stop him!" Cameron rapidly pushed button after button until he shut off the sound and video in the room, awakening everyone from their stupor.

Tears streaming down her swollen cheek, Christine laughed. "He's stopping you! He's stopping you! Now everyone will know!"

"How is this happening?!" Cameron screamed.

"Someone's hijacked the equipment!" replied one of the men.

"What floor?" asked Cameron, running around the room in a panic. "What floor is he on?"

"I don't know! He could be anywhere!"

"Well, it has to be in this building, right, you idiot?! Right? Get up there and kill him! Just kill him!" Cameron let out a growl of anger, his eyes insane with rage. "I am going on stage! Get me on camera! Now! Get him off the screen and me on this instant!" He turned toward Christine, sneering. "And keep her alive for now! I may need her in a few moments." He stormed out of the room and raced outside. Several of the men ran upstairs to search for Erik and to try to reclaim the screens, and the rest followed Cameron. One guard remained with Christine.

"—and once the economy crumbled, there was no hope. Your crime rates skyrocketed. Your birth rates plummeted. Only Cameron Lourdes seemed to thrive. And that was no coincidence."

He was telling them everything.

"Bring her out here!" Cameron screamed. She gasped as she was forced up and out onto the stage. An unsettling mob had begun to surround it. Most of the audience was still transfixed by Erik's speech. Some people were crying. Some were marching toward the stage, hungry for revenge. Some were staring into space, too stunned to do anything.

Cameron and his men had managed to get control of one of the screens. He didn't have too many guards at his service by this point. But he did have a few loyal forces remaining, maybe those who had been at least vaguely aware of the plot all along. Or those who didn't care what crimes Cameron had committed so long as they had power.

"Listen!" Cameron exclaimed, raising his hands in the air and trying to reclaim the attention of his people. Sweat dripped from his forehead and into his beard. "Listen to me! These are all lies! Ungodly lies told to you by the Devil!" He gestured to the screen where Erik was still speaking. "That is the Devil! Don't you see what he's trying to do? He's trying to tempt you away from our blessed community! The Devil is trying to trick you!"

"So you see," Erik continued. "It was not the work of God. Quite the opposite—"

Erik's voice overpowered Cameron's in a million different ways. It wasn't hard to tell who had a stronger grip on the audience.

She shrieked as two hands gripped her arms and dragged her to the middle of the stage.

"Here's our little singer," said Cameron, using her to lure Erik away from his mission. But Erik didn't react on the screen. He didn't flinch. Maybe he didn't even know. "Too bad she'll never sing again, eh, Erik?" Still no reaction. *"Erik!* Look at what I'm going to do to her!" Cameron grabbed Christine's hair, jerking her head back. "Do you want to see what happens to disobedient women?" he asked. His voice was desperate. He knew the game was about over, which, while wonderful for the rest of society, was horrible for her. Cameron literally had nothing to lose and only revenge to take.

A gunshot rang into the air. Screams as everyone around her lurched backward. Cameron grabbed his right shoulder with his left hand

and sank to his knees, now bleeding through his gnarled fingers. Someone had shot him.

Clutching his arm, Cameron stared at her with pure hatred. "All this trouble over you? And for *what*? These people are all doomed to Hell all because of you. You've doomed the entire country to Hell!"

Two other men circled around on both sides, blurred at the corners of her vision. "Do it now," Cameron ordered from the ground, his voice growing weaker. "Take out her tongue. I don't care if it kills her. Just do it. Maybe it'll get his attention." She clamped her mouth shut, grinding her teeth together. One man squeezed her nose closed so that she couldn't breathe. The other forced her head back.

"Open it, or I'll take out an eye first!" the man spat. He yanked her hair out of her face. "Open up now."

A sharp object was dangerously close to her eyeballs. And she needed to breathe anyway. Her lips slowly parted.

Erik's heavenly voice floated all around them as he continued to speak. As Christine tried to turn her head and delay the inevitable, she felt a sharp pain slice through her cheek. The metallic taste of blood filled her mouth, causing her to gag and sputter. She sensed a sharp point against the back of her tongue. Christine squeezed her eyes shut and braced herself.

A gust of air brushed against her face.

Pop.

Chapter 39

The man who held the knife fell away from her, his head twisted unnaturally on his neck as he crumpled to the ground. The other guard who had been near her was now twitching a few feet away, his expression one of agony. Cameron stared at the scene with his mouth hanging open. His face was pale as he bled from the gunshot wound. Christine blinked, disoriented. She sat up on her elbows and looked back and forth.

A tall silhouette detached itself from the other shadows behind the stage. With one arm, the shadow scooped up Christine. She understood. A recording was playing on the screen. Erik was here.

"Demon! Devil!" Cameron's voice growled nearby. He attempted to stand and then half-stumbled, half-crawled toward Erik. "I hate you! I hate you! I would have given you everything! I hate you!"

Erik turned toward him. The masked man took several slow, calculated steps toward Mr. Lourdes. Cameron backed up toward the edge of the stage, still waving his good arm and insanely shouting, "Devil! Demon! You're Satan! Away Satan! Devil! Devil!"

"Mr. Lourdes," began Erik in a calm, cold voice. "It sounds like your people want a word with you. Why don't you...*inspire* them?" Erik barely touched Cameron's chest with his free hand, but it was enough to cause Cameron to go flying off the stage and into the enraged audience. An agonized scream of horror followed. Several morbid crackling sounds pierced the smoke-scented air. She shuddered and turned away as the deceived people descended upon Cameron Lourdes.

Chaos completely consumed the background. Crying and shouting and the clatter of metal against metal. Children bawling and people shouting to the sky over and over, "Oh, God. Oh, God. Help me! Help me!"

A huge white cloud of smoke puffed out around them, a shield of sorts. They headed behind the stage and into the passage behind the curtains. Into a dark tunnel. Then they were outside again. There was an "oomph" as Erik threw someone out of their way. Debris flew through the air. She heard a soft shattering noise, and it sounded like something had broken. Erik cursed but didn't slow down.

Through a shed, and they were soon moving downwards; the cacophony above became less audible. The air was still and much cooler. Erik spoke to her, one hand behind her skull as he maintained her in a sitting position. "Keep your head up. We will be fine soon."

Erik slowed to a fast stride. "Christine, we are safe now. But you must open your mouth and let me look." Her arms were around his neck, and her fingers were curled into his jacket for dear life. She resisted in her panic. "You must. So I know what to do next." With a soft groan, she finally did so. Erik gently tilted her face from side to side, examining her.

"Do I have a tongue?" she murmured.

Erik laughed. "You would not be able to ask if you did not. Can't you feel it?"

A pause. "Yes." She gave a shuddery sigh and put her head back against his shoulder. Then she glanced up again and raised a hand to his face, her expression softening. His mask had fallen off.

"What in God's name were you doing up there?"

"Abby. Outside the room. They were torturing—I couldn't let…"

"It is fine. It is fine." He quickly calmed her. "We will talk later. We must leave now."

"I'm okay to walk. We'll go faster that way." He set her down.

They wandered together a long way through the tunnels. Her steps were heavy, and her head was pounding with pain and exhaustion. Still, there was relief. And far too much to think about. She could feel him watching her from the corner of his eye. Erik led her up a set of steps to the surface and into an underground parking garage, lit only with a few dim bulbs. There were two black cars in the entire dark lot. He approached one. "Do you have hidden cars everywhere?"

"Here and there," he replied distantly. Erik stared at her before climbing inside. "Christine—"

"Yes?"

"Never mind." He turned on the radio, and they listened to the news.

"—many things we don't know. We don't know if that was a prank, Tim. You know, someone's idea of a sick joke. It's—Oh, we have some aerial shots, and one look will tell you all you need to know. It's chaos there tonight."

"What about the cities?" asked another man. "Have we gotten reports on the reactions there?"

"A few reports of riots and looting here and there. But I think, like you and I, most people are just waiting to see what's found. If, and that's a very big if—*if* that strange broadcast turns out to be true—well, you know, it would—"

"It'd change everything," the other announcer agreed. "We'd have to look at the last several years with a giant magnifying glass, wouldn't we?"

"Exactly, exactly. Ladies and gentlemen, please stay with us as we continue to cover this possibly historical evening…"

Everyone was either discussing Erik's broadcast or the demise of Cameron's world. They all questioned whether Erik's words were true. How could one man be responsible for all that? It had to be a hoax, right? Maybe someone had become angry at Cameron and made up an entire story to destroy him. That's what some of his supporters seemed to think.

"Oh, well, we just got some good news," said the announcer. "We've now gotten word that Phillip Chandler, the eldest son of Ethan Chandler, is safe. Now, we don't know if he was ever in danger. Or if he was abroad. All of this is coming in as we speak. But we can now tell you that he is confirmed to be alive and safe. Let's go to Rick with more details."

She took a breath. "Erik?"

"Yes, the other one is alive, too. He's in a more private location. I'll have to release him myself."

They continued to listen to the radio. "So if we take apart that weird broadcast—we basically get a single man. And we're assuming it's a man. Um…right. So this man—"

"They sound very confused," she said.

"Yes," Erik replied. "They will not have solid evidence until I carefully reveal my home. I will do that within days. And then we will leave this country. Since you appeared on stage that night, you may also be wanted for questioning."

"You think I'd be in trouble?"

He shrugged. "You were Cameron's spokeswoman. They will interrogate everyone. The investigation will go on for years, but they will only find what I want them to."

She leaned back into the seat. *I did it. I really did it. I stopped everything. Raoul and Phillip are alive.* She glanced at Erik. And now…Now it was done. She would be okay. She felt calm and hopeful.

Silence followed them all the way back. The streets were quiet, only a few other cars on the road. Everyone else was probably glued to their television sets.

When they were back underground, Erik fixed her an iced herbal tea. The bleeding had long stopped, and the cold liquid felt good on her mouth. "Sleep, if you would like," he said. He had replaced his mask.

She needed sleep, likely weeks' worth of it. "What will you be doing?" she cautiously asked.

"Sorting it all out," he replied. "What to take. What to leave as evidence. And what to destroy."

"Can I help?"

"You do not need to."

"I want to," she said. "If I can."

He was silent for a moment, his focus on some documents. For a second, she thought Erik was just going to ignore her. Finally, he said, "In the room with the cabinets—you can take the files and put them into boxes. Then tape the boxes shut."

She nodded and went forward. They worked throughout that entire night. They labeled and sorted and collected it all together. She didn't ask about the more sinister looking papers, maps with circled locations and charts that showed the sharp downturn of the economy. She just labored at his side, stopping occasionally for a snack or a glass of water.

"What will you do with the furniture?" she asked during a break, gazing at the sofas and decorations.

"It can all be replaced," he replied. "That was a delightful piano. But I will not haul these things with me. It's time to start anew, as you said, Christine. We will forget all of this and begin again."

Near sunrise, he walked beneath the ceiling door. "I must go down," he said. "That is where they will find most of their evidence. Within the main system. You may come or stay."

"I'll go, too," she replied. She slipped on some comfortable shoes, climbed out, and followed him through the familiar tunnel.

When they reached the bottom, he headed toward the other systems and typed into the keyboards. Christine didn't know enough to help with this process, so she stood back and watched him. Erik seemed to be deleting some things and ridding other documents of security walls. There were beeps and hums as billions upon billions of bytes of information were processed. Finally he looked at her.

"Come," he said. "I think you might enjoy this part."

Curious, she followed him out of the room. They rode the third elevator, and then they went to the surface, toward the theater exit. He led her to a broken window. Christine looked out. "I don't see anything," she said.

"Wait," he whispered.

And then she saw them. Blues and oranges and yellows and reds. Butterflies and hummingbirds and other beautiful creatures. All flying across the fields. They were not too packed together to draw attention but instead came more subtly in little groups. Still, it was quite a vision.

She knew they were the fake ones, all returning home to their true master. They swarmed into the theater, many heading downwards toward the basement stairs. A few crashed into the walls and then lay uselessly on the ground, their artificial wings fluttering every so often. It was both lovely and disturbing. She watched them arrive for a long time.

"What will you do with them?" she asked as Erik looked on with her.

"I am going to destroy them. While the current administration is a billion times more benevolent than Cameron's society, this sort of technology is still far too tempting." He sighed. "I doubt I will ever find all of them. But many. The most powerful ones will self-destruct from a distance."

He quickly gathered up the insects that had already broken into his bony hands. She grabbed some as well, studying them for signs that they were artificial. It was amazing how difficult it was to find such signs; the creatures were near perfection. Erik finished some work in the computer room as she collected the bugs. After tirelessly continuing their massive project through the rest of the day, she nearly slumped into her soup bowl that evening.

Erik touched her shoulder. "Sleep now," he said. "You have done more than enough. I will finish the rest."

She started to protest but then stood. Before she left, Christine gazed over the room and at all they had accomplished together in less than twenty-four hours. Her slumber was long and dreamless.

When she awoke and came out of her room, washed and dressed, a bowl of oatmeal awaited her. Soft food for her sore mouth. Slowly, she sipped the warm, sweet mixture. Erik moved in and out of the rooms at a rapid pace, grabbing items now and then for storage. Then he stopped and looked at her.

"We will leave this evening," he said. "The authorities will swarm in faster than the butterflies once notified."

"Where are we going?" she asked.

"First, Chandler. Then–" He gestured widely as though to say: *Everywhere!*

"Erik, I wanted to thank you for what you did. It meant everything to me. I...thank you." He didn't respond.

Christine headed into her bedroom closet and began to sort through her clothes. The ones that reminded her of Cameron would be left behind or destroyed, especially the dresses that looked more like creepy costumes. Outside of her clothing, she didn't see much that she wanted. Then again, she hadn't had many possessions since she was a small child; that had been part of giving up the world.

After stuffing a hairbrush and hand mirror into the suitcase, she moved to gather Cocoa's things. As she tried to force the cat into a plastic traveling kennel, Cocoa struggled and ran in the opposite direction and meowed in protest. "Come on, kitty. You can't stay down here. Do you want to get arrested?" The cat swiped at her hand and left a small scratch near her wrist. "Ouch!" Christine finally managed to push Cocoa inside and latch the door. She went to the sink to wash out the cut.

Erik glanced in. "I heard you cry out," he said.

"Yeah. Cocoa was less than happy about leaving." Christine paused. "She's going to have to be locked up a lot while we travel, isn't she?"

"I am afraid so. If she is vocal, there may also be situations where she will need to be sedated. For our own security."

"Hmm."

He must have seen her expression. "But we will manage. We will manage." Erik glanced at her suitcase. "Are you ready?"

"I do believe I am," she replied with a tired smile. Grabbing her suitcase and the kennel, Christine followed him out of the room. To her surprise, he entered the single locked room that she'd never seen. Curious, she followed him into the dim space.

"What's this?" she asked.

"My bedroom. If you could call it that."

The room was the size of a large closet. There were no pictures or decorations, and the only ornate piece of furniture was a cedar dresser with four drawers stacked on top of each other. His shirts and jackets were neatly hung up on a silver rack against the wall, like in a clothing store. A long metal cot with plain white sheets and a lonely pillow stood in the center. The place looked like a prison cell. "Erik, how did you sleep here?"

"I don't sleep often. Therefore, it is silly to devote much space to the task, isn't it? This did just fine."

It further confirmed the idea that this entire mission had been one of anger and revenge—not power or wealth.

Erik opened the drawers and removed several objects, a digital watch with multiple buttons, a strange silver sphere the size of a tennis ball, and a...black gun. She gasped. "My dear," he said upon seeing her expression. "I have no plans to use these items. I simply do not want anyone else to get their hands on them. But if you think that we are going to travel countries and oceans without any sort of protection—"

"I understand," she said. "Are all of those things weapons?"

"Yes." He shrugged. "When I became bored, especially before I first saw you, I created. Music. Computer programs. Tunnels. Weapons. Anything that came to mind."

She shook her head in disbelief. "Erik, I know you'll do many more amazing things."

He continued to rummage through the drawers. "I cannot believe how much time I spent here, making and collecting all this nonsense." He stopped searching. "I suppose that is enough for now." He took her suitcase from her, lifting it high above the ground. Erik headed for the ceiling entrance, and the stairs descended one last time. "Say your adieus to this place. I am sure you will miss it terribly. So many happy memories." There was a touch of sadness amongst the sarcasm.

"Good and bad, this place changed everything," she replied, looking it over one last time. "I'll never forget it."

Goodbye strange little home…

It was cloudy and mid-afternoon when they reached the surface. She inhaled the fresh air and hoped that their new home would be aboveground, where she could always feel the sunshine. They walked the long distance to the car, and he placed her belongings into the trunk. She sat in the passenger's seat and waited. Erik climbed in. He sat there without starting the car, staring forward.

"Is everything okay?" she asked, playing with her ring.

He shook his head but answered, "Yes."

They reached what looked like a smaller abandoned warehouse. It was made of metal, now rusted, and half the windows were broken out or boarded up. Overgrown weeds grew up the walls and fences, inviting moths and gnats.

"Can I tell him goodbye, please?" she asked. "Otherwise, he'll just keep looking for me…" It hurt a little, but perhaps not as badly as she'd imagined it would when this moment arrived.

"I will give you five minutes." Hugging her arms against herself, she followed Erik inside. "Watch your step," he said. "There are nails."

Brown and grey birds flew over them, twittering, and sunlight streaked in from above. She stepped over broken boxes and wooden planks. She sneezed several times from the stirred-up dust.

"Here," he said. They were in front of a grey door. He unlocked it, opened it, folded his arms, and stepped back. She looked inside.

Chapter 40

Thinner than she remembered him, Raoul was sitting on the concrete floor, his arms hugging his knees. He wore the same clothes, and they were dirty and torn. Still, her friend appeared uninjured. He looked up in disbelief. Then he slowly grinned. Raoul jumped up and walked unsteadily toward her. His dusty hands reached outwards. "Christine!" She wrapped her arms around him. "Christine!" he choked out. "I can't believe it! I didn't think I'd ever see you again!"

"I know. Me neither!" She leaned back and gave him a watery smile.

"Are you okay? What's happened? What the hell is going on out there?" He glanced toward the open door.

"It's over," she said, a hand resting on his upper arm. "Erik exposed everything that happened, that there's no Spirit. So Cameron is done. Dead. I think everything's going to be okay now." She told him a few more details and about Erik's announcement on the screen. About Cameron and the mob of angry people. She didn't include her interaction with Erik. She left out the battles and described the end of the war.

"That's awesome!" he exclaimed. "Great. So-so who brought you here?"

"Erik."

His smile disappeared, and his jaw tightened. Raoul half-glared at the empty doorway. "All right. So what happens next? Does he want some kind of pardon because I don't think—"

"Your brother's okay, too!" Good news first. "And your mom!"

"That's great, Christine. You did it!" He gave her another hug. "I knew you could."

"I did," she whispered.

"But now what? Where do we go?" He again looked at that open door and tugged on her hand. Her heart ached for him.

"You're going to go back home with your family. That's where you belong. You'll be safe there. You can help everyone get back to normal."

"What about you? You'll come with me, right?"

She swallowed. "Everything's going to be okay, Raoul. I promise."

"Where are you going?"

"I don't know yet, but I'll be okay. It's like a new adventure. I'm kind of excited." That wasn't really a lie.

Raoul's eyes widened and then narrowed in furious understanding. "No! He can't make you go with him just because he stopped terrorizing the country! He can't do that! I'll get the cops! I'll get the army! He can't do that!" Raoul nearly ran for the door. She held him back with both hands.

"Shh." She held his shoulders, massaging them with her thumbs. Christine leaned and whispered into his ear. "It's going to be okay. You can give the country hope again. I know you will. You and your brother. Everyone will want to hear from you. You have an important part in all this."

"No! I won't let him do this to you! There has to be a way!"

"I'm so, so sorry." She saw Erik come in silently behind them. "I'll never forget you," she whispered. "Thank you for everything. I couldn't have done this without you. You helped me see the truth." Before Raoul could turn around, Erik had taken out a syringe and pierced the back of his upper arm.

"You evil monster!" Raoul growled in anguish, whirling toward Erik and slumping to the floor.

"It's going to be okay," she said, helping him down as he faded from consciousness. She gently laid him on the cement. "I will be okay."

"I'll never quit looking," Raoul murmured, staring up at her with the saddest blue eyes she'd ever seen. "I'll never stop trying to get you back. I love you. This isn't fair. I love you."

She didn't say it back. She'd never said those three words to him, and maybe that was for the best. Christine just stroked his cheek one last time. "Did you call his family?" she asked Erik as she stood.

"They will be notified as soon as we leave." His tone was grim. It was time to go.

She left Cocoa there with a note. "I know you'll take very good care of her." At least she could leave Raoul with someone she loved.

* * *

Christine saw Cocoa once on the television months later. Phillip easily won his election, and Raoul's whole family was on the screen. Along with Meg and Caroline. Most of them were grinning, their faces glowing. Raoul's expression was gloomy, and he could barely fake a smile for the camera. But he was alive. That's what mattered. She never knew how much effort he put into finding her afterwards, but Christine hoped it wasn't a lot.

While Erik finished cleaning up the evidence, he briefly left her at an apartment that had multiple deadbolts on the inside, a safe house. She was surprised that she wasn't locked in. Christine could have easily left and found help, told the authorities whom and where Erik was. But she didn't. Mostly, she watched the confusion on television for several hours. They were showing all the members of Cameron's sect, thousands upon thousands of them, standing around and appearing utterly bewildered as investigators sorted through the mess. Some were hugging each other and crying, their hair soaked from the recent rains.

"Lies!" one bearded man yelled as he thrust his finger at the camera. "Lies by the feds to destroy Cameron Lourdes! There will be the justice of the almighty!"

More than a few people seemed to share that opinion.

But it was on that day when the first story about the girls at the medical center came out. The horror that Christine had felt upon seeing them spread throughout the country.

"We found young women missing feet," said a government spokesman into a microphone, his face pale as he tried to keep his composure. "One missing a hand..."

Christine felt nauseated all over again. Still, opinions began to change rapidly after that. Erik's evidence would push it all over the edge. Only the craziest people could still support Cameron after all of this was revealed.

Several hours after they left the region, the authorities found Erik's home. Or, rather, Erik allowed them to find it. There was still confusion. "We'll find him," the government assured the people. "We'll figure it out." They wouldn't. She could hear it in their voices. "We know he's at least five foot ten."

"How tall are you?" she asked.

"Six, six."

They wouldn't find him.

Still, the country was finally escaping from the shadows that had plagued it over the last five years. And maybe they would never quite understand what had happened. But they could look back on that year, 2034, with relief and new hope.

***

Their last days were spent in New England, a cold rain bearing down upon them. They were waiting for a ship from a European aid organization that was delivering supplies and goods to the United States and then returning.

"Are we going to hide on the ship?" she asked, concerned. She certainly wasn't as good at being quiet as Erik was.

"Not quite. You will wear a wig, and we will be under false identities for quite a while, I am afraid."

"Why are we going by boat?"

"Because it will give us more freedom of movement than a plane," he explained. "There is nothing worse than being entrapped in a tiny space. If in trouble, we can swim. But we cannot fly."

"I haven't gone swimming forever," she replied with a laugh. "My mother bought me swimming lessons when I was really little. But then, well, bathing suits were a big *no*."

"I taught myself when I was twenty-two. Before then, I had never been submerged in water."

"Twenty-two?!"

"No one wants to see an ugly, pale child in a bathing suit, I suppose."

"How'd you learn then?" she asked.

"After an altercation over, ah—that does not matter, I dove into a lake to avoid a worse fate. One learns quickly under those circumstances."

There was so much about him that she didn't know. Prying information from him was still difficult, and he was quieter than ever during those days.

Now that it was all over, Christine finally allowed herself to wonder what was going to happen to her.

"It's too bad we can't have music here," she said on the evening before they left. "We'll have to get another piano."

"But we can, in a sense," Erik replied. "This is not the nineteenth century. It is not the same as a real instrument, but it is adequate." He typed something into the computer, and some sort of intimidating software popped up. "I have used it to compose while running from place to place. Listen."

The song was composed of a medley of instruments, beginning with a piano and then several string instruments, maybe a violin and a cello. She should have known that something like this existed, but the world was still new to her. The music picked up speed and then reached a crescendo before softening.

"That's amazing!"

"Here," he said. "You may try."

She played with the program, adding notes and tempo based on what she knew of music. Christine laughed as it came out sounding horrible. "I guess I'll stick to singing?" She paused. "Or wait. Maybe I'll just add in tuba sounds, and that'll fix it?"

He stared down at her and then seemed to realize she was kidding. He chuckled, but the sound was kind of sad. "You may play with it whenever you wish."

She had tried to bring music back into their lives, and she had succeeded for a couple hours. But it wasn't enough.

When they departed in the early morning, Erik grew very tense. His hands clenched, and his shoulders were thrown back in that commanding way. He glanced backward every so often. Perhaps the enormity of his sacrifice had dawned upon him.

"You can let go now, Erik," she murmured. "You can let go."

At the sound of her voice, Erik's hands slowly unclenched. He looked down at her, eyes softening. She could feel the shadows receding behind them, falling away as the tide came in.

She felt a little sad as they boarded. A loss of another future that she'd once imagined. The enormity of her sacrifice. It lasted only a moment, though. She felt ready to go forward on this adventure. The boat began its journey, and miles and miles of ocean stretched out before them. She appreciated the intricacies of the waves and the expanse of grey sky. Maybe she wasn't free, but she no longer felt trapped.

She expected their new lives to begin—whatever that meant. Maybe they would continue to have conversations about music or history, with no more mentions of the past. Maybe he would want to marry her immediately, and she would keep her promise to him. But, in the days that followed, Erik became very distant. Not cruel but silent. She would try to start a discussion, try to offer a gentle touch. She would ask questions, and he would give her one syllable answers. Christine wondered if he regretted his decision—her companionship instead of power and revenge. He didn't even keep an eye on her. Then again, there weren't many places she could run off to.

One cloudy night, barely a star in sight, she found him staring over the railing and at the frigid water. He blended in with the darkness. She briefly wondered if they were even supposed to be out there. All was quiet except for the waves against the side of the ship and an occasional creak from the frame. "Hi," she said. "How are you?" She zipped up her red jacket and shivered, standing beside him.

"Fine. How are you?" His voice was hollow.

"Okay. A little cold."

"Then you should go back inside."

"I'm also kind of lonely," she admitted, looking down.

"I imagine you are."

"How much longer till we're there?"

"Another day, I think." A long silence passed between them. Still staring outwards, Erik said, "That was quite a…a task you took on, wasn't it? All those people you saved from me." She didn't respond. "Yes, it was," he agreed with himself.

"Are you upset that you left?"

"Not in the slightest. You kept your promise. I kept waiting for you to run. You had chances to escape, to betray me, but you didn't. Why didn't you tell the authorities? There were many at the port." He looked down at her.

She shrugged and folded her arms. "I don't know. We made an agreement. It didn't seem right to go back on that. And, Erik, I didn't want you to get arrested. I don't want anything bad to happen to you."

"That is very kind of you." He stared forward again. "All I simply wanted was to not die alone."

"You won't."

"No. I am not alone." His shoulders moved slowly up and down. He took a shuddery breath. He gripped the cold railing with his gloved hands, staring at the ocean as though he wanted to embrace it.

"What are you doing?"

"Thinking."

"Thinking about what?" She took a cautious step forward.

"You shouldn't be here. You think I do not know that? You don't want to be here. You are here because you are so good. You are the most wonderful girl in the world. You could go to bed now, you know? And close your eyes and dream of happier times."

"Erik—"

"In the morning, you could say you want to go home. Back to him. And we will both have what we want. I will know that you did not leave me. You kept your promise. I think that is good enough."

"Erik!" She grabbed his arm as he leaned over the railing. "Stop it! *Don't make it all worth nothing!*" His head swerved toward her. The look in his eyes nearly undid her. "Come here. It's all right," she whispered, pulling him toward her and away from the water. "Come here right now."

"It is not all right! I tried to give you the world. But you did not want that. Now I will leave for you. I will do anything for you!"

"I know. I know—"

"But you do not want me. You do not want me. No one wants me!"

"Erik." She wrapped her arms around his waist. "Erik, I want you. I do. I want you. We're fine. It's going to be fine. I promise."

A sob emerged from behind the mask. They sank down onto their knees together, onto the cold deck with a soft thud. Her arms wrapped around his neck as she embraced his shaking body. Her fingers found the tiny strings to the mask around the back of his head. "I want to see you. Please let me see you." He was too defeated and weak to stop her. She untied them.

With her left hand, Christine removed the mask and stared at him, at the tear-stained skeleton face. He gazed back as though she might strike him. She smiled, her left hand dropping to the side. With her right hand on the back of his head, she gently kissed his tattered left cheek. And then his other cheek. Then the center of his forehead. And finally she pressed a kiss to his thin, pale mouth. Her lips tingled. He moaned but made no effort to respond. He was motionless, watching her with yellow eyes buried in their deep sockets. "I want you," she said.

It was rather the brightest sight she had ever seen in her twenty years—a work of art, watching a faint glint of humanity return to those indifferent eyes. She could feel it warm her from the inside out, radiating from her heart. She held him as he wept, his bare face buried deeply in her shoulder. "I love you," she heard him say over and over. "I love you."

"We'll be okay," she reassured him. She was going to kiss him again, as a wife might kiss a husband, but he only wanted to be held. "Breathe," she whispered. "Breathe, Erik."

"Oh, what have I done?" His words were muffled by her shirt, barely audible.

"I want you. I want you here and alive. Breathe."

"But you don't want to be—"

"I told you we'd start all over."

"But only because—"

"No. Do you remember when we sat together at the piano?" she interrupted. She hadn't been ready for this conversation. She'd never be ready but... "And I told you, 'slowly'?"

"How could I ever forget? I almost believed you!"

"Good. Because I meant it, you know? After the way I grew up, you were the most baffling person in the entire world. And I knew that something wasn't right about it all. But still I had feelings for you. Even back when you were the Spirit. You were so smart and interesting and talented. You were you."

Erik exhaled. "I never wanted to be me. I have always hated being me."

She stroked the back of his head, fingers threading through his sparse hair. "When I found out about Anthony, I felt terrible. When I found out the rest, I nearly wanted to die. Not just because you lied to me and involved me in all that. But because I cared so much about someone who was doing those terrible things! I tried to protect you until doing that meant millions of people were going to suffer. So who was I?" she whispered. "What kind of person was I to feel so strongly for someone who was...?"

"A monster," he murmured.

"Erik. You're not a monster. But some of the things you did were…"

"And now you love *him.*"

"Raoul, he was the only person that seemed to make any sense. I wanted him to take me away from all the pain. I wanted to forget."

"You love him."

She hesitated. "There were moments when I was happy with him. There were moments when I was also very happy with you. Until you hurt me. I left because you hurt me. Not because of Raoul."

"I know I was monstrous to you," he finally said. "I just did not think you ever would stay unless I could give you something that you could obtain nowhere else. I was too ugly. Too wretched. But the more I tried to give you, the more you hated me."

"I told you what I wanted."

"You did. And I did not listen. And I cannot go back."

"No," she agreed, watching his shoulder slump. "But there is forward. And that's only because of you, Erik. That's only because of what you did in the end."

"I did it for you. Looking at you and touching you and simply being around you—everything about you makes me want to stay alive."

"I know," she said after a moment. "And I'm here. And I want you to keep living. I'm not going back there; I can't."

"I could turn myself in, if that would help clear your name. I would do that for you."

"I don't want that. I want to stay here. But I hope—I hope you'll let me be something, now that we're out here. I hope we can help each other. I told you we'd start over together. And I meant it. I think I even want it. I think we have lives to live. New ones. Don't we?"

"Christine." He looked at her with slight disbelief. She knew he'd be haunted for a long time to come. She would be, too.

There were probably many who would say she should have let him jump, freed herself and let an evil man die. They would label her a martyr, a sacrifice.

They would call him a terrorist and a monster.

Maybe they didn't really matter now. She was tired of doing what everyone thought she should do.

Christine took him back inside, threw a blanket over both of them, and held him. Every so often, he'd murmur, "You are still here. You are still here." She kissed the top of his head. A spark of life returned to his defeated eyes. An ember of hope stirred in her heart.

Tired of the past, she spoke only of the future. "Tell me everywhere we're going, Erik. Tell me everything we'll see."

The End